CAST A LONG SHADOW

CAST A LONG SHADOW

A saga of three generations
of a Southern Illinois family,
reaching from
Williamson County
to
Belgaum, India

Ruth Childers Seamands

Other books by Ruth Seamands

Missionary Mama
House by the Bo Tree
Land of the Snake Charmer
Sandy and Stories for Sandy
Pearls in the Rain
Engineered for Glory (with J.T. Seamands)

CAST A LONG SHADOW

ISBN: 0-9644387-0-4

Ruth Seamands
407 Talbott Drive
Wilmore, KY 40390
606 - 858 - 3920

Cover design by David Caldwell

For

BRANDILYN

(Lindie)

My Daughter

A Tough, Loving Critic

PREFACE

Cast A Long Shadow
is written in loving memory
of my family who came before me,
and to honor those still living today—
especially Helen, Arthur, and Irene.
Events are historical
but some are fictionalized to
bring them alive for the reader.
Some names have been changed.

Ruth Childers Seamands
1994

CAST A LONG SHADOW

Book I

J U L I A

Part I

1877 - 1884

CHAPTER ONE
Spring Love

Julia was thirteen, and she owned the world. She smiled at herself, bending her face close to the pond, trying to see a clear reflection. But it wasn't clear—her smile looked more like a grimace in the breeze-stirred water. Surely she didn't look like that! Who would ever love such a face? Thinking about love made her cheeks burn a little—but why shouldn't she think about it? She *wanted* to love a man some day. After all, the Lord *had* made both male and female! The preacher said so.

What would it be like to be held in a man's arms with his face close to hers? She'd seen engaged couples walking to church or at a square dance, and she always watched them. They looked only at each other and paid no attention to anybody else. The man would kiss his girl and she would lean close for a hug when she thought no one else was looking. Julia shivered with joy at the thought. Could it be like that for her? She scooped up water in both hands and washed her face and neck under the mop of black hair. Drying her face on her long brown skirt, she heard a whistle. Seth was whistling for her—and just when she was thinking about love, too. Suddenly a little shy, she peeked out. Seth was down by the rail fence on the lane. She waved.

"Hey, Julia, come on down!"

She started to run, then slowed to a sedate walk. No use letting Seth think she was overjoyed to see him! As she walked with her eyes down, she sneaked a look at the two little mounds in her dress. Weren't her bosoms *ever* going to grow? Were they just a little more noticeable than they were a week ago? Why was she so tall and skinny?

But she felt too good today to worry about retarded bosoms. Seth was waiting for her! Julia was tall for her age—about five-feet-six, and she held herself ramrod straight. Because an Indian brave had fathered James King, *her* father, she had been taught to be proud of the blood flowing in her veins. She never knew her Indian kinfolks, but she had always known her family was not plain folks.

She had some different blood. When she looked in the mirror she could see signs of her Indian heritage. Her father had been tall and she was tall. Her hair was black like her father's—but instead of Indian straight, it was like her mother's—thick and curly. Besides her physical likeness to her father, she knew in her heart that she had the same proud, determined spirit her father had possessed, though he had been more stoic. Like her mother, Julia usually bubbled excitement.

And she felt bubbly today. She hoped she was beautiful and though only thirteen, she knew she loved Seth. She couldn't know that, beginning today, her life and the lives of her children would be drastically changed for generations—even forever.

Julia King was born near Lake Creek in Southern Illinois, May 8, 1864, and was welcomed by her four older brothers, Joe, Caleb, William, and Matthew. Not only welcomed; her brothers adored her, each one taking a personal responsibility to teach her things and help her grow up safe.

As long as any of the boys were at home, Julia tagged at their heels constantly. At thirteen she had never been in any other part of Illinois in her short life, but she was convinced that *her* part was better than any other place in the whole world.

Seth lived on the farm next to theirs. They'd grown up knowing each other, so she knew Seth liked her as a friend. She had a most terrible crush on him. Neither of them had ever been able to go to school—it was too far away to walk in winter, and in spring, summer, and fall they were needed on their farms.

She joined Seth and they sat on the rail fence. "What you doin' over here, Seth? I didn't expect to see you. I'm glad you came, though!"

"I was just workin' down by your property line and saw you up there by the pond. What 'er you doin'?"

"Oh, just a little hoen' and washin' my face."

"Are you goin' to do anything special this summer?"

"Well, Ma and I are goin' to start sewin' on my hope chest if she feels like it. She's been poorly lately. Says she has some heart pains. I already got a couple of quilts, some pillows, and I been cross-stitchin' a Sunday tablecloth. Then we'll do the cannin'—nothin' special.

Seth sat and just looked over the fields. "Did you ever wish you could go to school, Julia? I do. I wish I could read."

She nodded. "I have thought about it. But when my brothers all got married and went to their own places, I knew I had to stay and help Ma. She couldn't do all the things by herself. And I like working on the farm. It's nice our places join each other— I'm glad we're neighbors, Seth."

"Me too."

Their farms lay a few miles outside of Jeffersonville (called "Shake Rag" by some and "Lake Creek" more recently). Their land stretched green and flat. Southern Illinois had proved so rich for growing corn and other grains that it had been dubbed "Egypt" by early settlers in the first part of the 1800s. Later many people called the area "Little Egypt."

Their settlement was called "Shake Rag" in the beginning, because of an ingenious practice. At first, delivery of whiskey to the one saloon on the hill was sporadic. In his enthusiasm to advertise a new shipment, the saloon-keeper nailed a large white rag on a pole which he kept to hoist and shake in the wind. Eager men with sharp eyes and dry throats would see the banner and beat a path to the barrel on the hilltop. Long after the saloon was torn down and the more sophisticated name of "Jeffersonville" was adopted, people still called the village "Shake Rag."

When the post office was established in 1852, they changed the name, this time to "Lake Creek." Many men enlisting as soldiers in the Civil War—though they came from all over Little Egypt—gave Lake Creek as a postal reference. At that time the community boasted of a tobacco warehouse, blacksmith shop, sawmill, a provisions store, and a post office.

Julia's father had died when she was very young, and her mother had raised her four brothers and Julia on a rented farm. Many farms were leased out because so few families had enough money to buy one, and everyone in every family worked. Now her four brothers labored hard on their own places with their own families and Julia and her mother were left at home. Julia and her mother didn't plow all the fields for wheat and corn as they used to do. Now they just raised their vegetable garden. Of course they kept a few pigs, chickens, their cow, and two horses, so they had barn chores to do every day.

They canned hundreds of quarts of vegetables, apples, and berries every summer. They also "cooked down" sausage and other meats to can—enough to last through the hard, cold winters. The boys always came over at hog-killin' time to do that job for them. Their lives were no different than other farmers in their community. After harvests were in every year, her brothers took turns coming over to chop and store their firewood close to the house. Winters were long and hard but fun, because the family often flew over the snow in their horse-drawn sled to house parties of their friends. There they pulled taffy and made fudge and popped corn and danced a hoedown sometimes. She liked dancin' the hoedown with Seth. Yes, life was good and Julia couldn't even imagine any other.

Seth broke into her daydreaming when he turned his head sideways and looked at her. "You look purty in that dress, Julia. Did your ma make it for you?"

She was amazed at the question. "Of course! Who else would make it? Ma makes all my clothes, sometimes she sews at night after garden work. I tell her it's hard on her eyes 'cause that coal-oil lamp light is dim, but she says she can't keep up with my spurt of growin' lately. She's teachin' me how to sew, but I don't do too good with fittin' dresses yet."

Seth looked at her more critically. "That's right! You *are* a-growin."

She giggled and looked briefly down at the dress she was wearing—where it strained at the side seams. She wiggled her shoulders and felt the dress pull under her arms. She was glad because that meant she was growing in the bosoms department! She had just about decided she was a woman now. And maybe Seth would think—just maybe—they ought to get married before too many years—say like when she was fifteen! Her face flushed a little just thinking about it and her giggle was happy.

"What 'er you laughin' about?" Seth asked. When she just smiled and shook her head, Seth said, "Let's walk down the lane a little. Do you have to hurry?"

"No." She hopped off the fence and just for fun she grabbed his hand and pulled him off,

Seth held on to her hand and smiled and Julia thought his eyes looked as blue as the sky on a bright spring day. Even though she was tall, Seth was much taller. Looking up at him she loved the way the sunlight danced down through his corn-colored hair.

He said, "Pa and I are goin' to work fixin' up the place this summer. It's sorta gone down since my ma died. That and farmin'—that's what I like to do best. To have a hammer or a saw or a plow in my hand—well, nothin' makes me feel any better. And sometimes I *need* to feel better. I miss Ma a lot—it takes a woman on the place to make it feel like home." He swung Julia's hand. "You thirteen now?"

She nodded.

"Well, I'm sixteen. Uh—can you set for a spell?"

Joy raced around in her heart and she hunched her shoulders to try to keep the feeling. "I guess so. Far as I know Ma don't need me for anything special."

Across the lane was a woods with some fallen logs that made good sittin' places. They chose a shady spot, Julia straightening her long brown calico skirt. Seth followed her. The ground was spongy after last night's rain and the odor of pines was all around. Julia sniffed the fresh, pungent air and felt so happy she thought her heart was going to jump right out. She loved these woods—she'd played in them all her life with her brothers and Seth and his older sisters. Now, of course, she was too big to play like that, but she felt like it sometimes. Only she didn't want anybody to know.

Seth sat beside her on the log, his long legs sticking straight out. "Julie, I might not see you for a spell—it's goin' to be a busy summer for Pa and me."

"Won't you even be comin' to church and to camp meetin' when the preacher is 'round here? I'll be real lonesome if I don't get to see you in church sometimes."

"Oh, I reckon we'll come there. Pa likes to come to church. But even if we do, I probably wouldn't get much chance to talk to you all by yourself."

"I always like goin' to meetin'," Julia said. "I like all the singin' and when somebody plays the pump organ, I like that." She paused. "And I like to hear the preachin' too— sometimes them preachers git people worked up to such a pitch it takes 'em days to simmer down agin. And I like the Bible readin'. Always wished I could read the Bible." She paused and watched a frisky squirrel run down a long tree limb, and a sassy bluejay peck for worms under some damp leaves. "You know, Seth, sometimes I think about my Pa up in heaven, lookin' down and seein' me in church. I bet your Ma looks down and sees you and she's happy because you're there. Do you think about God very much?"

Seth sat quietly for a while. Then, "I do think about God and I do like to go to church. But lately I've been thinkin' about somethin' else." He swallowed. "J—Julie, I want you to be my girl. Would you let me kiss you—just once? And if you will, *will* you be my girl?" He shook his head. "I don't know anybody else I'd want to be my girl."

Julia was suddenly so happy she thought she'd burst. But she pretended to consider it for a spell, because she didn't want to seem too anxious. Then she nodded.

Remembering later, it seemed to her that time stood still

and she knew she would never forget that moment. Sunlight sifted through green branches while a young, blond head bent down over black, curly hair. Blue eyes looked down into happy brown eyes as their lips touched lightly. For both of them their first kiss was one recollection they would always treasure.

When he lifted his head, they smiled at each other and Julia was radiant. "Yes, Seth, I *want* to be your girl. I don't know anybody else whose girl I'd think about bein'."

Seth looked triumphant, sighed, and lightly held her hand. "Well, so you *are* my girl! Don't forget it now!"

Her eyes opened wide. "Forget you! I *kissed* you, didn't I? So how in the world could I ever forget you?"

"Well, lots of other fellers live 'round here. Some of them are soon goin' to notice how pretty you are, and you might just forget all about me!"

She shook her head. "Never! Do you really think I'm pretty?"

"I shore do!"

"Then don't worry. I'll never forget you, Seth. Anyway, how could I ever forget you? I'll see you at church sometimes." She teased him, "And if I *did* forget you durin' the week, then I'd remember who you was on Sunday!"

"Yeah—"

"Are you goin' to tell anybody else I'm your girl?" She didn't care if the whole world knew.

"If I see any other fellers makin' them slant-eyes at you, I shore will tell 'em!"

She laughed. "Anyway, I wouldn't make slant-eyes back at 'em. I use my eyes for other things." With a practiced calculation, she squinted at the sun. "It's still a couple of hours till evenin'. Would you like to come up to the house and say howdy to Ma? I think she's got some apple pie to go with fresh buttermilk. And she's not seen you in quite a spell."

"Well, just for a little while. That apple pie shore sounds good. Neither Pa nor I can make pies. Do *you* know how to make apple pies?"

She nodded. "I know how."

"Then you'll make a good wife some day."

Her face flushed. "You don't want me just because I know how to make pies, do you?"

He looked at her and grinned. "Now, Julie, you know better'n that! You know I wouldn't mind some kissin' once in a while between your pie-makin'." He stood up.

"You have to go now?" Julia asked.

He pulled her up. "I hate to leave here, but if I'm goin' up to your house, we best go. I can't stay too long—I got to get back to Pa. He'll be wonderin' what happened to me. I didn't tell him I was comin' over to your place."

They sprinted up the hill, Julia's thoughts racing faster than her feet. *I can't wait to tell Ma he wants me to be his girl! She likes Seth a lot—she'll be glad!*

Reaching Julia's place, they jumped up on the back porch steps, Julia calling, "Ma, Ma, we got company——" She burst happily into the kitchen door and stopped short, not believing what she saw. "Oh, Ma! Ma! What's the matter, Ma?"

Lucinda White King was lying unconscious on the kitchen floor.

Julia fell on her knees beside her mother. "Oh, Seth! Help me put her on the bed! It must be her heart—she's been havin' some pains lately, but I didn't think too much about it."

Lucinda's frail body seemed to weigh nothing as Seth picked her up, carried her into the other room and gently laid her on the bed.

"I'm so thankful you're here, Seth—"

"So'm I, Julie. I'll go and try to find Doc Cooper— it'll take me a while, you know—"

"Yes, yes—take old Gray. He's in the field. I'll git him for you."

She ran down the back steps and whistled her own particular call for her horse. Old Gray galloped up to the fence and she hurridly rubbed his nose. "Now, Gray, you take Seth to find the doctor for Ma."

Seth was quick to get him ready and very soon Old Gray's hoofs pounded down the lane.

Julia ran back into the house, looked into the bedroom and saw that Lucinda was still in a sort of stupor. She took a pan of cold water near the bed, dipped a rag into it and began to rub it on her mother's face. She softly spoke, "Ma, Ma, wake up! You're goin' to be all right. The doctor's comin' after a while—Seth went to get him."

Lucinda's eyes opened once and she clutched her chest. "It hurts, Julie—get me some water to drink."

The moon was shining in the bedroom window making shadows on the hooked rug, before Seth came back with the doctor.

"Hope he can help her, Julia!"

Julia nodded and pointed the doctor to the bedroom. "I'm much beholdin' to you, Seth. Ma's livin' but her chest hurts. I never saw her this sick before. Seth, you better go on home, your Pa's goin' to be worried about you."

Seth nodded. "I'll come to see about her—and you too, Julia." He hesitated before walking out the door. "I'll never forget today and what we talked about."

"I won't forget either." Her eyes sparkled with unshed tears.

She tiptoed into the bedroom and stood watching Doctor Cooper listen to Lucinda's heart. When he was finished, he stood up and motioned Julia back into the kitchen.

"Your Ma is pretty sick, Julia—her heart's bad. She'll have to rest a good bit; I've left some pills for her. I don't know anything else to do for her right now. In time her heart may get a little stronger, but—" He shook his head. "I'll come when you need me—just send word." He left in his buggy.

As the doctor's tired horse plodded out of the yard, Julia sank against the door. She knew her mother would never again be well, and her life would be changed, too. She didn't know how much.

CHAPTER TWO
A Time To Live, A Time To Die

The next year was a hard and busy one for Julia. Over the whole year, Julia watched her mother grow weaker and more frail, in spite of all that she and the doctor could do. Sometimes Lucinda got up and sat on the porch in the sun, or in the rocking chair by the fireplace in the kitchen. But she didn't improve. Julia kept trying to tempt her mother's feeble appetite with good food, and prayed that God would take away that white, tired look.

During that year, Julia did all the chores alone. She milked their cow, fed pigs and chickens, raised the vegetables, cared for the horses, prepared food, washed and dried dishes, and cleaned the house. Julia did all the canning, her mother directing from her rocking chair.

Lucinda had enjoyed knitting so much that she had put off teaching Julia how to do it. But Julia needed to know. So during the winter months' short daylight hours, over and over again Lucinda patiently guided Julia's unskilled hands in how to hold the yarn, how to twist the needles, knit and purl into ridges, and to take out knitting mistakes. She said, "You may have to knit all our socks for next year, Julia. I'm so no good and feel so poorly, I can't do much anymore."

"I like it, Ma. The needles clickin' make a kind of friendly sound." Though Julia's fingers still felt a little awkward on the needles, she learned fast and by spring she had already knitted new socks for both of them. Then feeling brave, she started a new sweater for her mother.

Sometimes Julia was so tired when darkness came that she fell into her bed without undressing. Often her mother would need attention in the night, so Julia's days and nights were spent in a daze of sleeplessness.

Neighbors and her brothers came by as often as they could, but everybody else had farm work too. Several times Seth and his father came to see them. Seth looked at her entreatingly; but much as she wanted to, Julia couldn't even go for a walk with him or talk to him alone. Matthew, Caleb, William, and Joe helped her with chores, repaired things for her, and came just to sit and talk when they could.

One morning Lucinda made no effort to get out of bed. Julia woke up beside her very early because her mother was restless. "I'll get you some breakfast, Ma," Julia whispered as she rubbed her eyes and crawled out of bed. Once in the kitchen, she opened the back door and sighed at the beauty of a rising sun shining on green fields and the pond. Roosters crowed and strutted, and jaybirds chattered in the trees. How she loved the farm scenes!

She dipped water from a bucket into the washbasin, wrung out a washrag and brought it to the bedroom, gently sponging her mother's face. "Don't worry about gettin' up today, Ma. You just stay here and rest and I'll bring your breakfast to the bed. Think you could eat some cornmeal mush this mornin'? I could put some cream in it for you, and a little sugar."

Out at the fireplace she blew on the banked coals, fed some brittle branches and soon the blaze started up. Once the coffee was beginning to boil, she peeked in the bedroom. Lucinda seemed to be sleeping. As Julia came near the bed, her mother tried to sit up with a choking gasp. Julia quickly raised her head from the pillow. Her mother groaned and pressed both hands against her chest, and fell over on Julia's arm. She didn't breathe again.

Julia gently laid her back on the pillow. She put her head on Lucinda's chest, listening for a heartbeat. Silence. Then on her knees with her head on her mother's chest, she cried like a four-year-old.

Memories flooded over her—scenes of running after her mother as a little girl, of Lucinda baking bread and corn pone, churning and sewing and telling Julia stories while knitting. "Ma, Oh, Ma, how'm I goin' to live without you? I want you to come back, Ma, I just can't do without you!" Her tears soaked her mother's nightgown. She rocked herself back and forth as she cried, then cried and rocked some more. Finally, her storm of weeping was over. She straightened up and dried her face on the bed sheet. Now she had another task.

Automatically, she took the boiling coffee pot away from the fire, heated the basin of water to warm, took some soap and went back into the bedroom. She undressed her mother, washed her body, then dressed her in her Sunday best. Julia was shocked again at her thinness. Every time she had bathed Lucinda she had grieved, for Lucinda was nothing but skin and bones. Julia combed her mother's hair and folded her hands on her breast.

Her sight blurred by tears, Julia stumbled a little on the back steps on her way down to the barn. But she kept doggedly on. Once there, she stopped a moment to rub the cow's sleek side. "You'll have to wait a while, Old Bossie, I can't milk you right now. I gotta go get Joe." She whistled for Old Gray, got on him without any saddle, and rode two miles to tell her brother.

Joe and Martha lived on a farm two miles north of theirs. Martha, a tall blond, blue-eyed lady of Norwegian descent, ran to the door when she heard the horse gallop up, and Julia slid off into her arms. "Ma's gone, Marthie," she said, and burst into sobs on Martha's shoulder.

Martha didn't say a word but rang the big dinner bell, by the kitchen door to call Joe in from the barn. Then she set Julia down at the kitchen table and made her drink a cup of hot coffee, strong, with sugar and fresh cream.

Julia accepted it gratefully, almost in a daze.

Joe's feet came pounding through the woodlot, and he burst into the kitchen. "What's the matter, Martha, is one of the children hur—?"

Julia looked up from her coffee, so exhausted she was nearly past feeling. "Ma's gone, Joe."

Joe's tall body sagged and he crumpled down into a chair. Martha thrust a cup of coffee toward him and he drank it without a word. Then, "I been expectin' it, Julie, but that don't make it any easier." His shoulders hunched and he hid his face in his hands, dark hair falling over his fingers.

Two of his smaller children stood wide-eyed in shock when they heard their father sob. That was something they'd never seen or heard before. In fear they hid their faces in Martha's apron and began to cry too. Martha stooped down, hugged them and wiped their tears. "Mama, your face got some tears too! Why is everybody cryin'?"

"Your grandma just died this mornin'."

"Grandma Lucinda?"

"Yes. She's gone to Heaven and we're gonna miss her. It'll be real lonesome without her."

"Why did she have to die?"

"Well, you know she was sick a long time. You remember that lots of times when you went to see her she didn't feel like playin' with you? She had a bad heart and her body just plain wore out. She was too weak to live any more. She'll be better off in Heaven because Jesus will take all her pain away."

The children nodded. They'd heard the preacher talk about Jesus in church.

Joe dug a well-worn handkerchief out of his pocket, wiped his eyes and blew his nose. Regaining his composure he said, "Well Julia, after everything is over, you pack your things and come home with us."

Julia looked straight at him and felt her stubbornness rising, even amidst her grief. "No! I ain't goin' to come here and make you one more mouth to feed. You got all you can do to take care of your own five kids and this house and farm. And I ain't goin' to be beholdin' to anybody. I'm a big strong girl and I can hire out and earn my keep." She stopped suddenly, too tired to argue further. It could wait until later. "Come on, Joe, let's go."

Joe called his oldest son, James, and told him, "Go get on your pony and ride around to tell all the neighbors. And when you come back, finish up the milkin' in the barn." Then he said, "Martha, when James gets back, you and the children come in the wagon. I'll go with Julia now."

"I didn't milk Old Bossie yet either," Julia said.

"I'll do it when we get there," Joe answered. "The cow's gotta be milked, no matter who lives or dies."

Word of Lucinda King's death spread quickly through the farming community, and by noon wagons were arriving at Julia's mother's place. Her brothers' families came, friends and neighbors came. Seth and his father came first, for they lived the closest. Julia and Seth looked at each other and she saw compassion in his eyes. But this was not the time to speak to each other alone.

Neighboring women brought fresh bread and pots of beans and ham, fried chicken, boiled potatoes, or whatever they were cooking when the news came. They spread all the food on the kitchen table. While the men and boys ate first, the women sat and talked quietly in the small bedroom where Julia's mother lay so peacefully. They sympathized with Julia and wondered where she would live after this.

When the men finished their meal, they silently took shovels out of their wagons and went off up the hill to the grave lot. It was their custom—neighbors buried neighbors.

Julia watched them go in a daze. Her mother—dead! How could she ever do without her mother—the dearest person in the world to her? She hardly knew what was going on around her, and when anybody spoke to her she didn't remember whether she answered or not.

The men came back with dirt on their overalls and shoes, and lifted from their wagons long hewn white pine boards. They deposited them under the spreading oak in the back yard and took tool boxes from under the wagon seats. When their hammers started nailing together a plain box, Julia could stand it no longer. She fled to her own special place in the haymow, sobbing her heart out. She heard them calling her but would not answer, because she couldn't stand to see anybody. The sound of nails being driven into a wooden box made her stop her ears and sob even harder. She felt her life was ending too.

Then the hammering stopped and she lay exhausted for a few minutes in the hay. Joe found her and gently helped her up, keeping a tight grip on her arm as they followed their friends carrying their mother up the hill in a new-made box.

Their itinerant minister was away somewhere in the countryside, and not being able to find him, family and friends buried Julia's loving mother without his comforting words. Joe spoke a few sentences of love and appreciation over her fresh-dug grave and recited some treasured verses from the Bible. *Let not your heart be troubled: ye believe in God, believe also in me. In my Father's house are many mansions: If it were not so, I would have told you. I go to prepare a place for you. And if I go and prepare a place for you, I will come again and receive you unto myself; that where I am, there ye may be also."* (John 14:1-4)

Martha wiped her eyes and said she was thankful to have had such a fine mother-in-law. Some of Lucinda's close friends told of helpful things she had done for them in the past and how they would miss her. At that moment, Julia could say nothing at all.

Late afternoon sun slanted down on the farmers and their families in their everyday clothes standing in front of the high mound of dirt. Shovels were sticking out of the top of the pile. Women in their working dresses stood close to Julia beside the pine coffin. Julia put out her hand and touched it just before it was lowered with ropes into the fresh-opened earth. "I love you, Ma," she whispered.

Friends wiped their eyes and nodded. "Your ma was a good woman, Julia. We will miss her, but we know she's better off now. She won't suffer no more."

The sad women walked silently back to the house while men shoveled the loose dirt down into the grave. Julia couldn't look around and see that, but she heard it.

The neighbor women went with Julia into the house to collect their kitchen utensils. By the time the men returned from the hill, they had washed things and cleaned up Julia's kitchen for her. Then they hugged her as they climbed back into their wagons. "Julie, we've got to go and do our evenin' chores. But we'll do anything we can to help you—you know that. Just let us know—"

"I am much obliged to all of you," Julia said, her voice shaking. "The Lord gave us good neighbors and I'm obliged to Him, too." As the wagons rolled away, Julia sobbed on William's shoulder. "It's so hard to believe she's gone! But I know she is better off." Somehow, at that moment, the thought was little consolation.

Two of Julia's brothers, Caleb and Matthew and their families, went back to their own farms for the night, but Joe and William stayed with Julia. The plan was to meet here again the next day to talk about some family matters— meaning, Julia knew, "What about Julia? She must come and live with one of us. She cannot stay here alone." But Julia was so mentally and emotionally exhausted that she could not think about anything at all—except about her mother in a pine box.

The families all came back the next morning, and some of their closest friends also came. The small children were given some bread spread with butter and jam and sent out to play. The adults sat around the kitchen table drinking coffee, not knowing how to broach the subject.

Finally, Will said, "Julia, we've been talkin' this over amongst us, and we all agree. You can't stay here. We don't own this farm, and even if we did, you couldn't stay here alone. It ain't safe. You got to pack your clothes and come home with us. We want you to be with us."

"No!" said Julia stubbornly.

Joe looked worried. At thirty he was the father of five children, with the heavy burden of making a living for them from his small farm. "Julie, you know you can come to our house. We can always make room for you, and the children will like to have you."

Caleb and Matthew also pleaded with her to come and live with them. Each said, "My family wants you to come. You must live with some of your own family."

"I ain't goin' to," Julia repeated for the tenth time. "I ain't goin' to be draggin' around any of your places. Anyway, if I went to any one of your houses, I'd just be crowdin' you. You all got a housefull of kids, and I aim to earn my keep."

"You could help us on our farms! Our kids are purty small and any of us could use another hand."

"No—it ain't the same. I can hire out to somebody. I'm a big strong girl; I'm fourteen-years-old, and I can do the work of any man. You all got more'n you can handle right now. I'll stay right here 'till I find somethin' else."

"NO YOU WON'T!" thundered Joe, Caleb, Matthew, and William altogether. "No young girl can stay here alone. You got to come with one of us!"

Mrs. Crawford, a small, thin, frail woman with wispy, grey hair, who was Julia's mother's best friend, spoke in a shaky voice. "Maybe nobody's thought of us. We're like Julie's own kin, and we got no chick or child of our own. Julia can come and live with us. She will be company for me. And you all know we got a big farm and plenty to eat. And it's not so far from all you brothers. All of you can come over and see her any time you want to. I know Solly won't care if she comes, will you, Solly?"

Her husband, the thick-set, red-faced man called Solly, looked up with cold blue eyes from the coffee he was drinking and said shortly, "She's welcome."

Joe's wife, Martha, caught her breath. Julia to live at *Solly's*? Her mind flew back to just a few Sundays ago when the small congregation was coming out of their country church. Martha's good friend Amanda was walking out with her, and Mrs. Crawford was taking to someone else behind them.

Martha said "Hello" to Mrs. Crawford, then she and Amanda went on ahead. "Where's Solly, I wonder?" she asked. "He never comes to church with her, does he?"

"I didn't see him," Amanda answered. "We came by and picked up Miss Ellie and brought her in our wagon like we usually do. We never do see Solly. But I've got a pretty good idea where he might be." Amanda sounded disgusted.

"Where?" Martha asked curiously.

"Well, not long ago I was in the Marion feed store with my husband. As we came out the door, we saw Solly come out of the saloon across the street and go back to that house in the back. I asked my husband who lived there and he said I wouldn't care to know. But Solly knocked on the door and a woman opened the door, grabbed Solly's arm and pulled him inside. She acted like an old friend—and I bet she was!"

Martha was surprised. "Solly goes to that whore house?"

"Well, I saw him go in! Poor Miss Ellie. No wonder he won't come to church with her. I bet he goes there every Sunday while she comes to church!"

Martha saw Miss Ellie coming closer and whispered to Amanda, "Well, I guess he's got enough money to afford to do that." She turned. "Miss Ellie, I'm glad to see you this mornin'. You feelin' all right today?"

Now, sitting with family and friends, including the Crawfords, at Julia's table, Martha bit her lip. Should she object to Julia's going there? She *did* object, but she'd have to say why she did. How could she do that here? But surely Solly wouldn't do anything to Julia with Ellie there. But what if . . .

Silence was all around the table as the family thought about Miss Ellie's offer.

Julia had known Solly all her life, but as she looked at him she couldn't see any welcome. Ever since she was a small child, she had been afraid of Solly Crawford. Now that Miss Ellie had asked her to come and live with them, she felt confused. She wanted to hire out but felt scared to live in the same house with Solly, and she wasn't sure why.

Would he be kind to me? she wondered. *I've never seen him be kind to anybody. Why did sweet Miss Ellie marry him? Was he ever any different? Has he ever been loving to Miss Ellie or to anybody? Well, with Miss Ellie in the house, I ought to be safe enough. At least I wouldn't be crowding anybody.*

Julia had always loved Mrs. Crawford and knew she would like to be with her. She was silent for a while, thinking what her life might be like. Some premonition flitted like a shadow through her senses, but she quickly shook it away. She didn't live by premonitions or shadows. Her life as a farm child had always been practical—simply to do whatever had to be done.

"Well, Miss Ellie I hadn't thought about livin' with you before. But I think my Ma would be pleased to know I was with you. If I come, I intend to earn my keep there on your big farm. I might be an orphan now—" though her voice broke, she swallowed and went on, "but I'm not a charity case. I must work."

But Martha thought to herself, *I don't like Solly Crawford and I don't like what I heard about him.* She asked one more time, "Julia, please come and live with us. I'd be so happy to have you. Would you?"

Julia shook her head. "Martha, I do appreciate all you've done for me, but I'd crowd you too much. I'd better go with Miss Ellie."

Martha knew that Julia, once her mind was made up . . . so she said, "I'll stay today and tonight and help you pack up, Julia. Is it all right if the children stay too? They can help us. Joe can come back tomorrow."

Julia's brothers looked at each other around the table with questioning eyebrows. They all nodded in silent assent. Julia would be well cared for and would live close by so they could keep an eye on their little sister. The matter was settled. Everybody breathed a great sigh of relief.

Miss Ellie smiled and nodded. "If you will be ready by tomorrow, we will come back and get you in the wagon. I'll be most pleased to have you live with us, Julia. It'll be sort of like havin' Lucinda back again—you're like her in lots of ways." She hugged Julia and Julia felt truly wanted. It made her feel warm inside.

Solly showed no more reaction, but walked out the door saying, "Come on, Ellie, got to go clean the barn." He climbed up into his wagon, picked up the reins, and his wife struggled up over the wheel on the other side just before it started to turn.

Will, Caleb and Matthew all came back the next day with their wives and wagons. When Joe arrived they set to work. They gathered all the tools, farm equipment, and stock, and divided it among themselves. Julia and her four sisters-in-law divided all the canned food. "I'll take my share of this to Miss Ellie's. That way I don't have to go empty-handed," Julia said.

They stacked all the other household items in the kitchen and first filled Julia's "hope chests"—a humpbacked trunk and strong oak boxes—with quilts, dresser scarves, towels, dishes, and kitchen utensils. "You'll need all these things when you get your own place with your own man, Julia. It won't be too many years, probably. And we've got enough in our houses already."

"Joe," Julia asked, "would you take my trunk and these boxes and keep them in your barn—or someplace—for me? I don't want to lose these things of Ma's. And I don't want to take them to Miss Ellie's. I'll only take my clothes. Joe, can I have Ma's rockin' chair for mine?"

"Course, Julie. I'll keep your boxes and the chair all safe for you. Not too long and you'll be wantin' them, I reckon. You're near growed up."

Julia's sisters-in-law then divided everything else that Julia didn't want to keep. In the middle of the afternoon, her four brothers' wagons crunched slowly out of the yard loaded with Lucinda's tools, and chickens in crates. Her livestock, tied to the wagons, followed along. That caravan took with it the living of the last forty years. Julia stared after them for a few minutes, until the dust settled. Then she saw it. The house, the barn, the barnlot, and the land were all dead. A desolation that Julia had never known existed, crowded her heart and crushed her lungs until she thought she could not breathe anymore. She didn't know whether she would ever feel any more dead.

But Indian stoicism took over and she clenched her jaw so tight it gave her a headache. She paid no attention to it. The first part of her life was now over. This was not the time to question whether she had chosen the right path—to go with a friend instead of her family. Some work still remained to be done.

So without looking around for any signs of life, Julia carefully stacked her share of the canned goods in some old bushel baskets, and stuffed her own clothes into a pillow case. When the Crawfords came, she said, "Howdy," as Solly and Ellie got down. Miss Ellie hugged her and she thought she heard a grunt from Solly. But she wasn't sure.

Without many words, they stowed the rest of Julia's belongings in Solly's wagon and climbed in. As they clattered over rocks and ruts in the yard and road, through tears she looked back at the little brown farmhouse fading in the distance. It had nurtured her all her life. She wept quietly, *Seth won't even be close any more!*

CHAPTER THREE
The Barn Raisin'

Julia's mother died in the summer of 1878, and all through the next cold winter, she and Mrs. Crawford sat by their big iron range in the kitchen, pieced quilts, made hooked rugs, knitted and talked. The frail woman drew a great deal of comfort from Julia's presence. Miss Ellie always made Julia feel wanted—like the daughter she never had. Julia did most of the inside work, and Mrs. Crawford, never strong, was glad to have Julia "do" for her. Julia was strong and quick.

Julia loved to work—she always wanted her hands busy. While her hands were busy doing the never-ending household tasks, her thoughts were conjuring up dreams all centered around Seth. She hadn't seen him in such a long time now. Was he thinking about her? Did he still want her to be his girl? How she would like to go back to her old home, sit on the fence and talk to Seth!

Solly Crawford was not at all friendly to Julia in front of Ellie, and was often harsh when telling her some special work he wanted done. After living in his house for many months, Julia liked him no better than before. He never showed any appreciation of Miss Ellie—he acted like the sun rose and set because of Solly Crawford. Of course Julia had to be near him during mealtimes, but at other times when he was inside, she found work in another part of the house. Wherever he *was,* Julia wasn't! She couldn't stand him because he was crude and disagreeable.

A few times at the table, Julia caught him looking at her with a speculative glance. And since she was fearful, she gave him no opportunity to be alone with her. But once when Ellie got up from the table to go down to the cellar for some special pickles, Solly reached over and put his heavy arm around Julia's shoulder. "Kind of like havin' you here, Julia. Makes the place cheerful."

Julia shrugged away and said, "I like it here, Mr. Crawford. You got a fine farm, and come spring, if Miss Ellie feels better and I don't have to help in the house so much, I'll work in the fields and begin to pay for my keep. I like workin' in the fields—I'm used to it."

"Oh well, course I can always use some more help outside,

but you ain't got no cause to worry about that, Julia. Guess we can always help a friend."

Julia liked his friendliness even less than she liked his sullenness and was relieved to hear Ellie coming back upstairs.

* * * *

When spring of 1879 came, Julia felt it in her bones with a rising eagerness. She could plow a straight furrow, and took great pleasure in the feel of newly-turned moist earth in her fingers. She didn't mind getting all hot and sweaty from scattering seed and covering the seed rows. She often scanned the skies and talked to God about sending rain at the right time. Eagerly watching the first shoots of corn thrusting out of the ground, she would pause to thank the Lord for the joy of working with Him to bring in crops. Southern Illinois in the spring was God's chosen place!

In May, shortly after Julia turned fifteen, they heard about a barn raising. Some friends were planning it for a newly married couple near Shake Rag, and they heard that everyone for miles around was set on going. Farmers didn't like taking a day off from their own work, 'specially this time of year, but this young couple did need a new barn. Their other barn had just burned down. They'd planted for a big crop and if they didn't get a new barn, they'd have no storage place for the harvest.

"Are we goin', Miss Ellie?" Julia asked.

"Yes, we are. Neighbors must help neighbors."

Julia was excited. A barn raisin'! Seth would be there—and now she was fifteen, close to marryin' age!

Julia and Miss Ellie, who had been feeling better since she had help in the house, sewed for days on a new dress for Julia. They cleared off the kitchen table and spread out the cloth to cut it.

"Make the skirt big and whirly, Miss Ellie." Julia's eyes sparkled. "Got enough goods for that?"

"I have, and that's what I'm goin' to do, Julie. This cloth was just made for you. For your black hair and brown eyes, no prettier goods could be found."

"Where did you find this—did you already have it?"

"I did. Some time ago when I was in Marion, I saw this piece in the drygoods store. I didn't need it, but somethin' just made me buy it. All the way home in the wagon, Solly fussed at me for spendin' the money, but I didn't care. Part of that money is mine anyhow. I put the goods in my trunk and didn't think of it again 'til the other day when we heard about this barn raisin.' I guess the Lord wanted you to have a pretty new dress."

"But don't you want it for yourself?"

Miss Ellie shook her head. "No,this is not for me. I want you to go to that barn raisin' and be the prettiest girl there. We got to catch a beau for you!"

Julia's face flushed. She already had her beau, but that was still her secret.

The dress was a red-flowered print, with a full skirt, tight bodice with a white lace collar, and Julia knew she looked beautiful in it.

When she got dressed on the day of the barn raisin', she was astonished at how grown-up she looked. The red set off the flush in her cheeks, and her eyes sparkled. She had put up her hair for the first time but some stray black curls fell around her face. She was excited and felt happier than she had since her mother died.

When she was dressed, Miss Ellie walked round and round her exclaiming, "Never saw anybody prettier than you, Julia!" When she climbed into the wagon, Solly looked at her with a new gleam in his eye. She saw it and looked away. Solly wasn't going to spoil this day for her.

The wagon crunched two miles over the rutted spring road toward the barn raising. As they came up the turn-off lane, they saw that all the neigbor men—young and old—were just beginning their work. Tools were being unloaded and long boards were laid out on the grass. Soon the sawing and hammering started. For a few moments Julia closed her eyes when she heard the hammers beause it took her back to last year and crying in the hay. But she told herself she could not always grieve for her mother; Lucinda would want her to be happy today.

All the country women—married and free—swished around in their new ginghams and calicos, talking, admiring new babies, and unloading victuals. Every woman had brought her most bragged-on food. Piles of crispy fried chicken sat in the center of boards-over-sawhorses tables. Children parked themselves alongside, some with their noses barely visible over the tops of the tables. Their eyes scrutinized the dishes of relishes, green beans cooked with ham, corn—in fritters, plain from glass jars, and 'scalloped, sweet potatoes which had been baked in hot ashes, boiled potatoes, and huge loaves of bread. Their eyes lingered longest on the different kinds of cakes and pies, including fried peach pies and apple turnovers, and they yelled at their mothers, "Ma! When 'er we gonna eat?"

At the end of the tables, pots of coffee waited to be warmed up over an open fire.

Julia was helping to set out the food when her quick eyes caught Seth's blond head towering over some of the others and her heart raced. Would he try to speak to her? Did he still want her to be his girl?

The thought struck her again with terrific force—*I want to marry Seth! He is so handsome.* Now he was a man—he was a real man who stood out from among the other men. He was taller than a year ago, light hair still sparkling in the sun, and his dancing blue eyes were smiling into hers. She knew he had arms strong to hold her, and a happiness in life which infected everybody. As she helped at the tables, Seth came over to her. She was so flustered she dropped a spoon, but it looked like he didn't care who heard him say, "Hello, Julie, hoped you'd be comin' today."

Her face flushed nearly as red as her dress and she smiled at him with her heart in her eyes.

Solly, watching Julia, looked at Seth with daggers in *his* eyes.

Mr. Jones Martin was a photographer who had a small shop in his home in Marion. He had heard about the barn raisin' and realized that many women and children would be there. That would be an ideal time for him to drum up some trade. The farm families probably wouldn't have much ready cash at the barn raisin', but in his business he was paid when he delivered the finished product.

So about ten-thirty, he drove his wagon up the lane and parked it alongside all the others. A few women and children recognized him and greeted him gladly when he began to unload his picture-taking paraphernalia.

"Did'ja come to take our pitchers?" they asked. "We ain't had no pitchers taken in a long time and some of them new babies—I bet they never had one."

"That's what I come for," replied Jones Martin. If your ma and your pa say yes, then I will. Go ask them."

He set all his equipment out on his own folding table. When he was ready, he ambled over to where the mothers were working around the long sawhorse tables. "Howdy, ladies. I'm so happy to see you all looking so well today. And bless my soul, I think you are the prettiest bunch of ladies I've seen lately. Now maybe some of you will want me to take your picture, or maybe a picture of your young'uns. I charge you only fifty cents today, and another fifty cents when I deliver the picture to your place." He waited, looking expectantly around the table. His eyes fell on Julia King—*What a beautiful girl! That black curly hair, brown eyes, and high cheek bones—what a combination! And that well-fitted bright red dress!* He sighed and his artistic soul mourned. It's too bad that nobody can do a picture in color! She'd take any photographic prize if that were possible!

Martha King said to him, "I'll go over and see if my man has fifty cents in his pocket. If he does, I want a picture of my young'uns."

"So do I," agreed several others and they started over toward where the men were working.

During the lull, Miss Ellie said, "Julia, I want to have your picture made. I got fifty cents in my pocket here of my own money and I don't have to ask Solly nothin'." To the photographer she said, "Come take Julia's picture first."

"Is she your daughter, Madam?"

"No, but I love her like one. And I want this picture made so I can give it to her. Some day she'll have a family who wants to see how purty their ma was."

So Julia sat at his little table and looked straight into the camera. When he was finished, after taking several trial photographs, she asked him, "Do you remember me, Mr. Martin?"

"I don't see how I could ever forget you. Didn't you come to my place with your mother a few years ago?"

"Yes. My Ma and I come into town one day with my brother Joe. I still got that picture—my Ma was well then and we stood up with our arms around each other."

"Yes. That's right. And how is your mother now?"

She bowed her head and her lips trembled. "My Ma died nearly a year ago. Now I live at Miss Ellie's place."

"I am very sorry, Miss Julia. His eyes rested on her for a moment. Miss Ellie, I will deliver this photograph to your place in about a week. Thank you," he said, as Miss Ellie gave him a fifty cent piece.

Their conversation was interrupted with mothers coming back, their lively children in tow. For the rest of the day, Mr. Martin was busy doing what he loved best—taking pictures of happy people.

At twelve o'clock the men stopped working and everybody gathered around the laden tables, including Mr. Jones Martin whom they asked to share their bounty. They heaped their plates and sat in the shade to eat. Seth followed Julia down the food line and whispered to her, "Come eat with me."

Not even knowing what food she chose, she took her plate and walked with him. They wandered away from mothers watching their young children, away from men looking critically at the half-framed barn, and headed down toward the spring. Some women who had marriageable-age daughters, saw them go and raised jealous eyebrows. Mrs. Crawford, who kept a special eye out for Julia said to Joe's wife, Martha, "Looks like we might have a *house* raisin' come next year!"

Seth and Julia sat by the spring and Julia didn't know whether she was eating ham or turnip greens. She looked into Seth's eyes and felt her heart go soft like butter fresh out of the churn. He almost forgot to eat because he was looking at her so straight. Then he spoke softly, "Julie, you're so awful pretty, but you're awful young, too."

So he *did* still think she was pretty! "I'm fifteen —just had a birthday—and I am grown up now. I'm not a little girl any more, Seth, even though I'm not as old as you. I've missed seein' you—Solly won't take us to church and he don't want us to go neither."

"Yeah—we been goin', Pa and me, and I been lookin' for you every time. Been sorry not to see you. What's the matter with Solly Crawford, anyway? Is he just mean?"

"Oh, he's always grouchy—just born that way I guess. Wish he *would* go to church—it might do him some good."

"Does he treat you all right, Julie?"

"He's all right—I just don't get too close to him. But I do love Miss Ellie and she's awful good to me."

"Well, he better not do anything to hurt you!"

"Let's don't talk about Solly. Are you and your pa workin' on your house? Said you was goin' to fix it up."

"We're workin' on it. We fixed the back steps—our bull got loose and started chasin' me. I run up the steps and he stood there and pawed the ground and horned the steps. Took a while to get him settled down."

Julia's laughter rang out. "Good thing there's no bulls 'round here—and me with this red dress on!"

"And you shore are pretty in that red dress. You look like a fine lady! Did Miss Ellie make it for you?"

Julia nodded. "I worked on it too, but she did the most. What else are you doin' to the house?"

"We're fixin the floor—makin' it more level." He chuckled. "Poor Ma—she always said that floor made her tired just walkin' back and forth, cause it was so hilly. I was up on the roof yesterday, repairin' that. Chimney was about to fall down." He sighed. "Lots of tinkerin' to do. Windows still got to be fixed, we're goin' to rehang the door, and saw some new slats for the bed. But we had to get the crops in so we ain't been doin much inside lately. What you been doin' mostly, Julia? Does Solly make you work hard?"

"Nothin' I don't really want to do. I like workin' outside. Course, durin' the winter I just stayed inside with Miss Ellie and we made quilts and knitted some. It's a nice house the Crawfords got and Miss Ellie likes it clean, so there's plenty of inside work. But I like helpin' her."

A silence fell while they sat and watched some fish swimming around in the pond, jumping to grab a morsel they threw on top of the water. They simply enjoyed each other's company. Then Seth asked, "Are you still my girl, Julie? Anybody else been around lookin' wall-eyed at you?"

She giggled and looked straight at him. "No wall-eyed men 'round me! Been two years now, but I'm still your girl if you want me to be. I think about you a lot, Seth." She pondered something for a while, then decided to say it. "What about you? You're a man and you can go anywhere. Any girls been flippin' their skirts in your direction?" She blushed at being so bold, and looked back at the pond.

Seth grinned. "Well, I been goin' around some and I seen some girls—there's girls ever'where. But I didn't see no skirt flippers that *I* wanted." He gazed at her, shook his head and sighed. "I wish you was sixteen or seventeen. I'm eighteen already, and Pa's been talkin' about it lately. He says I ought to get wed soon and that I'm old enough. Says he has a hankerin' for kids about the place again—it's too lonesome since Ma died. But I told him I still don't know any girl I like as well as you."

"What did he say when you told him that?"

"He says you're too young and lots of things can happen before you grow up. But he don't know you well as I do. Think you'll still like me in another year or two?"

"Yes, Seth, I will," she smiled, her cheeks flaming. He bent his head to kiss her—a kiss Julia had been waiting for the last two years. The sweetness of his lips on hers sent a shiver through her spine and set her heart to pounding 'till she was sure he must hear it. She didn't know the word "romance," but she felt that way. And she usually blurted out what popped into her head. So after he kissed her she opened her eyes, looked into his, and exclaimed, "Seth, I'm shore glad you don't chew no tabacker."

Seth howled with laughter and hugged her close to him. "Don't never intend to, Julie. It's nasty stuff." He lifted her face and began to kiss her again and was interrupted by a clanging bell calling him back to work on the barn. "Oh," he said, "I'd rather kiss you than work on a barn, but guess we better get on back. This barn's gotta be raised today. But I hope I can see you soon, Julie."

Julia jumped up and brushed the grass off her skirt. She really didn't want to join the others but knew she had to. She couldn't lollygag here.

All afternoon she sat with the other women, most of whom had brought knitting or quilt pieces to work on. Farm housewives' hands were always busy while gossipin' was goin' on. Children were running all about playing games and shouting at one another. Julia watched them and remembered not too many years ago when she and Seth used to play together. Now they were grown up, and in a new way Seth had become much more important to her. As she sat knitting and listening to all the goin's on of the county, she often raised her eyes and looked over toward the barn, her eyes searching for Seth among the other men. When she saw him straddling the top ridgepole, bent over and hammering, she shivered and closed her eyes. Oh, what if he fell? Nothing must happen to hurt Seth!

By the time the doors were hung and the barn stood finished—shining and new, the western sun was slanting long, red rays across the fields. The men stood for a few minutes, scrutinizing their craftsmanship, then set to putting their tools away in their wagons. Nodding satisfaction, they all straggled down to the pond to wash their hands and sweaty faces, drying them on their big red bandana handkerchiefs as they walked back to the tables.

The women folded up their dishcloths which had covered the food, protecting it from the flies. Not so much food this time—children had been raiding under the cloths all afternoon—but enough for everybody to have something before they went home. They had made more coffee and the men drank that thirstily.

By the time the moon came up—a great, round orange globe rising over the pine trees—wagons were packed and children rounded up. Shouting, "Much obliged" and good-byes to each other, the men slapped the reins on horses' broad backs and one by one strong farm wagons pulled out and rumbled toward home. This neighborly deed was completed and a happy young couple had a new barn.

Miss Ellie chattered to Julia most of the way home, commenting on all the news she'd learned that day. For a woman, a barn raisin' was much better than a newspaper. Not everybody could read a newspaper anyway. Solly drove hunched over the reins, and never said a word.

This was one time when Julia wished Miss Ellie wouldn't talk so much. It interfered with her memories of beside-the-pond-sittin'-time with Seth. She'd hoped he'd have a chance to say something to her at the last, but his pa had said, "Let's go, Seth," almost before he wiped his mouth after his last cup of coffee. Julia thought it wasn't because his pa wasn't friendly to her; he just looked tired. But it kept her and Seth from saying good-bye to each other.

She closed her eyes, ignoring the jiggling of the wagon, and thought about Seth kissing her and how she enjoyed it. Seth didn't think she was old enough to get married, but *she* thought she was. Maybe Miss Ellie would go with her to church even if Solly didn't go. Not only did she miss seeing Seth by not going to church; she missed hearing the Bible readings and the sermons too. She liked thinkin' about the Lord and hearin' stories from the Bible. She liked knowin' more about salvation.

When they got home she had a chance to speak to Miss Ellie alone while Solly was putting up the horses. She hugged Miss Ellie and said, "I'm much obliged to you for makin' this dress for me."

Miss Ellie beamed. "What did Seth say about it?"

"He said it was pretty. And he asked me if you made it for me. I told him yes, but that I had helped a little. He's very nice, Miss Ellie and—though I've knowed him all my life, well—it's kinda different now."

Ellie nodded wisely. "I saw how he looked at you. And I saw how you looked at him, and I was a'thinkin' we might have a new house raisin'—maybe next year. Is he in a marryin' frame of mind?"

"Yes. But his pa says I'm too young and he wants Seth to hurry up and marry with somebody else. Says he wants young'uns around the house because it's too lonesome."

Ellie comforted her. "Well, I could see that Seth favored you. Maybe he can just hold off a while and not listen to his pa."

"I hope so, Miss Ellie."

Before Julia climbed into bed that night, she knelt and looked out at the big moon sailing high and wondered if Seth was lookin' at the moon and thinkin' about her.

CHAPTER FOUR
Violation

One morning in August Solly said at breakfast, "Julia, I want you to go down to the south quarter today—the corn's ready. I'll be workin' the east quarter." And without waiting for an answer he tramped out of the kitchen.

"Don't see why he wants you to work outside," exclaimed Ellie to Julia. "He's got plenty of money to hire anybody he wants to help him."

"I don't mind, Miss Ellie. Hard work won't hurt me. Anyway, I like workin' in the corn."

"Well, don't forget your sunbonnet—you'd be burned to a cinder."

Julia finished her breakfast, enjoying her slice of fried, thick-cut country ham, and coffee. "Heard about any more barn or house raisin's?" she asked with a twinkle in her eyes. "Maybe if there was one, I'd get to see Seth again. Seems like a long time since last May."

Miss Ellie smiled. "Ain't heard nothin' about anything like that. If I had, I'd 've told you first thing. I know how anxious you are to see him."

Julia sighed. She had been thinking about Seth all summer, ever since last May. But she knew he must be busy at his own place.

She tied on her sunbonnet, waved to Miss Ellie and ambled out the back door. She first filled a quart jar with water from the water bucket on the porch. Picking up a couple of towsacks from a heap by the steps, she put her water jar in one and slung both of them over her shoulder. It was a long walk down to the south quarter and Julia swung through the fields with her usual lengthy strides, checking out the squirrels and birds. Looking up at the sky she said, "Lord, it's been some days since I thanked you for the sunshine and the crops and the critters. Much obliged, Lord. And bless Seth at whatever he's doin' now." She was sure the Lord liked to be thanked for His handiwork.

Entering the south quarter corn patch between the first two rows, Julia dropped the sacks on the ground, set her drinking water aside, and turned to pulling the ears of corn. Gathering an armful at a time, she stooped and stowed them in the towsacks, raised up again and gathered more as she worked her way down. It was so peaceful and quiet in the field and she reveled in the feeling of being alone there. Her bonnet sheltered her face from the sun and kept buzzing flies from her eyes. She liked the rustle the corn stalks made as they gently blew together—that raspy, dry, papery sound. She liked stretching for high ears and feeling her breasts ripple under her tight bodice. She was busy with rosy dreams of herself and Seth on their own farm—maybe come next year.

Suddenly someone caught her from behind in a bear-like grip, nearly stopping her breath. She dropped half an armful of corn, twisted around in this vise and looked up into a sensual face—much too near her own. Solly! And his narrowed eyes viewed her with an expression she'd never encountered before. "Mr. Crawford!" she gasped. "Let me go! Mr. Crawford! What's the matter with you—what do you want—have you gone crazy?"

She was pushing, squirming, trying to duck and run, trying to bring her knee up to shove him away, and closing her eyes at the same time to shut out the sight of him. For all her struggling, Solly only laughed and held her tighter against him. With one hand he held her, with his other he was exploring her body. "I been watchin' you fer a long time now and you're gettin' awful purty." He shook his head. "Why ain't you nicer to me, Julia? I'm good to you. You're livin' in my house and I ain't a goin' ta hurt you none."

He sounded almost pleading. For a moment he loosed his stranglehold on her and she kicked out, turned, broke free and stumbled down the row, trying to pick up her skirt so she could run. And just as quickly he lumbered after her, swift in spite of his bulk. He caught her and again she was a captive against his sweaty overalls. In an instant his mood had changed and he pushed his face closer to hers. He began pawing at her, panting and behaving like an animal, relentless—like a bull after a heifer in the field.

Her breast heaved—she could not bear the look in his eyes. She pushed him and she kicked, but she was no match for his brutish strength. "Fight all you want, Julia, I aim to have you. You been settin' me on fire all winter and summer long. You're mine and you'll *stay* mine too. If you tell anybody about this, I'll horsewhip you!" He tore off her sunbonnet, grabbed a handful of her thick black hair, pulled her head back, and his thick lips crushed hers.

She jerked her head around far as she could, and spat. Some of her spit hit his cheek and a sudden stab of gladness pierced her mind. But gladness faded instantly and she cried out, "You dirty, filthy hog! Don't you know my brothers will kill you for this?!"

Solly's mouth turned down and his head jerked. "Ha—they'll never know. I'll watch you and keep you for mine. I won't let you get away, no use to try. And Ellie with her snifflin' ways won't believe you if you tell her. But if you do, I'll kill you." All the time he was threatening her, he was also trying to subdue her flailing arms. When she continued to fight him, he softened his voice and coaxed, "Aw—come on now, be a little nicer to me." Then his jaw jutted out, his neck grew redder than ever and he muttered, "Whether you do or not, don't matter none."

Weeping, struggling, cold with fear in spite of the blazing August sun, Julia was flung to the ground between rustling corn stalks and his heavy body fell on top of her. He folded one arm tight against her throat to hold her down, and she felt his other thick hand pulling up her long skirt. "No—No!," she screamed. "Don't—" But his bulky arm muffled her scream and she closed her eyes against his savage face. His mouth bruised hers again.

She wanted to vomit, felt her stomach surge, then she screamed again at seering, brutal pain.

Solly only grunted. Finally he hoisted his body off her and stood up.

Sobbing, she rolled over on her side, drew her knees up into a fetal position, and hid her face in her arms. She lay there weeping for a long time after he had finished with her. Finally, she groaned and sat up, brushed the hair out of her eyes and struggled to her feet. Her skirt was a mess and automatically she started knocking dirt off it, turned, and stumbled a few steps toward the house. Hearing a sound, she whirled and there sat Solly watching her, smoking one of his hand-rolled cigarettes.

He threw down his cigarette, scrambled up and grabbed her arm. She tried to jerk away, but it was no use. She had no more strength than a baby. Never in her life had she felt so afraid and so helpless.

"Guess you've worked enough for one day." He smirked. "I'll come to the house with you. Tell Ellie you had a faintin' spell, and don't forget what I said. You don't tell nobody nothin'!" He shook her. "You hear that? You're goin' to work with me ever' day and you never say anything about this to Ellie."

Uttering not a word and sick to her very soul, Julia shambled back over the field beside Solly, sometimes falling to her knees in weakness. Then his hateful hands lifted her up with no gentleness.

Her head hung down and her hair fell over her face, and as she walked she noticed nothing of God's beautiful, plentiful earth. She looked only at her feet moving over the ground and wondered if they belonged to her. Numb and almost beyond pain, she thought of nothing at all except that one foot must be shoved in front of the other. Finally she tottered up the steps and into the house alongside of Solly.

Ellie gasped and jumped from her chair when she saw Julia. "What in the world happened to you, Julie? You look like you're 'bout to fall down!" She held out her arms toward Julia.

Julia didn't seem to see the loving arms. She shook her head and brushed past Ellie on the way to her bedroom. She simply couldn't speak.

Ellie trailed after her. "It's too hot in that field for you today. Where's your bonnet? Get into bed and I'll put a wet cloth on your head." She stopped at the door to Julia's room and turned to her husband. "Solly, you got no cause to make Julie work so hard on a hot day like this!"

"Aw—she's all right," he said, his voice as cold as pond ice before a spring thaw. "She must 've just had a faintin' spell. I found her on the ground when I went to see how she was workin'." He sat down in his chair at the kitchen table. "I want t' eat some dinner."

"With spirit Ellie replied, "It ain't dinner time yet! I didn't know you was a'comin in early, so you'll jest have to set a spell and wait while I get it ready."

"Ain't gonna wait. Heat up that coffee and give me some o' that cold chicken and cornbread we had yesterday. And bring me some peaches from the cellar."

Ellie pursed her mouth and didn't answer, but took the chicken and cornbread from the meat safe, put it on a plate and plopped it down in front of him. Then she blew up the coals under the pan of their left-over morning coffee. "You can git it fer yerself when it's hot—the peaches too. I'm goin' in there to see about Julia. I don't like it that she worked so hard she fainted."

"Nothin's the matter with her," he shouted. "Soon as she's in bed, git out of her room and let her sleep. I want her to work tomorrow." He picked up a chicken leg.

Ellie stood with her hands on her hips. "Well, she'll work outside tomorrow only if she feels like it!"

Solly looked at her, his brows drawn together and his hand holding the chicken stopped half way to his mouth. "What's the matter with you, Woman? You act like an old bear growlin' about her cub. Only she don't belong to *you!* So leave her alone."

Ellie looked at him with narrowed-eyes disdain, turned her back and strode to Julia's room.

Julia, once in her room and in spite of the heat, pulled the curtains tight over her windows. She wanted only darkness. She got undressed and into her nightgown though it wasn't yet noon. She'd never worn a nightgown this time of day before, but she'd never felt this way before. She longed to be able to wash herself, but with Solly in the kitchen, she couldn't ask Miss Ellie for any hot water. She just lay rigid and sleepless in total soul sickness through the rest of the day and the whole night.

At daybreak the next morning still numb with shock and terror she shot up in bed, covers pulled tight around her neck. Solly was at her door calling, "Julia!" Oh, was he coming in? What was he planning to do to her now?

"Time to git up! You can go back to the south quarter—'twon't be so hot today. Ellie's got breakfast a'waitin'." His heavy steps clomped toward the kitchen.

Julia rolled out of bed, every muscle screaming in protest. Her arms hurt so much she could barely take off her nightgown and put on her work clothes. As she pulled the dress on over her head, some stray dirt from the cornfield fell into her hair. As if she didn't already have enough cornfield dirt in her hair!

Like a zombie she walked through the kitchen and down the steps to the outhouse. When she emerged a few minutes later, Solly was standing nearby under some fruit trees. He came up close to her and she drew back. "Leave me alone," she pleaded. "Do you even have to come out here and follow me?"

"I don't want you to think you can run away. And if Ellie's watchin, I'm just lookin' at my fruit trees. And I don't want you to fergit what I said yesterday. You're gonna work with me ever' day and you ain't goin' nowheres, and you ain't tellin' nobody nothin." He leered at her. "Think you can remember that and behave yourself?"

Hatred flooded her soul. She said nothing but walked back to the house and tried, for Ellie's sake, to eat some breakfast. But how could she eat anything with Solly's hateful presence there? She never looked at him once.

Ellie hovered over her like a mother hen—she knew Ellie loved her. How she longed to throw herself into Ellie's arms and tell her what Solly did. It wouldn't change the fact that he did it, but at least she'd have some comfort. But she didn't doubt for a minute that Solly *would* kill her. And if she told Miss Ellie, then Solly might kill her too, so nobody would be left to tell on him. She had to protect Miss Ellie.

She was caught in this horrible web like a fly, and she had *chosen* to come here! The big red spider, Solly, watched her day and night. She longed to kill him with a fury that turned her faint, but Ellie suspected nothing.

For a month Solly made her go with him to the fields and work alongside him and he possessed her day after day. After some time the physical pain was less, but her soul pain was piercing. She felt vile and degraded. She could barely think, she simply did her tasks with his hateful eyes on her. Her most basic instinct was raw survival, and after a while she felt that she was nothing more than a farm animal. She never knew when he would decide to throw her down again, and she never looked him in the eyes. He was a beast in stinking, sweaty overalls. He guarded the door every time she went to the outhouse, so she knew it was useless to even think of running away from him. How could she live with such hatred and shock all mixed up in her brain?

She dully began to think about God. He must still be up there! So she tried to pray but felt only blackness in her soul. *Oh, God, did you ferget all about me? Let one of my brothers come to visit me! But I know they are all covered up in their own work! They think I'm all right. Lord, send <u>somebody</u> for me to talk to!* But nobody came.

One evening when Solly was out by the back steps cutting wood, Miss Ellie said to her, "Julie, you ain't talked much to me fer a while. Don't you wonder how Seth is gettin' along? Maybe he'll come over sometime to say howdy. You still think about him, don't you?"

Miss Ellie's face showed total bewilderment when Julia's eyes grew wide, then she burst into tears and ran to her room. Ellie followed her to her door. "Julie, is somethin' wrong between you and Seth? You used to talk about him." She listened for a while but Julia only sobbed.

Julia lived for four weeks in perpetual shock, for Solly never left her. When he left the house he made her come—always on the pretext of a job for Julia to do. Every time Solly forced her, the revulsion was so great that she vomited. Solly only laughed.

Then one day Julia realized her monthlies should have started a week before. But she had seen no sign. They probably hadn't started because she had been so hurt. The next day and the next, she looked expectantly. When two weeks had passed and they hadn't started, in great bitterness she knew she was carrying Solly's baby. *Now what will happen to me? How can I live and have Solly's baby? Everybody will say I'm a bad girl, but Seth will never believe them. Seth! He would take care of me—How can I ever get to Seth to tell him—how can I? Solly watches me all the time!*

But after a month Solly began to grow weary of his new role as jailer and lover of a fractious fifteen-year old. He began to think about a woman in Marion. She appreciated him. And she didn't vomit. Well, he'd just have to take a trip into Marion—he needed supplies anyhow. But what about Julia? *I'll threaten her good and she'll be scared enough to behave herself. She wouldn't dare disobey me!* The next morning at breakfast he announced, "I got to go to Marion today for some business."

Julia said nothing. *He'll probably make me go with him.*

"Bring me some flour and sugar," Ellie requested.

"Well, if I have time I'll try and git 'em. I got lots to buy—ain't been there for a month!"

"If you don't git 'em, you won't have anymore of them biscuits 'er cakes. Why *wouldn't* you have time? You got all day!"

"What you bein' so sassy fer? No need fer you to git so riled up. I'll git 'em." He turned to Julia. "No cause for you to work outside today. Ellie ain't feelin' well and I want you to stay with her. Understand?"

Julia barely glanced up at him and that enraged him. He bellowed, "Julia! Listen to me!"

She raised her eyes briefly to his face—that revolting face which so often had been close to hers.

"You heard me?" She nodded and he looked hard at her; his meaning clear. He strode outside.

Ellie said, "Julia, what in the world do you think is the matter with him today?"

Julia just shook her head and stared at her plate, her thoughts beginning to whirl. She couldn't believe that at last her chance might be here! She had known that *sometime* Solly would have to go to town for supplies and would probably make her go with him. But he must have thought he had secured her forever—that she would never disobey him. But he *was* going and leaving her at home! Her heart pounded at the possibility of freedom.

Solly went out to the barn, hitched up the wagon and drove out his gate without looking back. Julia waited until his wagon disappeared in dust and then said, "Miss Ellie, there *is* some more work in the field—I can get it done while he's gone. I know you don't need me inside today."

"Child, I don't know where he got the idy I ain't feelin' well—I'm feelin' fine. And I don't need you inside. You look plum white and peaked here lately. Go on outside, but don't work. Set down under some tree and rest."

Julia's heart thundered so hard she was afraid Miss Ellie could hear it. *Can I get away? I feel bad to leave Miss Ellie without tellin' her the reason. Maybe I oughta tell her everything. But I can't! If I don't go now, I might never get away. I'll tell Miss Ellie some other time! I got to go now!*

Was Solly only pretending to leave so he could trick her? Had he stopped down the lane just waiting to pounce on her again? She wouldn't put anything past him. But maybe it was true. Maybe she *could* get away.

Julia walked slowly out the door and waved to Miss Ellie from the steps. Once out of sight of the house, she started running down beside the lane, keeping to one side so she could quickly disappear into the woods, in case she saw him. But she saw no sign of Solly's wagon. When she reached the main road, she knew which way he would take to get to Marion—if he really went to Marion. She peered fearfully out from the trees at the crossroad and saw no one. *Wouldn't surprise me none if he was hidin' out around here.*

She darted out onto the main road, turned toward her brother Joe's place opposite from the Marion route, and began running as fast as she could. She was desperate. She knew her very life depended on reaching Joe. He was her nearest brother. She hadn't dared take anything with her so was not burdened by any bundles. She ran 'til her legs gave out then slowed to a stumbling walk. *Oh, Lord, let somebody come along and give me a ride before Solly changes his mind and comes back looking for me!* The autumn sun was merciless and her shoulders drooped. She wiped her sweaty face with her sleeve and wished for a drink of water as she plodded on down the road.

Clop-clopping of a horse in the distance jerked her to awareness. Some rider was coming toward her! She dashed into scrub beside the road, hid behind some tall bushes and peered out. Was it anybody she knew—or anybody she could trust? Her legs began to shake and her heart leaped as she recognized the rider. Seth!

With a cry she staggered out into the road and flagged him. *How can it be that Seth come along here and found me? What will I tell him? If I tell him the truth, will he think I'm dirty and not have anything to do with me? But he said in the spring he still wanted me to be his girl. Yes—but that was last spring before Solly— Now he won't want me. Now he will be ashamed of me!* Thoughts swarmed in her tired brain like flies droning over spoiled food. She had been held captive too long!

In surprise Seth recognized her and when he jumped down from his horse, she completely lost control of her emotions. Gone was her stoicism. She threw herself against him in a storm of tears.

"Julie! Oh, Julie, what's the matter with you? You look like you're half dead. What are you doin' this far from the Crawfords, and *walkin'* down this road?"

"Oh, Seth, it's Mr. Crawford. Take me away from here! You got to get me away from here—I want to kill him. I hate him, I hate him! Oh, Seth, he threw me down in the corn lots of times and now I'm carryin' a baby. Seth, I'm not a bad girl, he made me! I feel so dirty! Take me to Joe's. Take me away with you—take me with you anywhere—" She heard herself babbling and shrieking and wanted to stop, but had no power to. She simply shuddered moaning on his shoulder.

Seth didn't understand. He shook her shoulders. "Julia! Stop! What are you sayin'? Who threw you down?"

"Mr. Crawford!" she sobbed.

"Solly Crawford? And you're carryin' his *baby* now?"

"Yes, yes yes!" she wailed. "I've been a prisoner for a month—he won't let me alone. He even watched the outhouse when I went there. He went to Marion today and I ran away soon as he was out of the barnlot—"

Seth's face showed shock and consternation, and he pulled Julia close to him, holding her head on his shoulder and smoothing her touseled hair. "Ssssh, Julie— quieten down now. Let me understand. Is all this true? Solly Crawford held you prisoner for a month and used you?"

"Yes! It's true, Seth! He made me go to the fields with him every day, and he used me whenever he wanted to in the field. He's a filthy pig, Seth. He made me work beside him all the time and he watched me all the time. Said he'd kill me if I told anybody. But I couldn't get away to tell anybody. Miss Ellie—"

"What about Miss Ellie? Did she know what he was doin' to you? Why didn't you get her to help you?"

"No—I was afraid to tell her. She knew somethin' was wrong, but she couldn't even think of what he was a doin'. And I was afraid if I told her he would kill me. He said he would. I thought he might kill Miss Ellie, too, then nobody would know. It ain't her fault, Seth, and it ain't my fault. He's a beast in the field!" She sagged in his arms.

As this horrible news began to sink in, Seth put his face down on Julia's hair for a minute, his heart pounding in anger and sorrow, his eyes streaming. He hugged her to him for a while longer to try to comfort her and slow down her tears. Then he lifted her gently onto his horse. "I'll take you to your brother Joe's," he said.

They rode for some time, her sobs lessening, as she leaned against Seth's back—a wonderful haven. Her arms encircled him as they rode. She felt safe now—Seth was here to take care of her. But she was tired—so tired that she was afraid she'd fall off the horse. Her mind ran on in jumbled relief, full of dreams. She was with Seth now.

Suddenly a thought leaped at her. She sat up and raised her head. "Seth! Why'd you come by here today? You goin' to Marion to get supplies?"

He hesitated for a long time—as if he didn't want to tell her the reason he had come riding down this road instead of working on his harvest. She didn't know why, but she began to dread his answer.

"Seth?—"

He shook his head in despair. "Oh, Julie, how can I tell you? It don't seem right to tell you now . . ."

"Well, you sound like it's bad. Just tell me straight out—" Her voice had the spark of the old Julia.

Seth drew a long breath. "When I heard what you just told me, I nearly forgot what I was ridin' over this way for. This ain't no time to tell you my news, but you have to know I guess." He stopped and couldn't seem to go on.

A cold chill made her shiver. "Seth—?"

"Julie, I was on my way to the Crawfords to see you. I was a comin' by to give you an invite to my weddin'."

CHAPTER FIVE
Repercussions

Julia didn't understand. "Your *weddin'?*"

"Yes, Julie. I'm awful fond of you; last year you was my girl. But you're too young and Pa wants me to marry. I wanted you to be the first to know that I aim to wed with Hattie Knight."

Weakness snaked down Julia's spine, inundating her. She had to lean against Seth's back again to keep from falling off the horse, and she tasted bitterness in her soul. She shook her head from side to side, rubbing her face against his back. *I can't stand it! All the time I've been goin' through awful things, Seth wasn't thinkin' about me at all. He was plannin' to get wed to somebody else. I don't care if I don't live any longer! But people don't just die when they want to.* With dry lips she asked, "Hattie Knight? Who's she?"

"They're a new family over by Makanda. Hattie's the oldest girl. She's awful pretty—nearly as pretty as you, Julia."

"Where'd you meet her if she lives in Makanda?" Her voice sounded like the voice of a stranger.

"I met her at a protracted meetin' in June."

"How old is she, Seth?"

"Seventeen."

"I'm fifteen," she said, her voice flat and dull. "And even if you didn't marry with Hattie Knight, you wouldn't want to marry with me. I ain't fittin' to marry nobody now."

Anger stiffened his body again and he said tenderly, "To me you'll always be the same Julie." He shook his head. "That Solly Crawford ain't worth killin'—to do that to you. You're not even growed up yet! Killin's too good for him!"

Julia, in total despair whispered, "I'm all growed up now."

They didn't talk anymore. By the time they reached Joe's house, Julia was almost dead with fatigue.

Martha came running out at the sound of the horse and when she saw Julia's face, she put her hand over her mouth to keep from crying out. Then she held out her arms. Martha was the closest to a real sister that Julia ever had. In spite of bearing five children, Martha was still a lovely woman—tall and straight with blue eyes and wavy blond hair. Her hair was rolled in a knot in back, but loose curls escaped the knot, framing and softening her face.

Julia slid off Seth's horse, her face crumpled on Martha's shoulder. "Ring the dinner bell, Marthie—I need to talk to Joe."

In the field Joe heard the bell, glanced at the sun high in the sky, dropped the bucket he was holding, left the bags of harvested corn on the ground, and made for the house. He found his wife, Seth, and Julia sitting stiffly around the kitchen table waiting for him. One look at Julia's face told him she was almost ready to collapse.

Joe rushed to put his arm around Julia's shoulders and asked, "Julie, what's happened to you?"

Without any more tears then, her face like granite, Julia told the three of them the whole story of what Solly had done to her. A month ago she would not have been able to recite such unspeakable things, but now it was as if she were talking about them happening to another person. She talked about the pain of it, the shame of it, the threats, the fear, and of being a prisoner so that she could be used over and over. And the worst part was that now she was going to have a baby—a lifetime reminder.

Joe sat in stunned silence, staring at nothing and shaking his head back and forth. By the time Julia was done telling her horrible story, his face was in his hands, tears running through his fingers. There was silence around the table as they looked at Joe, waiting for him to speak.

Finally he raised his head. His mouth was tight and his face so angry that Martha was afraid for him. Joe was always an easy-going man; she had never before seen her husband like he was now. But he controlled his voice and said evenly, "I'll get Matthew and Will and Caleb. Don't know when I'll be home, Marthie."

He jerked down his shotgun from a nail by the kitchen door, rammed open a drawer and pulled out a bag of buckshot. Jamming on his old felt hat he banged open the door. "You stay here, Julie. Martha's got another gun and if Solly comes lookin' for you, she'll use it. You'll be safe here." Before going out the door his arms encircled Julia for a few moments. He wiped his eyes.

"I'll go with you, Joe!" Seth said, following him outside. "I'd like to help you get Solly Crawford."

"Thank you, Seth—you're a good friend. But this is a job for brothers!" Joe whistled for his horse, jumped up, wheeled and galloped out of the yard.

Seth hung his head and walked around for a spell. When he went back inside, Julia was still sitting at the kitchen table. He touched her shoulder and said in great sorrow, "Julie, I wish I could do somethin' to help you."

She looked up with deep melancholy. "Ain't nothin' nobody can do for me, Seth. But I hope you and Hattie Knight will have a good life."

"Good-bye, Julie." Seth's eyes burned as he walked out of Martha's kitchen. In the yard, his shoulders hunched and tears rolled down his face. He thought about Julia, his good friend, Julia—spirited, independent—Julia reduced to this. How could this thing happen to the beautiful girl he had known all his life?

Julia watched him go. *There goes my man,* she thought. *I always thought he'd be mine, but he never will. How can I stand to see him go now when I need him the most? I've been sorrowful and hopeless for the last month, but this must be the worst because this will last forever.*

Martha seemed frozen in her chair for a while as they both watched Seth climb on his horse and slowly walk him out of the gate. Seth was hunched over wiping his eyes and even the horse drooped.

Finally, Martha seemed to remember that Julia needed attention and she touched her arm. "Are you hungry, Julia? Let me fix you something—"

"No. Can I go to bed, Martha—even if it's the middle of the day? I've had no safe sleep for a month. Solly never come in my room but I was always afraid he was a goin' to. And all I want to do now is sleep."

Martha took her to the children's room, turned down a bed and pulled the heavy curtains over the windows. She brought Julie a thick slice of fresh-made bread with new-churned butter and a glass of cool spring water. "Here, Julia, eat this first and sleep. You need 'em both. First, let me help you off with this sweaty dress—I'll wash it while you sleep and it'll be dry when you wake up. I won't leave the house and my gun is ready for Solly if he comes here."

Julia looked at Martha standing by the bed and suddenly realized the house was quiet. "Where are all your young'uns? I just now thought about 'em."

"They're all over at my mama's place today, helpin' her pick apples. Goin' to stay a few days and help her put 'em up—that and pears too. My young'uns are not growed up yet, but they know how to work. This is a good time for you to rest and the Lord knows you need it, Julia."

"Marthie, I know this is a heap of trouble for you, but first could I have some water in one of your washin' tubs? I am so dirty.

Ain't had no decent bath lately because Solly wouldn't leave me alone long enough to ever get washed."

Martha tried not to look shocked again, so she turned away from Julia's face. "I'll get it ready in the kitchen. I've got a big kettle of water already hot and a bucket by the kitchen door."

Martha had to help her with her bath because Julia swayed and felt too weak to step into the tub by herself. At last feeling clean—on the outside—Julia sat on the side of the turned-down bed, her head drooping. "Marthie, I feel so bad that I had to come here and put this on you. When Ma died I was only thinkin' that I could be independent and make my own way and hire out. I never ever thought that Solly Crawford was the kind of man he is. He is evil! I had to have some help—I had to get away!" She wiped her eyes. "I guess nobody can ever be independent like I wanted to be. Now ever'body will soon know about me and they'll all think it's my fault I'm in this shape—"

"NO!" Martha said, her mouth tight. "NObody will think it's your fault. Solly Crawford has never been a good man—I should have paid attention to some of the things I heard about him. I just thought he'd behave himself at home with you there. I should have told Joe. If he'd have known what Solly was like, he'd never have let you go there. It's partly my fault." She put her arm around Julia.

"People only put up with him because they like Miss Ellie," Martha continued, "and feel sorry for her. And after this gets out, ever' woman in this county will want to kill him. Ever' woman will think, *What if it was my daughter?"* Martha sat beside Julia with her arm around her, smoothing her hair. "Julia, this is hard, I know, but you can count on us. We are your family. We'll just tell people the truth. That's the best way. They won't blame you."

Tears rolled down her cheeks, and Julia said, "Marthie, if I'd had a sister, I wouldn't love her more than you. Right now all I can say is, 'Much obliged.'"

Martha kissed her cheek, stood up and went out. At the door she turned around and said gently, "Eat your bread, Julia. I'll call you when supper is ready. Sleep now. And Julie, welcome to our home. I know you wanted to make your own way, and you will sometime. But this is your home now. You are like my own sister and I know that Joe would say, 'This is your home, Julie.'"

She closed the door, went to the farthest corner of the kitchen, and sobbed into her bunched up apron.

* * * *

Joe left Julia and Martha, racing his horse first to Caleb's house. His thoughts were a tangle of hatred for Solly and anger at himself for allowing Julia to go there. He blamed himself—he was the oldest of Julia's brothers, and he should not have allowed her to go. He'd never had any love for Solly Crawford, but always liked Miss Ellie. No one could ever have forseen this. *Lord God, forgive me for not takin' better care of my little sister!*

Caleb, tall, dark hair and high cheekbones like Joe, was just sitting down to a noon dinner of beans and cornbread. When he heard the horse he went out, stood and listened to Joe for a spell. His wife, Mary, looking out the back door, saw her husband's face change from surprise to shock to fury. Then both men tramped into the house and Caleb got his gun and shells and put them on the back porch.

Mary stood in fear but she asked quietly, "What's the matter, Joe? What's happened that both of you are goin' out with guns?"

Joe quickly repeated the story he'd just told Caleb. "We're goin' first to William and Matthew's to get them, then we're goin' to divide up and try to find Solly."

"Come on, Joe," urged Caleb. "Might as well eat first. No tellin' when we can git any more."

"Yeah, but let's eat fast." He shook his head. "I can't tell you how awful I feel. Julia looked like she was more than half dead-—and I'm aimin' to kill Solly Crawford if I get a chance. I ain't heard nothin' like this goin on for many a year. But now it's happened to our sister!"

Caleb nodded, took out his bandana and swiped it across his eyes. "I hope we all get a shot at him. Filthy dog like that's lost all his livin' rights!"

Mary shook her head. "I shore feel sorry for Julia. But you two just might get yourselves killed and I'm warnin' you to be careful. That Solly might have a gun with him too. If he's that mean, he's liable to do anything. I've heard a few things about him but couldn't hardly believe all of 'em."

The two men left Caleb's and rounded up Matthew and Will, again repeating the story. Anger filled each heart as they tramped up and down in Will's barn lot rehashing the story and again questioning Joe on parts of it. Sorrow was visible as each one in his own way accepted part of the blame for not doing more to care for their young sister. They knew their family would never be the same.

The four of them together made their plans. Joe and Caleb would go into Marion to look for Solly; Matthew and Will would ride to Solly's house. Whatever was done, they would meet at Joe's house when they finished.

When Matthew and Will arrived in Solly's yard that afternoon, they saw Ellie Crawford sitting in the kitchen door in her rocking chair, peering anxiously out. Her eyes widened when she saw the guns in their hands. She stood up from her chair, and moved it away from the door.

"Come on in, Matthew and Will," she said, her hands visibly shaking. "Ain't seen you since the barn raisin. Why're you bringin' them guns in here?"

"Howdy, Mis' Crawford. You better set down agin."

Ellie backed down into the rocker and Will and Matthew stood holding their guns. They both were shorter and heavier than Joe and Caleb, but there was a strong family resemblence to each other. "Is Solly here?"

"Tell me first what'r you boys carryin' guns for?"

"We'll tell you, Miss Ellie. Is Solly around?"

"No, he said he was goin' in to Marion— but I'm worried about Julia. She left this mornin'—said she had some work in the field she wanted to do, and she didn't come when I rung the dinner bell. You know where she is?"

"Yes, we know, but we're lookin' for Solly."

"It's nearly evenin' now. Solly ought to be home soon. But shorely you don't need to look for Solly with your guns in your hands! Why don't you lean 'em over there against the corner?"

When Matthew and Will made no move to do what she asked, she grew more nervous. "What you want him for? You say you know where Julia is?"

"We'll tell you. Mis' Crawford, has Solly been actin' funny lately? Has he been doin' unusual kinds of things?"

"Well—" she thought for a time. "I didn't pay too much 'tention to it, but I reckon he has, kinda. He's been awful grumpy, but he is most of the time anyhow. Why? I'm more worried about Julia. She ain't been lookin' too good here lately—she looks peaked; and don't talk much. But she's went ever' day to the fields with Solly so I guess she's all right." Her brows creased in anxiety. "Ain't she all right? Why didn't she come back home?"

"Julia is at Joe's," Will said. "She's at Joe's place with Martha." Will's face flushed—he despised doing to Ellie Crawford what he now had to do. "We hate to tell you this, Mis' Ellie, but we have to say it straight out. Solly's been forcin' Julia, throwin' her down in the fields and abusin' her. He made her go with him ever' day. And he told her he'd kill her if she done any reportin' to you. She was afraid he might kill you both. Now she's carryin' his baby—"

Ellie gasped. "What are you a sayin'? That Julie is carryin' *Solly's baby?"*

"Yes," Matthew picked up the tale because Will was having a hard time saying it. "She's tried to get away from him but he watched her like a hawk, so she couldn't go tell nobody or get any help. He even guarded the outhouse door when she went there!"

Ellie's face crumpled. "I didn't know what to think of it but I did see him foller her outside sometimes. Then he'd come in after her. But I never suspected——Are you shore of what you're a' sayin?"

"Shore as the sun risin' tomorrow. Julia didn't want to hurt you, Miss Ellie, and we don't like hurtin' you now. But Julia's our sister and we know she don't lie. She's just about dead over this. Today when Solly said he had to go to Marion, was the first time she had any chance to get away. She started off runnin', then she walked fer a while. Seth Boyd come acrost her on the road and he brought her to Joe's on his horse. She told Joe and Martha and Seth ever'thing that Solly's been doin' to her over the last month. It's the worst story we've ever heard."

At the beginning of that unimaginable recital, Ellie's eyes widened, and her mouth hung open. Now her thoughts were so muddled she shut her eyes and tried to will order out of chaos in her brain. *These boys are not tellin' the truth,* she said to herself. *This just ain't possible!*

"Miss Ellie, we are sorry fer you," Will said. "We don't fault you none. Julia's gonna stay at Joe's."

Ellie seemed calm, but she felt hysterical inside. "Julie must hate me fer not watchin' out for her better. I'd promised to take good care of her."

"No. She knows you couldn't help it none. You didn't think Solly would do the things he's done to her."

Miss Ellie was weeping hopelessly into her apron. "I thought I was a' helpin' Julie to bring her here and give her a home. But it looks like it was the worst thing that ever happened to her."

"'T'werent your fault," Matthew said. "Miss Ellie, don't mourn over Solly. He's worse than ary lowdown snake I ever saw, takin' a fifteen-year-old innocent girl! Why didn't he visit that house behind the saloon oftener? I guess because he knowed he'd have to pay money for that! When my wife heard about this today, she said she did hear once about Solly a'goin' to that place."

"I knowed he done things like that sometimes," Ellie confessed to Matthew and Will, "but I couldn't do nothin' about it. And I never thought he'd do anything like this right at his own place and to a friend's daughter! It's awful hard for me to believe this."

She stood up and wiped her eyes. "Jest wait here and I'll pack up Julia's things. She come over with 'em in a pillowcase and I'll send 'em the same way. You can take ever'thing to her. Tell her I'm shorely sorry 'bout this."

"You got time to get 'em together," Will said. "We ain't goin' jest yet."

Ellie stopped suddenly. "So that's what your guns are for. You're intendin' to kill Solly, ain't you?"

Both men nodded. "We are. Joe and Caleb's gone to Marion to get Solly there if they can. Will and me—we aim to stay here and we'll get him if he sneaks home. We don't want to hurt you, Mis' Ellie, and we know you ain't to be blamed, but we're goin' to kill Solly. He ain't worth the powder and lead it'll take to blow his brains out, but we're goin' to do it anyhow. It's too bad he'll die so quick and Julie will suffer all her life for what he done to her!" Matthew turned his back, his shoulders shaking.

Ellie's face was fixed into a screwed-up pucker. "But——but Matthew—but Will—surely you don't aim to kill him——? He may not be much of a man, but he is my husband. What'm I goin' to do here by myself?"

"Like we said, we feel sorry for you, Miss Ellie. But he's gonna get what he deserves." Matthew's face was like stone. "What he done is about to kill Julia. Joe said he never seed anybody sufferin' any more—skeered fer a month, and livin' ever' day wonderin' what he'd think up to do to her! Nobody ought to be put through that kind of hell."

Miss Ellie stumbled into Julia's room with her head bowed.

Will and Matthew shook their heads in sympathy—but their minds were not changed. They moved two kitchen chairs to good watching positions—one by the door and one by the window. They sat there with rifles across their knees.

After some time Ellie came back with a bulging pillowcase and put it close to her rocking chair. She sat down silent for a while, thinking. Then she drew a deep breath and said, "I'd like to say somethin' else to you boys. Will you hear me out?"

Matthew and Will nodded.

"It's jest this. I don't blame you for what you want to do. If I was in your place I'd probly want to do the same thing. But now

I'm thinkin' about you. I've known you four brothers all your lives. I was with your Ma when you was born. She was my good friend. I'm now askin you to think long and hard, about killin' Solly.

"If you kill him, all your lives you'll have guilt on your soul. Even if you never went to jail for it, it would be there, inside you. Solly's got to be punished. But it ain't a good idy for you brothers to do the punishin'. Jest think about it because I care what happens to you all."

Will and Matthew listened with sober faces. Yes, she'd been their friend all their lives. They stared at her in silence for a while, then Will said, "But Miss Ellie, we can't do nothin' else!" They got up and went outside.

Ellie sat there for a while, her thoughts whirling. What would she do if they did kill Solly? She knew he was a man she could no longer respect, but did she want him *dead?* Of course not. She didn't want to *see* it happen either. Poor little Julie. She loved that girl! But she had failed to protect her—even though she never thought about her *needing* protection. Busy—she must keep busy. If she was working with her hands, maybe her brain wouldn't work so much. *It don't matter what I think about what Matthew and Will are gonna to do to Solly, it's nearly evenin'. I have to give 'em their supper.*

She went outside on shaky legs—forgetting to put on her sunbonnet—and saw Will and Matthew walking around back of her house, watching the lane. She stood looking at her land, her cows and her horse, down to the barn lot, the corn crib, chickens clucking in the yard, and they all looked strange to her. She shook her head. *Ain't nothin' changed but me. And I won't never be the same again.*

Not speaking, she gathered up an armload of small kindling from the wood stacked by the kitchen door. Squatting down, she laid the kindling criss-cross under the big three-legged iron kettle sitting on three stones in the back yard. A wood splinter drove itself into her hand but she barely noticed—just pulled it out with a finger and thumb of her other hand. Like a sleep-walker she crossed over to the well, and dropped the hitched-up bucket into its depths, the pulley creaking as the rope turned it around. Three buckets of water she pulled up and filled the kettle.

Rattling of a team pulling a wagon drifted up from the road at the foot of her lane. Instantly immobile, dripping bucket in her hand, Ellie held her breath and waited to see whether the wagon would turn in. She could see a trail of dust kicked up by the horses, but it went by her gate and the sound receded. She found herself staring at the kettle of water and wondering what she was doing out in the yard. But her brain began to work again, and she hooked the bucket back at the top of its pulley as she had done hundreds of times before. *Got to git the fire!*

Like a puppet, she turned back toward her kitchen, picked up her small shovel, and scraped together a few live coals from her cook stove. Though she didn't remember feeding the fire past noon, coals were still there. Taking a shovel full, she walked back outside and dumped the fire onto the kindling under the big pot. A breeze blew some smoke into her eyes, but she was surprised when she felt a few tears on her cheeks.

Without hurry, she sat stiffly down on the back steps waiting for the water to boil. She felt frozen, in body and mind, as she stared at the fire. Now and then she plodded back toward it to push some wood further under the kettle. Her favorite barn kitten mewed and rubbed against her long skirt, but Ellie's hand had no welcome caress. She stared at the kitten and never saw it. *How could he do it!? What Will and Matthew said must be true, but how could Solly be so rotten? Sweet Julia—only fifteen years old!*

When steam bumped the big iron lid up and down, Ellie rose slowly from the step and lifted a bag of feed corn from the porch. Measuring two handfuls, she scattered the grain near her feet. A dozen greedy chickens ran to the corn, and she grabbed one and wrung its neck. Standing ramrod straight, she watched the chicken's death struggle. When it quit flopping on the grass, she held it by the feet, and dipped it into the scalding water in her kettle. She swished it round and round until all the feathers were soaking wet and then plucked it, tossing the wet feathers into a pile on the grass. Force of habit. She always collected the feathers later, spread them out on the porch to dry, and used them in pillows for her house.

When the light feathers were all off and heavy pin-feathers pulled out, she took the chicken into the house to clean out and cut up.

Outside, Matthew and Will watched Miss Ellie perform these familiar tasks of a farm wife with no comment. They knew she was going to cook supper for them, even though they were there waiting to kill her husband. Farm hospitality guided her actions, but her face revealed the death-cold hopelessness she felt in her soul.

Ellie built up her stove fire, put the chicken on to boil, and brought up vegetables from the cellar. These she peeled and cut up, putting them in the pot with the chicken. She also made cornbread and coffee. All the while the two men walked around outside, watching the road silently, occasionally scanning the fields and flicking their eyes toward the kitchen window to check on Miss Ellie.

When the cooking was done, Ellie called them to supper. She couldn't eat anything, and wouldn't sit down with them. Like most farm wives, she stood by the stove to refill plates and coffee cups while men ate. Her eyes were blank and staring.

Will muttered to Matthew, "When you watch her it looks like she's just a body there but she ain't got no soul."

Matthew glanced at Ellie, nodded and whispered, "Ain't never seen a woman change as fast as Miss Ellie did today."

Ellie didn't even know they were talking.

The men ate in silence after that. When they finished, they took up their guns again and went outside.

Ellie sank down into her rocking chair, and, totally exhausted, leaned her head back. *Guess I ought to eat somethin', but don't know how I could swaller it. Might as well go on out to the barn and do the milkin'. But I'll just rest a mite first.*

Ten minutes later, *No use tryin' to rest, better I keep on workin'.* So she struggled out of her rocker, took the milk bucket from its hook on the porch wall, and started toward the barn. Matthew caught up with her and said, "Let me have the bucket, Miss Ellie. Will can watch for Sollie and I'll do your milkin'."

Ellie simply nodded, gave Matthew the milk bucket and turned back toward the house. Passing by the small pile of feathers on the grass, she stopped and stared at them as if in a trance. *What are them feathers there for?*

Suddenly like a wilted rag doll, she slumped to her knees on the ground and gathered all the feathers into her apron. Her mouth was trembling and tears were coursing down her cheeks. When she could get up again, she walked stiff-legged straight to the kitchen stove and threw the feathers by handfuls onto the glowing coals. *I'll never make another piller for this house!* The wet feathers began to sizzle and smoke, and the putrid odor penetrated her kitchen. Her mouth twisted and she said aloud, "That stink ain't near as bad as what Solly done!"

The three of them waited in vain for Solly the whole night, listening to all the night sounds, the men walking around the yard often. No one slept. The next morning Will and Matthew milked the cows for Ellie, and did the other outside chores, still on the lookout for Solly.

She had breakfast ready when they brought in the fresh milk. "Much obliged for doin' the chores," she said, her eyes scratchy from lack of sleep. "Have some breakfast." She shuffled to the stove and brought the coffee pot—she suddenly seemed very old.

"We thank you kindly, Miss Ellie. We appreciate your hospitality." They ate her breakfast of thick sliced bacon and fried eggs, homemade bread and coffee. While eating, Matthew said, "Looks like Solly ain't goin' t' show up. Maybe he's got wind we're waitin' fer him."

Ellie shook her head. "I can't imagine where he is. He's never done this before."

The rest of the morning, Matthew and Will walked around the yard, carrying their rifles, searching the place one more time. By noon they decided Solly wasn't coming home, so they said good-bye to Miss Ellie, mounted their horses and rode over to Joe's. Ellie watched them go with jumbled thoughts. *I'm glad he didn't come home,* she said to herself. *But where is he? Will he come back and kill me because I don't aim to have nothin' more to do with him? What am I goin' to do now?*

* * * *

During the night Martha had barely slept, keeping her rifle beside her. Julia, feeling safe for the first night in a month, slept and dreamed, cried and slept again.

CHAPTER SIX
The Search

When Julia had been running for her life on Tuesday morning, the county sheriff, George Thomas, was sitting on a porch near the grist mill in Marion. While talking to four cronies, he saw Solly drive his team into Marion and stop in front of the mill. Solly climbed down, tied his team to the hitching post, and grunted a howdy to the fellows on the porch. Then he went inside the mill, carried out two sacks of feed and put them in his wagon without saying anything more. He acted like he always did, so the sheriff had no reason to suspect him of anything.

When Solly went into the boarding house to eat his dinner, one of the fellows said to the sheriff, "I don't like that Solly Crawford. Because he owns that big farm, he thinks he's better'n anyone else. He's got a mean streak in him a yard wide—some of the girls across the way told me about him." The man angled his chin toward the house behind the saloon. The sheriff only nodded in reply.

Since it was nearly noon, Sheriff Thomas said to his friends, "Guess I'll go on in and eat my dinner at the boarding house. My wife told me to eat in town today. She wants to finish her cannin'." He went inside and sat down at the table where Solly was eating. People who knew Solly, knew that he was sour and never talked very much to anybody. So nobody talked to him, either. When Solly left the dining room, the sheriff got up too, and went back outside. He walked around the square for a while, checking to be sure everything was peaceful, then went back to sitting on the porch.

About 2:30 in the afternoon, Joe and Caleb King came riding up hard, both of them carrying guns. The sheriff let down his tilted-back-chair and stood up. He watched as Joe and Caleb tethered their horses. The hard, angry look on their faces spelled trouble. "Joe, Caleb, what're you men carrying shotguns for?"

"We're huntin' a mad dog, Sheriff."

The sheriff said, "Well, now, I ain't heard of any mad dog around here. If I saw a mad dog I'd shoot him. Who said they's one here?"

"They's one, Sheriff," Caleb said. "We aim to get him and we won't bother you none. Tilt your chair back and set." With determination they started toward the saloon.

Sheriff Thomas was off the porch in an instant, took three long strides and planted himself in front of the two angry men.

"Now boys, I don't want to arrest you—ain't got no cause to yet. Who's the mad dog?"

Joe took a deep breath, then let it out kinda slow and said, "Might as well tell you, Sheriff. You'll have to know anyhow—everybody will. It's Solly Crawford. Our sister Julia has been stayin' with him and Mis' Crawford since Ma died, and now he's ruined her. He raped her in the cornfield one day, then kept her pisoner, and he's made her work with him outside every day, so he could rape her whenever he wanted to."

"Didn't she try to get away?" Thomas asked.

"Sheriff, he watched her all the time—even guarded the outhouse when she went there. She couldn't get away from him—said he'd kill her if she told. Now she's carryin' his baby and we aim to kill him. No jury will convict us for avengin' our sister—" Joe spied Solly's wagon with the feed in it. "Ain't that his wagon settin' there?"

The sheriff nodded, "It's been there nearly all day."

Hiram Grey, on the porch said, "I saw Solly go over to the saloon from the boardin' house and after awhile he went to that other house." He jerked his head toward the house back of the saloon. "Guess he's been busy."

Thomas said to Joe and Caleb, "Let's go, boys. But put your guns down. Even if we get Solly, we got to have a trial. You're not goin' to take the law into your own hands."

Joe and Caleb stood with their feet planted broad apart. Joe said, "I don't see lettin' Solly live another day if we find him." They gripped their guns.

But Sheriff Thomas said, "I got my gun and if he tries anything, I'll get him. I'll put him in jail—everybody gets a fair trial. You two boys think now! What'd happen to your families if you killed him? *You'd* both go to jail."

They finally put their guns down on the porch.

"Hiram, I deputize you to watch them guns," the sheriff said. "Come on, boys, we'll catch us a mad dog."

They strode to that particular house behind the saloon, which every woman in town, except those who lived there, hated. They searched every room, but Solly'd gone. "He's been here," Mae said, "but he left in a hurry."

Joe, Caleb, and the sheriff looked all the rest of the day. They checked every business and every house nearby, but found no trace of him. Nobody knew anything.

The sheriff was puzzled. He tried to think of anybody in town who would benefit from hiding Solly Crawford. He thought of a few, and decided he'd do a little investigating on his own. He said to Caleb and Joe, "Fellers, it's been a long hard day for you. It's late. I think you better go over to the boarding house and eat and sleep. I'm goin' to investigate a few things. But I better do this alone."

"Couldn't we help?"

"This is my job, Caleb. Maybe I can get people to talk to me who wouldn't talk if you came with me. You go get a room, and I'll take care of your horses. Maybe we'll know something tomorrow. I promise you I'll do all I can to find that criminal. Somebody is bound to know *something.*"

Sheriff Thomas saw to their horses, and Will and Caleb went to the boarding house and rented a room. "Don't think I'll ever sleep," Joe said.

"Don't think I will, either," Caleb replied.

Joe was snoring before Caleb came in from the outhouse. And Caleb barely unlaced his shoes before he fell onto the bed beside him.

After they had gone, the sheriff went straight to the saloon. Al Jordon, slight of figure with a long face was cleaning off the bar with a dingy rag. The sheriff heard him say, "This time it's on the house. Free drinks for ever'body."

Sheriff Thomas said "Howdy" to all the fellows at the bar, then turned to the bartender. "Wanta talk to you, Al. Over here in the corner." He motioned with his head.

Al sauntered over and sat down on a sturdy wooden chair at a small round table, opposite George Thomas. He looked a little uneasy. His watery blue eyes kept flicking around and his hand kept pushing at his lank, blond hair.

"Yeah, Sheriff. Whatta you want with me?"

"Al," Thomas asked, "what do you know about Solly Crawford? I saw him come in here today."

"Solly Crawford? Yeah, I know him. He comes in here once in a while. Now let me see—he did come in here today. But I don't know nothin' else about 'im."

"What time did he come?"

"Oh—about one, I guess. He come in and got a drink and

then left. He never talks to nobody. He's kinda stuck-up, you know, and maybe thinks he's better'n other people."

"Where'd he go after that?"

Al's head motioned to the house back of the saloon.

"Did you see him after that?"

"Uh—no, he didn't come back in here."

The sheriff sat pondering for a while then took another line of questioning. "Did you see the King boys— Joe and Caleb—come into town today?"

Al thought for a while, then nodded. "Y—yes."

"Know what they came for?" the sheriff asked. "It just happens, Al, that while I was talkin' to the King boys, I saw you. You was standing in your front door with a broom in your hand, but you wasn't sweepin'. You was listenin'. You was bending your head and trying to hear the story they told. And I'm thinkin' that probably your saloon is close enough that you heard what they said. That right?"

Al was getting more fidgity. "Well—I was just sweepin' out the saloon and was in the door when they come up. I seed them a talkin' to you over there on the porch."

"Did you hear what they were talkin' about?"

"I—heerd them say somethin' about their sister and Solly Crawford— They looked purty tore up."

"Then what did you do?"

"Nothin'! I jest came back to mindin' my own business."

"Sure you didn't do anything?"

"No, Sheriff!"

George Thomas pondered for a while. Then casually he said, "When I came in just now, I heard you givin' free drinks to everybody. How come you can do that? These'r kinda hard times. Been makin' any extra money lately?"

Al looked surprised. "No!"

"Then how come you can buy free drinks for everybody? I thought booze was expensive—"

Al seemed to have trouble with the Adam's apple moving in his skinny neck.

Sheriff Thomas reached across the small table, clutched Al by his collar and pulled his face close. "Want to know what else I think? *I* think you are withholding information about a criminal. You know who I've been lookin' for. You know I'm wantin' to arrest Solly Crawford."

Al stiffened. "What fer? What's he done?"

"You don't have to know that—but I think you already do. And I can put *you* in jail if you're not tellin' me what you know about his disappearance. That's called 'aiding and abetting a criminal'. You know everything that goes on around here." Thomas sat quietly for a while and watched Al squirm. He could see Al was weighing his options.

Sheriff Thomas continued, "Now Solly must'of got out of town mighty fast to leave his team and wagon in front, and I think you know somethin' about it." The sheriff pulled out his handcuffs. "Maybe a few days in the jail house will help to bring back your memory."

Al Jordon slumped back in his chair and breathed out a great sigh. "All right—all right! I'll tell you. I don't want to go to jail to save him—he ain't worth savin' anyway. And I got a big family of my own to think about, Sheriff!"

Thomas nodded. "That's better. Let's have it all."

"Well, Sheriff," Al confided, "you're right. I heerd somethin' of what the King boys was a tellin' you, but I couldn't quite make it all out. Anyway, I thought I ought to warn Solly—he's a good customer—that he jest might get killed. I knowed where he'd gone—he allus goes back there. Soon as I heerd Joe say he's a goin' to shoot Solly, I run through the back o' the saloon and over to the house. And I swear, Sheriff, this is just what happened!"

"Go on with it."

"Well, I run in the door and asked Maggie in the front room, 'Where's Solly?'

"She said, 'He's not here!'

"And I yelled, 'I know he *is* here! This is important. What room's he in?'

"She told me, 'He's in Mae's room.'

"So I run up and beat on Mae's door hard and Solly shouted, 'Quit bangin' on that door and get outa here!'

"I called out loud to him, 'You better come out quick, Solly, it's awful important.'

"Then I heard some gigglin' and some groanin' and after a few minutes Solly come out into the hall pullin' up his suspenders. 'Well, what's the matter, Al?' he asked me. And he was mad. 'What you botherin' me fer?'

"So I leaned agin' the top of the steps, real casual like, and asked him, 'I was just wonderin', Solly. You got any cause to be afraid of the King boys?'

"You know, Sheriff, Solly's face is nachuly red, but it got

redder, and his neck sorta bulged out and he shouted, 'No, I ain't! I ain't done nothin' to them!'

"'Okay,' I says. 'Don't get mad at *me,*' I says. 'If you ain't done nothin', then I guess you won't care if I tell 'em where you are. They been lookin' all over the place fer you.' Then I looked him straight in the eye and says, 'Funny thing, though, they's both carryin' shotguns and I heered 'em say they's lookin' for you.'"

Al shrugged and said, "Then I just squinted sideways at Solly and started down the stairs.

"But Solly's face wasn't red any more. It had turned a dead white and his lips was a'shakin'. He grabbed my arm and said, 'Al, wait. Don't tell them King boys where I am! I know they *will* kill me if they find me. Help me, Al! How can I best get out of town now? They'll kill me!'

"'Aha!' I says, 'So you DID do somethin' to their sister! Might take a sum of money to make me ferget where you are. Want me to tell you where to hide? H-mmm — saw you with a roll of bills in the saloon. How about fifty dollars? Worth it, ain't it?'" Al looked at the sheriff like he was satisfied with himself.

Sheriff Thomas' face grew hard, his arms grabbed Al across the table and shook him like a cat shaking a rat. "You dirty skunk—you're as bad as he is! So if it hadn't 'of been for you, we'd of found him."

"Now wait, Sheriff, I don't want to go to no jail, so let me tell you the rest of it."

When Thomas sat back down, Al went on, "Solly and me, we clomped down the stairs and on the way down he handed me fifty dollars. I told him how to get to a cellar I knew about—he could hide there. I guess he did and then when it got dark he must 'of left. He ain't there now—I went to see about him jist a few minutes ago. No—I swear I don't know no more about him. He must 'of took the train to Carbondale—or over to Shawneetown—or maybe he went to Chicago. Course, he might 'of gone across to Kentucky."

Thomas got up in disgust. "Too bad for us Marion folks, we have to live with people like you! If you hadn't been so greedy, I'd have had him. As it was, we probably missed him by just a very few minutes. I'll see to it that the judge knows how you aided and abetted a criminal."

Al's face turned white. "B—but Sheriff, you said—"

George Thomas looked at him like a bird eyeing a worm. "I said you'd go to jail if you didn't tell me what you knew. I didn't promise you anything if you *did!* You helped a criminal. That calls for punishment." He stalked out of the saloon, the men at the bar looking after him and shaking their heads. One of them took a swig of his whiskey and remarked, "That sheriff'll git you, Al."

* * * *

When Solly Crawford and Al ran out the back door of Mae's house, they were only a few minutes ahead of the sheriff, Joe, and Caleb. But Solly didn't have far to run. Al pointed to a place and Solly literally dived into it. Al ran back to the saloon and nobody noticed his absence.

The place was only a stone's throw from the Marion square, and near the railroad. At one time its owner had intended to build a log cabin there, but when he dug an area to put down a foundation log, he discovered a spring on that very spot. He decided to build a little farther south.

The "cellar" was really little more than a hole in the ground with a log abandoned over it, and brush grown up around it. Solly felt safe enough in this hiding place. The cellar seemed like a grave—only in a grave, he'd be laid out flat. Here, he was all cramped double, with his knees up to his chin, trying to keep himself dry from the spring water seeping through the ground. *Well, I can stand it fer a while. Then I got to get out of here; clear out o' town. Lucky I brought two hundred dollars with me this mornin'. That'll take me somewhere.*

How did I ever git myself in such a spot as this! It's all Ellie's fault! She's the one who brought that girl into the house—then expected me to keep my hands off her! If she'd had any sense at all, she'd have knowed better. She's the whole cause of this! After all, I'm only a man. Even sittin' in disgrace, there in that hole with his pants gettin' wet from the spring, Solly had to grin a little. Julia was still worth it! Her fightin' ways had made him most determined to have her. He sighed. *Well—maybe I made a little mistake, but for a time there I was crazy for her. Just couldn't let her alone. She's a real looker. If she'd been a little older, and Ellie'd been a little sicker*—he didn't finish that thought. He squirmed around to get a'hold of his money, removed it from his pants and put it up into his shirt pocket. *No use lettin' all my money get wet!*

Maybe he should have come to Mae's place more often—but that cost him money. He liked Mae, though, and she always seemed like she appreciated him. Now he'd probably never see her again.

Solly peeked cautiously out between the scrub to see where the sun was in the sky. Soon it would be dark. He'd leave Williamson County for a while, then after a few months, when this thing had all blown over, he'd come back to his farm where he belonged. But right now, he'd have to run from them two brothers of Julia.

Wasn't it just a little ridiculous that Solly Crawford, big land-owner and respected citizen, was doing his best to evade the law? He hated to admit that he was frightened. But who wanted to tangle with a couple of shotguns? He couldn't help it—and after all, what he done wasn't so bad. If takin' a young girl was a thing people talked about, they'd hear a lot more of that kind of goin's on in the country.

Finally the summer day was over, and darkness seemed to smother him. He could faintly see a few lanterns in the square, and some at the railroad station, but here where he crouched, was pitch blackness. He heard the whistle of an approaching train. He peered out again, saw no one and heard nothing else. So he crept out, ran as lightly as his heavy legs would allow to the station, keeping in the shadows until the train stopped and some people got off. He saw the trainmen go into the small depot, and waited a few more minutes. The way was clear. Only a few lanterns shown here and there and shadows were plentiful.

In case someone did see him, he straightened up and walked up the steps into a coach—just like a passenger who had got off for a spell. He made his way down the long coach's aisle and sat in the very last row, facing the car's back wall. He didn't know where the train was going, and didn't care. Solly folded his legs and lay on his side in the seat, put his hat over his face and was soon snoring.

He didn't know the train was moving until he was poked awake by the conductor. "Got your ticket, Buddy?"

Solly didn't dare ask him where the train was heading; the fellow would think he was crazy. "Uh— no, didn't have time. Thought the train might leave without me and I was tired. I'll pay fer it—how much do I owe you?"

He dug some money out of his pocket and gave the conductor a twenty dollar bill. He took the change the man handed him and put it back into his pocket without counting it. The trainman walked on to the next car.

Whew! I'm safe and on my way. Don't matter where I'm goin', I'll find out when I get there. Solly was snoring when the conductor yelled, "All aboard for Chicago!"

* * * *

The next morning Sheriff Thomas met Joe and Caleb for an early breakfast at the boarding house. While they were eating, he recounted the whole story of his conversation with Al Jordon after he'd left them last night. He could see the anger welling in Joe and Caleb's faces.

"That filthy hog!" exclaimed Joe. "I ought to kill that Al Jordon! If it hadn't been for him, we'd have got Solly!"

"Maybe we would," Sheriff Thomas said. "And maybe we wouldn't. But fact is, Joe, in sight of the law, what Al done was to help a friend hide himself when he saw two men with guns after him. Nothin' we can do about that."

"One of these days," Caleb predicted, "Solly Crawford will get what's comin' to him. I hope I can see it happen."

"Soon as we finish eating," the sheriff told them, "I'm goin' to hitch up Solly's horses and drive his wagon home. Miss Ellie's got to know what's happened. After we talk to her—if you both will come with me—I want to ride out to your place, Joe, and talk to your sister Julia. It's a job I don't relish, but I've got to get a signed statement from her."

Joe and Caleb rode first, while the Sheriff rode in Solly's wagon and led his own horse. They were wondering how they could bear to be in the place where Julia had been so violated. They could be sympathetic to Miss Ellie—none of it was her fault. But how could such a thing go on right under her nose for a month and she never suspect anything?

When they drove into Solly's yard, Miss Ellie got up from her rocking chair near the door and came out to meet them. One look at her face and all three men were full of pity. Obviously she had not slept last night and was in a state of fear and shock. She led them into the house and they saw that two people had recently eaten a meal there. Probability was she'd eaten nothing. Neither had she bothered to do anything about cleaning up.

"Will and Matthew left about twenty minutes ago, Joe," she said. "They stayed here all night and watched for Solly. They told me all about what he done to Julia and I've been mourning about it all night." In agitation her hands were clenching and unclenching and folding themselves together. She didn't even know she was doing it. "There ain't nothin' you boys could say to me that would make me feel any worse. I'll never get over what he done to Julia. Joe and

Caleb—you must know that I love Julia like my own child. I can't never undo anything about this awful treatment she's been receivin' right here on our farm. No, I'll never get over it—" She was sobbing into her apron.

Joe and Caleb were wiping their eyes too. Sheriff Thomas said, "Sit down, Miss Ellie. We came by to bring back your horses and wagon, and to tell you what happened yesterday. I'm sorry, I don't think Solly will come back. . . ." Sheriff Thomas paced the floor. "Now yesterday morning I saw Solly when he drove into Marion—" And he told her the whole story.

Ellie sat in her chair through the long recitation, looking down at her hands in her lap. Hopeless tears rolled down her face. None of the three men could make things any easier for her. All she could think about was days stretching into weeks and years, all alone with such a burden on her soul. How could a Christian woman live with such sorrow?

When the sheriff finished, they sat quietly for a time, not knowing what else to say. Finally Thomas said, "I'll come back in a day or two, Miss Ellie, and see about you. Right now we've got to go out to Joe's place and talk to Julia. I have to get a statement from her. You must know that a warrant will be out for Solly's arrest, so I don't think he'll ever come back here—even if he does own this fine farm. I am so sorry, and if I can help you, just send me word."

Joe and Caleb rose to go. "Good-bye, Miss Ellie," they said, touching her arm in sympathy.

"Good-bye," she sobbed. "Tell Julia I . . ." She could not go on. She could only weep.

As the three men rode out of her yard, Sheriff Thomas voiced their common concern, "I don't know how in the world she's going to come out of this. She'll probably just pine away in that kitchen. No wife ought to ever have to hear things like that about a man she's been married to for twenty-five years."

When they arrived at Joe's, they had to tell the story over again to Will, Matthew, Julia and Martha. The sheriff finished, and said, "Miss Julia, I know you're feeling mighty bad. But for the law to work right, I got to get a statement from you and have you sign it. I need to know exactly what Solly Crawford did to you."

Julia, who'd had only one good night's sleep in a month—last night—looked totally exhausted. Her cheeks flushed a deep red and she looked down at her hands in her lap. "It's goin' to be mighty hard to tell it to you, Sheriff."

"I understand, Miss Julia. If it would help, your brothers and Miss Martha can stay in here with you. I have to write down what you say."

So with red eyes and a stony face, Julia told him what Solly Crawford had done to her. Shame washed over her, and the sheriff had to look away at her torrent of tears. He wrote down her words as she told him the whole ugly story, and the sheriff couldn't help but think, *What if this happened to my daughter? I'd want to kill him, too.*

Telling it to her own family and telling it to a total stranger—those were two different things. Julia felt so humiliated recounting some of the scenes but she knew she had to be truthful. And she was embarrassed again as he read back to her what she'd said before she signed it. She signed an X on the paper with Martha as a witness.

The sheriff shook his head. "These are awful bad things you've gone through, Miss Julia. I hope we can find that criminal. But I don't know if we ever will."

Thank you kindly, Sheriff," said Julia. You done what you could. I don't reckon he'll ever come back here."

"No, I don't reckon he ever will."

CHAPTER SEVEN
For A Rainy Day

The sheriff rode over to Mrs. Crawford's place. She was sitting at her kitchen table, picking at some food when he came up the back porch steps. She looked frail and worn and Sheriff Thomas felt as sorry for her as he did for Julia. And he felt nothing but revulsion for the man who had brought all this sorrow upon two fine women—one whose adult life was just beginning, and one whose life was nearly over. He knocked. "Afternoon, Mis' Crawford."

"Afternoon, Sheriff. Come on in and have some milk and cornbread. That's all I had an appetite fer today."

Thomas took off his battered hat, pulled out a chair and sat at the table filled with several dirty dishes. He couldn't help but notice her appearance. Ellie looked as if she had slept in her clothes and not combed her hair since his last visit. *She probably doesn't even realize it.* "Thank you kindly, Mis' Crawford. This is pretty hot weather for autumn here in Southern Illinois."

She nodded, got up from her chair, went to the cellar and brought up a crock of cool, fresh milk. She poured a glass for him and dished up a pie-shaped slab of hot cornbread from an iron skillet in the warming oven of her stove. Her hands and lips were shaking. What news did he bring? Was Solly dead somewhere? Did she care if he was? Was he in jail? If he was, she knew he'd be there a long time. She blurted out, "It's been two days, Sheriff. Heard anything about Solly?"

Sheriff Thomas had never pitied any woman more than he now pitied Ellie Crawford. "Mis' Crawford, I wish I knew something more about him, but I don't. Because of Al Jordon, Solly was able to hide and get away. My hunch is that he got away Tuesday night on some train—can't prove it, but that seems most likely."

Ellie was sitting silently, her eyes down, staring at the tears dropping on her folded hands. She couldn't eat any more. *How could I have lived so long with Solly and never suspected he could do such awful things? He was grouchy but he wasn't ever really mean to me.* "Sheriff, what in the world makes a man act like that? Don't he know he's got to meet his Maker with such a sin on his soul?"

"Don't know what it is, Mis' Crawford. Just wickedness, I reckon. Looks like he just went crazy." He sat shaking his head. "We don't blame you none, Mis' Crawford. It wasn't your fault. Solly probably won't come back here—he knows there'd be keen eyes squintin' down shotgun sights if he did. Will you be all right out here, Mis' Crawford? Can I do anything to help you?"

"Yes, you can deliver somethin' to Julia for me." She sat shaking her head. "Oh, I wish I could make it up to Julia what he's done to her. But nobody ever could, I know."

She took a large crumpled handkerchief out of her pocket and unwrapped a roll of bills, then wiped her eyes with the handkerchief. "But I can do one thing for her. I want you to take this money and give it all to Julia. It's three hundred dollars. I found it last night, hid away in Solly's things."

The sheriff was taken aback. "If you give this all to Julia, do you have any left for yourself to live on? You'll need *some* money, you know."

"I know Solly has a bank account, Sheriff. Maybe you could help me get that money." Her anger flared. "He owes me *somethin'!* He allus told me he didn't have no money 'round here when I wanted to buy somethin'. But I was sure he did b'cause when *he* wanted somethin' he allus got it. I started searchin' last night—I jest had a feelin' I'd find some somewheres."

The sheriff nodded. "I will help you with the papers to get your hands on his account. When the judge and the bank people hear what he done, I'm sure they'll give it to you. And we better do it soon before Solly authorizes somebody else to get it for him. You'll have to come in to Marion to sign some papers and when they get 'em ready, I'll come and fetch you. It won't be long."

"Well—I won't need much, I reckon—wish I had more to send to Julie. This will help pay for her keep at Joe's."

Sheriff Thomas took the money, rolled it up and put it into his pocket. "Mis' Crawford, you're doing a real neighborly deed."

"'T'weren't nothin' I shouldn't do."

"I'll deliver this money to Julia. She'll need it. It won't be easy for her. But I don't like leavin' you out here all by yourself. How can you manage? Don't you have any relatives you can go and live with? Or somebody who can come and live with you?"

She shook her head. "No, I can do for myself."

Thomas was genuinely concerned. "How *can* you do all these things for yourself? It takes a heap of muscle to take care of the stock, do all the milkin' and plantin'. You're not able to do that."

Ellie looked a little uncertain. "Well—I guess I'll sell some things. I don't need but one horse and cow. Guess I can make a little garden, and when I need help, I'll ride over and get a neighbor boy to help me."

"Well, Mis' Ellie. If you need me, just send word."

"Thank you kindly, Sheriff, fer thinkin' about me and takin' this money to Julia. Looks like you're doin' a lot to help her. It's a terrible thing Solly's done. He's ruined the girl that's like my own child, and I'll never get over it."

"Some day he'll pay for it. Much obliged for the milk and cornbread—it tasted good." The sheriff stood up, put on his hat and Ellie walked with him to the back porch.

"Good-bye, Sheriff. Much obliged."

George Thomas waved, and rode down the lane.

Miss Ellie, dazed by all the happenings of the past week, tried to tidy up her kitchen. But in the middle of washing dishes, she sat down in her rocking chair and sobbed. She had put on a good brave face for the sheriff, but how could she do farm work? How could she take care of even one horse or milk even one cow? Some days she simply felt too tired to get out of bed. Could she live alone?

She had no respect now for Solly, but she knew he was a good farmer and took very good care of the farm and livestock. With wry humor, she realized he'd taken much better care of the livestock than he ever had of her or Julia!

* * * *

The next day George Thomas went back to Joe's farm and found Julia and Martha carrying out blankets and pillows and putting them in the sun to air. They were spread all over the yard.

"Good morning, Sheriff," greeted Julia. She looked hollow-eyed as if she hadn't slept much lately.

"Looks like house cleanin' time."

"Yes—well, these are nice days and I thought we better do this now," Martha said, breathing heavily as she threw a thick comforter over the clothesline. "Pretty soon it will be hog killin' time and lots to do then."

"How are you feeling, Miss Julia?" asked Thomas.

"I'm doin' all right. Got to go on livin'——" her voice trailed off. Then she breathed heavily and asked, "You heard anything about Solly? He's not come back home, has he?"

"No, Miss Julia. And I don't think he ever will. He knows

the weather 'round here'd be pretty dangerous for him. No—I don't think he'll ever show up."

"I just can't sleep for dreadin' he'll come back. He said he'd kill me if I told anybody, you know. And he knows I told my brothers and you!" She shuddered and looked over her shoulder. "You don't have any idy how it is to be afraid all the time."

The sheriff looked at her in sympathy. "I don't think you ought to worry like that. You're safe here with Martha and Joe. Solly wouldn't come around here—he'd know better." Sheriff Thomas thought for a moment. "Yesterday I went over to see Mis' Crawford after I left here, and she . . ."

"How is she? I feel so bad for her."

"She's takin' Solly's shameless deeds hard. And now she's alone—I don't see how she can manage that big place."

"I didn't know either, Sheriff, but I can't stay there!

"Oh, no! Absolutely not!" agreed Sheriff Thomas. "You could never feel safe. But, Miss Julie, I hope that after some time you will find it in your heart to go see Ellie. She thinks of you like a daughter."

"I know it." Julia bowed her head. "But I do shorely know I can't go now. Maybe sometime . . ."

"Well, she has sent you something." George Thomas took the roll of bills from his pocket. "Ellie Crawford gave me this money to give to you. It's three hundred dollars. She wants you to have it." He held it out to Julia.

Her eyes widened and she drew back. "All that money—? Oh, I can't take that money!"

"Now, Miss Julie, you must be reasonable. You *have* to live. You will *need* money—for your own keep and for your baby that's comin.' This is from Ellie—not from Solly. She found it at home and believe me, Solly would never dare to come back for it. She *wants* you to have it and she wished she could have more to give you."

Julia put both her hands behind her back and shook her head. "Takin this money would be like gettin' paid for what Solly done to me!" She thought, *If I keep this money, every time I looked at it I'd hate him all over again. I know Miss Ellie loves me and I love her, but would she think I hate her if I don't take this? I can't go over and talk to her about it.*

"No! It's not like you were getting paid for what he did to you," Sheriff Thomas insisted. "This is from *Ellie!* She could have kept this money for *herself* to live on, but she wanted *you* to have it. She is showin' her love and sympathy for you with this gift and you mustn't refuse it. No use hurtin' her any more than she's already been hurt."

Martha was standing listening to this conversation and now she spoke up. "Julie, Sheriff Thomas is right. You ought to take this money because this comes from love and not wickedness. You cannot refuse a love gift. Poor Miss Ellie is doin' what she can to help you and you must not say no to that help. She loves you——"

"Well, I love her too. She's a good woman and treated me like her own child but——" Julia sobbed.

"Don't say, 'But,' Miss Julia. Ellie will feel better knowin' you are bein' helped with this money. If you don't need it now, then save it. The time'll come when it's right for you to use it. It'll be a bank account for you."

Julia sighed, and looked straight at Sheriff Thomas to see if he was really saying what he thought was the right thing for her to do. She saw only honesty in his face, so she held out her hand. "All right, Sheriff. I'll save it. Some day I'll go to see Ellie—when Joe can come with me—and I will thank her for it. And I thank you too, Sheriff. You are a good friend."

"Sheriff Thomas, will you come in for some coffee?" asked Martha.

"Thank you kindly, Mrs. King, but not today. I got to get on back to town—I'll be there by noon and I'll eat then. Tell Joe I said 'Howdy.'"

"He's back out in the fields today. I'll tell him. He's tryin' to catch up on his work."

The sheriff tipped his hat and rode out of the yard.

Julia watched him go then turned to Martha. "Martha, do you actually think I ought to take this money? I don't want nothin' that ever belonged to Solly."

"You are right to take it. Money can belong to anybody—in this case it belonged to Ellie. *She* gave it to you and you know that Solly—as stingy as he is—would never give it to you. I'm a practical woman, Julie. I know it might seem like tainted money to you. But someday it may be that your baby might need somethin' special that only this money could buy for it. If that happens, you'll be thankful to have it. If that never happens, then use it for your own life to make it better in some ways. Besides, Solly owes you ten times that much money for what he did to you. Of course we both know that no money in the world could ever be enough to repay you for all your sufferin'. But keep the money Julie, and hide it. Don't tell anybody else you got it."

"You and Joe are the ones who deserve this—for all the help you're givin' me."

"No. We are family and we help each other. You'll be a great help to me, too. You can do work that my kids are not big enough to do. And when your baby comes, we'll welcome it, too."

Julia hugged Martha in among all the blankets. Her thoughts whirled. *My baby—oh, why couldn't I have been a little older and married Seth and had his baby! How I wish it was Seth's baby.* She couldn't help her tears. "I'm so thankful Joe married you, Martha. Nobody could be better to me than you are." She looked at the wad of bills in her hands. "Did you ever see this much money all at once?"

"No. I'm glad you've got it."

"I'm goin' in to put it away."

Julia had very few clothes and kept everything, except two dresses, in the trunk which had belonged to her mother. A year ago, after her mother died, Joe had brought it home with him and put it in his children's bedroom. The day she ran away from Solly's house was the first time in a year she had seen it. The sight of that trunk made her cry harder and miss her mother more.

When Matthew and William had brought all of her belongings from Miss Ellie's a few days ago, she had tossed them into the trunk. She owned only two good dresses—the nice dress Miss Ellie had helped her make to wear to the barn raisin', and the other dress which had been her Sunday one. They were hanging with Joe's family's clothes.

Julia took the money inside, found her oldest black stocking, put the money clear down into the toe of it, rolled it all up and stashed it in the corner of her mother's trunk. On top of the stocking—which she determined never to touch unless the need was dire—she spread out all her underthings and working clothes. *Three hundred dollars!* she thought. *Men have killed other men for less money than that.*

Under any other circumstances in her life, she would have been able to thank God for this much money, but she couldn't now. Before—when she was a virgin—she had no money at all. And she was the happiest girl in Southern Illinois. Now she was rich but no longer a virgin, and her life was broken in pieces. Only because she had been so violated did she have money. Such a bankroll—but at such a price!

CHAPTER EIGHT
Old Chores . . . New Love

Weeks passed, and Julia worked alongside Martha and Joe, getting ready for winter. They harvested hay and grain and stored it in the barn for the animals. They dug sweet potatoes, white potatoes and onions and laid them in the cellar on shelves. Pumpkins were ripening in the fields. For weeks she and Martha canned and dried vegetables and fruits, made pickles and jams—so their cellar was filling up. With Joe's five kids, Martha, Joe, and Julia, they had to think about preserving enough food for many meals for eight people until next spring. No small task!

Aside from not being able to eat breakfast once in a while, Julia felt well, even though she worked very hard. She was determined to do her share. Martha kept a watchful eye on her and often said, "Julia, we're nearly done now. Go and rest a bit. I'll call you when I need a little help."

Julia knew they tried to help her forget. But that didn't stop her clamorous thoughts. Over and over again an incident with Solly came unbidden to her mind, turning her faint with fear and loathing. The feelings seemed to roll over her—like a wave on a pond when a big fish jumps—and leave her shivering. She wondered whether she could ever feel normal again.

Harvesting corn was the worst. She simply could not go by herself into long rows of harvest-ready corn. To her its rasping, brooding stance high over her head, filled her with terror. She smothered and choked, and she was sure that at any moment Solly might grab her.

Julia could work in the corn rows only if somebody else worked alongside her. Joe and Martha understood and one of them always helped in that very same row, or else they ordered some of their children to be with her. Of course the children kept up a lively conversation so Julia didn't have time to think or remember.

When the harvest was all stored away for animals and family, they began to plan for hog butchering day. This always took place around the time of the first frost when the countryside was a mass of red and gold leaves.

One day at breakfast Joe announced, "William and Caleb'll be over tomorrow to help butcher the hogs, and Matthew'll come if he can. We think this good weather'll hold. So let's get things ready today. You kids take your baskets and gather a great big pile of cracklin' dry firewood. I don't want to see no wet nor damp wood, either. This fire's gotta burn!"

Joe and Martha and Julia all lifted and tugged together to move their large cast iron kettle—forty to fifty-gallon size, from the barn to an open place in the yard not far from the well. Then began the parade to and from the well carrying buckets of water to fill up the kettle. The children began to bring in their baskets of wood and to stack it nearby. They drove the hogs to be butchered into a special pen apart from the others. They laid wood criss-cross under the huge three-legged kettle, all ready to set fire to it the next morning, and set up boards over sawhorses for tables under some maple trees. Next they brought four large wooden barrels from the barn, rinsed them out with clean water, and set them up near the kettle. Near the day's end, Joe cleaned his rifle, and sharpened his big knives. Finally everything was ready.

They practically fell into their chairs at the supper table. While Joe was working with his rifle and knives, Martha and Julia had come in and prepared the meal of chicken and dumplings, boiled sweet potatoes and cornbread. That evening Joe squinted at a breathtaking sunset streaking red and gold across the sky, and remarked, "Red at night, sailor's delight. Well, it's goin t' be a clear day tomorrow. Let's get to bed early—got t' be up early." Nobody argued with him about going to bed.

The whole family woke up with a start before daylight the next morning, because Martha was banging loudly on a piepan with a wooden spoon. From the oldest to the youngest, they grunted, protested, rolled out of bed, and each one started a particular chore.

The small girls made up the beds and helped each other get dressed. The younger boys pulled up their suspenders and brought wood into the kitchen. The largest boy went with Joe to milk the cows. With her small-sized fire shovel, Martha carried out some coals from her fire in the kitchen, and lighted the wood under the big kettle outside. By the time Joe was back from milking, strong coffee and thick slices of sourdough bread were on the table and the house was cleaned up for the day. Caleb, William, and Matthew rode in, ate breakfast with them, then all four men went out to do the job that women didn't usually take part in. The girls didn't like to watch it either.

But the boys did. At least they *said* they did. They watched as their father took his .22 rifle and shot four hogs smack-dab between the eyes. As soon as the animals fell over, each of the men took a sharp knife and stuck it into a hog's jugular vein. Bleeding the animal was necessary.

They dipped boiling water into the barrels, and holding the hogs by the feet, eased them down into the scalding water so that all the hair could be scraped off. After that, they hung them from a pole with ropes and wires, and removed all the innards. Cutting up the carcasses required strong arms and hands. The four King brothers, though not heavy men, were adept at this work. From the sharp knives on the saw-horse tables came shoulders, hams, side meat, ribs, backbone and head. Every piece was used. After they emptied the kettle, it was dried over the fire, then they dumped all the carefully trimmed hog-fat into it and built the fire up again. The fat was turned into lard and cracklins. Lard and flour made the best piecrusts. They cut some of the meat into small pieces and then ground it into sausage with heavy hand grinders—tubs filled with meat sprinkled with salt and sage and all mixed by hand. Sausage up to the elbows!

Julia and Martha cooked a big noon dinner for the men—ribs and backbones, with potatoes baked in iron pans at the edge of the fire, and squash and onions fried together. Fresh cucumber pickles were served along with canned green beans, applesauce and cornbread. After such a morning, hungry men and boys made short work of the food.

But Julia couldn't eat a thing. In fact she could barely help serve the men their dinner. Seeing so much fresh meat with all the blood on those outside tables, made her stomach begin to heave. "Martha, I've seen hog-killin's many times on the farm, but I ain't been in the family way before." She wiped the sweat off her face. " I've had about all the sight of fresh meat I can stand for today. I've got to get out into some air and away from it. Can you manage alone here for a while?"

"Yes!" Martha's bright blue eyes gazed at Julia with sympathy. "Go on out for a spell, Julie. I remember how I felt helpin' with butcherin' every time I was expectin' too."

After dinner the men began salting the big hams and shoulders and sides and putting them into the smokehouse. Joe looked at all his meat hanging and said to his brothers, "Well, that saltin' ought t' be enough to set 'em for a while. Then after they get cured with all that good old hickory smoke, they'll make fer some mighty good eatin'. Looks like I can feed my family for another year. I shore do appreciate your help. Just let me know when you're a wantin' to do yours and I'll be there. Now—before you go home, wrap up some sausage to take for your supper."

His brothers each took about two pounds of sausage from the tub. They wrapped it up in some old cloths and put it in their saddle bags. "Come on, Joe. Before we go, we'll draw some more water and help you clean up around here. Martha, where's Julie?"

"She was feelin poorly—seein' all that hog-killin' and she had to walk away from it. Just natural, you know."

"Pore little Julia!" said Matthew. "It's goin' t' take her a long time before she gets over this— It just makes me killin' mad ever' time I think about Solly Crawford!"

"Me too," agreed Caleb. " And of course, Julie never will get over it."

* * * *

Truth soon made its rounds, and neighbors learned that Julia King was carrying Solly Crawford's baby and the awful circumstances under which such a thing happened. The King family made no attempt to cover anything up, and their forthrightness was appreciated. Women in the area felt afraid to walk or to be alone for a time, because they feared they might meet up with Solly. But Solly was gone. After people realized he wouldn't dare come back, every woman around agreed: "I'll gladly shoot him if I have a chance! The King family has always been respected, and now just because one of them is an orphan, she's been spoiled by that devilish Crawford."

So they rallied to Julia and strengthened her with their friendship. But Julia, who wouldn't be sixteen until spring, carried her child with silent shame. She didn't feel quite so self-conscious when she was around women who already had children. But when she was near a group of girls her own age, they looked at her in a strange way. She could tell they knew all about her. She felt like she was on display. She had said to Joe and Martha, "I'll go to church with you until I begin to show, then I'm not goin' anywhere. People already got enough to talk about!"

But her self-imposed exile was hard. She missed being with friends at church; she missed the careless fun they used to have before her mother died. It seemed like a thousand years ago when she felt like laughing. She felt old. But more than anything else, she missed Seth.

After Seth had left Joe's that day in September, she'd kept alive a secret hope that he would change his mind. Maybe he would forget about Hattie Knight and come back and marry her. Surely his father would think she was old enough to get married now that she was pregnant! But of course, the very fact that she *was* pregnant would turn his father against her forever—even though it wasn't her fault.

So her spirit died a little more when she heard that Seth and Hattie Knight were married the last of October, and soon afterward Hattie got in the family way.

I guess I'll never marry now, she thought. *Nobody would ever want to marry a ruined girl like me. I reckon I'll always be just "the sister that lives with her brother Joe."* But it was hard, and from time to time she still dreamed of Seth's arms about her. Of course, she always woke up feeling guilty—he belonged to someone else, in God's sight.

* * * *

Julia's sixteenth birthday was like many other days. Though she was very large and uncomfortable, she insisted on helping Joe with some planting and hoeing. True, she had to straighten up and rub her back often, but she refused to stop. What would she do with herself if she couldn't work? She'd just have to think all the time. And every time she got to thinking, she realized more and more that she did *not* want this baby. Martha often tried to tell her that she would love it, that it was *her* baby and not the baby's fault, but she could not feel any stir of loving anticipation. This pregnancy was simply a fact of life to be lived through.

When they came in from the fields for the noon dinner, Martha surprised her with a birthday cake and a knitted baby blanket. "Oh, Martha, you are so good to me! What in the world would I do if Joe was married to somebody else?"

Martha laughed. "Well now, I have no idea! I'm just glad that Joe's married to me!"

Joe looked at her with love in his eyes.

Julia enjoyed eating a piece of cake, but the new knitted baby blanket did not move her at all, even though it was beautiful and she thanked Martha for it. She did not want this baby and didn't even want to be reminded that it would soon be born.

* * * *

This must be it! A slight pain had nudged Julia out of sleep. She lay and thought about it for a while. Maybe she'd been mistaken. But no—about the time she was drifting back to sleep, another catch began in her lower back and fanned out from side to side. This must be the day! Not a day she had been looking forward to, except to ease her of being so heavy. The pain wasn't very bad, she thought, so she wouldn't call Martha yet.

By the time the sun was rising on another spring day, she'd felt several twinges that made her very uncomfortable. When she heard Martha in the kitchen, she crawled out of bed and with difficulty shuffled out. "Martha—" she said, easing into a kitchen chair. "I—"

"You're having pain?" she asked.

Julia nodded.

Martha went toward the bedrooms calling, "Joe— Everybody. Get up! Get dressed. You young'uns are going to your grandma's today."

She'd already told her children that when Julia's baby was coming, they'd have to go to her mother's house.

"Why do we have to be sent off when such an excitin' thing's goin' to happen here? We want to stay here!"

But Martha was adamant. "No—I already told you you'd have to go. Now hurry up and eat."

Joe went out to hitch up the wagon and by the time the children finished eating, he was ready to go. "I'll have some breakfast at your mother's," he said as he kissed her. "I'll come back and be nearby. Ring the bell if you need me."

Martha was Julia's midwife—she'd already helped in many birthings. "Walk around some while you still can, Julia. It might help things along. But when you want to go to bed, I'll help you." Martha was busy getting water to heat, taking out a pile of clean white cloths, getting scissors and twine ready.

"Oh, Martha," Julia cried, "I wish this didn't have to happen! I don't want to have a baby!"

"Julia, you will love your baby. All that happened is not your baby's fault. When it comes, you'll feel different."

Julia shook her head as a searing pain wrapped around her. She bent over and whispered, "I want to go to bed now."

The birth was long and hard. As Julia's pains came closer

and with more intensity, her stoicism deserted her. When agony overwhelmed her, she screamed, "I don't want to live! I don't want this baby!"

Martha kept calm and tried to soothe Julia. "You're going to have a fine baby, Julia. It'll be *yours!* You'll love it because that's God's way." Finally she ordered, "Now push—hard—one more time and your baby will be here!"

With intense anguish, Julia gritted her teeth, arched her back and pushed. She saw Martha lift up a small, wet bit of humanity, heard a "Smack!" and a responding cry as the baby began to breathe. Then she turned her face to the wall and wouldn't even look at the baby. Her body felt so battered she wanted to sleep for a week.

But Martha was excited. "It's a girl, Julia! My goodness, it's the spittin' image of you! Look at her, Julia!"

But Julia couldn't look. "I don't want that baby!" she insisted, and closed her eyes.

Martha said nothing more to Julia then, but cleaned the baby, wrapped her tightly in a blanket, and put her in a crib beside Julia's bed. Martha's babies had all slept in it. Then she finished cleaning up Julia. Julia slept, the baby was quiet for a few hours, and Martha kept watch.

Finally the wee child began to cry, and Julia woke up but she didn't turn over.

"Julia, "Martha urged, "Look at your baby. She's beautiful! She looks exactly like you. She's hungry, too!"

Julia felt nothing but complete exhaustion. "I don't want to look at her. I might think she looks like Solly."

"She does *not* look anything like Solly. But even if she did, she's *your* baby. She needs to nurse. Julia, you've got to let her nurse. Your breasts may not feel full right now, but you've got some milky water in there and that's very good for babies. When she nurses that out, it will help to bring the real milk in. So you must feed her."

Julia finally gave in—she was too tired to argue any more. No doubt breasts were made to satisfy babies; never mind the remarks Solly had made about hers.

Groaning, she rolled over away from the wall and with tired eyes looked into the crib at her own face in miniature. Arching dark brows over lightly slanted eyes, rosy complexion, high cheek bones, a mop of black hair, and a wide-open mouth screaming for attention. The baby was so *small!* How could her belly have been so big for such a tiny mite?

Julia simply held up her arms and Martha laid the baby on her chest. Julia opened her nightgown and turned stiffly on her side. Martha turned the baby toward Julia and helped her touch Julia's breast. Mother Nature then began to assert her rights. As the baby began first to blindly nuzzle and then to pull on her breast, Julia began to feel a faint stirring of emotion—so faint that at first she hardly felt anything. Her nipple slipped out of the baby's mouth and the nuzzling started again. Julia laughed and helped the baby to find her breast again.

Several times this happened and Julia looked up to Martha. "That's just the way baby pigs do it. They lose it and find it again—only they squeal more."

Martha nodded.

The baby didn't nurse long before she fell asleep, her little head lolling back against Julia's arm.

"When she wakes up," Martha instructed, "put her to your other breast. You can sleep awhile—she's satisfied for now. I'll be working in the kitchen."

Both the baby and Julia slept for an hour. Then the baby began to grunt and squirm, and Julia turned on her other side and drew the baby to that breast. Julia felt awkward trying to get the baby in the right position, but soon the baby was nuzzling again. Julia put one finger into the baby's tiny hands and the baby clenched tight. "Martha, she's strong!" Julia exclaimed, as Martha came in from the kitchen.

"She's a beautiful, perfect, healthy baby, Julia."

Sixteen-year-old Julia lay still watching her baby nurse, hearing the tiny greedy, grunting and swallowing sounds. *She is actually being fed from me. I hadn't even thought about nursing or how it would make me love my baby. The Lord sure did think up somethin' great when He thought up this plan.*

She was amazed. As her baby was being filled and satisfied, she began to feel life flowing both out of her and into her. Love she never expected. Love for her baby. Unbelievable love.

"Her name is Eva Jane," she said later. "I don't know where I got it from, but it sounds like a good old-fashioned name. I like it."

CHAPTER NINE
A Chapter Is Closed

As Julia cared for her growing baby and helped on Martha and Joe's farm, miles down the road, Ellie Crawford rocked her life away in front of her kitchen door.

When Solly had first left, she was afraid to go to bed at night. After what he'd already done, if he came home in the dark, no tellin' what he might do to her. She had nothing to do but think, and many memories crowded in upon her. She rocked and thought about when they were first married—she was strong then, and was sure that Solly loved her.

If she hadn't been so sick after losing a baby that time, things might have been different. After that, she was always frail and never could have a child. Maybe if Solly'd had a son who looked up to him, he wouldn't have become the surly kind of person he was. But it was too late to change anything now.

During his last few years on the farm, he'd shown no consideration at all for her. He acted like he merely tolerated her because he needed her to wait on him. He never wanted to give her any money and pretended he didn't have any to give. But she knew better. Just like she told the sheriff—she was sure he had a sizeable bank account.

With the help of the sheriff and the bank president, and because Solly was declared a fugitive from justice, his account was turned over to her. She was amazed at the size of it, and realized she'd never have to work in the fields and raise any of her food if she didn't want to. She could buy all her supplies, hire people to fetch her what she needed, live a long time and still have some left. She could have moved into Marion and had some close neighbors, but she still loved her home and didn't want to leave it. Once a week— from a mile away—a lady came in to clean the house for her and that's about the only time she saw anyone else. Sometimes, when she was able, she worked in her flower garden.

Mostly, Ellie just sat in her rocking chair looking out the kitchen door, realizing money doesn't bring happiness. When Julia ran away and she knew the kind of man she'd been living with, she lost all interest in everything. For her, life was over—nothing was really worth getting out of bed for. She ate as little as she could to live, and didn't mind if she died.

Sitting in the doorway nearly two years later, Ellie heard a wagon rumbling up the lane. She couldn't believe her ears. She shaded her eyes with her hands, squinting, trying to see who was coming. She had very few visitors. The wagon bumped closer and she could make out three people and a child.

The team pulled the wagon up by the kitchen door and Joe King, Martha, and Julia all jumped down to greet her. Ellie was totally taken by surprise. She thought they would never ever come near her again. But her heart pounded when she looked at Julia. Julia was now a lovely young woman of seventeen, with her hair up. And in Julia's arms was her beautiful year-old baby, which looked just like Julia had looked as a one-year old. Ellie began to sob into her apron, and Julia stooped and put her arms around her.

"Don't cry, Miss Ellie."

"Oh, Julia, I am most powerful glad to see you!"

"And I'm glad to see you, Miss Ellie."

"I didn't think you'd ever come back over here, Julia. I wanted to talk to you so many times and tell you how sorry I am about—about—"

"I wanted to see you, too—you was always nice to me." Julia sat down on the floor beside Ellie's chair. "But I just couldn't come before—I couldn't get over the bad things that Solly done. Before I left here I wanted most powerful to tell you what was goin' on, but I was afraid to. Solly'd said he'd kill me if I did. I thought he might kill you, too—I just run when I got the chance."

Ellie looked totally flustered. "Joe, Martha! Please pull up them chairs and set. I'm so surprised at havin' you come that I ain't got no manners at all." Looking at Eva Jane, she continued, "Can I hold your baby, Julia?"

Julia wiped her eyes, picked up Eva Jane and put her in Miss Ellie's lap. "This is Eva Jane, the only good that come out of that bad time."

Eva Jane looked up at Miss Ellie for a moment, smiled showing perfect little teeth, then scrambled back off her lap.

"She's just beginnin' to walk," explained Julia, "and she's never still a minute."

Ellie sat watching the baby and shaking her head. "She's so much like you! Thank the Lord she don't look a bit like Solly."

Eva Jane was trying to walk to her mother, when her little fat foot caught on a chair leg and she went rolling like a kitten over the floor. She began to scream.

"She shore has a healthy voice!" Ellie remarked.

Julia laughed. "She shore does, Miss Ellie. Sometimes when Eva Jane screams like that, people stop dead in their tracks. They can't imagine how such a loud noise could come from such a small young'un." She picked Eva Jane up and soothed her.

"Miss Ellie, I want to thank you for the three hundred dollars you sent me. I'm still savin' it for that rainy day. I've not needed it before because Joe and Martha have been takin' such good care of me—"

"Miss Ellie, Julia has earned every bit of care we've tried to give her. She just won't be beholdin' to anybody. She thinks she's got to pay for every little thing," said Martha.

The three of them talked for a while, watching Eva Jane crawl around investigating every inch of the kitchen. Ellie finally remembered her manners enough to get up and make some coffee for everybody. She also served them some cake, saying, "My neighbor who cleans my house brought me this cake yesterday. When she brought it I didn't think I'd ever be able to use it all."

Julia appreciated seeing Miss Ellie, but the longer she was there, the harder it was to sit still in that house. Bad memories threatened to swamp her. Her hands began to shake and her eyes clouded up.

Joe and Martha saw her agitation, and stood up saying, "We better git goin', Julia. Be time to do the chores when we git home."

"Will you come back and see me—and bring the baby?" Ellie asked as they climbed into the wagon.

"Yes," promised Julia. I can do it now, but I still need Joe with me when I come here. You understand?"

Ellie nodded. But she knew Julia need not worry. "Solly will never come back, Julia."

From time to time during the next three years, Julia kept her promise and she and Joe came bringing little Eva Jane with them. Ellie looked forward from week to week hoping they would come, and she seemed to be comforted and more content. Each time they brought Eva Jane, Ellie kept exclaiming how she was growing and had some small gift for her. They always found Ellie in her rocking chair in front of the kitchen door, but with each visit they could see Ellie's strength and awareness was fast failing.

Finally, near the last, they found her babbling to herself and Julia knew Ellie did not recognize her. Julia hated to leave her but her neighbor, Mrs. Archer, was there taking care of Miss Ellie all the time. Julia shook her head in sadness. "Oh, she's bad off! She's so shrunk up, I don't see how she's livin'. We'll come back soon. She's been rockin' in that doorway for nearly five years and I don't think she'll last long now."

Mrs. Archer answered, "She's a sweet lady but I can't get her to eat or do anything else. All she wants to do is just set in that rockin' chair and look out the door."

Joe said to Julia on the way home, "I wonder if she keeps hopin' that Solly'll come back sometime. I hope not."

* * *

The following week, the sheriff in Marion sent word to the four King brothers to come in. He had news for them. When they arrived in his office the next day, he said, "I wanted to tell you fellers some news. Miss Ellie Crawford died last Saturday—"

Joe gasped. "She did? We just went to see her on Friday. We thought she looked awful bad."

"Yes," the sheriff said, "she died in her rockin' chair. The neighbor lady, Mrs. Archer, sent her son in to tell me. I got some men together and we buried her. Poor Miss Ellie—she's better off".

"Don't suppose you've ever heard anything about Solly, have you, Sheriff?"

"No, I never did. He may be dead after all this time, but if he isn't, then I suppose we'll hear about him when he does die. World's better off without men like him anyway!"

Julia's brothers nodded their heads. "You're shore right about that, Sheriff!"

When Julia heard the news, she wept into her apron for Miss Ellie. She went in and lay down on the bed while Eva Jane napped. *Poor Miss Ellie!* she said to herself. *She deserved so much better than him! But where is Solly and will he ever come back here? I worry about seein' him somewhere. I still don't like goin' out by myself—don't like goin' into a corn patch alone, either. I'm afraid I'll meet him—then what would I do?*

J U L I A

Part II

1884 - 1885

CHAPTER TEN
Hotel Interlude

Eva Jane was a husky four-year-old, playing outside with a puppy when Joe came back from Lake Creek bringing supplies. While riding home, Joe had been thinking. He'd heard some news at Lake Creek which might be good for Julia. She'd been with them for five years, and she was welcome. She was family, and both Joe and Martha loved her dearly. But was it good for her to stay here so long? Julia was a wonderful girl, and she was smart too. Maybe it would be good if she tried something else. And his news sounded good. Joe realized he'd have to be careful because he certainly didn't want Julia to think she wasn't wanted.

As he got off his horse he waved to Julia who was busy taking clothes off the line. "Heard somethin' you might like to know about," he said. "I'll tell you at supper."

She nodded.

When the nine gathered around the table, he looked at each one of his family—his wife, their five children, and Julia with Eva Jane. He bowed his head and said, "Lord, I'm thankful for every one at this table. Our family is well and we're in debt to You, Lord. We thank You for all this food which keeps us goin'. Bless us, keep us from sin, and keep us a' servin' You. Amen." Then he filled his plate with ham hock, beans, and cornbread.

"Julie, I heard some news today. People talkin' at the post office said they's a finishin' a new hotel down in Creal Springs. They's wantin' some young women to work there—makin' beds, cookin', cleanin' and such."

"What's the hotel like? How far is Creal Springs from here?"

"I reckon it must be about ten or twelve miles south of here—maybe a little more. It's a different kind of a hotel. Seems this hotel got started in a strange way."

"What's that?"

"Well, the talk I heard in the post office was that they're a lot of people coming to Creal because of some spring water that cures just about ever'thing.

"The story goes that about four years ago, a family with six young'uns came in a covered wagon from Missouri. I—don't know how far they was goin' to travel. But when they got to Creal, they was all bad sick with malaria fever. They couldn't go any further. So they stopped and made camp by some springs down there. They begin drinkin' that spring water and the first thing you know they all got well. They stayed there for a spell and all their thin, pale yellow faces got flushed and healthy. Their malaria was gone!"

"I guess they told people about that spring water?"

"They did. They's a Mr. Creal who lived there. Now for a long time he had been noticin' some fish livin' in a small rock basin near the springs. They was bigger and healthier than the same kind of fish in other ponds around there. So after he heard about the family gettin well from malaria drinkin' that water, he got excited. Mr. Creal took some of that spring water north, all the way up to the Keeley Cure Clinic at Dwight, Illinois. I don't even know what that place is. But Mr. Creal told everybody that he had that Creal Springs water analyzed. They found the spring water had powerful chemicals—the kind like they put in medicines."

"That must've made Mr. Creal more excited than ever!" Joe's children were interested in the tale.

"It did! It seems the news about the springs a'curin' people got around the country and people started comin' to Creal—people with malaria, rheumatism, lumbago, heart trouble—all kinds of aches and pains. They swore that after they took baths in that warm spring water and drunk it for a few days, they was well. So a Doctor Brown from Herrin's Prairie left his practice and went there and built a hotel for sick people to come and stay in while they's layin' in the water and drinkin' it. I hear the hotel's full all the time—and they's a'needin' more people to work there."

Julia sat thinking. Maybe she could get a job there. But would she dare to leave her shelter here and take a job so far away? What about Eva Jane? She'd have to leave her. It would be good, though, if she could get a job and make some money to take care of herself and Eva Jane.

"Do you think there's a chance I could get a job there, Joe? If I could, I'd pay you money for stayin' here so long." Julia's eyes sparkled. "If I could work there, Marthie, would you keep Eva Jane? I could pay you for it."

"No call to do that, Julia. We don't take money from family. Anyhow, you've always earned your keep here, workin' in our fields and house—"

"I know, Marthie, but you've been so good to me. You

wouldn't take any of that money Miss Ellie gave me—it's still hid away. But I know you work awful hard keepin' Eva Jane with your own little'uns when I'm in the fields. And if I get a job I intend to pay my own way. Martha—that would help you too. Your kids need shoes and things and you want them to go to school. It would help everybody. "What do you think, Joe?"

Joe considered for a while. Should he really let her leave the security of his house? She'd had such a hard time and he would always worry about her safety. But she was old enough to make up her own mind. Finally he nodded. "Well, Julie, you're all growed up—you're twenty years old. I can't keep you from tryin' to get work. If you're sure you want to go, I'll ride down there with you whenever you're ready and we'll look it over."

"Well, it sounds like somethin' I might ought to be doin'. I don't know of any other way to bring in some money. And I can't depend on you forever."

Eva Jane was listening to this unusual supper-table conversation. She looked at Julia with tears rolling down her face. "Mama, did you say you was a'goin' to leave me?"

Julia took her from the table and they went outside and sat on the porch. "My sweet baby, I might have to leave you for a while. I'm thinkin' about it—it might mean a job for me. Even if I go to Creal Springs, I don't know if I'll stay. But if I do, it's because we need some money."

"Mama, you said Aunt Marthie would keep me. Why can't I go with you? I'll be a good girl!"

Julia hugged her tight. "I know you would, Eva Jane. But this is a workin' place. I couldn't take care of you."

"But I could drink that water and get strong and take care of myself! Uncle Joe said——"

"But you're already strong and healthy. You don't need that water. No, you have to stay here where you have other young'uns to play with. And I will come home to see you, or Joe would bring you down to see me. You'd like that, wouldn't you? So dry your face, and let's go back and eat our supper. I have to think about this for a while."

She finally got Eva Jane settled for the night, but it wasn't easy for Julia to sleep. Over and over in her mind rolled reasons why she should try to get a job away from here, and reasons why she shouldn't. The decision was hard.

All the next day as she worked with Joe, they talked and reasoned. At the supper table she said, "I've made up my mind, Joe.

If you'll go with me, I'll go to Creal Springs tomorrow. How long will it take us to ride down there?"

"Oh—maybe about three hours."

"All right. I'll get my things together tonight." She put Eva Jane to bed, but it was hard for the little girl to settle down, knowing her mother would leave the next day. Before she went to bed, Julia put her two best dresses, some working clothes, underwear, her other pair of shoes, a nightgown, and her comb and brush in an old pillowcase. She tied the top with a small rope. She'd hold that in front of her on the horse tomorrow.

What about the money still hidden away in her trunk? She certainly didn't want to take it with her. She decided to tell Martha that she was leaving the money where it was. If they needed anything, they could use it. Her excitement was so great that she scarcely slept.

Up at daylight, she and Joe ate a working breakfast—coffee and eggs with hot biscuits. Martha had been up for an hour and a half already, to heat up the stove and cook their breakfast. When she finished eating, Julia tiptoed back into the bedroom and brushed a good-bye kiss on the round, rosy face of a sleeping little girl. She smoothed back a mop of curly black hair and asked God to take care of her baby. Holding her packed pillowcase, she and Joe mounted their horses and trotted out the gate. Where the lane met the main road, they turned south.

Though Marion was only about five miles away, Julia had been there very few times. She was surprised to see how the town had grown—blocks of businesses and houses all clustered around the courthouse in the center of town.

As they rode, leaving the courthouse behind them, Joe asked, "Did you ever hear about Steal-Easy?"

"No—what's that?"

"Well, Steal-Easy is a little place about five miles east of here. Like most other early settlements, one of the most important things there was the grist mill. I've been told they had a mill-hand there named Bob Goe who sold customers their ground-up grain. He'd always make sure he showed the customers that the weight of their already-ground grain was right. But he used to wear great big cuffs on his sleeves and, not bein' a very honest feller, he learned to pour the weighed meal down into their sacks so that part of it fell into his big cuffs. That way, he could collect nearly a pound of meal there. His customers went away with part of their meal down in Bob Goe's cuffs, and he simply sold it and made himself some extra money."

"So why did they call the place Steal-Easy?"

"Because everybody there said that Bob Goe could steal easier with his cuffs than he could with a gun!"

"Did they ever catch him at it?"

"I think they did. When they got a post office there some years later, they called the place Crab Orchard because of so many crab apple trees around."

From Marion, riding east and south, the flat land of Little Egypt began to edge up into the Ozarks. Hills were higher than Julia had ever seen before and from some crests she looked out over great expanses of nothing but timberland marching up and down mountains and valleys. She gasped at the grandeur of it. "I didn't know it was so purty down in these parts!"

Joe pointed ahead to a hill they had to climb. "All this is called the Ozark mountain range and it runs through the states of Illinois, Kentucky, Missouri and Arkansas. You know they called our part of the country 'Egypt' because the land is so good. Then others called it 'Little Egypt' so I guess it don't matter which we call it."

"We raise lots of corn too. Don't the Bible talk about the corn in Egypt?"

"It does. And these mineral springs we're goin' to see down in Creal Springs are called 'Pharaoh's Waters.'"

Julia said, "I remember the preacher one time preached about old Pharaoh in Egypt who wouldn't let Moses' people go. Was his water special, too?"

Joe shook his head. "Don't know if it was or not. But I do remember the Bible story about Joseph and old Pharaoh in Egypt—and that's where the name come from. I guess them old people who settled around here first must have knowed a lot about their Bibles—they called these places so many Bible names."

In the early afternoon they cantered into a small village. Alongside the road was a brand new building—the biggest Julia had ever seen—the Brown's Creal Springs Hotel. They hitched their horses in front with other horses and wagons, and climbed down. "I must be gettin' old!" Julia exclaimed. "Ain't rode so far in a long time and I feel stiff!"

They entered a mammoth reception room. Huge, elegant sofas and chairs upholstered in red plush were scattered around. Julia had never seen anything so fine. A young desk clerk stood behind a counter assisting a line of people. Some were old and crippled, being escorted by their much younger children. Joe and Julia stood in line while the clerk pushed a huge register from one guest to another for signing. Then he gave each one a big numbered room key. *This ought to be a fine place to work,* Julia thought. Finally, she was at the counter.

"What can I do for you, Miss?" the clerk asked.

Julia answered timidly, "I—I hear that you need some women to work in your hotel. I've come to get a job."

He looked her over while Joe stood silently by. "What is your name and how old are you, Miss?"

"My name is Julia King and I am twenty years old. This is my brother Joe."

"Are you married?'

"No."

"Could you live here at the hotel? We'd give you a room and you would be expected to work from sunup 'till eight at night. Think you could do that?"

"I've worked in the house and fields all my life. Reckon I could work in a fancy place like this."

"Can you start today? Our guest rooms are full and we need help now. Dr. Brown will talk to you first. You would be on trial for the first month."

"I could start today."

Joe pulled himself to his full height of six-feet-two inches and looked straight at the hotel clerk. "Sir, I am sure you will be responsible to see that my sister is safe if she is working here. I will hold you to account for her."

"You can rest easy, Mr. King. We have a very fine establishment here with the highest standards. Dr. Brown, our owner, won't have things any other way. We take very good care of all our young women. She will be safe."

"Where can we find Dr. Brown?"

The clerk pointed to a door across the room. "He's in there. Don't be afraid, Miss King. He's a very nice man."

Julia and Joe walked across the room and knocked on the door. A fine looking, white-haired man opened it. "Come in—I am Dr. Brown. What can I do for you?"

Julia liked him on sight. "My name is Julia King and I heard you need women to work in this hotel. I come to see if I could get a job. This is my brother Joe—we rode from up near Shake Rag today."

Dr. Brown smiled. "Shake Rag! I laugh every time I hear that name. But I know the place because I came from Herrin, which isn't far from there. Please have a seat."

Julia and Joe sank down in a soft chair and Dr. Brown seated himself behind his desk.

"Have you worked for anybody before, Miss King?"

"Well, I—uh grew up on a farm and I've worked all my life in the house and fields."

"You understand that this would all be inside work? We need women who can clean the rooms, make beds, and help out in the kitchen at mealtimes. We have certain rules of cleanliness which must be followed. Would you be willing to learn to do things our way?"

Julia nodded. "Yes, I would."

"How old are you? And is there anything else that I should know about you—anything you'd like to tell me about yourself?"

"I am twenty years old." His other question confused her and she wasn't sure how to answer. Hesitantly, she began, "M-my Ma and Pa are both dead and I——"

Joe broke in. "Dr. Brown I suppose you ought to know somethin' which is hard for Julia to talk about. But if we don't tell you, it might not be right because you ought to know about them that works for you. You see, somethin' bad happened to her that ought never to have took place."

Joe breathed deeply—telling this to a stranger was painful, but Joe had a strong sense of fairness in all his dealings. "My sister is a good girl. She was stayin' with some friends and workin' for them after Ma died, and she was only fifteen years old. The man who lived there raped her over and over and kept her his prisoner for a month. None of that was caused by any of her doin'. Finally she got a chance to run away. But she had a little girl by him—she's four years old—and they've been livin' in my house ever since that time. If me and my brothers could've caught that man, we'd a shot him. But he got away and ain't been seen since. We recently heard from the sheriff that Miss Ellie, his wife died. She just set in her rockin' chair and mourned her life away over that man.

"People back home know all about this and they don't blame Julia none. If she works for you here, I don't think you'll have cause to be sorry you hired her."

Dr. Brown looked at Julia with great compassion. What a beautiful young woman she was! Brown eyes under dark brows, black curls which didn't want to be swept up in such a severe band, a sweet smile, a tall, strong figure, and having to deal with such a stain on her soul.

When Joe began to tell Dr. Brown her story, Julia bowed her

head. Now she was afraid to look up—surely the big doctor would say he didn't want her kind in his hotel.

But Dr. Brown got up out of his chair and came around in front of his desk and took Julia's hand. "I am very sorry for all that happened to you, Miss King. And I don't hold you responsible. It's a sad thing to have people like that man in the world."

Julia nodded and a tear stole down her cheek and dropped onto her folded hands.

Dr. Brown then spoke to Joe. "Mr. King, this story will go no further than the walls of this room. No one else needs to know what has happened to Julia, so she can do her work here without thinking that everybody is talking about her or blaming her. I appreciate your being honest with me. Julia, if you want the job, it's yours."

Julia raised her head, looked at him, and a smile lighted her face. "You mean I have the job? You want me to work at your hotel?"

"Yes, I do," answered Dr. Brown.

"Oh! I'm much obliged to you. I will work hard and no trouble will be caused by me!"

"She will be safe here?" Joe had to ask it one more time.

The doctor understood what Joe was asking. "We see to it that our employees are well protected and taken care of. We run a safe place. If anyone ever gives you any trouble, Julia, all you have to do is report it to me."

"I thank you, Dr. Brown. I need to have a job. The only thing I worry about is that sometime I might see that awful man again. I'm still scared of him, even though it's been five years."

"Julia, if you ever see anybody around here that looks like him, you come straight to me. If he comes around here, we will see to it that he is locked away in jail for a long time."

"Thank you, Dr. Brown. You have a very nice hotel and I think I'll like it here."

"Then she can stay if she wants to." Joe picked up his hat and looked questioningly at Julia. She nodded to him. "Thank you, Dr. Brown. Looks like you have a fine place here."

The doctor shook hands with both Joe and Julia. "Tell the desk clerk to show you to your room, Julia. You can have a little rest and then—" he pulled his gold watch from his vest pocket and its gold chain swung while he studied it for a moment—"you can report to the dining room at six o'clock. They will furnish you with an apron. I'm glad to have you working with us, and hope you will be happy here, Julia."

Julia and Joe walked back outside and stood beside their horses. "Goodbye, Julie. Here—don't forget your clothes." He handed her the old pillow case. "You can try workin' here for a month. Then me and Marthie will bring the young'uns down to see you. Eva Jane will be wantin' to see her ma by then. If you don't like the job, you can come back home with us. One month from today we'll be back."

Her lips were trembling and she held his arm for a few extra minutes. She had suddenly realized how lonely she would feel, and was gathering strength to tide her over the coming weeks. "Goodbye, Joe. Take good care of my little girl. See you in a month!"

He climbed on his horse and led the one she had ridden. "We all like takin' care of Eva Jane, Julie. See you in a month."

A great sinking sensation hit her chest and she had to blink fast to keep the tears from her brown eyes as she watched Joe ride northward. She was farther from home than she'd ever been in her life, and this was the first time she was ever away from Eva Jane. She longed to feel those little arms around her neck. But now she was truly grown up, so she had to prove it. She straightened her shoulders, held her head high and went in to her new life.

* * * *

Julia's days in the Creal Springs Hotel began before sunup, but that was no hardship—she'd been doing that for all of her twenty years. The help breakfasted in the kitchen at five o'clock. After the kitchen was cleaned of all signs of their breakfast, instructions were issued for the rest of the day.

Julia's job was to clean ten rooms each day and help in the kitchen at meal times. The rooms she cleaned were inspected every day and they had to be spotless. She was taught to wash her hands thoroughly, scrubbing them with soap and water before touching any food in the kitchen, and her apron had to be immaculate at all times. She did not have to wash her own aprons—a clean one was given to her each time she entered the kitchen. If any food was ever spilled on herself, she was to change her apron immediately.

She liked the hotel. She liked seeing people get well. Many came in pain, and returned to health before they left. Julia was always pleasant to everyone, but did not try to make any close friends. She performed her tasks and minded her own business.

Julia's beauty was not dimmed with the work and hardships she had endured all her life, but she took no notice of it. Her curly black hair strained at the bonds of the tight knot at the back of her head. Her cheeks had the glow of health, her clear brown eyes under curving black brows looked at the world asking no favors. Her shoulders were broad, and she stood straight and tall. She had two good dresses and three work dresses, all with voluminous skirts. Large aprons, supplied by the hotel, covered the worn spots in her every-day clothes. She wore high-laced black shoes and black cotton stockings.

Her habit had been in winter to wear two petticoats and long underwear, a corset and a vest. She needed that many layers of clothing then, because houses were warm only in the kitchens. In summer she took off the long underwear and one petticoat. Her sleeves were always rolled to her elbows, showing strong, shapely hands and arms. Only on Sundays when she put on her brown chambray dress for church, did she wear the sleeves long.

Julia made up her mind to pay strict attention to her business, so she spoke to the male guests only if spoken to. She answered their questions but never offered friendship. Because of Solly and what he had done to her five years ago, she could never trust any man again. She had built up a wall around her heart that was solid as a tomb and she would allow no one to penetrate it.

Of course, she met many men while she worked in the hotel—that was inevitable. Many of them were cheered at the sight of her and tried to talk to her. But if she thought any man was trying to be a little too cordial, a few cool words were enough to chill the stoutest heart.

She didn't allow herself to be friendly toward any of the young women she worked with, either. She was too afraid they would find out about her and then judge her as being poor white trash—women liked to gossip.

Julia earned two dollars a week and her keep. She put aside seventy-five cents to pay Martha for taking care of Eva Jane, and except for buying another work dress, most of the rest she saved. The life-long constriction of poverty was on her and she grudged every penny which had to be spent. If she ever wanted something, she always told herself that some day she'd have a greater need than what she was now thinking about. That was a rule she lived by.

The first month of working in the Creal Springs Hotel was the hardest. She missed Joe and all his family, but most of all she missed Eva Jane. Especially at night she missed her—they had slept in the same bed ever since Eva Jane was born. Eva Jane loved to cuddle up to her mother at night. Most of her life, except for the time at the Crawford house, she had slept in a bed with someone. Now this small single bed at the hotel spelled loneliness.

A month later, on the day she was expecting Joe and Martha and all the children, she was more excited than she could ever remember. She kept looking down the road when near a front window, until finally she saw the wagon coming. She raced to the front door.

Little Eva Jane jumped out of the wagon like a whirlwind and threw herself into Julia's arms. "Mama! I missed you! Did you know we were having a long ride in the wagon today to come here? I even went to sleep."

Julia hugged her. "I'm so glad to see you, Eva Jane. I missed you, too!"

"Can I stay here with you, Mama?"

"No, sweet child. I don't have any time to take care of you and there are no other boys or girls for you to play with here. You'll be better off at Martha's."

"What do you do all day, Mama? Field work?"

"No. I make beds for sick people and I serve food in the dining room to them, too. I work 'til after dark at night and I just couldn't have any time with you."

"B—but couldn't I help you work?"

"No, Eva Jane. Only big people work here."

Eva Jane considered, sighed, then gave up and changed the subject. "Did you know we've got new kittens? The mama kitty catches rats and eats them—ugh!"

"Are there any new puppies yet?"

"Oh, yes. They are big now and when I run, they nip at my toes and they make a big noise barkin', too."

"Eva Jane, are you learning to do some work to help Martha in the kitchen?"

"Oh, yes! She lets me churn and I pound the bread dough. Sometimes she lets me lick the cream spoon and sop gravy in the big skillet—if the big kids don't beat me to it!"

Julia put Eva Jane down. "You children can all go walkin' around and see where I work. But don't touch anything, don't go into any of the bedrooms, and be quiet! Some people here don't feel too good." As the children jumped up, she cautioned, "Walk soft now."

The children danced with eagerness to explore this fascinating place. Sally, Joe's oldest daughter, said excitedly, "We just peeked in the door, and we want to see this whole place with all the big, soft chairs. We ain't never in our lives seen any chairs like 'em. And we want to walk around and say 'Howdy' to all the dressed-up people."

"All right, Sally. See that you keep the others quiet." Julia, Joe, and Martha watched the little procession tiptoe inside, looking at everything on the way.

"Are you satisfied workin' here, Julia?" asked Joe as they sat in a porch swing. "Anybody cause you any trouble?"

"I'm satisfied, Joe. I like makin' my own money and I work hard to earn it—but I don't mind. She handed Martha a rolled up handkerchief. "Here, Marthie. Here's your money for keepin' Eva Jane last month. It's a great help to me to know that she has a good home and people to love her when I'm away—I don't like being away from her—that's the *only* bad part about workin' here."

Martha accepted the money. "But you have no call to pay me, Julie. We're family."

"I know, but I'd have to pay anybody else, and I know you earn it. I like makin' my own money and it is good for you, too. I miss you all—but I'm goin' to stay here."

"We miss you too, Julie. I got used to havin' you there. But I'm glad you are happy," Martha said.

"Yes," Julia admitted, "Guess I'm about as happy here as I'll ever be anywhere. Everybody is nice to me. Sometimes I talk to Doctor Brown—he and Mrs. Brown are extra nice to me. He said he'd like to meet Eva Jane today and that havin' her made no difference in the way he thought of me. It weren't my fault, he knows."

Joe heaved a sigh of relief. "Well, it's a load off my mind, to know that you're settled, Julie. I was all ready to take you home if you wanted to come, and I still will. I was a little worried about you bein' safe."

"I feel very safe, Joe. The sick people who come are feelin' too bad to try anything with the girls here. And if any of the men who work here tried it, Doctor Brown would get rid of 'em quick. So I do feel safe."

Dr. Brown had given Julia the afternoon free to spend with her family. Julia escorted Joe and Martha all around the hotel and also showed them the main attraction—the springs. "I wonder where the young'uns are."

"We'll run onto them somewhere here abouts," Martha promised. They finally caught up with the children at the springs—in the bath house. They were just about to stick their feet into the water.

Julia called sharply, "No! You can't do that!"

But the children wailed, "We want to see if this water feels like any other water. Is it hot? Is it cold? Will it make our feet tingle? How're we goin' to know if you won't let us splash in there a little bit?"

"No—it would probably just make your feet clean. But you're not a guest here so you're not supposed to do that. You can go home and wade in the creek."

"But that's just old creek water—that does no healin.'"

"Anything wrong with your feet that you want healed? Got any crooked toes, broken ankles, or rheumatism in your feet?" Julia laughed. "Course, it might even cure cross- eyes or a turned-up nose or a freckled face."

"N—no," they giggled. "We ain't got none of them."

Julia peered closely at them. "W—well, I do think I see a couple of turned-up noses and some freckles——"

Joe called, "Come on, all of you. We gotta get back, we got a long ride home."

"Oh——" Amid protestations they were soon back in front of the hotel and loading into the wagon. Julia kissed them all and gave Eva Jane a special hug. "Joe, come back soon as you can. I sure love to see you. Be a good girl, Eva Jane, and mind Martha. Your Mama loves you."

"Bye, Mama."

"Bye, Aunt Julia—"

Julia stood and watched the wagon as far as she could see Eva Jane and the other children waving to her. She went back to work with a lighter heart.

CHAPTER ELEVEN
Falling Shell

Julia had no close friends and at twenty was a sober woman with a child but with no illusions and no dreams. She had lived like that for more than four years now but finally she began to thaw a little. Sometimes while she worked at the hotel, her mind played with the idea of Seth as her husband, and living in his house and having his children. When that happened, she had to shake herself and come back to reality, for a life with Seth would never be.

She sighed because she knew there *were* happy people in the world who liked to laugh and hoedown, go for buggy rides and picnics, and take walks together. She used to be like that, too, but now fun things in life were over for her. Life hadn't been fun for a long time.

One day, however, after she had been working at Creal Springs Hotel for about six months, a stranger hobbled into her life and, try as she would, she could not ignore him.

"Julia," said Dr. Brown that day, "I have a special job for you in room number nine—a man by the name of John Childers. He has a broken ankle and it hasn't been healing as it should. Horse stumbled and threw him. He will have to eat in his room for a while and needs a little extra help. You're a sensible girl and I think you can earn a little extra money waiting on him."

Julia knocked on the door of Mr. Childers' room as she had been taught to do. When she heard, "Come in," and walked into the room, she saw John Childers sitting in one chair with his bandaged foot propped on another. An open valise was on his knees, and he was trying to reach the dresser drawers to put his clothes away. He was breathing heavily, his forehead wrinkled in pain.

"I reckon you need some help, Sir. I'm Julia King. Dr. Brown sent me."

He looked up at her. "Proud to know you, Miss King. My name is John Childers. Reckon this is the first time I've ever been laid up like this." He shook his head. "Been takin' care of myself for quite a spell now, and I don't like to have to be waited on."

Julia nodded but made no reply. She lifted the valise off his knees and quickly put his few things away in the drawers. She shut the drawers and asked, "It's about dinner time—are you hungry? I'll bring it to you here."

"I hate to have you do that." His voice sounded gentle. "But I sure can't get to the dinin' room with my foot a'hurtin' like it is right now." He leaned back in his chair and sighed and closed his eyes.

She brought his food from the kitchen. She set the tray on his knees and went over to the washstand, dipped a cloth into water in the big white china bowl, and handed the cloth to Mr. Childers to wash his hands.

"I'm beholdin' to you, Miss King." He looked at the plate of sausage and vegetables and continued, "Didn't know I was so hungry 'til I saw all this. It smells good!"

As she went about her job of cleaning the room and changing the bed, Julia felt a little strange to be working with a man sitting in the room. Usually the guests were out at the springs while the rooms were being put in order.

But John Childers spoke again, "I'm sorry to be in your way when you're gettin' your work done. The Doc says tomorrow they'll take me out in a chair with some wheels. Then I won't be such a bother to you in here." As he ate he continued, "I hope these springs do all the good they're claiming they do. I've got to get back home and get to workin' again." His words put her at ease because she knew what it was like to want to get out and work.

When she finished cleaning the room, she took his empty plate. "I'll bring your supper too, Mr. Childers. Rest this afternoon and stay off that foot."

"I'm thankful for your help, Miss King. I don't rightly know how long it's been since I been waited on like this. Makes a man feel like he ain't worth much!"

Julia glanced at him and smiled a little. "Don't feel like that, Mr. Childers. Lots of people come here who need help. I'm glad I can do somethin'." She was suddenly aware that she was looking straight at a man because she liked his manner. Before she looked away, she saw he had a face that she might be able to trust—sharp, blue eyes, brown hair and a neatly trimmed brown beard. His nose was straight, and his lips were firm but gentle.

"Don't worry, Mr. Childers. Your ankle will heal soon and you'll be all right. Everybody needs help now and again." She was amazed at how easily she could talk to John Childers. She hadn't talked that much to any male guest for the last six months— ever since she'd been working here. And she didn't feel strange about it! That amazed her, too.

For the next five days when she went in to room nine, Mr. Childers was gone. *He must be spending a lot of time down at the springs with his injured foot in the water,* Julia thought. *Well, that's what he came for, and that's what he needs.* Still, she missed him in the room.

About a week passed, and Julia went in to make his bed one day. She was late in getting to this room because some new guests had come in and she had to make up their rooms. One of the other girls had a bad toothache and couldn't work that day. When she reached his room, Julia found John Childers hobbling restlessly around, using a chair as a crutch, and trying to put some weight on his injured foot. "Mr. Childers! You're walkin' on it too soon! Let it heal first."

"Miss King, I guess you're right, but you don't know how hard it is to be like this! I'm used to workin'!"

"I know, but you just have to forget about workin' for a spell. You're soakin' your foot in these springs every day—it's bound to be cured soon. And now with your push-chair you can go eat in the dining room, and you don't have to keep your leg up all the time. So you're gettin' better."

"Yes—but it's sure pokin' along. I need to be gettin' on home—my family needs me."

Julia had been wondering about a family. Did he have a wife? He never mentioned her. This was the first time he had spoken of anyone else. "You got a big family, Mr. Childers?"

"Well, Miss King, I guess it's big enough. I got five young'uns—their ages are from fourteen down to six. My wife died nearly three year ago. Been takin' care of them by myself 'til I got my foot hurt."

"Oh. You have any more family nearby? Who's takin' care of them while you are here?"

"My wife's sister. If I had to get hurt, I guess this would be about the best time. My wife's sister and her husband had come up from Tennessee to visit during the winter. It's a good thing they're at the house or I couldn't have come here to get this foot healed."

Julia nodded. "I'm sure their aunt will take good care of them so you shouldn't worry."

"I appreciate the good care you've been givin' me here, Miss King. I know that is part of your job, but still, you've been helpin' me a lot."

Julia smiled at him and John Childers thought, *She's the prettiest girl I've seen in many a year.*

Friendship came slowly to Julia. She was still partially wrapped in her shell of mistrust, but she could not deny to herself that with each morning she became more eager to get to room nine. The sun shone brighter and her spirits seemed to be lifting. Maybe she couldn't trust other men, but John Childers—for some reason she felt he was different. She began to dread the time—she could barely stand to think about the time—when he would walk down the steps of the hotel and out of her life.

From day to day when they did meet, Julia felt more at home with him. She was not so shy; she felt free to be natural near him, and was more willing to talk. She realized she did not feel the same way in the presence of any other man. Only John Childers seemed to make her at ease.

Sometimes they talked about farming, which both of them loved, and how, every winter, they looked forward to planting season. "Of course," she said, "workin' here I'm goin' to miss all the plantin' season. It'll be the first time in my life I've not helped with plantin'—it'll be hard to stay inside." "What do you like to raise most on your farm, Mr. Childers?"

"Oh—of course I always have a big garden—got to put stuff away for winter. But mostly I raise corn. I make the purtiest corn crop in the country. I shore appreciate to look at them long rows of corn just before harvest time."

Involuntarily, Julia shuddered and her face changed. She looked almost haunted, she was nervous, glancing toward the door. "I—I'd better go—got other rooms to do up." And before John could say anything to her, she was gone.

Outside his door she leaned against the wall trembling, her face in her hands.

Dr. Brown going on his rounds, happened to be walking down the long hall, saw Julia and stopped. "Julia, is something wrong? Did Mr. Childers say anything to make you upset?"

Julia wiped her eyes on her sleeve. "N—no, Dr. Brown. He has treated me just fine. It's—I get a spell now and again when I think about Solly Crawford and what he done to me. Mr. Childers just mentioned he always had a good corn crop and liked lookin at the long rows—and sudden like that—fear just washed over me again." She sniffed. It was in a cornfield that Mr. Crawford—" she couldn't go on.

Dr. Brown took a large clean, white handkerchief out of his

pocket and handed it over to her. She took it gratefully, wiped her eyes and blew her nose. Then with a nervous laugh she looked up. "I'll wash it for you, Dr. Brown. I know I oughtn't to take on like this. Just sometimes that awful remembrance of a cornfield sweeps over me and I can't help it. I'll try not to let it happen again."

"Don't apologize, Julia. I do understand. But I hope you will try to forget your bad memories here. As for the crying—I don't know any lady who doesn't need a good cry once in a while. You're a fine girl, Julia, and we all appreciate you."

"Much obliged, Dr. Brown." She sniffed again. "I'll go do up the other rooms now."

He watched her walk with determined steps down the hall.

John Childers pondered what he'd said that upset Julia so, but he couldn't figure it out. *That Julia King is one fine girl*, he thought.

When Julia came the next day to do his room, he asked, "Miss King, I hope I didn't say somethin' yesterday to make you feel bad? You looked kinda agitated when you left in such a hurry."

"No, Mr. Childers," she shook her head and looked at him earnestly. "No, it wasn't you. I just remembered somethin' from years ago and I know I didn't act right. I hope it didn't bother you too much."

"If I can ever do anything to help you, Miss King, please tell me. I don't want to ever say anything that makes you feel bad."

"'Twasn't you—just me. Don't worry none about it. We was talkin' about plantin' and I do love to plant things and watch 'em grow. God gives us such good land around here."

"Yes, He does."

After that, he noticed a slight thawing in her manner toward him, but he made no mention of it. But she noticed the eagerness in his eyes when he greeted her. And she felt eagerness beginning to stir in her own heart too.

Weeks passed and even Julia could see that the swelling was lessening in his injured foot. "It's better, but don't walk on it too soon," she cautioned. To herself she said, *and I can't stand to think about the time when it gets well and you have to go back to your family!*

One day she came in and found him standing without a chair, but still grimacing with some pain. "Mr. Childers! Don't do that or your foot won't ever heal right. Sit down now and wait 'til it's all well."

"Julia—I hope I am not oversteppin' any bounds to call you Julia—I'm glad we've been gettin' acquainted. But I'm a workin' man and I can't stand this sittin' all day long." He sat down in his chair, stretched his leg out in front of him on a footstool, and ran his fingers through his thick, brown hair. "Come over here, Julia, I want to say something to you. Been thinkin' about this for some weeks now."

He leaned back in his chair and looked up at her as she stood near. She looked straight at him and thought she had never seen kinder eyes. "Julia, I've not known you for very long, and I hope it's not too soon to say this. But I got a heap of likin' and respect for you. You're awful purty and you're a good girl. I know you are. As I been watchin' you come and go every day, I been thinkin' more and more about you—"

Julia's eyes widened, and she hoped he wouldn't hear the pounding of her heart.

He reached up and gently took one of her hands and held it. "Since my wife died more than two years ago, I've been a lonely man and never looked at another woman. But since I've been here and got to know you, Julia, I've been thinkin' that I'm too lonesome. A man oughtn't be alone like I am, but I never even wanted to marry again before I met you. But now that I know you, I'd like to marry you. What do you say? Could you find it in your heart to care anything about me?"

Julia gazed at him and pressed her lips together, tears filling her eyes. Her heart was pounding because of what he had said—that he wanted to marry her. She knew—because of the way she'd been feeling about him lately—that she could love him. She also knew that as soon as he heard all about her, he wouldn't want her.

When she could control her trembling mouth, she shook her head and said, "I *would* like to marry you, I think you're a fine man. But I don't think any man could ever love me after they know the truth about me, and I've got no hope that you would either, Mr. Childers." She paused and breathed deeply. "I ain't fittin' to marry you. What you don't know about me is I got a four-year-old daughter and I've never been married." She turned to go but he held on to her hand.

She was shocked then, when John Childers said gently, "Yes, I know that, Julia. You see, I been talkin' to Doctor Brown. When I got to thinkin' about you all the time, I went to him and told him that I'd like to marry you and asked him to tell me what he knows about you. I asked him if he thought that might be the right thing to do. Then he told me your story, Julia. Don't feel bad at him though—he hadn't ever talked about you to anybody else. We both know you ain't to blame for what happened. If I could get my hands on the filthy hog who treated you like that, I'd beat him to a pulp."

"My four brothers all went after him with shotguns, but he got away. Nobody's heard from him since five years ago, but I'm still afraid of him. That's what was wrong when you talked about the corn rows. It was in his cornfield that he treated me so bad, and sometimes the awful shame washes over me. I just can't help it. But I don't think you'd want to live with me with all that on my mind sometimes."

"But I do want you, Julia. Whatever happened in that cornfield wasn't your fault, and nobody can hold it against you. I don't hold it against you, and I know God won't. We can make a new life together and I will love you the way a man ought to love his wife. And nobody will ever find out about what that man did to you from me! Do you think you could ever love me, Julia?"

She tried not to cry, but still tears welled up in her eyes. She couldn't say a word—her throat was tight with unbelief at what was happening. This good man wantin' her after all! She'd seen lots of men here at the hotel—some who wanted to be friendly with her. But John Childers was the only one she ever thought twice about. She wiped her eyes on the handkerchief she took from her apron pocket and just stood waiting.

Now it was John's turn for doubting.

"Julia, even if you could love me, you might not want to marry me because of all my young'uns. It wouldn't be easy for you to come into a house with five young'uns already there. And I'm fifteen years older than you. My wife, Moriah, and I got married young. She was sick a long time after our last girl was born, and I've had a hard time raisin' my young'uns since she died. I got two boys, Ed and Milton, and three girls, Dora, Dona, and Ada. I don't know what you'd think, but they're purty good young'uns."

When she could finally speak, she asked, "What do you think they would say about you gettin' a wife?"

"I think they would say I done good!" He smiled. "I guess I've done all right raisin' the boys, but them girls—I don't know all I need to know. They need a mother and I think you would be good. I ain't got much money, Julia. I don't own a farm, I rent one a few miles from here."

"You shouldn't worry about rentin'. Most people don't own their farms—they just rent 'em. So did we—"

John nodded. "I know—only rich men can afford to *own* their farms. Anyway, I try to bring my young'uns up right. I've always taught them right from wrong and I take them to church. And I make them mind me, too."

He hesitated. "But I don't know if you'd like farm life after workin' here. You said you was raised on a farm and that's what I like too. Would you ever want to go back to a farm again?"

"Oh, yes! I love livin' on a farm. I was raised to work, too, and I can work as good outside as any man."

"My father was a veterinarian," John said, "and he taught me all about how to care for animals, so that's always helped me make a livin'." He watched her face for some sign of hope. Then, "Well, what do you think, Julia? Will you marry me?"

She stood there thinking for a few moments. He was still holding her hand and all of a sudden she started to giggle. She laughed and laughed, then had to wipe her eyes again. "I'm not laughin' at you, Mr. Childers. But—we'd start our married life with a family of *six children* between us. Can you see me with six young'uns? I've had my doubts about raisin' one' and all of a sudden I'd have *six!*"

He laughed with her then he grew serious. "But workin' together, we could. You need a home and a father to help you with your young'un, and I need a good wife to help me with all of mine, and we both need somebody to love. Let's do it, Julia. I'll take good care of you and your little girl, and I will love you, too. What do you say?"

Julia looked straight at him—and she knew she could trust him and love him. His blue eyes looked steadily at her and he was smiling. Her heart was again suddenly thudding against her ribs, the whole world seemed to open up, and a great invisible weight fell from her. She put out both hands and he caught them and drew her down to his lap. His lips were clean and sweet, and his beard tickled her cheeks a little. For the first time in a long time, she wanted a man to kiss her—*this* man. She smiled at him and her tears dampened his coat as he held her head against his shoulder. She felt the last of her cold shell crack and fall into bits.

She had come home.

CHAPTER TWELVE
Preparations

Alone in her room at the hotel after telling John she would marry him, Julia cried into her pillow—her pillows had known many tears since she was fifteen. She was crying this time because the realization suddenly struck her that she couldn't wear a white wedding dress. How ashamed she was that she could not come in purity to her wedding. More than anything in the world, she desired to be able to wear white when she stood up with John for their vows. But everyone knew it was impossible—only a virgin wore a white dress at her wedding! And everyone at *her* wedding would know, of course, that she wasn't a virgin. Sorrow and shame overwhelmed her that night.

The next day when she went to clean room nine, John stood waiting for her, and she walked straight into his open arms. He kissed her and looked anxious. "You've been crying, I can see. Why? You've not changed your mind, have you, Julia?"

Her eyes searched his face, then she shook her head. "Not if you're sure you still want me."

"I've got no intention of mind changin'. But you didn't say why you cried."

She was ashamed to talk about it. But he was going to be her husband, and this must not stand between them. So she said, "I was cryin' last night because I can't wear a white dress at our wedding. And more than anything, I wish I could—for your sake."

He smoothed her face with his hands. "Julia, I understand how you could feel like that. But it is nothing that you could ever have helped, nor ever can. That part of your life is behind you and we have to go on. I love you for what you are right now, and I don't ever want to dwell on the bad things that happened to you. I can't stand to think about it, and I hope you won't either. Let's just love each other, and let God help us both."

She nodded and buried her face against his vest. "I'll try not to let it bother me any more, John. You are a wonderful man and I'm lucky you want me." She wiped her eyes. "How does your foot feel to be standin' on it?"

He looked down at his ankle—still a little swollen—and answered with a grin, "When my foot saw you come in, it forgot about bein' hurt." Holding her hand, he sat down in the easy chair and she sat on the footstool looking up at him. "Julia, it's goin' to be a while yet 'til this foot is completely well. But I hope you will marry me as soon as I can get back to walkin' right. Will you?"

"Yes. But I think I better work on here for a while and give Doctor Brown a chance to get somebody else in my place. And I can save a little money too, because I want to get some goods and make a proper weddin' dress. It's already February—you think we can have a weddin' in April? Then I can help you get your crop in."

He looked at her in amazement and started to laugh. "What? Here I am just askin' my girl to marry me and she's talkin' about a crop already!" He tilted her chin up and looked straight into her eyes. "Julia, I don't want you to marry me just to help me put a crop in the ground! I want to love you. I want to see you ever' night at supper—and I just want you to *be* with me."

She smiled and rubbed her face on his hand. "Well, I didn't think you wanted me just for a crop, but we've got to have one, don't we?" Her face flushed and she finished softly, "John, yes. I want to love you, too."

He nodded, and grinned at her.

"So," she continued, "I just want to help you put that crop in! It'll feel good to get back to the fields. I want to be a good wife to you, John—crop or no crop." She stood up. "But right now, I better get your room cleaned up, or Doctor Brown might tell me to leave today. Then the next girl that cleaned your room might start makin' eyes and swishin' skirts in your direction!"

John laughed aloud. "I'd never even look at her."

For the briefest instant Julia froze as she remembered someone she had once loved saying the very same words. Someone tall like John, but with blond hair. *That* love, just a young boy at the time, *had* looked at someone else and ended up marrying *her.* Julia shook off the thought. She and Seth had been just kids. Now she was a woman, and she had a man to love her—forever.

"When I get through workin' today, I'll go and tell Doctor Brown our news." So after Julia finished, she went through the lobby and knocked on Doctor Brown's door. When she entered, she found him sitting at his desk reading papers in big folders, by the light of two coal-oil lamps. "Doctor Brown, don't you ever quit workin'?"

"Come in, Julia." He rubbed his eyes. "How are you getting along? My goodness, is it time to quit already?"

She nodded and smiled, and her face was radiant. "I—I come to tell you somethin', Doctor Brown."

"Well, Julia, whatever it is, you look mighty happy. Please sit down." He motioned to a chair.

"Yes, I am," Julia replied as she lowered herself into the chair. "John Childers asked me to marry him and I said yes. And I want to say I'm much obliged that you told him about me. I didn't have to tell him and that's a big load off my mind. I think he is a fine man and he said even though he knows about me, he still wants to marry me."

Dr. Brown got up and came around the desk. "Julia, I am so happy for you. Yes, John came and talked to me one day about you. When he told me how much he admired you and that he was thinking he wanted to marry you, I decided it would be easier for me to tell him than for you. I'm pleased things turned out this way. Do you love him?"

She looked down at her shoes and her face flushed crimson. "Yes, I do. I've been thinkin' about him a lot since he come here, but I never thought— I've never been able to trust any man except him since—"

"I understand, Julia. I believe you are getting a good man. I've asked a few people about John Childers, and I get the same report from everybody that he is an upstanding, fine man. He takes good care of his children and I think he will take good care of you."

"I can't tell you how good I feel that he wants me. I never thought I'd get married—never thought any man would want me—"

"Don't ever think that, Julia! I know you were hurt. But you are still the fine person you were before any of that happppened. One wicked man couldn't kill your spirit. You're a beautiful woman and John Childers is lucky to have you—"

Julia's eyes opened wide. "You think he's lucky?"

"I do, Julia. And twenty years from now John will still think so. I'm convinced of that."

She wiped her eyes which seemed to be filled with tears often lately. But these were happy tears. "Thank you, Doctor Brown. You're a good friend." She rose and turned to leave, then had an idea. "Doctor Brown, I know you go to Herrin's Prairie sometimes. If you go soon, would you stop by my brother Joe's place and tell him about John Childers? Joe's been takin' care of me for the last four years and I want him to be the first to know about us gettin' married. Put in a good word for John, would you? When you go past Marion on the way to Herrin's Prairie, you go right by Joe's turn-off lane. I'd be much obliged." She laughed. "Joe is goin' to be surprised at this news!"

"I'll be glad to do that, Julia. When do you and John plan to have your wedding?"

"First part of April. I thought I'd work another month and give you a chance to fill my place."

When Julia left Dr. Brown's office, she had to lean against the wall for a spell to catch her breath over all the excitement. She had actually told another person she was getting married, but still could hardly believe it herself. She leaned there for a few minutes saying, *Thank You, God. This isn't all just luck. You are takin' care of me. You sent me a wonderful gift—a fine man who loves me and one I can love, and one who is willing to take care of Eva Jane. But Lord, he's handsome, too!* How could such joy and blessings be—after the past four years?

Julia went about her work in a daze of happiness the next two weeks. Of course she and John saw each other every day and every time she saw him, her eagerness grew for April to come. Julia cleaned room after room and later, if anyone had asked, she couldn't even remember working. No tired feeling—just excited all the time.

One day she reached John's room about two in the afternoon to do her usual cleaning there. She knocked and went in, stopped stone still in her tracks, and gasped. Five men were waiting for her in the room, and she couldn't believe her eyes. Her four brothers were sitting there talking to John! "Oh—Oh—Joe! Matthew! Caleb! William!" She flew over to hug them all. "I can't believe you're all here! Oh, I'm so glad to see you—why did you come? Is something wrong? D—Did anything happen to Eva Jane—?"

Her relief was visible when Joe said, "No—don't worry, Julie! We just come to see you and get acquainted with John Childers. Doctor Brown rode by three days ago and told us about this man, John Childers. We'd never heard of him, but we decided if he was goin' to marry you, we better get to know him. So we rode down today. We been here about two hours already."

She stood waiting. "W—well—?"

"Well," said Matthew, "he looks like a fine feller to me. Says he's got five young'uns. Think you could take care of all them?"

"I told John I'd do the best I can—"

Caleb spoke up, "It's not too late to change your mind. You ain't married yet and if you don't want to get married, you don't have to, you know."

"Oh, but—" Julia blushed, "but I *want* to marry John!"

John held out his hand to her and she went and stood next to him facing all her brothers. She looked up into John's face and said, "Yes, I want to marry him."

"That's what we wanted to make sure of," exclaimed William. "From the look on your face, you ain't doin' no thinkin' about changin' your mind. Now we been talkin' to John here, and he assured us he will be good to you. I believe him. Julie, I think you got an honorable man in John Childers. Far as I'm concerned, I'll vote fer him."

She looked around at the others. "Joe?"

"Yes, I'll vote fer him."

"Caleb?"

Caleb nodded. "He's got my vote."

"Matthew?"

Matthew walked over and shook hands with John. "My vote too. I know you, Julie. After what you been through, you'd trust only a good man."

Julie looked at all four of the dearest brothers any girl ever had, and nodded. "Well, I'm thinkin' if John had any idea of *not* bein' good to me, one look at the four of you would scare him to death. He'd change his mind about marryin' me. Now I don't see your rifles anywhere, but I bet he knows you've got 'em!" She smiled and her face was radiant. "No girl has ever been better taken care of than me. I'm glad you've all come—I did want John to meet the four best men that ever lived in Williamson County. And," she added, "don't ever forget that John stands right up there with all of you."

"Julie," Joe said, "John tells me that you're plannin' to get married in April. His foot ought to be well by then. So when you work out your time here before that, I hope you'll come back home. Martha wants to help you make your weddin' dress, and me and Martha want you to get married at our house. All our kin folks and friends want to get to know John. How about it?"

She looked at John and he nodded agreement. "Yes, Joe, I'd like that. That's been home to me for the last four years. I'd feel blessed to get married in your house."

"That's settled then. Well, we'll go along home and tell the news to ever'body. Eva Jane said tell you there's some new kittens under the house. She wants to take one of 'em with her to your new house! She's all excited about gettin' a new Pa."

Julia's eyes sparkled. "Tell her I'm excited that she's gettin' her own Pa, too."

Julia threw a shawl over her head and walked with her brothers to their horses. "You all made me happy that you like John. I'm glad you come. Joe, will you ride back for me in three weeks? By then we'll have our plans all made. If you see the preacher, tell him we want him to marry us. Good-bye—"

Whoever had such brothers? she asked herself, waving to them until they were out of sight.

During the rest of March together at the hotel, John and Julia's love for each other deepened and filled them both. As John began to hobble with a cane a little, the two of them took slow walks around the neighborhood after her working hours. Then they sat in a dimly lighted corner of the dining room and talked.

She felt so free to talk about her feelings with John. She told him about her terror of Solly Crawford—of how for all these years she'd been afraid he would come back. And John soothed her and said, "Well, I think that skunk would know full well that if he ever come back around here, somebody would blow his head off. He knows it'd never be safe for him. And now that I've heard it all, Julie, let's don't talk about it again. It hurts you too much to think about it. We've got plenty to think about now—thinkin' about us."

"But first, John, I want to know all about your life—where you lived as a little boy, where you got married, and about all your young'uns."

His eyes searched her face. "Do you worry about me havin' a wife before you?"

Julia looked straight at him. "No, I don't. Honest, John, I can say I don't feel jealous a bit. I know that you love me now. Anyway, I'm too busy gettin' over somethin' awful in my past. It's took me a long time."

"It's good that you're gettin' over it."

"And I'm not jealous that you had a wife and kids before you met me. I guess I ought to tell you that when I was fourteen, I thought I was in love with somebody else. And I thought he wanted to marry me some day—he'd said he did. But then the next year when bad things were happenin' to me, he was findin' another girl.

"When I run away from Solly's house, he was ridin' over to tell me about his weddin'. He's the one who put me on his horse and took me to Joe's. But when he told me why he was ridin' toward the Crawford place—to tell me he was goin' to marry with somebody else—well—I thought for a while I would rather die than live. Now I'm glad I didn't die! It would have been so awful if I *had* died then. Just think—I'd never have known you."

John looked at her and thought, *So that's part of why she always looked a little sad to me. 'Twasn't only what Solly done to her—it's because she was disappointed by the one who said he wanted to marry her. No wonder it was hard for her to talk to me or anybody else!* John's heart ached for her. His arm encircled her waist. "And now? How do you feel about him now?"

Julia leaned against his shoulder. "Truth is, John, I don't feel anything about him now. Since I got to know you I understand that was just first-time love. But my love for you is different—it's all grown up and I don't want the other kind at all. I'm a woman, and I know the Lord sent me here to Creal to find you. And these tears you see are joyful tears. I'm just thankful." She wiped her eyes on a handkerchief she took from her pocket. "Tell me—tell me about your life and your family—"

"Well—it may be a long story. I was born in Tennessee, and I remember movin' up here to Southern Illinois when I was a little boy—about three years old. We traveled with other families in a long wagon train. . . ." He stuck his weak leg out in front of him and leaned back in his chair. "It must'of been awful hard on all them people to make a plan, get all of 'em together at the same time, and get the big wagons rollin' to move from one place to another. Tennessee is far away, you know, and I can remember ridin' in the wagon and seeing nothin' but forests and prairies for days and weeks. Sometimes we'd stop and stay in one place for a few days if somebody got real sick.

"Our wagon train was guarded by sweethearts and husbands and fathers. The heavier wagons were pulled by large bulls and some oxen and horses, they were in the lead and in the rear. In the middle was the lighter wagons with women and children. I can remember sittin' on a high seat with my mother and seein' the big wagons ahead of us and behind us. Never could see the end of 'em.

"My dad told me stories about that trip as I was growin' up with my brothers and sisters. Used to tell us the stories by the firelight in the evenin's. He said that the women—includin' my mother—could shoot as good as the men. They took charge of some guns and ammunition, kept them loaded and ready for anything. They knew that fearful Indians was all around. Some wagon trains had been fired on. Ours moved all right. Some men drove the bulls and oxen, and the rest of the men walked ahead, alongside of and behind our train, carryin' their guns and on the lookout all the time.

"Women drove the lighter wagons. Babies was born in the wagons, with other travelers as midwives. And unless the women had a lot of trouble or died, the wagons kept movin'. They knowed they couldn't stay in one place too long—they had to get to Illinois before snow begun to fly. As we rode along, women and men would shoot deer, wild turkeys and geese, and cook 'em at night when we camped. . . "

"Just think," she interrupted, "you lived through all that quite a while before I was even born!"

John grinned at her. "You're just a young'un, you know!"

"Oh, John!"

He told her how they had cleared the land; he worked very hard. Then he grew up and got married close to Creal Springs. They'd always farmed. He spoke of the troubled times he had weathered after his wife died leaving him with five children to raise alone. John had tears in his eyes as he recounted the last two years.

Julia's sympathy was genuine. "Oh, John, I see that your life has not been easy." She kissed him and said, "There is no way we can forget all the things that's happened to us. We're bound to think about 'em sometimes and be sad. But now when we remember, we can thank the good Lord that we got each other to love. That's the important thing now, and I am thankful."

John held her close, "So am I, Julia."

By the time Julia was ready to go back to Joe's, Julia and John felt as if they had known each other forever.

When Joe came back for her, she had two pillow cases packed to go home instead of the old one she came with. Some of the girls at the hotel had given her some dresser scarves and pillow cases for wedding presents, and Dr. and Mrs. Brown had given her a bonus of twenty dollars. She felt very rich. The only sad part was saying good-bye to John. She dreaded it even if it was to be for only a very short while.

"I'll be there two weeks from tomorrow," John said when he kissed her good-bye. "After that, we'll be together all the time. I know my children will be happy to get a new Ma—'specially one as pretty as you. I'll bring 'em up for the wedding. That'll be a great day for me, Julia. God bless you 'til we meet for our wonderful day."

"Good-bye, John. I'll be ready." Wiping tears from her eyes she climbed on the horse Joe had brought for her. Julia hadn't been riding since she'd been here, and was happy for the ride home with Joe. While they rode, Julia told him all about how she and John had found each other.

Eva Jane, a two-inches-taller whirlwind, threw herself into her mother's arms when Julia jumped down from the horse at Joe's.

"Mama! Am I goin' to have a Pa? Is he nice, Mama? Will he like me? And he's already got some young'uns so I'll have some brothers and sisters? And can I take my new kittie—?" She stopped only because she had to get her breath.

Julia laughed and hugged her tight. "YES" to ever' one of your questions, Eva Jane. My goodness, how you've grown! Here. Can you carry in one of these pillow cases for me? You must be very strong by now!"

Eva Jane danced beside her, talking all the way to the house. Joe's children followed them in.

They sat down at the supper Martha had ready and Joe said, "You young'uns all be quiet now. We're goin' to thank the Lord for all these good things." He bowed his head on his folded hands. "Now, Lord, we are thankful for bringin' us together again. We're grateful for the food, for health, and because Julia's found the right man. Bless John Childers, Lord, and heal his ankle. Bring him up here at the right time. We're goin' to trust our Julia to him, so help him to live up to what she believes him to be. Amen."

The supper table rang with joy and conversation.

The next day, Martha and Julia took the wagon to the drygoods store in the Marion square. Julia had never been shopping in Marion before, and Martha went only seldom. First Julia bought a new pair of black, high buttoned shoes. Then they looked at the shelves of sewing materials. With so many bolts of cloth spread out to compare, choosing was hard for Julia. But she finally saw what she felt was exactly right. They bought twelve yards of pale pink flowered voile, a passel of buttons, and she found the exact shade of plain matching pink cloth. So she selected ten yards of that for the ruffles.

Sewing for two weeks, she and Martha made a lovely wedding dress with a high, ruffled neck, tiny pearl buttons down the front, long, ruffled sleeves, a tight waist and a full gathered skirt. At the final try-on session—with the family all shooed out the door—Martha exclaimed, "Oh, how beautiful you look, Julia!"

"I hope John thinks so!" she answered.

* * * *

When Julia first came home from the hotel, she knew one big job had to be done. She had to go through all her stored things, air them, and clean the boxes. But when she saw the trunks and boxes that had belonged to her mother in the corner of the barn, her heart failed her for a day or two. Finally, she went out saying to Martha, "I've got to do it today. It won't be easy."

Martha gazed at her with understanding in her eyes. "Do you want me to help you, Julia?"

"No. I better do it myself. It'll take me a while."

Once in the barn Julia dragged the boxes from against the wall and lined them up in a row. They had been closed since she was thirteen years old—more than seven years. One by one, she opened the lids and begin to lift out all the things she remembered from her childhood home. Pillow cases, towels, washrags, sheets, hooked rugs. Here was the last sweater she made for her mother—she smiled when she discovered the knitting mistakes. There were socks she had knitted for her—her feet had been so cold most of the time. Dresser scarves her mother had hemmed and embroidered reminded her of the dresser in her mother's room. The small mirror which had hung above was clouded and smaller than she remembered.

Pillows took up all the space in one trunk. They were mashed so flat that Julia took them out of the barn and spread them out on the grass. The sun would plump them up. Another box held the iron skillets and kettles her mother had kept the kitchen with. How many pots of beans and stews and chicken and dumplin's, cornbread, and biscuits had been cooked in them! The wooden spoons and forks, the bread board, egg beater, pancake turner, milk crocks, mixing bowls and all the little kitchen utensils were nested in the bottom of one box. Julia's tears flowed freely as she discovered them, one by one, and she remembered seeing her mother use them.

Tablecloths, dishes, old knives, spoons, and forks were tucked away in another trunk. Her childhood home came into focus through the tears as her treasures were re-discovered. So much had happened since she had seen these things! Her year with the Crawfords, the awful time with Solly, the year she waited for her baby—her shame and sorrow, and her loneliness even with Joe's family . . . they all paraded through her mind.

Yes—her early living was all here, all spread out in this barn. She thanked God for her mother she had loved so much and for all these things her mother had left to her. They would now be used in her own house, just as Joe had predicted many years ago. She thanked God for sending John to her. *Lord, help me to be a good wife to John.*

She worked in the barn all that afternoon and when she came back to the house Martha asked, "Are you all right, Julia?"

"Well, I cried a lot," Julia confessed, "and I lived my life over again. Now I'm ready to take all the things to John's and start my new life. When we packed these things up so long ago, I never dreamed how much I'd love them."

* * * *

John brought his family up the day before the wedding. When Julia, who'd been watching ever since noon, saw the wagon come into the yard, she flew out the door. John jumped from the wagon—forgetting his foot was still a little sore—and swept her up in his arms and kissed her. He held her so tightly she could hardly catch her breath. Over his shoulder she got her first look at John's children. They were just beginning to slowly climb out of the wagon when they saw their father hug Julia and lift her off the ground. They were first surprised to see that Julia was so beautiful. Their father had said she was, but they didn't expect her to be *this* purty! Their second shock came because they simply couldn't believe their father's actions!

He don't act like Pa a bit! each one thought. *And he looks so happy he don't even look like Pa! Why's he so fussed up crazy when he's old? But he don't look old, neither!*

Starting to get down from the wagon, they stood staring like statues, two of the children with one leg over the wagon side, and the other three balancing on the wheels. Only when their Pa put Julia down, did they climb down the rest of the way.

Joe's sons also watched the scene wide-eyed, winked at each other and one said, "He shore gave Aunt Julie some smackin' good kissin'!"

John heard the comment and said to them, "You boys want me to do it again so you can be sure you learn to do it right?" And he soundly kissed Julia again. The three boys slapped their knees and doubled over with laughter.

Julia, a little embarrassed, said, "Before you come, John, I had decided I would walk out and say howdy to you like a fine and quiet lady. But when I saw you I forgot to be quiet. I just run out the door like Eva Jane done when she saw me come home!"

John said, "You *are* a fine lady and you're just the fine lady I want! Don't ever forget it. Now I want you to get acquainted with our family." He reached out and pulled the tallest boy forward. "This is Ed, the oldest."

Julia shook hands with Ed and thought, *I'd better treat him like a grown man, so he'll feel like one.* "I'm proud to know you, Ed. You look like your Pa."

Ed was so embarrassed to be meeting his new step-mother-to-be that he just nodded, and didn't say anything.

"This is Milt," said John, motioning to the second boy. "Milt likes to work on a farm too, so you two ought to be good friends with each other. Milt is twelve."

"Hello, Milt. I hope we will be good friends," said Julia sincerely.

"Yes, Ma'am." nodded Milt. "You like to ride a horse?"

"Yes, I do," answered Julia. "Been ridin' horses all my life."

"That's good," Milt said.

"This is Dora," said John. "Dora is ten."

Julia smiled at Dora and nodded her head. Dora's hair was long, red and very curly, tied with a blue ribbon. Dora had plenty of freckles.

"Howdy, Ma'am," Dora ducked her head toward Julia.

"Hello, Dora. I'm glad to have some more girls in the family."

Dora's face flushed and she looked pleased.

"This is Dona, my second girl," said John. "She is eight. Dona likes to get out in the fields, so you two ought to have a lot to talk about."

"We will, won't we, Dona?" asked Julia.

Dona had long dark, straight hair, tied with a red ribbon. She nodded to Julia.

"And the youngest is Ada. She is six." John hugged his little girl.

Ada was a pretty child with light brown hair. She grinned, showing a vacant space where baby teeth used to be. She took a hesitant step toward Julia and suddenly lifted her arms, hugging Julia around the waist. Julia stooped down and hugged her too. Then she picked Ada up and Ada clung to her. Julia realized how much little Ada needed a mother. After all, she was only very little older than Eva Jane.

Julia stood holding Ada and said to the children, "I'd like to say somethin' now—I might forget it later. I hope you children are not scared of me. I just want to be a good mama to you. Now I'm not ever goin' to try to take your own mama's place—I know I never could. And I always want you to remember your mama if you can. But I do want to be a good wife to your Pa, and I'll do my best to make us all a good home. I hope you will try to like me—I will love you and do all I can for you.

"My little girl's name is Eva Jane and she is excited to have some new brothers and sisters. I hope we all will get along good and love each other."

Martha had made supper for all of John's family, so the kitchen was full that evening. Martha served them black-eyed peas, sweet potatoes, corn bread, apple sauce and blackberry cobbler. The children were noisy getting acquainted with each other.

When the hubub died down a bit, John said, "Martha, we sure do appreciate this good supper. I know it took a heap of cookin' to get so many vittles for all these young'uns. With your five and my five and Julia's one—you're feedin' an army here!"

"I'm used to cookin' for a big family," answered Martha. "John, I am thankful that you and Julia found each other. I've never seen Julia so happy."

Milt sneaked a look at his Pa and spoke up. "Yeah, Pa's happy too, I guess. When he told us about Miss Julia, we was thinkin' he'd gone plumb crazy. He was so ravin' over her he couldn't sleep nights."

Joe teased Julia. "Well now, Julie's been actin kinda funny here lately, too. For the last week, she's been walkin' around more nervous than a long-tailed cat in a roomful of rockin' chairs."

Everybody laughed and Julia blushed.

"I have to git to the chores, John. Want to come?"

"Sure. Got anything my young'uns can help with?"

The children all trooped outside to go with Joe's family to do the evening chores. Julia and Martha began cleaning up the kitchen. As they worked, they talked and counted off on their fingers the chores they'd planned to do and had done. "Friends and kin've all been invited for the weddin' and dinner afterward. We've been cookin' for two days so the victuals are ready. My dress is ready, and clothes all packed. The traveling preacher's promised to be here by noon. Ma's trunks and boxes that've been stored so long in the barn are all strapped to go."

"Julia, you know that you can't possibly load all that stuff on John's one wagon with all those young'uns."

"I know it—I thought about that," answered Julia. "I know Joe wants to get to his plantin', but do you think he could take a day and bring whatever we can't take? I don't know how much stuff John's got in his house, but I sure want my own things."

"We've talked about it already, Julia. Joe will bring 'em all down for you the next day. That way you don't have to do without things you might be needin'."

Julia looked out the kitchen door at Joe and John and the children all heading back toward the house. The sky behind them was streaked in long feathery trails of pink and red. She observed, "The sun's a settin' red tonight, so we won't have rain tomorrow. The sun's goin' to shine on our weddin'! Guess everything's finished that we meant to do."

"Yep," agreed Martha, "looks like we're ready for a weddin'."

"But, oh, Martha," Julia put her arms around Martha, "I'm gonna miss you when I go—no sister could ever be better. I love you—you are so good to me."

Martha wiped away a tear. "I'll miss you—and Eva Jane, too. She's just like one of mine now. But I'm so thankful you got a good man, Julia. You deserve that."

After they washed up, Joe took John and his children over to Matthew's to spend the night before the wedding. Julia walked out to the wagon with them. John held her hand and whispered, "Only one more night, my Julia, and we will be together. Tomorrow won't come too soon for me!"

"Me either, John."

As Julia watched the wagon fade into the darkness, she saw a bright star hanging low in the sky. *Let it be like this forever,* she wished on the distant light. Then she ran happily up the porch steps to spend her last night at Joe's house.

JULIA

Part III

1885 - 1888

CHAPTER THIRTEEN
Transitions

For five years Julia had doubted this day would ever come—her wedding day! But it dawned in a blaze of sunshine in April, 1885.

Julia woke up at daybreak with such happiness in her heart she thought she could not contain it. Today! She was marrying John today! The first thing she did was to thank the Lord while she was still in bed. *Lord, You know how I feel today. I am surely grateful because You have been so good to me. Bless John and his children today. Bless me too, and as we start our life together, help me to be a good wife and just the one he needs.*

She helped Martha get breakfast of thick slices of bacon and homemade bread, apple butter, and coffee on the table for her family. Julia was so excited she could hardly eat. Then they cleaned up the kitchen and immediately afterward began readying the table for the wedding dinner. Martha got out her best tablecloth and put all the plates she owned on the table. Forks and spoons, with cups, saucers, and glasses were set out, and pans of food set to slow warming. The cake was carefully lifted from the cellar and put at one end of the long table. When they had done everything they could think of that they needed to do, both women went to get dressed.

As Julia took her new pink flowered wedding dress off the hook in the small closet, she caressed her cheek in its folds. This one lovely, special dress represented everything she wanted—except virginity. It also represented everything else she thought would never be possible for her to have—most of all the love of a good man.

The clan began to gather at ten o'clock. As mothers and children climbed from buggies and wagons scattered over the yard, the women called, "You young'uns be careful now. Don't you get them clothes all dirty before the weddin'!"

The children immediately joined with others in the yard to play a few running games and to climb a few trees and fences. Mothers would not see them again before they pushed between grownup legs just as the ceremony started. Parents stood in small groups talking, the men conversing about Joe's planting, and the women admiring the fancy spread on the kitchen table, and being introduced to John Childers and his family.

The farmhouse began to fill up. Everyone around wanted to see what John Childers looked like and to exclaim about the fact that Julia would start with SIX young'uns. She'd have her hands full! But they all wished her well.

The parlor was not large enough to seat everyone, so when the preacher arrived they showed him to his corner and everybody else stood ringed in rows around the room. They left just enough space for Julia and John to walk through and take their vows before the man of God.

At twelve o'clock Julia came out of the bedroom to stand with John, and she was carrying her mother's family Bible. John gazed at the beautiful picture she made—smiling face, black hair and happy brown eyes. Her cheeks were as pink as her dress, and her hands holding the Bible were shaking. His eyes lighted up and when he smiled his total acceptance of her, she forgot her nervousness. She saw only John and his love for her.

The minister, looking very fine in his long black coat, stood with his Bible in his hand and looked out over his flock—people he had known for years. "Friends, I am glad to be a part of this happy occasion. I've not known John, but I hear only good things about him. I've known Julia all her life and now I rejoice to see her marrying this fine man.

"Marriage is a holy union, instituted by God, and we must enter into it prayerfully. It affects not only the two who are taking vows today, but it affects the whole family.

"Because it does, I want to ask John's five children and Julia's little girl if they will come and stand behind their parents while they take these holy vows. Children, come and be a part of this ceremony." He held out his hands.

John and Julia turned to face the people and held out their hands to their children. They had not planned this part, but were elated to have it happen. Their children, with surprise on their faces, squeezed through the crowded room, came and stood in a row behind John and Julia. Eva Jane reached out and held on to a bit of Julia's pink flowered skirt. John's older children, feeling strange to be the center of attention, stood looking at the floor. But Ada, the youngest, shyly looked up into John's face and smiled, then slipped her small hand into John's left hand and wrapped her fingers around one of his.

Their friends nodded and smiled approval, and some women

wiped their eyes. They'd not been to a wedding before where the bride had suffered as Julia had.

John and Julia turned back toward the minister.

"John, do you take Julia . . .?"

"Julia, do you take John to love him, keep him, honor and obey him . . .?"

"I do. . . ."

". . . I now pronounce you man and wife. . . . John, would you like to kiss your bride?"

The children all looked up and grinned at the wedding kiss.

"Now I pray that the mercy of God bless you and keep you forever more. Amen."

Then everybody talked at once. The women hugged Julia and the men shook John's hand and introduced themselves if they hadn't already met him. By that time the children eagerly led the way to the laden tables.

After a fine country dinner of chicken and dressing, dumplings, ham and beans, corn, tomatoes, cornbread, and a five-layered cake, they carried out part of Julia's belongings and put them into John's wagon. On top of one of the trunks they put Julia's big wicker rocking chair, pulled a heavy rope over the seat and tied it to the wagon sides. The chair was her favorite possession.

"I'm so thankful for all the things I brought from Ma's place seven years ago—they sure will come in handy now," she exclaimed to John as they were loading up.

Her mind flashed to yesterday. Before John came, she had gone into the bedroom to take her money out of the trunk. Maybe now she could handle it. In the beginning she couldn't bear to feel of it or even touch it. It had, at one time, been in Solly Crawford's pocket. It was tainted, dirty. And when Ellie Crawford had first sent it, she had thought she would never be able to accept it. It represented to her all the awful things that Solly was.

But lately, since she met John, she began to think about how they might be helped with it. She had not yet told John about this three hundred dollars that Ellie Crawford had given her; that information could be saved for later. All this time it had been in the wool sock in the corner of her trunk. Yesterday, feeling very brave, she had dug the money out. It was still tightly rolled, as she had put it away. She smoothed it flat, then wrapped it in a small handkerchief and fastened it in her corset. And she didn't feel dirty for having touched or accepted it! John's love had surely changed her spirit. She would use the money for her family when the need was dire. Also, in a small handbag with her underthings, was some extra money which she saved from working in the hotel.

John's new wagon was totally filled with their six children and some of Julia's household items. Eva Jane was jumping all over the wagon because she was so excited to be going to a new home. Joe promised to bring all the rest of Julia's oak chests full of blankets, pillows, and kitchen things down to her the next day.

With teasing, laughter, and tears of joy, they said good-bye to their friends and relatives, climbed into the wagon with the children and started back down to Creal. As their horses pulled them through the beautiful hills, they sat close together on the wagon seat and marveled how they had met. "Don't you think that God brought us together?" Julia asked. "Maybe He saw us both needin' somebody besides just ourselves. When I went to the hotel, I never thought about meetin' any man—I just thought about workin'."

"Well, I reckon God had somethin' to do with it. Don't seem to me that a thing like that can just happen all by itself. If God can make the corn grow and send the rain, He sure can bring a man and woman together! Anyway, Julia, I'm certain glad He brought you along. Last thing I thought about when I went to heal my foot at the hotel was comin' home with a wife."

"Do you ever thank the Lord for lettin' you grow up in this Southern Illinois, John? Course, I've not ever been far, but I know this is the best place anywhere."

John nodded and they smiled at each other.

After about an hour they heard, "I'm hungry!"

"An' I'm thirsty, too!"

John and Julia had almost forgotten that children are always hungry. "Here—" Julia said, "I got victuals in this basket under the seat. Pass the stuff around and eat what you want. There's some water in bottles up here, too."

The children, crowded into the back with all Julia's things, chewed on chicken legs and cornbread and wedding cake. Satisfied with food and water, they curled up between boxes and fell asleep. The wagon kept rumbling southward.

Julia looked at John on the seat beside her, reins loose in his hands. He was so handsome, strong and dependable, she trusted and adored him. For a moment, Seth's image flashed into her mind—but only for a moment. She realized that her girlish love for Seth was nothing at all compared to this. John was her whole life.

"John, when we get old and gray, let's never forget how we fell in love with each other and all the things we talked about down at the hotel. It's hard for me now to think about the time when I didn't know you."

He smiled. "Can't think about you gettin' old and gray. It'll happen to me long before it'll happen to you."

"Well, now that you're my husband I can tell you I think you are the handsomest man I ever saw. I've thought so for some time now—just didn't want your head to get swelled up before. Just think—I'm Mrs. John Childers! Hard to believe—but when I look at all those young'uns back there, I believe it!" She laughed and held his arm and leaned her head against him. He patted her cheek.

She sat quietly now, leaning against John and admiring him as well as the scenery, while the horses plodded on toward her new home. She would never forget this honeymoon ride with John.

About sundown the wagon stopped in front of the farmhouse. True—it was rented, but it was theirs. The children piled out, glad to be home again and run around to see their animals, but subdued because now they had a new mother.

"Mrs. Childers, this is your new home and all these children are all your new family." John smiled at them all, swung Julia down from the wagon and up into his arms, kissing her soundly while the children giggled. Julia was young enough to giggle too as John carried her through the front door, their six children trailing in behind them.

With great glee they began to unload the wagon, even the smallest child, Eva Jane, carrying in household things. Julia had wondered about John's house; now she was seeing the sparseness of the furnishings. Her things were coming tomorrow. They would help fill up the place and make it homey. Julia first put the eating and cooking things she'd brought with them in place in the kitchen.

"Looks like your sister-in-law took good care of your kitchen, John. It's nice and clean. I'm glad she and her husband came here to take care of your family while you was laid up."

"Yes, they're good people. Don't know what I'd have done without them. But I think they was relieved when I got home and told them I was gettin' a wife. They'd been here since fall and was feelin' homesick."

"Didn't they want to come to your wedding?"

John shook his head. No—they wanted to go home to Tennessee. So when I went north to get you, they went south. They'd helped me a lot."

John's oldest boy, Ed, fourteen, was a quiet, sober boy who immediately became Julia's special helper, and she needed help! At

Joe's house, he was very shy. But here, in his own home, he began to be more friendly.

The ride had been slow and bumpy, and after supper the children were tired enough to crawl into bed without any complaining. Since Julia, as yet, had no bed for Eva Jane, they made a pallet for her on the floor beside the girls. It wasn't long before the children stopped talking and were all sound asleep.

Now it was time for Julia and her husband to finally be alone. She had hardly known how to think about it. Of course Julia had wondered about her wedding night as all women do. She knew she trusted John; she knew he was a good man. But he *was* a man and she was apprehensive as to how she would respond to him. She wanted to love John and wanted him to love her. But would the ghost of Solly Crawford spoil this night?

Julia put on her nightgown while John was still in the kitchen, and was standing beside the bed waiting for him when he came into the bedroom. He simply held out his arms to her and she walked into them as naturally as if she'd always been there. He drew her close, his hand caressing her thick hair. "I've not seen you with your hair down before, Julia. You look so beautiful like that."

His body was strong, his touch was gentle. She knew she had nothing at all to fear. She reached up both hands, cupping his face and kissed him with all the love in her heart. He blew out the lamp on the dresser and lifted her onto the bed.

The ghost was gone forever.

* * * *

John's house furnishings were scanty, and with six children and a woman who really knew how to keep house, many more things were needed. By noon the next day, Joe's wagon, heavily loaded with all the rest of Julia's household items, rolled into the yard. Not only did Julia find all her own things left from her mother's home, but Martha had added new pans, dishrags, forks and spoons and sewing notions. "Oh, that's wonderful for her to send things to sew with! I never thought about how much I would need them. But I sure will—now that I have six young'uns to sew for!"

Before supper time the beds had sprouted clean bed sheets, covers, and spreads. The windows were hung with printed cotton curtains. Julia's rocking chair looked right at home beside the fireplace in the kitchen. As indeed it was.

Within a few days the house was straight and Julia said to John, "I want to go into Creal to get some provisions. Will you hitch up the wagon and take me?"

"What are you goin' to buy?"

"Oh—lots of things. Sugar, flour, cornmeal, more dishes, pickle crocks, cannin' jars, some goods to sew things for the children, some yarn so I can start knittin' socks for them for the winter, and maybe some goods to make you a new shirt—"

"All that's goin' to take some money. I'm not sure if I got that much."

Now was the time to tell him. Julia had purposely eased into this conversation by talking about buying things for their family. She wasn't sure how John would take the news about her long-saved nest egg from Ellie Crawford.

"I'll walk out to the barn with you, John." When they were out of hearing of the children, Julia said, "John, I want to tell you somethin' I've not told you yet. Been waitin' 'til the right time. See, I've got some savin's I've had for five years. It's some money that Mrs. Crawford gave me and I've kept it to use when I really wanted somethin'. It's the time—"

"Mrs. Crawford gave you money?" John's brow wrinkled as he pondered that fact for a moment.

Julia looked at him, then dropped her gaze down to her high buttoned shoes. "Besides Eva Jane, it's the only good thing that came out of that time, John," she said softly. "Anyway, it don't matter where it come from. What matters is, now we can spend some of it for things we need." Julia raised her chin and waited for John's reply.

"But I don't want you takin' any of your money to buy things for my young'uns," John said finally. "They'll get along without some of them things."

Julia put her arms around him. "John, when I married you, your family become my family. I want to do my best to take care of 'em. They've not had a Mama in a long time. Let me be Mama and do things for them their own Mama can't do. Your girls need new dresses, your boys could use some shirts, and they all need socks for the winter. I'm a good knitter, but I got to have yarn. And we have to get plenty of jars or we can't put up our garden—"

"But I don't want to take *your* money for all that—"

"Well, I didn't want to take this money from Mrs. Crawford either, at first, but Martha said I ought to. Now I'm thankful to have it. I also need to buy a cot for Eva Jane—at Joe's she was sleepin' in a bed with me. This money can help us all because I don't think about it as just *my* money any more. I give you the right to use it too, John. I got three hundred dollars—"

"Three hundred dollars!" John couldn't believe his ears. "That's a lot of money!"

Julia nodded. "I'm not goin' to spend it all today—I believe in savin' money too. We'll buy what we need and save the rest to use other times. We might need some for seed later. It'll help all of us. Because I love you, John—will you let me do it?"

John looked down at her and rubbed his eyes. "What a woman I married, Julia! I wish I had a thousand dollars to give you to fix up our place—I'd give it all to you."

"We don't need that much. It'll pleasure me to buy what we need now."

So John hitched up the horses and they went in to Creal Springs. On the way they decided to stop at the hotel to say howdy to Doctor Brown.

When they entered his office, he said in surprise, "Julia! John! Well, one look at your faces and I'd say you already got married. How's your foot, John?"

"My foot? Julia's done a miracle. I don't even think about my foot anymore." John grinned. "We come in to town today to buy some things for the house. She wants to fix it up up and start bein' a farm wife."

"Best life in the world," Julia declared. "Doctor Brown, I got a ready-made family. We started our married life with six young'uns. I think that'll test my mettle!"

"You're up to it, Julia. Good luck to you both."

When they left Julia said, "John, I'm so thankful for Doctor Brown. Do you realize that if it hadn't been for him, I would never have known you?"

"Yep. We owe him a lot."

Their wagon was full when they drove the horses into the back yard that afternoon. The children all came running out. "What did 'ja get?"

"What did 'ja bring?"

"Oh—is the new bed for Eva Jane?"

Dona was peeking into everything. "What's this? Looks like a lot a' new goods—are we goin' ta get some new dresses?"

"Oh—oh! There goes a ball of yarn a'rollin!"

"Pick it up quick," cried Julia. "Don't let it get all dirty or somebody's goin' to have dirty new socks!"

"Can you knit new socks?" asked Dora in awe?

Julia nodded. "Yes, I'll make you some."

"Whoooeee! I ain't never seen so many fixin's in my whole life!"

Julia smiled at them. "We got ever'thing from sacks of flour to knittin' yarn. We got some dishes, pots and pans, and food to stock the shelves in the cellar. All of you can help us carry it in. Yes, the new cot is for Eva Jane."

"What's all these glass jars for? Must be a hundred in these boxes."

"More than that, Dona. Your Pa's not been able to can anything, and your shelves are kinda bare. Looks like cannin' is just one thing a farm Pa don't do."

"Do *you* know how to do all that?" asked Dora.

"Just wait 'til our harvest, come this fall, and our shelves will be all full of home-canned victuals." Julia promised the family. "We're all goin' to work hard on our garden this summer," she told the children. "We're goin' to have the best garden around here and we'll have plenty to eat when winter comes. But I can't do it all by myself. I'll teach you and we'll all work together."

"That's good if we have a lot of canned stuff," Ed nodded. "This last winter was purty bad and it was worse when Pa broke his ankle."

"Com'on, with me, Milt," John called. "Let's go get the milkin' done. Rest of 'em can help Julia."

Young Milton was twelve years old. He liked to work outside and didn't cotton to any kind of housework, so Julia was very glad that the oldest boy, Ed, didn't mind helping her in the house. Ed even liked to cook sometimes. Dora, at ten, showed that someday she would be a very good housekeeper and mother. Her red curly hair accompanied a trigger-quick temper, and she was lively in whatever she did. She had learned to help with the younger children when her mother died, and now she was a big help to Julia.

Dona, eight years old, was quiet with brown hair and blue eyes. She enjoyed playing with the kittens and puppies in the barn. Any stray animal was Dona's friend.

Ada, the pretty little six-year-old, had light brown hair and big, brown eyes. She wanted to stay close to Julia, and Julia understood that she needed extra mothering. She had been very young when her mother died.

Julia's heart went out to all the children. Very quickly she learned to love them because they made her feel welcome and needed. They all needed loving—they had missed a great deal of mothering in the last few years.

The house had two large bedrooms and a big central room with a fireplace at one end and a black iron wood stove at the other. John owned three double beds—the big four-poster bed in one bedroom for Julia and himself, and the other two were set up in the other bedroom. Julia put the new cot for Eva Jane there also.

The two boys slept in one double bed, and John's three girls in the other. But six children in one bedroom can mean bedlam. Many a night John had to go into that room to settle them down. The girls fussed over not having enough room to sleep. "This bed is too little," they wailed. "And it's too hot in summer. If one of us wants to turn over, we *all* have to turn over!"

John's stern voice would answer, "Be thankful you have a bed. If you'd rather sleep on the floor, go to it. But I don't want to hear another thing out of any of you! Now all of you turn over on your other side and go to sleep."

Often the boys began to laugh and John would shut them up, too. Many nights when John came back to his bed, all the children would start to giggle. Dora would whisper, "You want Pa to come back in here with the strap? He'll whup you hard if he does. Now be still!"

Sometimes Dora said under her breath, "Eva Jane, you're the lucky one to have your Ma bring you a bed just for you by yourself. Nobody ever kicks you in their sleep. I wish somebody'd bring me a bed!"

Eva Jane, being the youngest of the six, sometimes told Julia that John's young'uns didn't like her, so she wasn't going to like them either. Julia would answer, "Well, Eva Jane, you be nice to them anyhow. You just be the best little girl you can be and do nice things for them. They will soon begin to like you."

But Eva Jane always tagged very close to Julia whether she was in the field or the house.

That year they kept two horses, two cows, several pigs and chickens, and made a big vegetable garden. At summer's end, as Julia promised, the dirt cellar was lined with vegetables—and after hog-killing time, canned meat. It would be enough to take them through 'til next garden time. Of course, Julia didn't do all that work by herself. Every one of the children helped. They picked and cleaned vegetables; they carried water and washed all the cans and lids; they carried wood and kept the outside fire going when lard was rendering or apple butter was simmering. Carrying water on washday to fill the round tubs and helping to hang up the clothes also kept the children out of mischief.

They also did other chores like farm children everywhere. The boys helped with the animals, and the whole family worked in the hay fields. Julia loved field work too, but she always had to leave a couple of hours early to go in, do her housework, and have food on the table for the others at noon and in the evening.

John and the boys liked to hunt. They were all good shots, so the table was frequently loaded with venison, quail, and rabbit. Very often it was a proud boy, instead of John, who brought in meat for the next day.

Money was not easy to come by. Sometimes John sold some produce, and the next spring they sold one calf. John's crop of winter wheat brought in some money. Sometimes a farmer would call him to help with a sick animal and John would make extra money that way. Now and then John would consent to use some of Julia's money to buy feed for the animals when she insisted, but usually he wanted to manage without touching her small savings. They both felt good to know a little money was there to fall back on in case of dire need. They told no one else about the money—not even the children knew about it.

John and Julia had been married in April—planting time. So when they arrived home to John's farm they had no time to call on their neighbors or go anywhere. Neither did their neighbors. And for a few months Julia had been wondering about something. One day she asked John.

"John, you must have told a few friends about marryin' me before I came here. Did you say anything to anybody about me havin' a baby?"

"I told a few friends I was goin' to marry a woman with a little girl. They just think that you had a husband and he died. I didn't tell any lies about it—I just didn't tell them any different. I think it's better this way. Nobody has ever asked me anything about it. If they do, I'll not tell them. Don't like nosey people anyway!"

Julia was relieved that nobody in her new neighborhood had ever dreamed what had happened to her. When she'd asked John the question, she knew he didn't even want to think about it. But Julia couldn't help but think about it sometimes, especially when she had to work in the cornfield. If John worked with her, she knew in her mind she was safe, even if she didn't *feel* safe.

If some of the children were near her, she could still manage. But she simply could not bring herself to go into the corn stand by herself, to do any kind of work at all. She never let John know how it made her feel, but she often began to tremble as she hoed weeds out of the rows—even with John hoeing in the next row. She felt worse when she was pulling heavy, ripe ears of corn and putting them into bags to take into the house.

She would have to bite her lips and clench her hands for a while to stop their shaking. Her fear was real; it just rolled over her, inundating her sometimes. It seemed to start with her hands, and go all through her body until her knees turned weak, like tomato vines bending under the weight of big red tomatoes. She was glad the children never noticed. But always the question was in her mind, *What if Solly came back and found me? What would happen?*

The next February, Julia became pregnant. This time it was a joy. She was so happy to have this baby that a little morning sickness didn't bother her. She worked in the fields along with the children and John that summer, and was able to do all her canning for that year—with the children's help. But she slowed down near time for birthing. She used her sittin' time to knit sweaters and socks. When November 1886 blustered in, every one of the children were thankful that she knew how to knit. She had bought many bright shades of yarn, and they all wore beautifully knitted sweaters. When the Childers family went to church, they were the most colorful in the congregation.

One night in November, the lusty cries of a healthy infant filled the house. George Childers—their seventh child—was born. Julia had a nearby neighbor as midwife, and the birth was not nearly as long nor as hard as her first.

Baby George was put into a new crib in their bedroom, and when he cried at night, Julia didn't even have to get up unless he needed to be washed. She just reached out and brought him into the bed with John and herself, changed him and nursed him.

Every day the house seemed to get smaller because now seven growing children—some nearly grown—were crowded into it. Julia's work never ended. But her health was excellent, she and John loved each other fully, and she was thankful for their family. Her biggest problem was cooking *enough* food for them. Usually when a meal was finished, leftovers were totally nonexistent. Julia wondered if she could ever fill them up.

CHAPTER FOURTEEN
Valley of the Shadow

George's chubby little body rested against Julia's arm as she nursed him in the stillness of midnight. When he had awakened for his late feeding, he needed to be washed. Julia had sleepily rolled out of bed and taken him into the kitchen. Such peace and quiet! That didn't happen very often in the Childers house.

George had nursed and gone back to sleep in Julia's arms when she heard whimpering coming from the children's room. *Now who's awake in the middle of the night?*

Julia gently carried her sleeping baby back into the bedroom and laid him in his crib. She heard John's gentle breathing as she tiptoed into the children's room to see what was wrong. It was little Ada, crying in her sleep. Julia bent over her. "Ssssh, Ada, don't cry. You had a bad dream."

Dona and Dora stirred restlessly and Julia soothed them. "Ada's not feeling very good," she whispered. "Just go on back to sleep—I'll take care of her."

The two girls turned over and were asleep immediately. In the dark, Julia pulled the covers up to Ada's chin and smoothed her hair back from her forehead. Her hand quickly slid to a stop. Ada's face felt so warm. It was only spring; the nights weren't that warm yet. Ada must have taken on a fever since she went to bed.

Julia lifted her out of bed and carried her to the kitchen. By the light of the coal-oil lamp, she could see how flushed Ada's face was. The child wasn't just warm, she was burning hot. Setting Ada gently into her rocking chair, Julia poured some cold water in a pan and quickly fetched a clean washrag from the cabinet drawer. Ada was limp—like a rag doll—as Julia put her on her lap and began sponging her face gently. Ada opened her eyes from time to time, but they always fell heavily shut again. Julia talked to her gently in whispers. Ada did not seem to hear her.

Over and over for the next two hours, Julia dipped the rag in water, wrung it out with one hand while she supported Ada with the other, and sponged her face. As the moments ticked by and Ada felt as hot as ever, Julia grew increasingly worried. *I better wake John.*

Slowly rising from the chair with Ada's full weight in her arms, Julia laid the little girl carefully on the floor before the banked fire. She silently entered the children's room to get Ada's pillow, which she tucked under her head. Then Julia covered her with the knitted shawl she always kept on her chair and tiptoed into their bedroom.

John was still sleeping soundly and she gently shook his shoulder, whispering, "John, wake up. Ada is sick."

John struggled awake at the unusual hour and sat up. "What's wrong, Julia?"

"Little Ada is sick. Come out to the kitchen."

John followed her and went down on his knees beside Ada, feeling her face. "She's awful hot!"

"Yes," said Julia. "I've been holding her for two hours and trying to get her fever down with washing her face. But she's no better. What caused the fever? She seemed all right last night. I tried to spoon some water down her and she swallowed a little. I don't know what else to do."

"When it gets daylight I'll ride out to see if I can find the doctor," said John.

"Has she ever had a fever like this before?"

"Not that I remember. She's always been healthy."

They sat together for a while, watching Ada. Julia wrung out the washrag many times, putting it on the hot little face. After a while she asked, "Why don't you go on back to bed, John? You got a hard day tomorrow, and need some more sleep. I'll watch her. Why don't you lift her and put her in my lap again? I'll hold her. It's easier to wet her face if she's up in my lap."

John lifted Ada when Julia again settled in her chair. "I hate to go to bed and leave you sittin' up here."

"But John, it don't seem to do any good for us both to lose sleep. And you can go and try to find the doctor when you get up. I'll just set and hold her."

John kissed her. "You're a fine mama, Julia."

Ada's high fever did not abate. Time after time Julia squeezed out the cloth, put it on Ada's forehead and face. And time after time it was warmed again. Julia's arm ached from holding the little girl so long but she couldn't stop trying to sponge the fever down. She prayed, asking God to touch the child and heal this fever, but never, throughout the long night, could she tell any difference.

John came out at daybreak, and found Julia asleep in her big rocking chair, holding his child. Ada seemed no different than when he'd last seen her. He touched Julia's face gently and kissed her forehead. "You're a wonderful woman, Julia Childers, takin' care of my little girl. But it looks like she's no better."

Julia struggled awake. "No—John, I don't know what more to do for her. She's been like this all night—burnin' up and sometimes talkin' wild—. Then she quieted down some and I slept a little."

"I'll stir up the fire first—we got to have that. Then I'll ride out and see if I can find the doctor." He hurried back to the bedroom to put on his clothes, but a cry from Julia brought him running out again.

"Oh—Oh, John! I think she's gone! She jerked a little like she was tryin' to wake up but then her head fell back and she just quit breathin'!"

John sprang to Julia's side and put a frantic hand on Ada's chest, trying desperately to feel a heartbeat. He felt none. He picked her up, shook her and felt again. But her head fell back. John couldn't believe this was happening—it had been so sudden. He sagged down beside the rocking chair, and Julia clutched hold of Ada's body to keep her from falling.

"Oh—my little girl!" John buried his face in his hands. Small Ada lay as if she were just lightly asleep in Julia's arms and there was no more struggle. Her eyes were half closed—her hands were quiet, she was at peace.

Julia sat stunned in the rocking chair, her eyes lingering on every detail of Ada's face. Her thoughts flashed back to the time when she was thirteen and her mother lay this still on her bed. For the second time Julia was in the valley with death. Her grief was just as real for Ada; she loved this child. Ada had responded to Julia from the first. How she would love to be able to ease John's grief. She put her hand on John's head, trying to hug him with one arm, holding Ada in the other. "I feel so bad, John," she said through a choked whisper. "She's just like my child, too. I didn't know what else to do for her."

John shook his head. "I didn't either."

Baby George, awakened by Julia's cry, began to scream in his crib. John stood up wiping his face on the back of his hand. Then he tenderly lifted his child from Julia's lap and carried her into their bedroom. Laying her on his own pillow, he smoothed her long, light brown hair back from her forehead, gently closed her eyes and folded the small hands over her breast.

While John was in the bedroom, Julia threw out the water in the basin, poured some fresh from the bucket on the water stand,

and washed her own face. Then she went to the crib in the bedroom, picked up angry baby George and stood in sorrow looking at little Ada. She put an arm around John and, holding the baby, leaned against him while he sobbed. They wept together, then she wiped her eyes. "I'll go wake the other children."

"Ed, Milt, Dora, Dona, Eva Jane!" When she called them, Dora and Dona grunted and rolled over half awake. Sitting up in bed, they rubbed sleepy eyes and asked, "Where's Ada? She up already?"

The two boys stretched in their bed and tried to settle back to sleep a little more.

"Everybody wake up." Julia's voice sounded odd even to her own ears.

The children had never heard her sound like that before and they were suddenly alert with solemn eyes. Julia looked strange—her eyes were red, her hair wasn't combed, and her mouth was shaking. She was trying to speak to them and at the same time to quiet the baby when Ed asked, "Is something wrong?"

Julia nodded and her eyes overflowed with tears. The children had never seen her cry before. "Little Ada— is—" her voice broke but she went on. "Little Ada has died—just a few minutes ago. I don't know what it was. She was sick all night and I tried to get her fever down—but—"

Their faces were frozen in shock for a time, then tears began to roll down Dona's cheeks. "I heard Ada cry in her sleep but you took her out of bed— so I thought she'd be all right. How could she die? How *did* she die so fast?"

"I don't know how she died so quick—it was the high fever. I kept wetting her face with a cold cloth, but the fever wouldn't go down. I woke up your Pa and we sat with her. He was goin' to get the doctor as soon as it got light. Just before he left, Ada sort of tried to sit up then her heart just stopped beating. Little Ada's soul is in Heaven now."

"Where's Pa?" asked Milt.

"He just carried Ada and put her on our bed."

"We want to see her—" The boys jumped out of bed and started toward the other room and the girls tumbled after them. "Ada just can't be dead—"

At the sight of their father inside the room, John's four children and little Eva Jane stopped in the doorway. Then they went in slowly, unbelieving. John was standing beside the bed with his head bowed, and they crowded in around him. His arms tried to encircle them all as they wept together because their little Ada was lying so still on the big bed. Julia stood with them holding the baby.

Finally, John wiped his eyes. Life on the farm needed tending to, even though their lives had been changed forever in the breaking dawn. "We got chores to do," he said in a cracked, husky whisper. "Animals have to be cared for, no matter how we feel. Come help me, Milt."

John and Milton went outside to milk the cows and do the other daily work. Julia, in the kitchen, directed Ed to mix up the corn pone and put it in the big black iron skillet to bake over the fire. She sat nursing her baby while Dora and Dona and Eva Jane made the beds, tidied up the large room, and set the table for breakfast. After John and Milton came inside, their pails brimming with milk, they all gathered around the kitchen table—a quiet, sad, forlorn family. They ate their corn pone and drank yesterday's milk in silence, not even seeming to be aware of what they were doing.

Julia put the baby back into his crib and tried to eat some breakfast. Then she strained the new milk through her special milk cloths, and put it into crocks to sit in the cool cellar. She wondered how they all could do their customary tasks so calmly when she knew they were crying inside—just as she was. But she also knew she shouldn't wonder—they lived in a world where the shadows of death hovered often. Sometimes those shadows crept out with a mother, sometimes a petted little kitten, and sometimes they left with a beloved child. Through it all, God's grace would sustain them, His Word would comfort them, and their faith that the loved one was in Heaven would lift them up.

"John, why don't you and the boys go 'round to our neighbors and friends and tell them? Maybe you can find our pastor at home—I hope so. I—I'll do the needful things here."

John nodded, and he and the two boys left to spread the news of their loss. Friends would soon arrive—that was the custom—and today Julia needn't worry about cooking any more food. Neighbors would bring it in. After John and the boys rode out of the barn lot, Julia took a deep breath. Now for her task. Silently she fetched water in a pan, and clothes to prepare Ada's body for burial. Had it only been last night she had done these same motions to soothe Ada's fever? It seemed so long ago.

Julia gently washed little Ada's body, dressed her in her favorite blue dress, and combed her long hair, bringing part of it to the front, over her shoulders. Julia marvelled at the silkiness of Ada's hair. She folded her small hands on her breast.

As she worked, Julia couldn't help but think about her mother's body in comparison. Her mother had been old and tired; so thin and frail. Ada's beautiful young body was so sweet and rounded, in a favored time between babyhood and growing up—a time of great promise. Now all the earthly promise would never be fulfilled. She would never grow up, never know the joy of children of her own. But her Heavenly Father would fulfill a much greater promise.

Dora, Dona, and Eva Jane stood and watched all the preparations with tears rolling down their cheeks. "Don't she look purty?" Dora asked in awe, shaking her head.

Dona nodded, wiping her eyes with her sleeve. "I just want to—" She reached over and lovingly touched Ada's hand and then drew back with a gasp. "Oh, she's so cold! I didn't know she would be so—" She began to sob and so did Eva Jane. Julia put her arms about all the girls and they wept together beside the bed.

The news spread quickly and soon neighbors began to come in, the women bringing dishes of whatever they had been cooking when they heard. They greeted Julia and the girls, their faces crumpled in sympathy, and wiping tears, put food out on the table. The men came bringing smooth, white boards, their hammers, saws, nails, and shovels. After eating the meal the women had spread out, the men all went out to a little hill where Ada had often played, and dug her grave under an oak tree.

John and the boys came back and stood watching sorrowfully while their friends were at work under the tree. They could barely comprehend that their Ada would soon be buried there.

The women ate their dinner, cleaned up Julia's kitchen, then sat around in the bedroom where Ada lay. They talked quietly together about children and the pain of losing a child. Nearly all of them had known that pain intimately.

When the men came back to the barn, they hammered together a small, stout pine box. Julia heard that hammering, and had to go alone to walk around under the trees for a while. Beside her grief for Ada, her memory was thrown back to the day when she felt such desolation over the loss of her mother. She had thought at that time her heart could never be healed. She prayed now for God to comfort and heal John and their children's despondency.

When the men were finished they brought the little home-made coffin inside. Together John and Julia kissed small Ada, then gently wrapped her in one of their clean, white sheets and lifted her body into the coffin. They walked outside holding tightly to each other's hand. Their friends nailed down the lid. As the men were carrying the casket out the kitchen door, the sheriff and their traveling minister rode up.

The minister grasped John and Julia's hands. "I can't tell you how sorry I am that you lost your little Ada. She was a fine little girl. I just happened to be on the road when I met the sheriff and he told me, and we came straight here."

"We are much obliged to you," John said, his lips trembling. "It's hard to bury your family without a preacher."

The pastor nodded. Julia went back inside, picked up her baby and bundled him up in his blanket. Then the small group of farmers and their families, sorrowing with John's family, carried the box up the hill and lowered it with ropes into the fresh-opened grave. As they all stood around the grave with bared heads, even though the wind was chill, the pastor opened his Bible and spoke to them.

"Though we are gathered here today in sorrow, Jesus has words of hope for us. We remember that He said, *Suffer the little children to come unto Me and forbid them not: for of such is the Kingdom of Heaven. And He took them up in His arms, put His hands upon them, and blessed them. (Mark 10: 14b-16)*

"We know that Jesus loves the children. And He has seen fit to take little Ada to Heaven to be with Him, so we know she is safe. We cannot help but grieve for our loss of her, but we also can rejoice because we know we can meet her again up there.

"Now, John and Julia, the Lord has some words today especially for you and your family. He says, *Let not your hearts be troubled. Ye believe in God—believe also in Me. In my Father's house are many mansions: if it were not so, I would have told you. I go to prepare a place for you. And if I go and prepare a place for you, I will come again and receive you unto Myself; that where I am, there ye may be also." (John 14:1-3)*

"I pray today that God would bless us all. Many of us have had this very same sorrow, and we know that God loves us and weeps with us. So let's trust Him, and believe His word. His promises are true. If we walk with Him, we'll see our loved ones again in glory. Amen."

When Julia heard these comforting words, she gripped John's arm and closed her eyes. Her mind flashed back to the time when Joe had recited these same words from the Bible as their mother's body was buried. A familiar pain clutched at her heart and she buried her face in John's sleeve. Baby George began to scream inside his blankets, so Julia loosed them a little and patted him.

The men shoveled dirt on top of the small lonely box, and then the band of neighbors, carrying their shovels, plodded slowly down the little hill to John and Julia's house. The men put their shovels back into their wagons and stood around outside—not knowing what else to do, and at a loss for words. John shook hands with them all. "I'm much obliged to you. Let me know when I can help you."

Women friends went back into the house with Julia and the children and tried to comfort them. They put their arms around them and said, "Come over to talk to us—let us help you if we can. Now you keep all the rest of this food that's left over. You're welcome to it—you don't have to do no cookin' today." Then all too soon, the neighbors had to leave to go back to their own farms—their work was waiting. The Childers family was alone.

Later, while the baby slept, they surrounded the supper table laden with extra food, and the children's faces were long and sad. John was very quiet and Julia had wiped many tears as she worked in the kitchen.

"Pa, is Ada in Heaven now?" asked Dona.

"Yes," answered John.

"Pa," asked Dora, "what did Jesus mean when He said somethin' about 'suffer the little children'? And what does 'forbid them not' mean?"

John explained simply, "'Suffer the little children to come unto Me' means *let* the children come to Me. And 'forbid them not' means *don't stop them from comin' to me.* See, Jesus is tellin' all us ma's and pa's that we must teach our young'uns about Him and we mustn't do anything to keep our young'uns from believin' in Him. I've tried to do that. You all *do* believe in Jesus, don't you? You all pray to Him and know He loves you, don't you?"

They nodded solemnly. Then Dona, needing to be assured again, asked, "Pa, is Ada really up in heaven with Jesus now?"

John nodded. "Yes. She is. Didn't you hear what Jesus said in the Good Book—that He was goin' to prepare a place for us? When we die, if we love Him, we will go to be there with Him."

"Well, before—when our Mama died, I remember that you told us our Mama went up to Heaven. Is Ada with Mama now? If Ada had to leave us, I like to think about her bein' with Mama. And when I die, I want to be with Mama, too."

The boys were listening intently to this conversation. Being older, they hadn't wanted to ask any questions, but they watched John closely and waited for the answer.

Julia answered for him first and told them all, "I think she has been with your Mama since she left us this mornin'. I think your Mama was waitin' for her—because she looked down from Heaven and saw how sick little Ada was. God took her spirit to Heaven when it left her body here. What we buried was only her body—not her spirit."

"You believe all that, Pa?"

John and Julia's eyes met across the table as John nodded. "I do."

Baby George was beginning to wake up in his crib and to make his hunger known. Julia got up to go nurse him, but first she went around the table, her arms encircling each of the children, her hand smoothing their hair while they cried.

"It's gonna be lonesome in bed without her—even if we do have more room to turn over," sniffed Dora, wiping her eyes on the bottom of her skirt.

Leftovers at the Childers table were plentiful as the children slowly trailed off to bed.

CHAPTER FIFTEEN
Addition and Change

The winter after little Ada left them was long and severe with below-zero weather for many days at a time. Snow was piled up around the window sills of Julia and John's little house, and the path to the barn was a white tunnel. Winters on a farm were always used to repair broken tools and to sharpen things. John spent a good deal of his time working on axes, knives, plows, hoes, and harnesses. Every day he brought some implement from the barn to work on in the kitchen. Always, moving around trying to get food on the table was hard for Julia because of the clutter of his repairs. Added to that was the children's clutter!

Of course, the livestock and chickens had to be fed and watered every day, and the eggs gathered. John, Milton, and Ed did those chores. That winter a calf was born too soon—before the weather warmed up in spring. John brought it in and laid it by the fire, then went back to the barn to try to save the life of the cow.

The girls took over the job of saving the tiny calf. Julia wrapped it in an old quilt, the three girls petted the newborn calf, talked to it and tried to feed it with a bottle. But it wasn't able to suck, so they dipped their fingers in milk and brushed the calf's tongue. Then they soaked a small wad of cloth in milk and squeezed the milk into its mouth. Before long the calf was trying to suck on the cloth. The next day they were able to feed it with a bottle.

The boys carried in wood every day, then had to clean off crusted snow, and dry the wood inside before it would burn. That meant two or three day's supply of wood stacked by the door of their already crammed household.

Julia cooked, then cleaned the kitchen so she could cook again. Washing clothes was a very difficult job because they had to be washed and dried by the fire. Tubs and a washboard were put on a small bench, clothes first rubbed on a piece of homemade soap, then rubbed on the board. On washday, wet clothing covered every piece of furniture while drying. The family wore long underwear, pants and shirts or dresses for two weeks at a time in winter, because washing and drying them all was simply too much for Julia to do.

Usually, Saturday was bath day—the only bath day of the week. Water was heated at the fireplace, a tub was put in a corner nearby, with a quilt hung in front of it for privacy. In a house as small as theirs, privacy was a much longed-for but seldom-realized commodity.

All the goin's-on around the fireplace got John to thinking. Their house was too small, no question about it 'specially now that Julia was pregnant again. "Been thinkin' about rentin' another farm," he told his family one cold night. "This house is too little with all our young'uns growin' so fast. And now with another one comin', we got to have more room."

Julia gazed at their family—all over the room. John, Milton, and Ed were fooling with harnesses. Eva Jane and Dona were trying to keep little George from getting all tangled up in the long harnesses stretched across the floor. Dora was helping Julia peel potatoes for supper. Julia laughed then sighed, "Looks like you're right. Everywhere I look there's a young'un—all ages, all kinds, and another one on the way!" She smiled, "And I wouldn't trade any of 'em off."

"If we get another house, Pa, will it be bigger?" Dora asked.

"No use to move unless it is," said Julia. This has been a good little place for us—our first house together."

"It will be bigger," John answered Dona. This has been a good home, but I've been lookin' for a while. I already found us a better place. It's not too far from here in the direction toward Creal. There's a school close, and you young'uns can go when the weather turns. House is bigger too—kitchen's bigger and it's got two more rooms than this and the farm is bigger. It'll mean more work, I guess—but you kids are bigger and can help more."

"Is the rent much higher?" Julia asked.

"It's about the same. Feller that owns it is too old to keep things goin' and he wants to rent it to somebody that'll take care of it. Said he'd rent it to me if I want to move. We'll have to wait a little longer 'til there's a break in the weather. Can't move in zero weather like this. But if we're movin', then we got to go before spring plantin' time."

"How'd you hear about this new place?"

"Met the owner of that farm in the feed store in Creal the other day and I said I'd talk to you about it. What do you think, Julia? Want to move to a bigger house?"

Julia was elated. "John! You know I'd like a bigger place! In one way it's nice not to own our own farm. We can move as our family increases, but if this land was ours, we'd be stuck forever in this little house."

Early in March a few warm days showed promise that the snow was past, so John loaded up the wagon with some of their pots, pans, and beds and took Julia and the smaller children to the new farm. Then he went back with the boys for other loads while Julia and the girls began to scrub up the house and settle in. Several days passed before all their things were moved over.

Julia and John reveled in the extra space. Now the boys could be in a bedroom by themselves and so could the girls. They could have a room to dry clothes in and for the children to play in, out from under her feet.

They were barely settled when it was time to get their crops into the ground. Everybody helped including Julia, though she was seven months pregnant. Even baby George toddled around and dropped a few seeds in the rows, managing mostly to get in everyone else's way.

* * * *

A few days before their baby was due, John rode up to Joe's place. Martha heard the horse gallop in and ran out the door, in surprise.

"John! Come in! It's good to see you. Is everybody all right?" She looked anxious. "I hope nothing's happened to Julia or your family."

"Don't be unsettled. They're fine. Julia's goin' to have another baby in a few days. She told me you're a good midwife. And I got to thinkin' that she's not seen you in some months."

"That's right—it's been a while."

"Yep. So I thought if I could get you to come for a short visit and to be Julia's midwife, it'd make her mighty happy. I know she thinks a heap of you."

Martha had been lonely for Julia. She thought for a few moments. "Oh, John, I'd be proud to come to see Julia if it's all right with Joe." When he comes in, I'll ask him. While we're waitin' for him, have a cup of coffee. And supper will be ready when he gets in."

When Joe heard why John had come he said, "Course you can go if you want to, Martha. I'd like to see Julia myself, but I can't go now. I'll take our two youngest over to your ma's—I think she'll be glad to have 'em for a while. The other three can stay and help me."

Martha sat up straight on the horse, threw her shoulders back and breathed deeply as they rode down through those fresh green hills to Creal Springs. "John, this is the best surprise I've ever had. It's been so long since I've had a horseback ride—I miss it, bein' in the house all the time. When I was a girl I used to practically live on a horse. And this country—I've never been down this far south before. It sure is pretty country through these Ozarks."

Julia expected John would come back today and she kept listening for horses. She was excited when she heard them coming and waddled down the steps as fast as she could manage that chore. Everything was a chore these days.

"Martha!" she cried, holding her arms wide. Martha tried to hug her, but Julia was so large with pregnancy that she had to hug her sideways. They both laughed. Martha said, "Sure won't be long now, Julia. Your baby's way down."

"I know it. I have a hard time walkin' like this. I guess ever' woman who's ever had a baby said the same thing."

Two days later, on May 14, 1888, Henry was born. Julia lay gazing at her new red-faced, husky boy. "He's so beautiful and I'm so glad to have you here, Martha. You're the best midwife ever! I can't help but remember the first time you done this for me—how different I feel about havin' a baby now. "Oh, Martha, look at that beautiful boy Henry!"

If Martha had also thought of that other birth, she made no mention of it. "He is beautiful, Julia. And he looks so healthy. I bet you're goin' to have a hard time keepin' up with him."

When Henry was born, John moved little George's new, small-sized bed into the room with his big brothers, and put Henry in George's crib beside their bed. Two-year-old George made it very clear he didn't like the new arrangement one bit and screamed most of his first night there. Ed and Milt called out to Julia, "Come and take this young'un out'a here or we're gonna choke him! We want to sleep!"

Henry was a robust, fat, lovable bundle of energy. Julia said to John, "This baby wants to eat all the time! I don't know how I'm ever goin' to have enough milk for him!"

Martha stayed with Julia for three weeks and by that time Julia was feeling strong again. They said tearful good-byes to each other when John was getting the horses ready to leave. "Tell Joe I hope he can come to see us soon," Julia said to Martha. "I miss him so much—he's a wonderful brother. And thank him for lettin' you come to visit me."

"I'll be back tomorrow, after I get Martha home, Julia," John called as their horses trotted out of the gate.

As soon as she regained her strength, Julia went back to work part of every day in their new fields. She carried little Henry out and put him on a blanket under a tree while they all worked. Sometimes Julia looked over her brood and wondered where she found all the energy to work so hard to care for them. *It's love*, she decided. *When people love each other, they can do anything.*

Their spring planting in the new place produced a bountiful vegetable crop, and by November, Julia's new cellar was full of her home-canned foods. The children were all healthy and happy, and the oldest ones were in school. Julia was so proud because they were learning to read!

They had no money to spend on extras. All the money they could scrape together went to pay rent on the farm and buy absolute necessities. John had figured out that they would not have enough feed for the animals to last until next year and that worried him. He and Julia talked about having to buy extra feed and putting it in the barn before the first snow fell. "Sometimes the first snow is on the ground a long time," she said. "I think we'd better do it."

So Julia spent the last of her savings on feed. "I have to do this, John. We can't let these animals starve. Next year will probably be better—we'll raise more here."

"I surely hate for you to take all your savin's, Julia. I just don't know what to do. Nobody's needed my services for their stock lately, and we didn't get in enough crop of our own for the animals. Barn's not full as it ought to be."

"It's *our* savin's, John, and we have to spend it now."

For John's sake, she acted as if it didn't bother her. But she'd had money in the corner of her trunk so long that she was frightened when they had to spend the last of it. *What if we don't make any more money?* she asked herself. *We'd have to sell the stock. Then what would we do?*

She hadn't realized before what a comfortable feeling came from having some money put away. But she did feel good knowing their stock would be well cared for until next spring. Then they'd have to put more land into feed for them.

That winter, like the last one, was a searing, cold, soul-pinching winter. Because the house had no heat in the bedrooms, they just had to undress down to their long underwear while they were by the fire, then run to bed. But Julia thanked the Lord for enough food to nourish them and enough wood to burn in the stove and fireplace. She had the children gather up several big rocks, which they took from their beds and laid beside the fireplace every morning. By nighttime they were warmed, and she wrapped the rocks up in cloths and put them at their feet in the beds. How shivery happy they felt to snuggle cold toes beside warm flannel-covered rocks! John got up at least twice every night to keep the fires burning.

That year, John had two changes of work clothes and two coats. One coat he wore to feed stock and do all the outside chores, the other he kept for good—which meant mostly wearing it to church.

Julia had only two house dresses, one church dress, and one pair of shoes. She washed a house dress twice a week at night and dried it in front of the fireplace while she slept. If the dress wasn't quite dry the next morning, then she wore her older one to work in. Most of the time while working inside, she went barefoot.

One day as Julia was cooking their noon meal of fried side-pork, black-eyed peas, and skillet corn bread, she was working without her shoes. John sat near the kitchen stove cleaning and oiling his shotgun. Baby Henry was sitting up against an old blanket playing with some empty spools, and the other children played checkers and dominos on the floor nearby. Snow was piled window-sill deep outside, and a cold wind blew under the house, sometimes gusting up between the floor boards. Nobody got very far away from the fire. Julia bent over to pick up baby Henry and as her long skirt swung forward, John noticed she was wearing no shoes.

"Julia! Why don't you put your shoes on? You'll catch a cold like that!"

"Oh, John, I was just savin' my shoes 'til I had to go outside. No use wearin' 'em full of holes in the house!" She didn't tell him she wasn't wearing the shoes because they were so worn out and run over that they gave her a backache. They were her wedding shoes.

John got up abruptly and left the kitchen and she heard him open the bedroom closet door. She knew he would see her shoes there and thought he might bring them to her and insist that she put them on. But he didn't.

After they finished their meal, John got up and put on his work coat. He said, "I have to go in to Creal. Got to see about somethin'—some business in there."

"In this awful weather?" exclaimed Julia. "John, you'll take your death of cold!"

"Oh, this weather ain't so bad. And the horse needs some exercise." John put on his work coat and went toward the barn carrying a large bundle under his arm. Julia wondered what it was but she didn't ask.

Late that afternoon, John came back riding his horse through deep snowdrifts. Snow was beginning to fall again and John entered the kitchen stamping his feet and blowing on his hands. His cheeks and nose were red, and snowflakes clung to his eyebrows and beard. He had a box under his arm. "This is for you, Julia. Hope they fit."

Presents in their house were rare, so in amazement she opened the box and there lay a pair of black, shiny, high-laced shoes, just her size. "John! You oughtn't to have done it! Where'd you get the money? Shoes like this must cost at least three dollars!"

"I saw your others, Julia. They ain't fittin' for nothin'. I'm not havin' my wife goin' barefooted, no matter what new shoes cost!"

"Oh, thank you, John. They look so pretty—nearly too pretty to wear." She tried them on and they fitted her perfectly.

The next Sunday morning as they bundled up against the cold and were climbing into the sled to go to church, Julia exclaimed, "John, you got on your work coat. Go and change it!"

"This one's all right, Julia. Won't see no strangers in church today, I reckon."

"No—you shouldn't wear that old coat to church. I'll get your good coat for you," she exclaimed. "Here, Dora, hold Henry for me."

And before John could stop her, she jumped down from the sled and ran back into the house. John followed slowly. Julia ran to the bedroom and opened the door—the closet was empty. She suddenly realized what the bundle had been under John's arm the day he brought her the shoes. John was waiting for her in the kitchen, sheepish, and she flung herself into his arms sobbing. "Oh, John, You sold your good coat to get me these shoes!"

"That ain't no reason for you to take on so," he answered patting her shoulder. "A man can't wear but one coat at a time anyhow, and my work coat is good enough for any man. Don't cry, Julia. These shoes ain't that much and you need them."

She kissed him with tears running down her cheeks. Then blinking through blurred eyes she looked at the shiny toes peeping from under her long skirt and said, "Truly, John, these are the prettiest shoes in the whole country!"

J U L I A

Part IV

1888 - 1915

CHAPTER SIXTEEN
Growing-Up Years

John's two older sons, Ed and Milt, sat nervously at the supper table after a hard day's work of plowing and planting. They looked at each member of the family seated there, then looked at each other and nodded.

"Pa—" Milt began. "Ed and me—we been talkin'." He stopped and pursed his lips.

"Been talkin?" John asked between bites of bacon, black-eyed peas, and cornbread. "What about?"

Milt drew a deep breath. "Well—we, uh—you won't like this, so I'll just say it straight out. We decided we're leavin' the farm." He ignored Julia's gasp. "We're goin' someplace else to make some money." Pent-up thoughts and feelings spilled out now. "You ain't never goin' to make anything here. You work all the time and you got nothin'! We work all day—all the time and we get nothin' for it!"

John's ire was rising. "You get a good home and good food for it! Julia works all the time seein' to it that you get fed. You get a bed. You get a family that cares whether you live or die, and you get neighbors who'll help you when you need helpin'! What's better than that?"

"Money! We want some money. We're old enough to meet some girls and have some fun sometimes, too."

Julia wanted to say something; to beg them not to go because John needed them, but these were John's boys. He'd have to handle this situation.

John leaned back in his chair, his hands on the table and was silent for a while. Then, "You done made up your minds about this?"

The boys nodded.

"Ed, you're quiet over there. You sure you want to go, too?"

Ed nodded again.

John expelled a long breath. "Well—you boys are welcome to stay here at home. But I know you got to leave sometime—that's only natural. So if you want to go, I'll do nothin' to stop you. I'll miss you here; a man thinks about his sons workin' with him—"

"We've *been* workin' with you!" Ed said.

John raised his hand. "I know. I won't say much more except I hope you'll both remember to live by the Book. Keep the Commandments and love the Lord. If you do that, people will respect you. Bring no disgrace on our Childers name." He sighed. "When you thinkin' of leavin'?"

"Tomorrow."

"Where you goin?"

"Well," Milt said, "I'm goin' to West Virginia. There's a lot of work there. Some fellers in Creal was talkin' about goin' the other day, and I decided to go with 'em."

"How are you goin'? I hear that's a long ways."

Milt continued, "We're ridin' in a wagon as far as Marion. Then we're catchin' a train. One of the fellers loaned me money to get my ticket—I'll pay him back after I get a job. We're goin' to work in the mines."

"Ed, what 're you goin' to do?"

"I'm goin' up to Carterville. Mines workin' up there all the time and they want workers. Good pay in the mines."

"I hear it's dangerous work—"

"We'll make it." The two boys stood up and Milt said, "We're gettin' our clothes together—be leavin' in the mornin'. Ed's goin' to ride with us to Marion and he can hitch a ride with somebody on to Carterville probably."

"All right," John said, his voice low with sadness. "Guess I can help a little. I'll give you five dollars apiece to eat on for a few days. If you two want to ride on one horse, I'll ride in with you to Creal and bring my horse back."

The boys nodded.

When they went to bed that night, Julia knew John was suffering. She put her arms around him. "I'm so sorry they're leavin', John. I know how bad you feel."

"It's hard, but I'll just have to live with it, I guess. Young'uns always grow up and leave—that's natural. It hurts, though." He turned over to try to sleep, then turned back again. "I'm thankful to the Lord for you, Julia."

The next morning Julia cooked a special breakfast for the boys. She cut one of their smoked hams, made biscuits, scrambled eggs, gravy, fried potatoes and coffee. The boys might not eat well when they left home, she knew. She fried two extra slices of ham and put them, along with some left-over biscuits and dried apples, in a lard pail for them to eat on the way.

The boys hugged Julia and the girls, patted George and baby Henry before mounting their horse. Their sisters were crying and both Milt and Ed surreptitiously dashed some moisture from their eyes. As they rode out the gate, Dora said, "I don't want them to go! But maybe when I grow up, I'll go too."

Dona nodded and sniffed. "Can I sleep by myself in their bed now, Mama Julia?"

* * * *

John's two daughters were growing up, too. Julia had taught both of them to knit and sew and now at ages fourteen and twelve, they were making things for themselves. And like all farm children, they knew how to plant, to reap, to can, and to keep house. Sometimes they whispered together about the big subject of BOYS, but they didn't want Julia to know about it. They did mention to Julia once that they would like to go to a square dance sometime. "Do you know how to square dance, Julia?"

"Well, I ain't been to a square dance in many a year. When I was real young, I used to go with my ma and my big brothers once in a while. I like the music and singin'."

"You think Pa will ever let us go?"

"Yes, I think he would—if anybody has one around here. I'll ask him to let us know when there is one and to take all of us. I'd enjoy it too."

Eva Jane also was growing like a weed in a tomato patch. At nine years of age she, too, could knit and sew and keep a house clean. She had inherited Julia's love for the land and for working in the gardens, and she never forgot her love for kittens and puppies.

When September came, most of their canning was done. Julia said to John one day, "John, we ought to have a little fun sometime. Is there ever a square dance around here that you know about? Do you like to square dance?"

"Tired of stayin' at home with me, are you, Julia?"

"Oh, John, you're teasin' me—you know better than that. But your big girls ought to get out once in a while and meet other people. It's not good to coop them up so close. Listen around the next time you go to buy supplies, and let's plan to take the whole family to somethin'."

"I guess you're right, Julia. I'm so satisfied just stayin' at home, I forget about how anybody else feels. I'm glad my girls have you for a mama."

October rolled around. George was a sturdy three-year-old and Henry was a feisty seventeen months, always into something and never still a minute.

John had been to Creal that day. When he sat down to supper he said, "You girls like to go to a hoedown next week?"

All three girls bounced in their chairs with excitement. "Oh, Pa! Is there goin' to be one? And you *will* take us?"

"I heard today there'll be one next Friday. If you want to go, we'll go." He winked at Julia. "I think Julia might like to square dance with some handsome man there."

"I sure would—and that handsome man is John Childers! I've never been to a hoedown with him, but I'm afixin' to enjoy it."

The next Friday afternoon John came in from the fields early. "Got the punkins piled up. Field looks good."

"Did you get all my broomcorn in the barn?"

"It's in there. I'll make you some new brooms before long. From the looks of them stubs you try to sweep with, you *need* some new brooms."

"Ready for your bath?"

"Yep. You done had yours?"

"Yes, and now I got things all ready for you."

One of their round tin washtubs was sitting beside the fireplace in one end of the room, and a quilt hung over some chairs in front of the tub. Julia poured a big kettle of boiling water into the tin tub and added plenty of cold water from the bucket to cool it down.

Dora, Dona, and Eva Jane had already soaked in their luxury bath in the tub before John came in. It took nearly all day for them to get finished. Now they were in their bedroom all trying to see themselves in the tiny dresser mirror at the same time. "Our girls been all day gettin' prettied up." Julia told John. "They're as jumpy as crickets too close to hot grease. I hope they enjoy things tonight."

"We heard you!" the girls called out. "We'll enjoy tonight!" They could overhear the splashing their father was making as he soaped and washed himself—a six-foot, four-inch man trying to get all of himself wet in a round washtub. He and Julia talked over the quilt and Julia made two trips with other buckets of warm water to pour over his head and back, to rinse the soap off him.

"You look mighty purty, Julia. You're goin' to be the purtiest one there tonight."

"And you are bound to be the handsomest man there. That nice straight nose and them blue eyes of yours, and your soft brown beard—I'll have to watch out for other women at that barn social tonight!"

John laughed.

Dona stuck her head out of the bedroom door. "She's right, Pa. You'll be the most handsome!"

"The girls 've been so excited all day," Julia said, "that I've hardly been able to get any work out of 'em. How long has it been since your girls went to a barn social? I know it's a long time since I went to one, and Eva Jane's never been."

"Well, I took my girls to one before I broke my ankle and met you. But they was little then, I guess. How long since you've had any fun like this, Julia?"

"I guess I must 've been about twelve. That was when my Ma was feelin' well. I remember that my brothers went with their families and they all danced with me. I'm excited you're takin' me to this. Hope I ain't forgot how to dance. It'll be good to meet all the neighbors again, too."

George and Henry were playing on the floor and Henry toddled over to the chairs and peeked around the quilt to look at his father in the tub.

Julia rescued him, "Look, baby, don't you get all wet! John, since it'll be dark by the time we get there, I just put Henry's nightshirt on him. He may be asleep anyway. He'll probably go to sleep in the wagon and may not even wake up when we carry him inside. I'll take some covers for him and his little pillow, and extra diapers. Guess I better take somethin' to put his wet ones in, too."

"Ain't it about time he got finished wearin' diapers?"

"Yes, about. I'm startin' to break him—"

John came out from behind his barricade, pulling on his clean clothes. His face sparkled and his beard and hair were wet and slicked down. He playfully kissed Julia on the cheek. They never did much kissing in front of the children. "Well, Missus, can I go to the dance with you now?"

She made a curtsy. "Yes you can, clean sir."

They ate an early supper of boiled ham, cabbage and baked pumpkin, and were soon ready to go. John had packed hay thickly in the wagon and they all climbed in and settled down. "This party's goin' to be at the Joneses, Pa?"

"Yes. Now listen, you girls. When we get there, you see to it that you stay inside the barn. I'll have no leavin' to take walks with nobody!"

"Oh, Pa! We're not thinkin' of takin' any walks!"

"Maybe not. But you might run into some of them young whippersnappers and they might be."

The girls giggled and teased him. "Maybe a walk with a *handsome* whippersnapper might be fun!"

John grunted. "You heard me!"

They reached the Jones barn under a big harvest moon and already twenty wagons were scattered around, with their horses tied to a nearby fence. Coal-oil lanterns were hung onto the trees with ropes and wires outside, and onto the barn rafters inside. As the Childers family went in, they were greeted by both old and new friends from all around the farm community.

"Howdy, John. Howdy, Julia. Come on in and make yourselves at home. We've got some sweet cider, popcorn and candy, pies and cakes."

Neighbor men were standing in bunches and women were sitting together talking. Chairs were placed all around inside the big barn and somebody was tuning up a fiddle.

Julia carried in an old pillow case containing clean diapers for Henry and a chamber pot to put the wet ones in. She stowed the pillow case behind an empty chair and sat down to talk to friends. Contrary to her expectations, little Henry was wide awake, so George took him by the hand and began to walk around through the crowd. "Take care of the baby now, George," cautioned Julia.

"Yes, Mama."

Mr. Jones was master of ceremonies for the evening. He now went to the middle of the hay-covered barn floor and made his speech. "Welcome, neighbors. We hope you all have a good time tonight. Ain't no strangers here and we can all just settle in for some fun. Tonight we're gonna do some singin', some dancin', and some eatin'. Got your fiddle ready, Grandpa? Yep—he has, and here comes Cousin Charlie with his banjo!"

The two musicians brought their chairs to the middle and Mr. Jones got the crowd to singing. Most people knew at least part of the songs, and if they didn't know all the verses, they hummed the tune and sang the choruses. It'd been a long time since they had a neighborhood singin' and everybody enjoyed being at one again. Old songs like *Comin' Thro the Rye, Billy Boy, Tenting Tonight, Aunt Dinah's Quilting Party, The Blue Tail Fly, You Get a Line and I'll Get a Pole, Honey* (the crawdad song), and many others floated out of the big barn on the night air.

Everybody then stood up and stretched and Mr. Jones made another announcement. "You'll be hearin' some of these songs again tonight, cause Grandpa's just a waitin' to play 'em while you dance. And now, we're gonna dance! I want ever'body whose bones are under seventy-five years old to come on out here and form a line. Come on now—old people and young people—we want you all. Even if you never square danced before, come on—it's easy!"

"Can we go out and dance too, Pa?" asked Dona.

"Shore can. Go on. If you don't know how, just watch somebody else, you'll learn."

"George," Julia said, "you stay right here in this chair and hold on to Henry. If he gets out in that dancin' crowd, he's gonna get stepped on. Watch him, now!"

"I will, Mama."

John and Julia got up and soon, with Mr. Jones calling the dance, the old barn literally rocked on its foundation. Everybody danced as hard as they could. Sometimes they couldn't hear the calls, but they kept time anyhow. Songs were lively, like: *Skip to My Lou, My Darling Clementine, Turkey in the Straw,* and many more.

To peek into that barn, a person would swear that the whole countryside was there bowing, skipping, sliding, turning, whirling. They made squares, stars and arches, they danced away from their partners and back again. They swung, circled and promenaded—all to calls when they could hear them:

"Hitch your suspenders, button your vest, and swing the little girl you love the best."

"Allemande left to the corner you go, grand chain eight around the row."

"Swing your girl and swing your ma, git over there and swing grandma."

"Bang your heel, don't stub your toe, chicken in a breadpan scratchin' out dough!"

Julia danced until she was breathless. She looked over at the spot where she'd told George to take care of baby Henry and saw that George was mesmerized with the music and thunderous dancing. Little Henry was facing a chair and holding onto it with both hands while he kept time to the music by dancing up and down in one spot. As Julia watched him, his soggy diaper fell off him and plopped between his feet on the floor. Henry didn't like that, so his face screwed up and he began to scream to the music.

Julia poked John, pointed to Henry and shouted over the noise, "I have to take care of him—"

John nodded and she left the line, went over and lifted Henry. She took a clean, hand-hemmed cotton cloth diaper out of the pillow case, laid Henry on her lap and pinned it on him. Once again standing up, the baby happily started jiggling to the rhythm. Julia then lifted the lid inside the pillow case, and stashed his wet diaper in the chamber pot.

She was shortly back on the floor doing the sashay and Do-Si-Do again. She felt so exhilarated and happy to be in the midst of such a good time. While grand chaining eight around the row again, she saw Henry dancing on his fat little legs with such enthusiasm, that his diaper fell off for the second time. But she couldn't leave that minute, so just watched him while she danced. This time Henry didn't cry. He simply stepped out of the soaked cloth, reached down and picked up his wet diaper, toddled around behind his chair, and all by himself, dropped the diaper into the chamber pot. He looked very pleased with himself. His long nightshirt covered the fact that he had nothing on underneath.

Finally, Mr. Jones was finishing his call with:

"That's the end, I do believe,

Kiss the caller before you leave!"

Fiddlin' Grandpa scraped his last chord on the fiddle, stood up and wiped his brow with his bandana. His banjo-pickin' partner stuck his celluloid pick in his shirt pocket and bowed. Then shaking hands with Grandpa, he said, "Gotta wet my whistle" and he walked toward the cider jug. The audience clapped and whistled for them both and then collapsed on chairs, breathing hard.

Julia rescued her half-dressed baby again and smiled at John.

"Now, folks," announced Mr. Jones, "there's plenty to eat and drink. If you all go home hungry or thirsty tonight, it's your own fault. Help yourselves from the tables down at the end of the barn."

Later, when the guests were full and the talking died down, people began to leave. Julia and John said goodnight to the host and hostess, some of the dancers, and to the musicians. The girls called goodnight to their friends, then climbed into the wagon and flopped down at full length in the hay next to George and Henry, giggling about the boys they had danced with.

John's horses pulled their wagon home through the crisp, full-moon October night. The children fell asleep in the sweet-smelling hay in the back, but John and Julia sat close together on the seat. John kissed her and she leaned against him as the wagon creaked home. They felt so young they almost forgot they had any kids behind them.

* * * *

John and Julia had lived in their second house for nearly two years when one day John came home from buying supplies in Creal. Julia looked out and saw him coming, and to her surprise and joy, she saw her brothers Joe and Caleb riding with him. She flew outside to hug them. "Oh, Joe! Caleb! Where'd you come from?"

"I met them on the road," John said. "They was just comin' to see us."

"Well, I wish I'd knowed you was a'comin. I'd have made you a big cake."

Young Henry and George exclaimed, "Well, they're here now, Ma. Why don't you go ahead and make it? We'll help 'em eat it."

"I know you would," Julia answered. Let me get some cider for you all. Just fresh, it is. Set right here in the kitchen and talk to me while I get dinner. We got ham and . . ."

John drank his cider and stood up. "Dora, Dona, Eva Jane—" he called.

"What'cha want, Pa?" they answered from their bedroom. "We're cleaning up this room."

"Well, come on out and say hello to your uncles Joe and Caleb. Then get on some old clothes because I want all five of you kids to come help me in the barn. Been puttin' off cleanin' it up for some days now."

Julia was surprised. "John! You gonna go out and clean the barn *now?* Why don't you stay and talk with us?"

She saw John look at Joe and Caleb and nod. They also nodded to John. "Well, Julia," John answered, "it's a good day and the kids have nothin' better to do. We'll do it now—you can call us when you want us in for dinner. Come on—all of you. Bring some brooms—rakes already out there. We got two big sacks there to haul out the rubbish."

He herded the three girls and two boys out the back door and silence settled over the country kitchen. A puzzled frown creased Julia's forehead. She sat down in a straight-backed chair facing her two brothers. "All right, what's the matter? Somethin's funny here—is some of the family . . .?"

Joe spoke up. "No, Julie—family's all fine. We come here today to give you some surprisin' news. But I think you'll be glad to know it. We told John while we was a ridin' here."

She sat rigid. "What news?"

"Well, yesterday," Joe continued, "the sheriff in Marion sent word for us and William and Matthew to all come in. Said he had some news for us. He'd heard of a death and thought we'd want to know. And we knowed *you'd* want to know."

"Yes, Julie—" Caleb broke in. "Now you can rest easy. Solly Crawford is dead!"

Julia's mouth fell open and she began to tremble. She hung onto the table edge like a drowning person. "He—he's dead? Are you sure?"

"Sheriff said it was him. He'd had an official message from the Chicago police saying, 'A man identified as Solly Crawford from Williamson county was shot in a brothel during a police raid. Not being able to find any kin to notify, the county buried him.' That's what the message said. So he's gone. We wanted to tell you ourselves."

Julia closed her eyes, then opened them slowly. "Twelve years! It's been twelve years and he was still foolin' around with women! Well, the Lord will have to judge him now." She sat for a spell. "How many times in the last twelve years I have been afraid of him! I never wanted to be alone. If I worked in the cornfield, I wanted John near me. I don't think John ever knowed how afraid of a cornfield I was! Now I can rest over it."

Joe touched her arm. "We all hated him, Julie. Of course, we didn't feel afraid of him, but we all hated him for what he done to you. Now I reckon we'll have to find it in our hearts to forgive him. That's what the Good Book says, and it makes sense. What we've all been feelin' can eat us alive, Julie. We'll just ask the Lord to help us forgive the dead and go on livin' with His peace now."

Caleb nodded. "Solly's dead and I ain't sorry. But the Bible says we do have to forgive."

Julia stood up and pulled a brown knitted sweater off a peg beside the door. "I just gotta go outside for a spell by myself. I'll be back soon—don't leave—I want to get your dinner." Blinking tears from her eyes she threw the sweater around her shoulders and ran out the door.

She ran toward the cornfield north of the house. Of course, since it was October, the corn was all in but John had not yet cut the shocks for cattle feed. They stood bare, row upon row, their dry, brown leaves drooping and blowing together in the wind. A parched, papery sound. She stopped at the edge of the field, looking at its density in the middle. If she went in between the rows, she could not be seen from the house, and the old terror of entering a cornfield threatened to overtake her again. She smelled the damp fall earth at the edge of the section, hesitated, and above the grating, scratching sound, she heard her heart thudding against her ribs.

She put her hand hard against her chest to slow the pounding, and looking up said, "Oh, Lord, he's dead! And I'm thankful today! I know in my mind I don't *have* to be afraid in this or any cornfield any more, but I *am* afraid. Just can't help it, Lord. And I need help to forgive Solly, because I can't forgive him by myself. I'm thankful for brothers and John who love me."

She watched a large blackbird wheeling overhead, looking for food on the ground. She thought, *That bird is so free—and I guess I'm free in a way, too. I can be free from fear of Solly—what a relief!*

She shook her head. "But, Lord, I need help to live through this relief! Sometimes when people are relieved they don't quite know how to act without worry in the back of their minds." She reached down, scooped up some of the moist earth and rubbed it between her hands and nodded. "Lord, You gave us fine land to work on, and I'm a thankin' You again for it. I can't be so scared when I'm thankful."

She reached out to feel of some raspy leaves, and with great determination took a deep breath, straightened her shoulders and stepped into the russet field. Resolutely she walked to the center, looked back and couldn't see the house. There, she'd done it! She was alone in a cornfield for the first time in twelve years. She caught her breath then raised her face, smiled a little, and waved both arms at the big blackbird.

* * * *

She rang the bell on the post and her family all trooped in from the barn. John's eyes searched her face and she nodded to him. Though her hands trembled as she put the food on the table, John knew that her mind would now be free.

"You're a good cook, Julie," Joe said. "This beans and ham and cornbread is as good as I ever ate."

"She's the best," John declared. While they were eating John said, "Julia, How'd you like to move up close to your brothers and close to Herrin's Prairie? I met a farmer in Creal today—he came down to the hotel to get cured of somethin'. Said he has a farm about two miles south of Herrin that he wants to rent. Says it has a house big enough for lots of kids."

"Oh, John, I'd like that! We've lived here only two years and it's a nice place. But if we lived up there we could see my brothers and their families often. If that place is a good one, I'd like the idy of our young'uns growin' up close to all their cousins. I think families ought always to be close to one another if they can."

"Well, I thought that's about what you'd say. I figured you'd like it livin' that close to 'em. So I'll ride up with Joe and Caleb tomorrow and see the farm."

"Joe, if we can get the place, will all you wonderful brothers each bring a wagon down and help us move? Will you ask Will and Matthew for me?"

"Course, Julie," answered Joe. "We'd be glad to have you move up there—we just don't get to see you enough."

"Did you say it's close to a school? What about a church? Any close to this farm?"

"Yep. And I know that farm," Caleb said. "It's a good one. We'll shore be glad to help you get there!"

"The man said young'uns only had to walk a mile and a half to school," said John. "Any young'un can do that. He said there's a church near too. Herrin's Prairie's gettin' to be a good-sized village, you know, lots of people comin' in. Maybe we can see Ed sometime. Carterville's not far away."

"Yes, I miss him, I miss Milt, too. Wonder how he's gettin' along in West Virginia with his new wife? I hear she's a fine girl."

Two weeks later the move was accomplished. A wagon train of five went north from Creal Springs, through those verdant Ozark hills and woodlands, and on up through Marion. Julia was amazed when she saw Marion again. How that town had grown during the last five years! Julia hadn't seen it since her wedding day when she and John had passed through on their way to their first home.

About eight miles on northwest from Marion they came to their new place. It would be home to them for many years. The house had four bedrooms and plenty of space for the children to play and run, live and work.

When they piled out of the wagons this time, Dora was nearly sixteen; Dona, thirteen, Eva Jane was ten and Julia could hardly believe it! George was five and Henry was a three-year-old mischief maker.

The girls helped to scrub up the house and get settled in. "I hope we stay here a long time," exclaimed Dora. "I'm tired of movin' ever' two years."

Julia, so happy to be near her brothers and their families again said, "I think we'll stay here a long, long time." And to herself she said, *And I don't have to be afraid of ever seeing Solly again.*

* * *

When Dora was sixteen, John knew love was in the air for her. She had met Wallace Nall, a fine looking tall young man who intended to become a preacher. Wallace rode out to John's farm several times to "call on Dora." At the end of the summer, Wallace asked, "Mr. Childers, I'd like to marry Dora. Will you give me your permission?"

John and Julia were not surprised, because they'd been noticing Dora's manner each time Wallace had come. They knew she was in love with him.

John answered, "Now, Wallace, you know Dora's pretty young—but then you are too. How are you going to make a living and support my daughter with your preaching? Are you goin' to be gone around the country all the time and leavin' her alone?"

"N—no, Sir," answered Wallace. "I intend to preach nearby. I aim to start and preach in a church. But I am also a good carpenter—my father and brothers—we are all carpenters. We build houses, and I can make a good living."

John already knew that. He had asked some people about Wallace and had received good reports about him. He called Dora to come in.

She came in looking at her shoes and trying to hide her shaking hands.

"Dora, you know what Wallace asked me. I want to know what you think about him."

"I want to marry him, Pa." Dora looked at Wallace and a deep red stained her cheeks, but she bravely went on, "I know he's a fine man. He's a Christian and gonna be a preacher. He will treat me real good."

"You think he can make a livin' for you?"

She nodded. "Yes, I know he will. And he'll make a good preacher, too!"

"Well, if you're sure you want to marry him, you can. We'll do well to have a preacher in the family. Who knows, we might need to have somebody baptized, or a funeral preached some day!"

"Oh, Pa!"

Wallace immediately began to build a small house for himself and Dora, and as soon as it was finished they were married. Dora seemed so young to John. He thought she looked like she was still "playing house." It didn't seem possible she was really grown up.

* * * *

The next year Dona met a farmer named Ed Hurley at a square dance. The first time Ed did the Do-Si-Do and grand chaining eight around a row with Dona, he wanted to marry her. She didn't take too much persuading, and they were married by the justice of peace in Marion without asking anyone's permission.

They came by John and Julia's house surprising them with the news. John had hoped she would wait a few years because she was so young. But since Dora had been married, Dona thought of doing nothing else but finding her own man. She had found him and her word was already given before John or Julia knew anything about it. What could they do then, except give Dona and Ed their blessing? They hugged her and wished them well.

While John took Ed out to show him their farm, Dona packed her clothes in pillow cases as Julia had done years ago. Julia opened up all her kitchen doors and drawers, gathered up a boxful of kitchen supplies for Dona, and put them with some canned food from her cellar in Ed's wagon. She and John kissed them good-bye.

Dona and Ed rode out of John's yard sitting close together on the wagon seat. It reminded Julia of her first ride after her wedding to John—how they'd sat like that on their wagon seat. But Dona and Ed didn't have six children riding behind them!

Ed's farm was five miles away outside of Lake Creek. Dona, in her new role as a wife, just kept on doing what she'd been taught to do all her life—farm work. But now she had someone of her own to do it with.

CHAPTER SEVENTEEN
More Additions

A year after their move to Herrin's Prairie, Julia began to give birth to girls. During the next nine years she had four—every one of them different, though a strong family resemblance existed in all of them.

Addie grew tall for her age with black hair and brown eyes. She had high cheekbones with a look of some Indian blood. Ola had brown hair and blue eyes and was sweet and quiet. She never wanted to hurt anybody's feelings. Ida had dark hair, grey-green eyes, and a temper which got her into trouble once in a while. Cena, born in 1900, was the wild one of the lot. She had curly brown hair, green eyes, was large-boned and sturdy, and she never saw anything or anyone—beast or man—that she was afraid of. Even from babyhood she adored her big brother Henry, and tagged after him all the time. They also strongly resembled one another.

How Julia accomplished it all, she could never figure out. She kept the house going, nursed every one of her babies—they were all crooned to and petted, and taken to the fields and put in the shade while she worked alongside of John. For that nine-year period of her life she was either nursing a baby or pregnant, all the while taking care of everyone else.

Those years for Julia were the same as for most farm wives and mothers—plowing, planting, growing, harvesting, garnering, loving, and giving birth. Julia was never still—how could she be? She always had food to cook, clothes to wash—in tubs on a wash board and hang out, or dry by the fire, and canning so they could eat during the next winter. The first freeze brought hog-killing time along with soap-making. In between were often crisis times with the children or the livestock.

Sometimes John sat up all night with a mare about to foal, and sometimes a sow rolled over and smothered two or three of her baby pigs.

With all the work was all the love. Julia never felt sorry for herself because she had so much work to do. She accepted this life as honorable. She had grown up a farm child, and farm life to her was what life ought to be. People ought to work. Her mother used to say, "Them that don't work, don't eat." And Julia often said the same thing to her children when they balked at doing an assigned chore.

Most of the time she could say to John, "I think we've got the best family of anybody around. Our kids all know how to work and get along with each other."

"We got a good family, Julia. We don't spoil 'em. Course, we got *some* problems once in a while . . . ."

Ida and Cena, the two youngest of the girls, were more than big handfuls for any mother, and sometimes Julia was at her wits' end in disciplining them.

One day when Ida was about seven, she and Ola, who was nine, walked home together after school. When they came into the kitchen, Ida's face was a thunder cloud. "Mama," she demanded of Julia, "how come you gave Ola a bigger apple in her lunch bucket than you gave me?"

Julia shook her head. "I'm surprised at you, Ida. You sound like a very selfish little girl. How can I get two apples exactly the same size, just so you won't get mad?"

Ida glowered at Ola and answered, "I don't want anybody to have anything bigger ner better than me!"

"Know what the Bible says, Ida?" Julia asked. "It says 'Thou shalt not covet.' That means you ought not to be jealous of what anybody else has. And it means don't be jealous of your sister's bigger apple. Behave yourself and one of these days *you* might get the biggest one." Julia caught Ida by the arm and gave her a little shake. "But listen to me now! I don't measure nor weigh the apples and I don't want to hear anything else like this again. If I do, you're goin' to get a hard smack."

Ida was partly repentant. "I'm sorry, Mama. I don't have to have the *biggest* all the time. Just give me one the same size as anybody else's!" But Ida couldn't stay contrite forever.

On Christmas morning she came out and found a doll with her name on it under the tree. She picked it up, looked it over and exclaimed, "Oh, you're a nice doll! I'm goin' to play with you."

Not long afterward, Ola came out and found a doll with *her* name on it under the tree. Ola's doll was bigger than Ida's because *she* was bigger. But taking one look at Ola's present, Ida couldn't stand the comparison. Her temper flared. She threw her smaller doll across the room and yelled, "I don't want no short-tailed doll for my Christmas!"

Julia came in just in time for the outburst, grabbed Ida and whacked her hard on the bottom. "Ida! Why don't you behave yourself and appreciate what you got? I'm plum ashamed of you for bein' so jealous of your sister's doll! And on Christmas, too."

"Yeah," goaded younger Cena who had just jumped out of bed. "You should never be jealous, Ida! Mean people does that and if you're jealous all your teeth might fall out."

"Oh, shut up, Cena!"

Though they often quarreled with each other, Ida and Cena were inseparable. Ida was more fearful of being hurt than Cena and tried to avoid any insecurity. Cena didn't seem to mind a little pain, and recklessly courted danger, charging like a bull into every situation. Ida usually tiptoed in.

Cena had reference to Ida's very loose front tooth which wobbled back and forth every time she talked. Though Cena teased her about it, Ida simply couldn't pull it out. She didn't want to see herself bleed.

"Why don'tcha pull that tooth out, Ida—it's just a rockin' in your gums?" Cena asked for the tenth time.

"I'm gonna pull it out when I want to. You just let me alone, Cena!"

"Cena!" ordered Julia, "let Ida alone—it's *her* tooth."

In fascination, Cena watched that loose tooth jiggle in Ida's mouth for a few more days. She was tired of Ida's procrastination. Younger but bigger than Ida, one day she just grabbed Ida, backed her up against the wall, and when Ida opened her mouth to yell, Cena jerked out the tooth.

"I was gonna pull it myself," wailed Ida, her hand holding her slightly bleeding mouth.

"Oh, you're such a big baby!" Cena was disgusted. "I bet that didn't hurt a bit. I hardly even touched it and I bet you can't squeeze even a penny's worth of blood out of it." Cena was nearly six years old.

Cena always worried Julia! She grew strong and seemed to be utterly fearless. She learned to ride a horse younger and rode it harder than any of the others. While she was very young, she learned to shoot a rifle, and could shoot straighter than any of her older sisters. Julia often hoped that with all her daring to do what the other girls wouldn't, Cena didn't kill herself some day.

* * * *

The family never forgot about the gingham. It was before Cena was old enough to go to school that Julia was in the barn lot one day, helping John hitch up the wagon.

"John, while you're in Herrin's Prairie today, if you have any money left over after buyin' flour and molasses and feed, buy some goods for us."

"Goods? What you need it for?"

"I need it for everything! The girls and I need dresses and the boys need shirts. I got to get to sewin' or them kids won't have anything to wear to school! And it's not goin' to be long before school starts, either."

"Well, what kind of goods do you want?"

"Oh, somethin' pretty. Red, maybe, for us and somethin' good for boys' shirts. Brown for them, I guess."

"How much do you want me to get?"

"Well, with all these dresses I guess you better get about thirty yards for us. Get ten yards for the boys."

"I'll see what I can find," he promised.

When John came home that evening, he hauled in a whole bolt of red-and-white-checked gingham and thumped it down on the eating table. "Hope you like this, Julia."

"John! So much of *this? All alike?* Didn't you get any goods for the boys' shirts?" She shook her head. "John, I've got to make 'em some school shirts!"

"Well now, Julia, I didn't see anything good for shirts and I didn't have time to waste." John took off his big hat and tossed it as he usually did. The hat sailed back through the air and like a homing pigeon landed on its peg by the door. "I saw this bolt—I know you like red—so I got plenty. You and the girls can have all the big skirts you want."

Thus began the worst year of George and Henry's lives. Julia had no money to buy any other cloth, so the boys wore shirts made of exactly the same gingham as their sisters' dresses. Three girls and two boys wearing the same fancy red and white!

The boys frequently came home from school looking quite messed up, but they marched home in triumph. The first time Julia saw swelled-up lips and bloody shirts, she asked, "What happened?"

"Some dumbbell made a big mistake," laughed Henry. "He said, 'Look at them sissies!' We showed him we ain't!"

* * *

Cena was almost six years old. The family had been growing fine, crops were good, children doing well in school (except Cena who hadn't started yet) and Julia was counting her blessings. Cooking supper and counting her blessings. During the counting, she suddenly realized she'd missed her monthlies—by three weeks already.

Oh, it can't be, she told herself. *I'm just gettin' old—I must be goin' into the change of life. Just a little tired lately. I ain't goin' to say anything about this to anybody!*

But three weeks later, she couldn't deny the symptoms any longer: no sign of monthlies, feeling tired, queasy stomach, wantin' to sleep more than usual. No doubt about it, she was pregnant again. She was forty-two years old and had already borne seven children.

She had to tell John, of course. "At first I thought it was the 'change of life' startin' early, John. After all I'm forty-two! But now I know I am goin' to have a 'change of life baby.' I declare, I thought we was through with havin' any more young'uns."

"I guess I thought so too, Julia. But it looks like this proves we're not old yet! Think you can do it again?"

"I'll do it again, and we'll love another one just as much as we love the ones we've got."

But many times during this pregnancy she thought she *was* too old to have a baby, she felt so listless and no'count. "John, sometimes I'm so weak I have to call the young'uns to take over some of my work."

"Well, call 'em! They're big enough to do a lot of your work and they know how, too! Julia, quit thinkin' you have to do everything. You need to rest more."

"But John, I've always been independent and I don't ever want to think I can't do what I want to do."

"Rest a mite, Julia," he coaxed. "You need it!"

Since Julia didn't know what the word "rest" meant, more than once she fainted in the effort to do hard physical labor. Most of the time the family didn't know when it happened. She was too proud to tell them.

One day a neighbor came over for an afternoon visit. Things like that didn't happen much in Julia's life. Mrs. Martin knocked.

"Well, hello, Gertrude. Come on in. Ain't seen you in quite a spell."

"Hello, Julia. No—guess we don't visit as much as neighbors ought to."

"Well, come in for some coffee. It's cold out today."

"Yes. I ain't seen you since I heard you was in the family way again, Julia. Baby comin' in March I heard. That won't be long now, from the looks of things!"

Julia laughed. "Not long—maybe another three weeks. How've you been? Your man Tom at home today?"

"No—he went into town. He's been in the house too long this winter and had to get out. How's your man?"

"He went into town too. Wanted to look up the doctor just to make sure he'd come when I need him. I ain't never had a doctor at a birth before. Always had a midwife. But John found a good doctor in Herrin's Prairie and he wants me to have him this time."

"Might be a good idea, Julia. You ain't as young as you used to be, you know. I brought you a present for your new little'un." Gertrude handed her a small package.

Julia opened it and found a beautifully embroidered, long white baby dress." "Oh, this is so pretty. I sure do appreciate this, Gertrude. You must 've spent a good long time makin' it. This is a baptizin' dress!"

"Well, Julia, it gave me somethin' to do. Most of my young'uns are gone now—just the one at home—and I like to do this kind of thing. Umm—this is good apple cake."

They drank their coffee, ate their cake and talked a bit. "You been feelin' well, Julia?"

"Just tolerable. Be glad when this baby comes, maybe I'll have a little more git up and go."

"Well, you got a good excuse to set around a bit. Us women don't have too much settin' time. I'll declare, Julia, I envy you. You are the luckiest woman! You got such a fine man and all these pretty young'uns, and another one a comin' and there's not a thing wrong with any of them. You know most people have at least one or two sickly children. Look at my family. Look at the Parkers and the Walters. All of us got one sickly child. Yes, you are lucky!"

"Sometimes I don't feel so lucky," Julia mumbled. "Sometimes I feel sorry for myself." She thought about little Ada. "We did lose a child—John's youngest—just after George was born. I loved that little girl. But now I'm goin' to have another one—I've had so many girls, guess I might as well expect another one."

"You oughta thank the Lord you got what you got! Lots of women would be glad to trade places with you!"

Julia nodded. "You're right. I ain't been thankful enough."

After Gertrude left, Julia sat quietly in her rocking chair with her eyes closed. She whispered,"Lord, excuse me for not bein' more thankful. Thank You, Lord for sendin' Gertrude and sayin' what she did. I ought to be more thankful—and I am. I appreciate my wonderful family. I thank You for John—my fine man. Couldn't be no finer anywhere. I hope You'll excuse me for not bein' more happy about this new baby comin' and feelin' sorry for myself. All You've ever done is to help me. So help me again to have this baby, make it healthy, and help me to be strong to raise it. Ever'thing good comes from Your good hand. Amen."

Early one morning in March, Julia knew it was time. She said to John, "Tell George and Henry to hitch up the wagon and take all the children to Joe's. I don't want any of them at home."

"We don't want to go to Uncle Joe's or anywhere else," Addie protested. "We'd rather be home for all the excitement. It's been a long time since you had a baby, Mama. We can help you here."

"Don't make us go, Mama! We want to stay with you." Addie, Ola, Ida, and Cena all begged her.

"You are all good young'uns and I'm proud to be your mama. But I don't want you here today. When the baby comes, you can come home. Be good at your Uncle Joe's, now. John, soon as they start, you go and bring the doctor. I'm gonna need him today."

By ten o'clock John was back with the doctor and Julia needed him.

The pains were far worse with this birth than Julia had ever felt before. *Probably because I'm so old,* she thought. *I guess anybody havin' their eighth baby ought to be used to it by now. But then a woman of forty-two shouldn't be havin' a baby at all!*

She felt strange—with a man attending to her while she was having a baby. Yet before long she was glad he was a real doctor. He gave her something to ease the pain a little. With the doctor coaching her at the last, she pushed harder and harder and finally heard the outraged squall. She was totally exhausted.

"You have a beautiful baby girl, Mrs. Childers."

John came in from the other room. He was wiping tears from his eyes. "I was shore worried because you had such a hard time, Julia." He smoothed her face and his hand felt good. "But we got another beautiful girl. What do you want to name her?"

They named her Olive. She *was* a beautiful baby with blond hair and big blue eyes. Julia looked down at her in awe. "John, how in the world can old people like us have a baby this purty?"

"You're not old, Julia—I'm the one that's old. But maybe the Lord just thought He'd give us an extra special blessin'." John smiled at the baby. "If that's what He thought, He sure worked it right."

That evening when the children all came back, they crowded close up around Julia's bed and looked with adoring wonder at the new baby. Cena exclaimed, "Mama, she's so little and her head is kinda pointed. I thought your baby would be lots bigger than that!"

"You was just about that size, Cena. And she'll soon grow out of her pointed head. It will be just as nice and round as all your heads are. This baby just had a hard time gettin' here."

"Can I hold her? When can I hold her?"

"In a few days, Now listen, all you girls. You are big girls now and you know how to do housework and cook for your Pa and your brothers. I've taught ever' one of you how to do things right. I want you to take over for a few days and let me rest. The doctor said I must stay in bed, and this will give you all a chance to show me how much you can do. Just let me rest and sleep all I can. Now go on, divide up the work and do it, and don't quarrel."

"What if we just can't do somethin'?" asked Ida.

"First you ask your Pa, or George or Henry. Only if they don't know the answer, then you can come and ask me. But between all of you, the work ought to be done right."

"Yes, Mama," they said, filing out of her bedroom. Then she heard them say, "Now I'll strain the milk and get the bread ready to bake." "I'll do the sweepin'." "You can do ironin'." "I'll do churnin'. "You can set the table and—"

"John, keep an eye on them. You know they're mischievous."

John leaned over her. "They'll do it. And you done well, Julia. You've had eight young'uns and you're still beautiful. We'll not have any more." He kissed her gently.

During the next few days Julia stayed in bed longer than she ever had in her life. She'd done hard physical work for so many years and never took much time for contemplation. *Now maybe my soul can take some time to catch up with my body.*

Her thoughts went back to the time when she and John were first married. Wasn't the Lord good to send John to her the way He did! Since that time their lives had been so full of work and children, that she'd simply not had time to reminisce. And, she thought, *I may not have any more time for years after I get up from here.* So during these few quiet days she took out many memories and examined them. Sometimes she cried and sometimes she laughed. And when John came to bed at night, she always had several happenings to remind him of.

CHAPTER EIGHTEEN
Family Ties

From the time John and Julia moved close to her four brothers and their families, they often enjoyed potluck dinners after church on Sundays. In the summertime, one of the brothers would put up saw-horses-and-board tables in his shady yard, and soon wagons full of kinfolks and victuals would arrive.

Milt, his lovely wife, Maud, and their family returned from West Virginia—he got homesick for southern Illinois. So they joined. Ed came too, and Dora and Dona with their families. Tables groaned with food, and children were supposed to shoo flies away with leafy branches. But they would forget about flies and climb trees or skip stones in the pond until their empty stomachs drove them back to the tables.

The men always sat down to eat first—and the children didn't like that one bit. The women and girls waited on the men while the kids hung around in the background. Their large hungry eyes peered over the edge of the tables and watched fried chicken disappear down big throats before it was time for them to eat. They always feared they'd never get anything, and the boys wanted to become men soon so they could eat first.

When young'uns had a smaller table of their own, an argument often broke out among the cousins over who had the shortest pulley-bone, who could rassle the best, who could play mumbley-peg the quickest, or who could shoot a sparrow off a limb with a sling-shot the farthest away. Sometimes they staged a tree-climbing contest, and mothers shuddered while their offspring soared in the heights. Sometimes they tamely skipped ropes, but not often. Cena always wanted to do something spectacular.

After the young'uns ate until near-bursting point, they'd wander off toward the pond, their mothers calling, "Now don't you go into that water 'til after at least an hour. You'll get a cramp."

Ida stuck close to Julia when the other children headed toward the pond. Cena usually teased her, "Come on in the water, baby Ida. I'll teach you how to swim and if you start to drown, I'll do the rescuin'. It's fun!"

"Fun for you, maybe," Ida would mutter. Terror struck Ida whenever she was near any water, because once Ola and Cena had thrown her into the pond and she landed beside a snake. She never forgot the panic of that moment and she never went swimming with them again.

After Olive was born, Julia was very proud to take her beautiful baby and show her off to everybody. The kids all wanted to hold her and when the others went swimming, Ida got her chance. But she never wanted to let anybody else hold baby Olive.

One Sunday afternoon, Julia said to Ida, "You can't always have things your way, Ida. You mustn't be jealous when somebody else wants to take a turn holding the baby."

"All right, Mama. Don't scold me. I'll try to do better."

Cena, listening, couldn't keep her nose out of Ida's affairs. "Yeah, Ida, you're jealous! You must grow up to be a good girl."

"Cena," Julia said sharply, "leave Ida alone and watch your own actions!"

"Yeah," answered Ida. "Look who's tellin' me not to be jealous. Do you remember what you done when you found out Mama was goin' to have another baby?"

"Na—I don't remember that. I didn't do nothin'."

"Yes, you did, Miss Cena. As soon as Addie told us Mama was goin' to have a baby and you wouldn't be the baby any more, you took to sittin' on Pa's lap all the time."

"I did not—"

"You did too! And one day he said to you, 'Cena, what's all this lap-sittin' you're doin' here lately?'

"And you said, 'Well, Pa, Addie says you'll soon be holdin' a new baby on your lap, so I'm gettin' my lap-sittin' in now before it comes!' And you nearly wore Pa out!"

Cena prissed around the table and said, "Well, Pa still holds me on his lap sometimes, so there."

In spite of their disagreements, Cena and Ida always stuck the closest together. If any mischief went on, Julia knew it would be caused by one or both of them.

They were about ten and eight years old when one spring Saturday John said, "I want you girls to plant corn today—here's the seed corn. Now do a good job." He sent them into the field with a huge bag full. That was hard work, putting all that corn into the ground, two or three grains in one spot, grains apart just so, and smoothing the dirt on top. They knew how to do it right—they'd been taught a long time before. But that didn't make them like it.

The sun was blistering, their bottle of drinking water was hot, and their bare feet burned. Their sun bonnets covered long, sweaty hair. They worked a good part of the afternoon but talked about something else.

"I wish we could just *go* somewhere," Ida said, sitting down on the ground for a few minutes. "I get tired of doin' nothin' but workin' all the time. Who wants to plant so much old corn all day?"

"Yeah, I'm tired too." Cena nodded. "Why don't we just quit?"

"We can't!" said Ida. "Pa told us to plant all this stuff."

"Well," argued practical Cena, "he don't have to know everything! Let's just bury the rest of this corn and go see some friends for a change. He'll never know anything about it."

"He will when no corn comes up!"

"But—maybe we'll be too big to whup by then!"

They didn't usually disobey their father—they had early learned it didn't pay. But before long they dug one big deep hole and dumped all the rest of the corn there. Then they scampered over the fields to see some friends, taking care to carry the empty bag home to their father in the evening.

The next Monday John said to them, "I'm goin' to town today to get some more corn. Don't you girls run off after school—I want you to plant it. You done such a good job on Saturday."

Cena and Ida dared not look at each other.

A month later John shook his head in wonderment, when a tangled mass of corn shoots humped above ground in a corner of his field. "Them girls! No wonder I had to buy more corn!" When he got to the house he called Julia. "Come go with me. I want to show you somethin.'"

Julia obediently walked with him to the corn corner. John pointed and said, "Look at that!"

Julia looked in surprise. "Well, I don't know what it is! I never saw anything like that before, John. What in the world could be growin' with such a big bump in that corner?"

"That's where all the corn went that Ida and Cena was supposed to plant. Remember?"

They both burst out laughing. "That's the funniest lookin' thing I ever did see," said Julia wiping her eyes. "What are you goin' to do about it?"

John was laughing too but he said, "We can't let them know we think it's funny. They didn't mind me—they didn't do what I told 'em to do, and they let us believe a lie. I'm not goin' to take the strap to 'em, but I'm not goin' to let them go to the school picnic this Saturday. They been countin' big on that, but they got to learn one way or another that it don't pay to be dishonest."

Two tearful, sorry little girls missed a school picnic and blamed each other.

"Nobody can ever predict what that Cena will do next," Julia told herself. "Things just seem to happen around her and Cena always does somethin' unexpected."

The unexpected happened three months later.

Henry, a handsome young man was still living at home and helping on the farm. One day after his noon dinner, Henry went out to lie down in the shade of the oak tree behind the house for a nap. As usual, Cena tagged after him, for she absolutely adored her big brother Henry.

Henry had just got comfortably situated in some soft grass with his straw hat over his eyes when Cena started a conversation.

"What 're you doin' today, Henry?"

"Weedin' the corn rows."

"Ma says I got to pick beans and tomatoes."

"You're good at that."

"Well, I oughta be good at it—sure have done plenty of bean and tomato pickin' in my lifetime!"

You sound like an old woman, Cena." He raised his hat brim off his eyes, "but you don't look that old. Now let me sleep before I have to get back to the field. I'm tired."

Cena obediently sauntered a short way off. She sat with her back against the house, her knees drawn up and her long skirt covering them. She kept humming and examining her bare toes.

"Cena," Henry shouted, "be still. Stop that singin' and let me sleep!"

"I ain't singin'. I'm hummin'."

"Then quit hummin'. I don't want to hear it!"

"All right then. I'll just watch all these bumblebees in the clover over here. And you wouldn't even care if I got stung with a dozen of 'em." She leaned back and warily contemplated one lone bumblebee harvesting a bunch of clover near her toes. She wasn't quite brave enough to swat it with her bare foot.

Julia's flock of chickens, as usual, was meandering and pecking in the yard. One old hen seemed particularly fond of Henry—she kept chirking close to his head and softly clucking near his ear as if crooning a lullaby for him. Finally Henry bellowed, "Cena, come over here and get this chicken away from me! This old hen is drivin' me crazy!"

Cena shot up from her bumblebee lesson. Always extreme in wanting to please Henry, she swiftly crept close, grabbed the hen, carried it squawking to the other side of the yard and skillfully wrung its neck. Henry, relieved, not realizing how she had accomplished the quiet, was already half asleep when Cena yelled, "Henry, you can sleep now! I wrung its neck and it's a floppin' in the rosebush!"

Julia heard the commotion from inside her kitchen and ran outside, wiping dishwater hands on her long apron. She grabbed Cena and smacked her bottom hard. Then, standing in judgment with hands on her hips she declared, "Well, I reckon we'll have chicken and dumplin's for supper. But Cena, you got to pluck ever' feather of that hen for me. I'll get water for the scaldin'."

Julia stalked back into the house still angry and still scolding Cena. "What's the matter with you? You know that was one of my best layin' hens. Ain't gettin' too many eggs these days. We need that hen a lot worse'n we need chicken and dumplin's for supper!"

Cena ambled over, stood beside Henry and Julia heard her say, "It's true them hens ain't layin' very good in this hot weather. But I won't tell Ma that I slip you some eggs ever' once in a while so's you can feed 'em to your horse! I know that raw eggs makes your horse's coat slick. And," with a shrug of her shoulders, "I don't mind thievin' for my big brother once in a while."

In spite of her frustration over the death of her good laying hen, Julia couldn't help but laugh when she reached her kitchen. She knew that Henry was Cena's favorite, and she'd noticed Cena's pride of Henry when he pranced down the lane on his beautiful horse.

* * * *

One sweltering day John went into town for some supplies. While he was in there, he got a shave and a haircut. And what a shave! He thought he was tired of wearing a beard—many men were clean shaven, and besides that his beard was too hot. So he told the barber to shave it off. When he looked in the mirror afterward, he didn't recognize himself. He'd worn a beard for years. His face felt very bare as he rode home and wondered what the family would say.

He was totally unprepared for the reception.

Julia came out to help him unhitch the wagon, took one look at him and wailed, "John! You've shaved off your beard! What did you do that for? I loved your beard—it was so pretty and brown and soft! And I remember how it tickled the first time you kissed me. But I liked the tickle. You just don't look like yourself at all."

"Well, Julia, I never thought it'd make any difference to you!"

"Oh, John, if I wake up in the night I'll probably be scared to death because I'll be sleepin' with a strange bare-faced man."

When the children came home from school they stood in the doorway and stared at the raw-faced, tall man sitting at the kitchen table. At first they didn't recognize him, but he said, "Well, come on in and shut the screen door. Don't stand there gapin' all day!"

All his girls started to lament, "Pa, you've ruined yourself. You don't look right any more."

Cena came over and sat on his lap. Tears were running down her cheeks. She put both her hands on his face and said, "Pa, you had the nicest beard of anybody and I liked it. I didn't want you to get rid of it—you just don't seem like my Pa any more!"

The children looked at Julia and asked, "You like him with his beard gone, Ma?"

Julia, looking sad, pursed her lips and shook her head.

John couldn't stand it any longer. "Well, if you all are gonna carry on so, I'll just have to grow it back."

"Will ya, Pa?" asked Cena. "That'd be nice—I like to rub your beard. You feel like a soft little puppy dog when you have a beard."

* * * *

Mike came not long after that. Mike was the children's favorite cousin—but more like a little brother than a cousin. He was George's son. George had been married very young, and shortly after Mike was born, his wife died. George could not raise a small child alone. His Grandma Julia took him. He was a little younger than Olive, so in her forties, Julia started all over again with two toddlers. Mike, small for his age, sped around the house like a squirrel, investigated everything, was quick-witted and funny. He always thought up stories and made everybody laugh. Julia loved Mike as much as the other children—and counting little Ada who died—Mike was the fourteenth child that Julia had cared for.

Discipline was strict but fair. She and John had always worked together and agreed on disciplining the family. From the beginning, John's wide leather strap that he honed his razor on was the main instrument of discipline. The children were never "abused," but they were taught to do right, were taught truth from lies, and were taught to respect their parents. If they didn't obey, they got a few whacks with the strap where it did the most good. John would never allow any of the children to "smart-mouth" or talk back to

Julia. They had to obey her and respect her, or John took action. He had to be strict; otherwise, with such a big family, chaos would have resulted.

There was one law—John's law. It was a fair, moral law that John got from the Bible: "Children, obey your parents"; and he and Julia also got their instructions from the Bible, "Parents, provoke not your children to wrath." Yes, discipline was present, but also love was present, and every child felt secure. As a result, the Childers family loved one another and would rather be with each other than with anyone else.

Julia and John took time to talk together about everything—their work, their children and themselves. John was a strong, good man. She knew she could never have found a better man, nor a man she could love more.

In cold weather when they rested from outside work, besides her knitting, she cut and sewed and pieced quilts, and taught her daughters to cook and sew and quilt.

No bit of cloth was ever thrown away. Even the tiniest piece, especially any bright-colored scrap, wound up in a quilt or comforter. The family could remember all their past clothes—and places where they wore those clothes, by just looking at their covers. Keeping a growing family warm on cold winter nights taxed all their fingers.

Julia never had a sewing machine. She sewed in her rocking chair which had belonged to her mother. When they had moved up close to Herrin, again it had rocked gently atop a trunk in the jolting wagon all the way up from Creal Springs. That rocking chair had been part of her own life and every one of her babies'. They'd all been nursed there. Julia loved to sit in it with her sewing on her lap, watching a quilt or comforter grow—row by row.

She didn't know where her mother had acquired the chair—it had always just been there. It was the most comfortable chair she ever sat in. Large, hand-woven wicker with wide arms. The arms were low enough to support an arm holding a nursing baby. The seat was wide enough for a mother with a couple of children climbing over her. Its high back angled at just the right height to rest a weary head for a nap. She couldn't imagine her home without the chair.

When the wicker in the seat grew frail, she turned it upside down and wove twine back and forth through the wicker strips for reinforcement. The chair was old—she sometimes thought she may be getting like the chair—old and tired.

CHAPTER NINETEEN
One by One

As happens in every family, one day the children are all underfoot; the next day they're grown up and gone. And the house whispers with memories.

Ed and Milt had been the first to go, then Dora and Dona. Julia began to dread the day when her own first daughter, Eva Jane, would find the man she couldn't live without.

About three years after Dona left, Eva Jane began mooning around the house with stars in her eyes. Bill Scott was in Eva Jane's class at school and they had known each other for a while, but suddenly he began to "notice her." And her whole world took on new meaning. She told Julia about him—how he looked at her and how she slanted her eyes at him—and with every glowing word, Julia knew the time was near. Mentally, she began to help Eva Jane pack her things.

At the end of the school year their class went on a picnic to the country churchyard. After finishing off their fried chicken and baked beans, Eva Jane and Bill strolled away from the rest of their friends. Once out of sight around a little hill, they pretended to be looking at the gravestones in the burial grounds but they looked at each other more. "You sure are a pretty girl, Eva Jane. You look a lot like your mother. You got her curly hair and brown eyes. . . " Bill caught her around the waist and began kissing her and she never even thought about resisting. A thought did cross her mind that Bill Scott was a handsome young man with bright blue eyes and light brown hair. He was not much taller than she was.

"You my girl, Eva Jane? Have you ever kissed anybody else like this?" Because he kept it up, she couldn't answer his questions. She just shook her head, but not so hard she'd have to leave his lips. She kept on enjoying all the new sensations flooding her whole body. They both felt new spring in their blood and rising hormones. Bill mumbled, "You like kissin' me as much as I like it?"

Eva Jane took a minute to catch her breath and looked back over her shoulder to see whether any friends had followed them to the cemetery. Nobody in sight. She looked up at Bill, kissed him again and nodded. "I like it." Then her face flushed a bright red.

"Eva Jane. let's get married. I think we've had enough goin' to school. What do you say? We're grown up now—we can get us our own house and I can get a job in the mines. No sense in fooling around and thinkin' about goin' to high school."

"I know my mother wants me to go to high school. But I'd rather marry you. Guess we better tell 'em when we get home."

They settled down on the north side of Herrin, and Eva Jane proved to everybody that her mother had taught her well. Her house was spotless, and when she had her first baby, he was petted and crooned to and cared for just as she had been. Eva Jane knew how to knit and sew, and as John had predicted, she was one of the best cooks in Herrin. Bill Scott was a fine husband and provided as well for his family as did any other miner. In the time when affection between husbands and wives was not demonstrated in public, Eva Jane didn't care who knew that she and Bill were very much in love!

George had left home to work in the mines when he was only eighteen, and before long he was married to a beautiful young girl.

Henry had gone only through the sixth grade when he quit school to work on the farm. For a few years he worked alongside Julia and John, but when he was sixteen he wanted more money and went to work in a Herrin Coal mine. Every payday, Henry tucked most of his money away. He was secretly saving it to fulfill a lifelong dream.

When they sat down to supper one evening he said, "Ma—got somethin' to tell you. I'm goin' to California."

Julia gasped and dropped her fork. "California! That's clear across the country. It's so far away it might as well be around the world. Why do you want to go there?"

"Well, Ma, I been workin' now for two years, and saved some money. I got 'California fever.' Lots of people got California fever and are goin' out there. I've seen pictures of California and it's summertime all the time there. They grow oranges and lemons—and a fellow can make a fortune."

"Oh, Henry, I don't want you to go!" cried Cena. "I'll never see you again!"

"Don't go, Henry. What'll we do without our big brother?" Ida was rubbing her eyes, but the tears rolled.

"Don't see what you got to go so far away for," grumbled John. "You're makin money here! You can find a nice girl and settle down."

"Well, Pa, it's awful hard work in that black hole in the ground. I'm just wantin' to do something different."

So Henry, over objections of the whole family, took a train over the wilderness and desert and landed in Pasadena. There he worked at various building jobs and seemed happy, but wrote that he missed them. They received many postcards with California scenes, some of them pictured Henry on golden, sun-warmed beaches, sitting with California girls in big hats.

"Look at them girls!" accused Julia. "I bet they're just throwin' theirselves at Henry. They probably never saw such a handsome man before! He's goin' to get in trouble out there. He ought to come home!"

"I imagine Henry can take care of himself," John commented.

"But with so many young'uns gone," lamented Julia, "I feel just like an old hen cluckin' around and only a few chicks to cluck over! And I don't want Henry out in California sittin' on beaches with California girls—hats or no hats. I want him to come home. He's just too far away—to me it's like he's clear over in China—wherever that is!"

Two years limped slowly by—everybody missed Henry. One afternoon Cena came galloping breathlessly from the mailbox on the lane. She was waving a letter and yelling at the top of her voice. "Henry's comin' home! Henry's comin' home!"

Julia jumped up from her churning on the back porch, forgetting her half-made butter. The dasher slowly settled to the bottom of the churn by itself. "He's comin' home?" she asked. "Henry's comin' home? Read me the letter, Cena."

Julia wept for joy. "I bet he never got no cookin' out there in California like he got at home!"

"Yeah, Ma," teased Cena. "He's comin' home just to get your cookin'!"

"Well, I tell you, Julia's cookin is worth comin' home for," exclaimed John.

"I just got homesick," said Henry two weeks later, sitting down at the table after he had arrived on the Marion train and hired a horse to ride home. "And Ma, nobody in California can fry chicken and make them biscuits like you can. They don't know how to fry chicken right, and they just eat store-bought bread in California! Got so I couldn't stand the stuff."

"I told you so!" said Julia to the family. And to Henry, "I'm glad you left all them girls in the big hats!"

Cena, now fifteen, had scooted her chair very close to Henry, and she broke in, "Yeah, Henry, Ma couldn't stand to look at them beach pictures with you and the California girls."

Henry laughed.

* * * *

Henry had been home a short time when he started to work in the coal mines again. This time he seemed satisfied. He came in after work one night and Julia was cooking supper. "Where's Pa?"

"He's out in the garden of course, he'll be in soon."

"Got something to tell you, Ma. Remember Wallace told me about the girl that's playin' the organ at his meetin's?"

"Yes. He likes her. Did you meet her? What's her name?"

"I met her. Her name is Pearl Baxley."

"You know, Henry, that Wallace is some powerful preacher! He's been holdin' meetin's ever since him and Dora got married. People just flock to hear him preach. Guess Dora's got a good man. What about that girl?"

Henry repeated, "Her name is Pearl Baxley."

"Where'd she come from? What kind of family did she come from?"

"She lives in Herrin. And Ma, she's the purtiest girl I ever saw. Wallace said he thought so too."

Julia pursed her lips and teased him. "Do you think she's purtier than some of them girls in the big hats in California?" She opened the big oven door.

Henry grinned, grabbed a towel from the back of a kitchen chair and lifted a pan of hot biscuits from the oven. He plopped the pan in the middle of the broad eating table, picked out a corner biscuit then tossed it from one hand to the other to cool it some. Biting down through half the biscuit, he threw back his head, closed his eyes and murmured, "She's purtier than all of 'em. Ummmm, if I just had sorghum and butter on this biscuit . . ."

"You can have it when we eat."

Henry swallowed the biscuit, leaned against the cabinet and looking straight at Julia said, "Ma, she's little—just five feet two inches tall, and she's got big blue eyes and light brown hair that glistens in the sun—like it's a sparkin' red. Thick, thick hair. I didn't see it down, but she said it's long enough she can sit on it!"

Julia sighed. "Sounds like you got it bad." Expertly she sliced part of a baked ham and laid the pink, juicy pieces on a platter. "I think you sound like you feel 'bout like I felt when I first saw your Pa. This must've come on you purty fast."

Henry nodded. "You'd like her. She's smart. She can read them music notes and play the organ just fine. She plays for Wallace when he has a revival, you know. And she's Wallace's niece—her mother was Wallace's sister who died when Pearl was little."

"Wallace's niece! I've not met her."

"Well, you will. She's had a hard life though—growin up in Makanda. She told me about it."

Makanda! For a moment Julia's hands stopped and her heart pounded hard. Though she had loved John all these many years, the name Makanda always brought sorrow to her mind. Seth, whom she had once loved, had met a girl in Makanda—and married her. When Julia lost Seth, she'd thought she'd never live through such sorrow. She couldn't help but think about it all sometimes.

"Ma—? What you thinkin' about?"

Instantly, Julia turned to dish up the green beans. "How long've you known this girl?"

"Oh—a few months."

"Seen her lots of times?"

"Uh-huh. She's good and sweet, Ma. A lot like you. And she's not so young—just a purty young woman."

"I was afraid you'd get caught by some gigglin' girl who didn't have sense enough to hook up her own corset!"

"Not me! I like Pearl. She's so purty and she can cook and sew . . . and she's got a job workin' in a laundry in Herrin. Works too hard. I want to marry her and get her out of that place."

Julia sighed again. But she knew Henry was bound to marry sometime. "Well, if you're thinkin' of marryin' her, bring her to dinner this Sunday after church and let us all get acquainted with her."

"I will. This Sunday. I'll bring 'em both."

Julia, already planning what to cook for Sunday dinner, missed Henry's last short sentence. Muttering to herself, "I got plenty of fryin' chickens, here's this ham, I'll get up early and make some apple pies . . ."

Julia dished up a mound of fried potatoes, filling a big bowl. Henry set it on the table for her. "Let's ask the rest of the family to come—Eva Jane, Addie, Ola, and all of them. I want them to meet Pearl. I'll have your Pa to ride in to Herrin this week and ask them. I want George and his new wife to come too. George's got one of them fancy picture-takin boxes—he can bring that out. We've had no pictures made lately. I see John a comin'. Call the girls and Mike—supper's ready."

The Childers family gathered that first Sunday in June of 1915. Excitement hung in the air as palpable as the odor of fried chicken and apple pies. Henry was bringing his girl home to meet the folks!

John, George, and the sons-in-law were sitting in kitchen chairs out under the trees in the back. Julia and the girls were in the kitchen turning chicken, stirring green beans and gravy, slicing ham, and watching the biscuits. Julia kept one eye on the lane watching for Henry. About one o'clock she saw Henry's high steppin' horse pull his buggy up close to the house.

"They're comin'! They're comin'!" yelled Ida, Cena, and Olive.

Henry stopped outside the kitchen and all action ceased—everybody's eyes on Henry's new girl. They saw Henry jump down, reach back in and, his hands around her waist, lift a lovely young woman from the buggy. Her thick hair shone like copper in sunlight, and she had on a cool, voile dress. She turned around, her big blue eyes taking in his family, a shy smile on her lips. But wait! Who else was in the buggy? Henry turned again, reached in and ceremoniously lifted down a dark-haired, sweet-faced little girl, about three years old. He set her lovingly down beside Pearl, took a deep breath and announced to them all, "Folks, meet Pearl Baxley. And this is her little girl, Helen. They're goin' to join our family in July!"

George's camera clicked and recorded for all time Henry, Pearl, little Helen, and the horse and buggy.

Standing outside the kitchen screen door, Julia's first reaction was shock. She hadn't known that Pearl had a child. Did Henry tell her that? Surely, if he had, she'd remember it. And something about Pearl's eyes, Julia thought they had a sad, almost a haunted look, as if she were afraid of being hurt.

Julia thought, *I wonder why she looks sad. Maybe she feels like I felt when I introduced Eva Jane to John thirty years ago. Thank you, Lord for John. Without him I wouldn't have had my fine family. Now John and me—we're gettin' old, but I hope we still have lots of years together. And Henry—we'll have to let him go.*

Henry—so handsome, standing there with his new wife-to-be. Blinking back her tears Julia prayed, *Lord, let this purty girl find in Henry the same kind of love I found in John. He's a lot like John, so he'll be good to her. And Lord, take her sadness away.* Stepping off the porch, she ran to meet Pearl and Helen, her arms wide open.

PEARL PROLOGUE

Gentle spring rain danced on the roof and slanted down the attic window, clearing ribbons in the dust. I hardly noticed. I, Ruth, sat misty-eyed on the attic floor gazing at my mother and father's first picture together. How happy they were! Still, as I looked at Pearl, my mother, I could see a kind of haunting sadness in her eyes.

Though Pearl and Julia had not known each other before, their spirits were inextricably bound together from the first meeting. Julia welcomed Pearl and little Helen into her large family and they were molded together in love.

As I leaned over the humpbacked trunk to tuck away Julia's cherished album, I felt on holy ground because of God's grace upon our family. Tomorrow I would open Pearl's album and be blessed anew.

CAST A LONG SHADOW

Book II

PEARL

1893 - 1915

CHAPTER TWENTY
Makanda

"Fanny Pearl! Where are you?"

Pearl and Bill had gone for a hike over the Makanda hills. The children walked down the curving road for a while, then struck up over a hill close to the Methodist Church. Pearl could climb like a wild goat. "I'll beat you to the top," she called, her strong, short legs leaving her brother behind. Soon out of sight in some scrub, she was hiding behind a big tree when Bill topped the ridge.

"Fanny Pearl! Come on out."

Fanny Pearl, six years old, slid out from behind her tree shelter. "Don't call me Fanny. You know I hate that name!"

"How come you hate it? It's your name."

"I know it's my name and I don't know where Pap got it. I will never tell ANYBODY that's my name. My name is just Pearl. And the Bible says I'm of great price!"

"So I'll call you 'Just Pearl.' I don't know anything about that great price."

She had to giggle. Bill could always tease her out of anger or disappointment. "Let's go over here and set and eat. Got the water?"

Bill reached inside his shirt and drew out a corked whiskey bottle. He had stashed it in the waistband of his ragged shorts and secured it with his suspenders.

Pearl looked at the bottle. "Sure that's WATER?"

"It's water. Pap finished the whiskey last night."

"And did you rench it out good? I don't want no whiskey smell in my drinkin' water."

"It's clean."

Pearl took from her skirt pocket a huge chunk of cornbread, broke it and gave half to Bill. They ate the bread and drank water from the bottle. Pearl wrinkled her nose. "Maybe YOU can't, but I can still smell that whiskey. I hate that smell!" She wiped her sweaty face on her long skirt—not a very clean skirt. "Hey, Bill. Let's ask Pap to take us to the circus."

"What circus?"

"Well, I heard him say they's a circus comin' to Carbondale. I guess that's far away but maybe we could go in the wagon."

"You know what happens ever' time we plan to do somethin' with Pap!"

She nodded—wise beyond her years. "Yes, but maybe it won't happen this time. Pap's always in a good humor when he ain't drunk. And he knows we don't get to go nowhere. All we can do is work in the garden and do dishes all the time." She sighed. She *did* work hard for a six-year-old. "I have to stand on a kitchen chair and wash dishes in them two big dishpans for all eight of us."

Bill kicked a stone. "Well, when I get a little bigger, I'll have to do farm work on the place or pick fruit for somebody else when the fruit is ripe."

Pearl sighed again. "We help stepmother in the house now—I'm glad you don't have to go to the fields yet. Course, sometimes she sends us to pick beans or tomatoes or corn."

"Aw, that don't hurt us—we help eat 'em. Just Pearl, guess we better be goin' home. We don't want to get yelled at again—by her."

Pearl nodded. "Maybe, but SHE won't do anything to us—and neither will Pap. He's asleep."

Pap was often asleep. William Jehu Gibbs was a drunk (they didn't use the no-blame word "alcoholic" in those days). And almost as much as he was at work, he was at home "sleepin' off a drunk." Pearl hated to go into the house and hear the snores and smell the stench of his clothes and of his whiskey bottles. Still, she loved Pap.

Pearl and Bill skidded down the grassy slope past the Methodist church on their way home. Pearl looked at the church and stood for a moment pushing an ant hill with her toe. "Wonder why we don't come to this church? Why do we always go to the Baptist?"

"I donno." Bill shook his head. Bill was eight. "Maybe only heathens come here. Somebody said they don't baptize right in this church."

Their bare feet raised plup-plups of dust on the road as they ambled home. When they entered their yard, all was quiet. "Stepmother must be taking a nap."

Their hound dog, from his favorite hollowed-out spot between the oak tree roots, raised his head and beat a few welcome thumps with his tail, but he didn't get up. The children stretched out on the slanting porch floor for a rest.

Fanny Pearl Gibbs was born in Makanda, Jackson County, in Southern Illinois on April 6, 1893. Her birthplace was a rough country house with one long main room, two bedrooms, a storm cellar dug into the side of a hill behind their kitchen door, and a path with an out-house at the end. When Pearl was born, already five children lived in the small house: Ella, eighteen years old at the time and engaged to be married, George, Sam, Henry, and Bill.

Makanda was a Republican village and hosted many a political rally. Some dyed-in-the-wool Republicans said, "I'd vote fer a yaller dog before I'd vote fer a Democrat!"

If any newcomer to Makanda happened to be sitting on the political fence with his feet dangling on the Democrat side, he soon squirmed around so he could dangle his feet in the other direction. That was especially true when a well-known Republican speaker was coming. Most Makanda children grew up thinking that Republicans would be the only people going through pearly gates.

When Pearl was born, her brother Bill became her keeper. He carried her around when she was a baby and he was only two, later taught her to climb trees, shoot a slingshot, play marbles and "mumbley-peg," and take long hikes over the Makanda hills. He told her stories—very funny stories. Both Bill and Pearl could laugh when nobody else saw anything funny. Their sense of humor and their closeness helped them survive the almost unsurvivable.

Their beautiful mother, Elizabeth Nall Gibbs, died when Pearl was a baby. And it wasn't long until Pap Gibbs brought in a succession of wives who did what they could to "bring up" little Pearl. Her first stepmother (whom she liked) was a young widow named Furlow who had a mischievous red-haired son. He and Bill and Pearl played together. But when Pearl was four, Mrs. Furlow Gibbs died, and now they had another stepmother. Pearl and Bill didn't think this one was so nice.

Living in Makanda was rugged. About 350 people lived between the two high, rocky hills, through which Old Drury Creek flowed and sometimes flooded. The village boasted a flour and feed mill, a shoe shop: shoes made new or repaired, a bank, post office, a place where coffins were fashioned, a drug store, two hotels, cooper shop, barber shop, a soda fountain, some general stores, and a saloon. The saloon was where Pap Gibbs could usually be found. A restaurant stood by the railroad tracks, handy for train crews to eat when the trains stopped for water.

The screen door opened and Pap Gibbs shuffled out onto the porch, rubbing his reddish-brown-stubbled beard and combing his hair with his fingers. Pearl and Bill sat up.

"Pap," exclaimed Pearl. "Didn't you say they's a circus coming to Carbondale? Can you take us, Pap? Huh? Can we go in the wagon, Pap?"

Pap squinted his sleepy eyes at the afternoon sun. "Well, now, I don't know, Pearl. That's purty far. Expensive, too."

"Oh, Pap—let's go. We ain't never seen a circus. When does it start?"

He sighed and sat down on the porch with his feet resting on the second step from the top. "I'll think about it. Starts tomorrow."

That night Pearl went to sleep dreaming of elephants and tigers, and pretty ladies flying through the air on swings—like she'd seen in some picture books.

The next day Pap worked in the field all day and came home only in time for supper. After gulping down some ham hock and pinto beans, he said, "I'm kinda thirsty—them ham and beans was too salty."

Pearl jumped up. "I'll get you some fresh water from the well, Pap."

"Don't bother, Pearlie. I'll just walk down the street and get a little drink there." He picked up his battered felt hat from beside his chair at the table, stuck it at a rakish angle on his head and started in the direction of the saloon.

That's exactly what Pearl was afraid of. She ran beside him. "Pap, come on back home." She tugged at his arm, "Don't go down there. If you go there, you'll forget all about takin' us to the circus tomorrow. Can we go, Pap?"

"I'll see, Pearlie. Go on back home. Gotta wet my whistle fer a while."

Pearl turned around and shuffled home, dragging a toe through the dust, wiping her tears with the bottom of her dress. She knew Pap wouldn't be fit to do anything the next day. And if he drank as much as he usually did, then he'd get sick and vomit on the floor. And Stepmother would make *her* clean it up.

That's the way it was. That's the way it *always* was. The next day when she woke up, Pap was snoring with a bad smell in the room and he wouldn't wake up when she called him.

Stepmother was in the kitchen, and when Pearl went there, Stepmother handed her an old mop and a bucket of water. "That floor needs cleanin', Pearl. You can have breakfast when you finish."

Pearl knew better than protest. She took the mop and bucket and performed the same filthy floor-cleaning job she'd already performed many times in her young life. Then she took the bucket back by the privy and poured out the stinking water, leaving the mop to dry in the sun. Maybe the heat would make the mop smell better, but it never did.

She thought she couldn't stand any more, and ran out onto the front porch, sat on the step, leaned over and buried her face in her skirt. It made her mad to cry like a baby, but she couldn't help it. *Why* were things always that way—*everything* ruined by whiskey. Oh, how she hated it! The smell of it turned her stomach—it always smelled to her like vomit. She vowed at the age of six that she would NEVER marry a man who drank anything else but water! And the man she married would be nice to her. He'd never vomit on the floor and he'd take her to the circus, too.

The circus came and went from Carbondale, but Pearl and Bill didn't see it. They had to think up their own games when they could get away from Stepmother for a while. They liked nothing better than picnics out on the hills where they couldn't see the house or the saloon. Their picnic food was seldom anything more than a piece of cornbread or a cold biscuit, but imagination made it fried chicken and cake.

In late summer one day Pearl told Bill, "I got a headache so I don't feel like goin' hikin'. I just want lay down on my bed."

Bill looked at her critically and touched her forehead. "You do look kinda peaked—have you got a fever?"

She rubbed her head. "Don't know—I just don't feel good. Tell Pap when he comes home." She rolled onto her small cot.

When Pap came in from the field, Bill said, "Pap, Pearl's kinda sick. She's been asleep all day."

"She's jest tryin' to git out of some work!" was the diagnosis from Stepmother.

Bill was indignant. "No! Pap, she's awful hot."

Pap clomped into the bedroom containing three beds and Pearl's cot in the corner. He looked down at Pearl's flushed face and when he touched her, he drew in a deep breath. "Yep, she's awful hot. I better get the doctor."

Pearl had been stricken with typhoid and almost died. She was sick a long time, and not able to start to school. When winter came she was still very weak. Her hair all came out and she wore a handkerchief tied around her head. All her brothers were nice to her, carrying her around when she couldn't walk. Stepmother was even nice, for Pap laid down the law that Pearl wasn't to do any work around the house. Stepmother had to mop the stinking floors.

She didn't go to school at all that year. When she finally felt normal the next spring, her family realized that she was not hearing as well as she did before her illness. Pap hired a horse and buggy and took her to a doctor in Carbondale. Bill went along and he and Pearl pretended they were rich and the horse and buggy belonged to them. They addressed each other as "Mister Doctor Bill" and "Miss Queen Pearl" all the way to Carbondale.

The doctor examined Pearl's ears and told Pap, "I'm sorry for your little girl. But she has lost about a quarter of her hearing. It will be that way the rest of her life. I'm very sorry but I can't do a thing about it."

"Don't worry about it, Pap," Pearl said. "I can hear you good enough. I just can't hear all the birds sing like I used to."

Bill wanted to cheer Pearl up, so that Easter he gave her a fancy Easter egg. He had boiled it, dyed it and drawn pictures of flowers on it. He asked, "Pearl, do you want to make five dollars?"

Her eyes widened. "Five dollars? That's a lot of money! How can I make all that much?"

"I know you'd like to eat that fancy boiled Easter egg. But if you keep it for a whole year, next year at Easter time I'll give you five dollars!"

"Where you goin' to get five dollars by next Easter?"

"I'll earn it workin on somebody's land."

"Then you'll give it all to *me*? And can I eat the egg then?"

Bill laughed. "Heck, no. It'll be good and rotten by then. I just want to see if you can do it."

Pearl marched over to the small dresser where everything she owned was stored in one drawer. She wrapped the egg up in an old ragged, long black stocking and put it in the back corner of the drawer. "There. Next Easter I want my five dollars. And don't forget it!"

Sure enough, next year when she was eight, she collected her five dollars and threw the egg down the hill.

CHAPTER TWENTY-ONE
Herrin

One evening during Pearl's eighth summer, Pap said at supper, "I heard they's lots of work in Herrin's Prairie these days. Coal mines all over the place, and they want men to work in 'em. I think we'll move to Herrin and I can get a steady job."

"And can I go to a big school?" Pearl asked. She had not yet been to school at all.

"Well, I reckon you can."

"I want to go to school and I want to read all the books in the world! Is that where my Uncle Wallace and Uncle Beverly live?"

"That's it, Pearlie. We'll go to see them."

So they planned to move to Herrin. Pearl's oldest sister, Ellie, had married and was living in East St. Louis. Pearl's two older brothers, Henry and George Gibbs, said they didn't want to leave Makanda; they just wanted to hang around where they were. Henry wanted to court a Makanda girl, so George decided to stay with him. He thought he might find himself a girl, too. George said, "We're young and strong, and we can take care of ourselves. We can keep on hiring out by the day to work on farms. Course, Henry here knows what he's gonna do at night."

Ever since the late 1890s, Herrin's population had begun to multiply after rich veins of coal were discovered on the prairie. Enterprising teams with money began sinking mine shafts all around the village, and before long, more than thirty coal mines were operating within six miles of Herrin. Hundreds of men came to make their fortune. Rooming houses and small hotels sprang up, many provision stores and department stores were built around the main street. Laundries were started—some owned by Chinese immigrants. Families began to follow their men to Herrin, and soon the population increased to more than 15,000.

Herrin streets were dirt—no sidewalks at first, but here and there some boards were laid down. Streets were wagon-wheel-hub-deep in mud after a rain. But little by little, as Herrin's economy improved, main streets were paved with brick. Side streets, where larger houses were built, continued to be dust-covered and dry in summers, and in winter the houses fronted on muddy, rutted roads.

Surrounding Herrin on all sides were small mining camps. Families could live in compact, company-owned houses and be close to the mines, but also near enough to Herrin to be able to do some trading there. To get into town one could either walk, ride his own horse, or rent one from a stable.

Mine owners and bosses made the rules. For the most part, the rules leaned more toward enriching the owners, than toward keeping the workers safe.

Just before the turn of the century came the union. John L. Lewis (with the bushy eyebrows) had appeared as a political force in Washington, and his campaign was for the safety of coal miners. He began to organize them into a union and they flocked in droves to him. At last *somebody* with some power was doing *something* for them! He backed them up when they went on strikes for better safety laws and a decent pay scale. At first, the average was between $1.25 and $2.00 for a long day's work.

Herrin soon became a strong union town. If a miner refused to join the United Mine Workers of America, he was thought to be on the side of the bosses and not the workers. Few men wanted to be in that position.

Very young and unmarried men could make a good living working in the mines, but a married man with a family found the pay totally inadequate. After the union was formed, a day's wages advanced from a paltry sum to more than $7.00 a day. Even so, some families barely "got by," and much of the fault lay at the "company stores."

Coal companies ran company stores near each mine, stocked with most provisions and clothing. Miners could easily stop at their mine store on their way home from work and find just about anything they needed. Then they could walk out without any money changing hands. Their purchases would be "checked off" their next two-weeks' wages. If the miners lived far away from town stores and had no transportation, the company store seemed like a blessing.

Convenient. Yes. But miners paid much, much more for their purchases than they would have paid anywhere else. On payday their envelopes held very little cash to take home, and most miners were always in debt to the store.

In summer of 1901, Pap, Stepmother, Sam, Bill, and Pearl moved their small possessions in a wagon to Herrin, and it seemed to Pearl that Herrin was so far away it must be nearly to the end of the world. They found a house on the edge of Herrin's Prairie (as it was called then), and not too far away from school. The house had a big yard, where Pap and Stepmother could have a garden and raise most of their vegetables. Pap found a job at Number 7 Mine outside of Herrin and started to work.

Pearl's dream came true; she finally began school in September at Herrin's North Side School. She was older than any other child in the first grade, but she was so bright and learned so fast that the teacher told her she could skip a grade. When her teacher realized Pearl had a hearing problem, she gave her a desk on the front row so she could hear clearly.

Back in Makanda, Henry Gibbs' dream of winning the girl he loved was not coming true. Henry found no favor in her eyes. Perhaps the habit of drinking he'd learned from his father interfered, or perhaps she had eyes for someone else. Whatever the reason, Henry was a very unhappy man. After a dozen attempts to interest her, when she continued to show no inclination to soften her heart toward Henry Gibbs, he started drinking in earnest. Then one day he simply went out into the barn and shot himself in the head.

Pearl sobbed for a long time when she heard about her big brother Henry. She had not been as close to him as she was to Bill, but she did look up to him. Pap did not take her back to Makanda for the funeral—she and Bill and Sam stayed in Herrin. Pearl wished her sister Ella was still at home, but she did not have the comfort of crying on her big sister's shoulder. Brother Bill comforted her as he always did.

To Pearl, school was wonderful. Her mind soaked up facts like a sponge, and she didn't want to do anything but read. Of course, she had to learn lessons in "numbers," but she thought arithmetic was a waste of time. Reading was everything. It didn't matter whether she was reading history, social subjects or anything except arithmetic, if it meant reading it in a book, she learned it fast. She looked with awe upon her teacher who knew how to pronounce and spell *so many* words! She vowed she would be like that too.

Sometimes she visited her mother's brothers, Beverly and Wallace Nall, but most of her time she spent in reading.

One day shortly after her ninth birthday, she was waiting for Pap, sitting on the porch step when he came home from work. "Pap, when can we go see Uncle Wallace and Uncle Bev again? I've not seen them in a long time now. Specially I want to see Uncle Bev."

Pap eased his tired body down beside her and let out a long sigh. "We'll go one of these days, Pearlie."

"Can we go today?

"No, not today. I gotta dig up the garden some today, and

after supper I wanta go downtown and wet my whistle a little."

"Oh, no, Pap! Don't do that."

Pap looked uncomfortable. "Well—I ain't had a drink in a while now. And this is Friday—no work tomorrow—now don't worry, Pearlie. I'll be all right!"

She turned away to hide the tears. He was *never* all right after he'd had booze. "Then can we go next week? I want to see Uncle Bev about somethin' very important."

"What's that?"

"You'll find out, Pap. Did I hear 'em say once that they're carpenters?"

"You did, and I hear they're the best in town."

"Do they build houses?"

"They do. They've built some of the nicest houses here in Herrin. You know your Uncle Wallace is a preacher, too, don't you?"

"A preacher? Has he got a church?"

"Well—I guess so—don't know for sure. But he preaches in lots of churches—holds protracted meetin's too."

"What about Uncle Bev?"

"Of course, he's a carpenter too—and nobody was ever any more particular than your Uncle Bev. And he always looks like he just stepped out of the dandy box—even when he's workin'. I used to tell your sister Ellie that she was just like him. But Bev's sure a good musician, too."

Pearl nodded. "I know, Pap, remember we heard him play the time we was over there when we first moved to Herrin? That's what I want to see him about."

"You want to see him about playin' music?"

"Yes, I do. Pap, I want to learn to play the pump organ. Will you take me soon to ask him? And if Uncle Wallace has a church here that he preaches in, I'm goin' to that church. I'd like to hear the music and I'd like to hear him preach, too. Would you go to church with me?"

Pap fidgeted. "Well now, I don't know 'bout that. Me and church ain't very well acquainted."

One evening not long after that conversation—when Pap had not been drinking—Pearl persuaded him to walk over to Uncle Bev's with her. She knew the way but she wanted some help in case she had to do some persuading of Uncle Bev. "Come on, Pap!"

"Why do you want to go today, Pearlie? I've worked all day and I'm tired!"

"Come on, Pap. You promised you'd come."

Finally he agreed and she skipped alongside her father, her reddish-brown hair flying up and down on her neck. After she had recovered from typhoid, her hair had come in thick and wavy.

Uncle Bev was sitting on his front porch practicing scales on his violin. "Hello, Pearlie. Come on up and sit a while. How are you, William? Haven't seen you folks in quite a spell now."

"I'm tired to the bone, Bev," Pap answered as he sank into a porch chair and put his feet up on the bannister. "But Pearl here, she just *had* to see you today."

"Now, that's nice, little Pearl. I'm glad you came to see me. I do declare, you're lookin' more like your mama, Elizabeth, all the time. Bless my sister's soul, I'm sure she's watching you from Heaven and she must be proud of her little girl."

"I hope so, Uncle Bev." She paused and turned sideways for a few moments so Uncle Bev couldn't see her brush away a stray tear. Then—"I've got something important to ask you, Uncle Bev. Been thinkin' about it a long time now—"

"Yes, Child. What do you want to ask me?"

Pearl's big blue eyes sparkled. "Well, Uncle Bev, I want to know if you'll teach me how to play your pump organ."

Uncle Bev played a few more trills on his violin, his chin quivering on its top. Then he put the instrument and bow carefully in its case. "How much do you really want to learn, Pearl? It takes a lot of practice, you know. How often would you be willing not to play outside after school, and come over here and practice instead? You'd have to learn to read music, too."

"I know. I've watched the ladies at church looking at the song books when they play the organ there. I'll practice a lot if you'll let me come over."

He got up. "Well, let your daddy rest here a spell and you come on in the house and I'll show you how the organ works. Maybe it's too big for you."

When they whirled the round organ stool into just the right height for Pearl, and scooted it close up under the keyboard, Pearl's feet could barely reach the big pedals. Bev began to explain how the stops worked and how, when you pumped, the note was sustained. And how, when you played certain two notes at the same time, you heard harmony and not just melody. Soon her legs were tired with pumping. Then Bev gave her the first lesson in reading music notes—lines: "Now Pearl, these are easy to remember. E G B D F, for Every Good Boy Does Fine; and spaces: F A C E.

"My goodness—what a lot to learn—with tired legs, too. But I still want to learn, Uncle Bev. Can I come back tomorrow? Is it too much trouble for you to teach me?"

"I would like nothing better than to teach you, Pearlie. Let's start with three times a week, just until we get some basics. We won't have long lessons, but we'll have them often—then you won't forget."

So Pearl began to learn to play the organ and to read music. By the time she was in the seventh grade, she sometimes played in church.

Pap, though still often so drunk that he couldn't go to work in the mornings, managed to keep his job in the mines. He paid Pearl's school expenses, her clothes and shoes, and food—though food was meager enough sometimes. But she *earned* her keep. Many times when Pap (between wives) got drunk and messed up the floor, Pearl was the one who had to clean it up. Not only the floor—she also had to wash all the sheets and towels too, scrubbing them on the washboard with a brush to get the spots out. Every time she washed a stinking, stained sheet, her revulsion against liquor grew. It was almost a phobia—the way she hated booze.

Books were her release. She could become engrossed in a book and lose all track of time. Because she couldn't hear everything being said, she could easily immerse herself in a lesson, a story, or poetry. She kept practicing the organ too, going to Uncle Bev's almost every day.

CHAPTER TWENTY-TWO
Ray

Pearl finished the eighth grade at sixteen, late because of her childhood illness and moving. She started to high school in the fall of 1909, but her heart wasn't in it. When half the first year was up, two things discouraged any further education. One was her lack of ambition to learn algebra or anything related to it. It made absolutely no sense to her that A equalled 15, or whatever it equalled. Why *should* A equal anything? The big reason she couldn't think about school was that she met a young man named Ray Baxley.

Actually, she had known Ray for some time because he went to the same Baptist Church that she did. But lately Ray had noticed her! That made a great deal of difference. Ray was six-feet tall, dark brown hair, blue, blue eyes, and a square chin.

One night she played the organ in church, and after the benediction, he caught up with her outside. "Pearl, can I walk you home?"

No young man had asked her that before—she had usually gone places only with her brother Bill. So her heart began to pound as she smiled way up at him from her height of five-feet two inches, and said, "Yes—I guess so."

On the way home he confessed, "I've been lookin' at you a long time, Pearl. Been tryin' to get up my courage to ask you."

"How come you asked me tonight? What did it take to get up your courage?"

"Well," he grinned at her, "while you were playin' the organ in church, you looked so pretty and I said to myself, 'Ray, if you don't say somethin' to that girl, some other feller is goin' to.' That kind of spurred me on."

She giggled and answered, "I'm glad you talked to yourself. Do you do that often?"

He nodded. "Sure—when I want to talk to a smart feller," and their laughter rang out.

They walked fast through the frosty February night, but Pearl didn't even think about being cold. She thought, *Ray is very handsome, but I'm not going to tell him so.* Before they got to her house she said, "I can't ask you to come inside. The house isn't very big and Pap's probably snoring."

"Oh, that's all right. Can I see you at church next Sunday night and walk you home again?"

"If you want to."

"I want to. Goodnight, Pearl. See you in a week."

He left her at her front porch and went whistling down the street, his hands in his pockets.

She went inside to bed, but was too excited to sleep.

They were together after church and on Saturday afternoons, and as often as possible after that. She hadn't said anything to him about Pap's drinking, but was sure he knew about it. Word like that gets around town. Then one evening in the spring when he brought her home, they found Pap sprawled out on the porch snoring, with the odor of whiskey all over him. Pearl was so ashamed she covered her face and turned away.

"Don't cry, Pearl. How often does he do that?"

He held her as she wept against his coat. "All the time! I never know when he's goin' to be drunk or sober. It's been that way all my life. And when he gets sick because he drinks too much, I have to clean up his mess. I love him, but sometimes I hate him!"

After that night, Ray began to "court her" in earnest. She thought about him night and day—He interferred with her thinking at school. *In this algebra class I don't know what A equals, but R equals Ray, and L equals love!*

One day Ray said, "Pearl, let's get married. I'll stop school and get a job in the Buckner mines. They want men there. We can live in a company house and have a good life."

"Are you sure you don't want to finish high school? Maybe sometime you'll wish you had."

"I'd rather be married to you. I love you, Pearl. How do you feel? Do you want to finish high school?"

"I thought I did at first, but I'll never pass any kind of algebra or geometry. I love to read, but I can do that at home. Yes, I will marry you. I love you, too, Ray."

Goodbye, high school! Besides loving Ray, Pearl was glad to get away from the booze at home. Ray came from a large church-going family of seven children, and none of them ever touched alcohol. She was very proud of Ray and loved his whole family.

One of Pearl's stepmothers had taught her to sew when she was young, so she made her own wedding dress of white batiste trimmed in lace, with a high neck, long sleeves, and shoe-top length. They were married by the Baptist preacher in the fall of 1910. She was seventeen.

Pearl had virtually nothing of her own except a few clothes as a dowry—Pap had drunk up all the money he ever made. So when Pearl and Ray moved into a company house at Buckner, about eighteen miles from Herrin and close to the mine, she took all her belongings in one small trunk. Ray's parents gave them some bedroom furniture and a couple of chairs. And little by little she and Ray collected other necessities. Ray bought her a New Home pedal sewing machine and she spent hours using it.

Pearl glowed with joy as mistress of her own house. Though small and square with four rooms like every other house on the row, it was theirs! Sometimes Pearl felt like she was playacting. She kept the house spotlessly clean. Water had to be carried into the house from a pump on the little back porch. In summer she washed clothes in two large tubs which sat on a bench under the pump. In winter she brought the bench and tubs into the kitchen and carried water in, heating it on her four burner kitchen coal stove.

Ray always helped her when he could and he never left for work without filling up two coal buckets for her. She cooked on a coal stove in the kitchen, and a coal heater in the front room kept the house warm in winter.

Ray was a gentle, quiet, thoughtful man. Pearl was the one who talked the most—she could always think up funny ways to tell him about simple happenings and gossip in the coal mining camp. She was happier than she'd ever been in her life.

Ray loved her dearly—gently, and took her on picnics and buggy rides on weekends when the weather turned warm. Sometimes on Saturday mornings they'd sleep later than usual and then just lie in bed and talk awhile. He'd ask, "Well, Pearlie, what do you want to do today?"

"Uh—can we go in to Herrin? Let's go see Uncle Bev. Then we can go and have supper with your Ma and Pa and spend the night. They'd probably like to see you."

"They like to see you, too, you know. They're proud of their little daughter-in-law."

"You think they really like me?"

"I know they do. Let's get up—I'll go hire us a buggy. By that time you'll have breakfast ready and then we'll go."

They always enjoyed the long ride into Herrin, and often visited Uncle Bev. Pearl played the organ and they delighted in singing hymns from the church book. Uncle Bev would get his violin from its case and accompany them. Afterward, a country supper at Ray's folks was a treat. Pearl enjoyed sitting around the long table with some of Ray's brothers and sisters and their families who lived nearby. The Baxleys never needed any reason to get together—they just did it often. Ma Baxley's table was always loaded with excellent food, and she had also taught her daughters to be good cooks. Her house was the first place Pearl had ever seen in which all the silverware was kept in a large, glass vase sitting in the middle of the dining room table. One never wanted for a fork, knife, or spoon——they were always there in the center of the food.

The next day after church Pearl and Ray would drive back to Buckner—letting the horse set his own pace, simply enjoying the countryside and each other's company.

Pearl could never get enough to read because Buckner was not close to a library. So while Ray was at work, Pearl spent most of her time working in her house, cooking things that Ray especially liked, and sewing. She hemmed many sheets, towels, and she embroidered dresser scarves and pillow cases. In the fall of 1911 came the time to begin making baby clothes.

Sailing through her pregnancy, she never felt morning sickness, and had plenty of energy to keep on doing her work. She was so happy they were going to have a baby—and at night she'd lie with her stomach against Ray so that he could feel the baby move.

Their love was complete when on June 2, 1912, their beautiful baby daughter, Helen, was born. She had dark hair and blue eyes like her father, but her facial features were like Pearl's. Pearl had an easy time with the birth for which she was thankful. She'd heard the screaming in other houses, of women struggling hour after hour in childbirth. What a joy to have her own baby to love and to learn all about taking care of her!

* * *

Along with thousands of other miners in and around Herrin, Illinois, Ray worked in very dangerous circumstances. Working even a few feet underground can spell disaster, but these mines were very deep and tunnels narrow. Miners sometimes lay in narrow passages, wet to the skin, digging coal from the walls beside them with a pick-axe. Sometimes they dug on their knees. As they dug, fanning out further from the shaft in all directions, tunnels were inadequately shored up with beams and crossties. Consequently, coal falls and cave-ins were frequent. They used all their muscles wedging props under sagging ceilings of coal. Sometimes water seeped into passageways, making the workers all the more uncomfortable.

Sometimes built-up gas pockets were set off by the open flame of a carbide lamp on a miner's cap. Then a deadly blast would roar through the tunnels, leaving men dead, or blinded and gasping for breath. Men were frequently buried under rock or killed by gas when a passage was blocked. The light of their flickering lamps attached to the front of their special caps was the only light they had.

Every time Pearl kissed Ray good-bye in the morning, she said a prayer, asking God to bring him safely up out of that mine. She was always afraid, as were all the other miners' wives. Other men, friends of theirs, had been killed, but Ray came home every night safe and sound.

* * * *

On October 16, 1913, Pearl and Ray got up at four o'clock as was their custom. Pearl lighted a fire in their coal stove and cooked a breakfast of rolled oats, eggs, biscuits, and coffee. While Ray ate, she fixed his dinner bucket. After he finished, he went out the back door carrying the coal buckets. She heard him say, "Hello, Big Red," to his beloved hunting dog, which was lying in its favorite place on the back porch. Big Red was just as much a member of the family as any of them. Ray had owned the dog when he and Pearl were married in Herrin, and Red was now at home with them in Buckner.

Ray loved to hunt. He had trained Big Red to be a fine hunting dog and they made an excellent team. The two of them were close companions. Red accepted Pearl and he allowed Helen to crawl all over him and pull his ears, but Ray was his first love. Every day that Ray worked, Big Red waited for him. An hour before his master was due home, Red parked himself on the front porch to watch for his homecoming.

Pearl opened the back door, "Ray, it's 5:30—time to go to work." Then, "Hello, Big Red, here's your breakfast." She patted the big dog as she put his bowls of food and water on the porch.

"Coming, Pearlie," called Ray from the coal shed.

He came back carrying the large buckets brimming with small chunk or "pea" coal for her kitchen stove and large lump coal for the heater. "Don't want you to have to carry in these heavy buckets. You're too little."

"Oh—not so little. I'm five-feet-two-inches, you know."

"Yes, you come just about to my shoulder. That's little!" He set the coal buckets down beside the stove, caught her around the waist and swung her in his arms. Her hair was still down—since it was early morning. He smoothed the soft waves. "You look so pretty with your hair like that—like you're about ten years old!"

"You're a very handsome man yourself, Mr. Baxley. And if you don't be quiet, you'll wake up Helen. It's too early for her to get up—she'd be fussy all day. By the way, I'm old enough to be your lovin' wife, and as your wife, I'm reminding you to go to work. Be careful! I want you back home tonight."

"Yes, Ma'am. I'll see you tonight." He shrugged on his heavy jacket, settled his miner's cap on his head, and hooked his carbide lamp on the front of his cap above the bill. She handed him his dinner bucket and gave him an extra kiss and hug as he went out.

She stood in the doorway with her shadow thrown by a coal-oil lamp, and waved to Ray as he went down the path in the rain. She went back inside, ate breakfast, drank a second cup of coffee, and propped the week-old newspaper up against the sugar bowl. She had barely started to read when she heard Helen waking up. Helen, sixteen months old, was sitting up in her crib and jabbering to herself. Pearl picked her up, dressed her and gave her some cooked oats covered with sugar and rich, creamy milk.

Helen, a blue-eyed, dark-haired beauty, toddled after Pearl all morning as she did her usual housekeeping chores—sweeping, dusting, cooking, and washing dishes. She baked a chocolate cake for supper (Ray's favorite) while Helen had her nap. All day—for some reason—Pearl felt uneasy. Recent mine accidents—coal falling and men dying—were on her mind. She wished Ray had a different kind of job. But like his buddies, Ray was not unhappy working there. He was robust and full of life and they were happy together. He didn't want her to worry.

Helen awoke from her nap and Pearl played with her for a while. Then about four o'clock she said, "Let me change your dress, Baby Helen. Your daddy will be home soon and he likes to see his little girl clean and neat."

She dressed Helen in a ruffled pink dress which she'd made for her, and put a tiny pink bow in Helen's dark hair. Then she combed and puffed out her own hair on each side of her face with a rolled knot in back. Supper was cooking on the stove and Helen was playing with her doll. "Your daddy's late—I wish he'd hurry up." Several times she peered out the window at the cool, October rain.

Finally, about six o'clock she heard a knock at the door.

When Pearl opened it, two men stood there in the dark. They had on their mine work clothes and coal dust covered their faces—they had not yet washed after working underground. One asked, "Are you Mis' Ray Baxley?"

Fear gripped Pearl as she said, "Yes," and Helen clutched at her skirt, hiding her face from the strange men.

"Mis' Baxley, we got a sad duty to perform. We are so sorry to have to break this news to you. But Ma'am, your husband, Ray, was killed about an hour ago as he was comin' out of the mine after work. You got our sympathy, Ma'am."

Pearl stared at the two men standing in the dark on her little porch. She heard the words, but they made no sense. She stood still in shock. Then, "Did you say *'killed'?* How *killed* when he was coming out?"

The other man explained. "You know, Ma'am, your man was tall. Well, as he was a'comin' out, there was a live wire that had sagged down too far from the ceilin'. One of the crossties holdin' it had come loose. In the dark nobody saw it, and Ray's carbide lamp touched it as he walked under it. He was electrocuted instantly. He had no pain. We are very sorry to tell you this, Mis' Baxley."

Pearl stood silently looking at the men for a full minute, then fell in a heap at their feet. She came to her senses with Helen screaming, but she didn't ever want to wake up. The two men were sitting beside her, one holding a wet cloth on her forehead, and the other trying to comfort little Helen. Big Red was barking on the front porch, and as Pearl began to stir, she looked past the men and saw many others standing quietly outside, holding their caps.

The next two days were a blurred nightmare. She never forgot the anguish of Ray's mine buddies carrying Ray's body inside the house and placing him on their bed. They had washed the coal dust off of Ray's face and hands, and he looked just as if he were sleeping. Big Red followed his master inside, he whined, licked Ray's face and lay down by the head of the bed, his nose on his paws. Pearl threw herself down on her knees beside the bed, shaking her husband, crying, "Ray! Ray, wake up—please wake up. Oh—" she simply was unable to believe he was dead.

A good friend of Ray's rode horseback to Herrin, to tell the Baxley family. After trying to console Ma Baxley, Ray's older brother, Stanley, rode from Herrin out to Buckner with the hearse.

Pearl had sat all night in a chair—some friends stayed with her. She could barely look at the bed, yet she couldn't *not* look. She had covered Ray with one of her best quilts and she kept looking at his face thinking, *He'll wake up. He's got to wake up!*

Helen was asleep in her own little bed, and Pearl thought, *She's too young to know that she'll never know her daddy.*

The hearse was a large, black, boxlike coach built on a high wagon bed with very large wheels, and drawn by two black horses. It drew up in front of the little mining camp house, and Pearl greeted Stanley in a daze. She sat in her chair nearly fainting, holding little Helen, while Stanley helped the driver carry out Ray's body and put it in the coach.

Big Red had stayed at Ray's side the whole night. As they carried Ray from the house, Big Red, with no sound, got up and quietly followed them outside, his head and tail drooping. When the horses began to move and the coach was drawn away, Big Red simply walked under the coach, between its wheels.

Many friends were watching in tears, and they called and called to Big Red, but the dog never looked back. The narrow road was full of deep ruts which must have hurt his feet. But he gave no sign. He walked all the way to Herrin under the hearse with his head down, and watched as Ray's body was carried inside the mortuary. Then he quietly stretched himself out on the porch beside the door.

A friend drove Pearl and Helen in his buggy and they followed the coach; Pearl, in anguish, watching Big Red all the way.

Pearl never forgot riding in the buggy then with Pa Baxley to find a burial plot in the Herrin cemetery. Nor could she ever forget the love of Ma and Pa's neighbors who brought in food and sympathy. Those days seemed to merge in a long, horrible dream of overpowering fear, shock, and tears.

The next morning, Ray's body was taken to his parents' house to lie in state until the funeral. Big Red followed the hearse there, and situated himself beside the Baxley's front door. During that time, many people spoke to him, patted his head and smoothed his red coat, but he seemed not to notice any of them. They tried to feed him but he ate nothing at all. They offered him water, but the bowls of food and water remained near him, untouched.

When the family followed the casket from the house to the church, Big Red walked under the hearse. He waited at the church door, then again walked between the wheels of the coach from there to the cemetery. When it stopped, the dog lay down beneath it.

To Pearl, this drama was totally unbelievable; that she was holding Helen's hand and they were standing beside her husband's grave. The rain had stopped and afternoon sun slanted down between some maple trees, but she paid no attention to the sun. She couldn't appreciate sunshine. This was her husband's grave! Her *husband! Ray!* Two days ago she had fixed his dinner bucket, kissed him good-bye, and waited for him to come home while supper was cooking on the kitchen stove. And he didn't even get a chance to have a piece of his favorite chocolate cake! Now he was gone. Now she had to decide how to do without him.

I'm only twenty-one years old and I'm a widow with a small child and Christmas is coming. I need Ray. I need a mother, too.

Never had she felt more bereft, even when the Baxley family, Uncle Wallace and Uncle Bev's families, and her own father and brothers were standing beside her. As she watched the six friends lower Ray's casket into the grave, feeding the ropes over their hands, she felt as if her life, too, was at an end.

Pearl wanted to go back home. So Stanley and Bill, Ray's brothers, took her the next day. Big Red was weak and limping. Though dazed, Pearl knew the dog had not eaten anything for three days, so she asked Bill and Stanley to lift him into the buggy. The dog then lay on her feet, his eyes closed, and Pearl soothed him. "I'm very worried about you, Big Red. Maybe you'll eat for me."

But when they reached the Buckner house, Big Red staggered underneath. All the company houses were built with cement blocks under the four corners, providing a crawl and storage space. Pearl got down on her hands and knees and called and called the dog, but he would not come out. Then she lay flat on the ground to look at him, and to let him see her. "Big Red come here. Please come out, Big Red. I need you."

Red opened his eyes and looked at her, but there was no welcome tail wagging. His head stayed on his paws, and he looked sorrowfully at Pearl. He was lying under the bedroom—under Ray and Pearl's bed.

It was too much for Pearl, and there on the ground, the sobbing started again. Stanley and Bill helped her up and into the house. They then put some food and water under the house as far as they could reach. "Maybe he'll eat it tomorrow," Bill said. "Surely he will eat now that he's at home."

Leaning against Stanley's shoulder, Pearl sobbed, "How am I ever going to live without Ray? The world is just not the same without him. He was wonderful to me."

Stanley shook his head, "Don't know how any of us are goin' to get along without Ray. We miss our brother somethin' fierce. Ma and Pa are just about dead over it too. But Pearl, you have to go on. Little Helen needs you now."

Pearl sat in her chair and Helen crawled up into her lap and smoothed her mother's face. "Mommie cry?"

The next morning Bill went outside and called the dog again. "Red, Red, come on out! You need to eat. Come on, boy."

But Red wouldn't come. "Poor Red!" exclaimed Pearl wiping her eyes. "He loved Ray more than anyone in the world." In the middle of the day she called him again, but this time he didn't even open his eyes.

She called two neighboring boys who used to play with Red. "Would you two boys please crawl under the house and pull Big Red out? He won't fight you, he's too weak. I need him with me, and Big Red needs to eat—he's not had anything since Ray died."

"He ain't eat nothin' since your husband died? Then he must be weak. We'll git him for you." The boys crawled under the house and began to tug at Big Red's legs as they crawled backward with him. Then one called out suddenly, "Oh, Mis' Baxley. Big Red ain't livin' no more. He's jest grieved hisself to death."

They pulled him out onto the grass and smoothed his rough red fur. "He was the best dog we ever saw—we played with him ever' day and we shore are gonna miss him." Tears ran down two freckled faces and dripped on Big Red's side.

The boys helped Stanley and Bill dig a grave for Big Red outside the mine camp. When they put the dog into the grave, the two boys cried and wiped their eyes on their shirttails. "We'll never find another dog like him."

This second loss in so few days made Pearl's heart all the heavier. She wondered when she would come out of this dark tunnel. She had no desire to go on living, but little Helen was needing to be loved. So she tried not to cry in front of Helen, and to act normally. She explained, "Sweet girl, your daddy can't be with us any more because now he is up in Heaven."

Helen nodded. "Daddy gone. Big Wed gone." But she played around in the house, looking behind doors and under the beds calling, "Daddy, Wed, Wed." Then she'd shake her head—she couldn't find her daddy or her playmate.

Ma and Pa Baxley, Ray's parents, came in their buggy to see Pearl when Bill and Stanley went back home. Ma Baxley had been born in Kentucky as Sarah Jane Westerfield. Pa, Julius Franklin Baxley, was also from Kentucky. They had been married forty years before in Sturgis, Kentucky. Julius was a policeman. But they decided to move, so early in their married life, they came to Herrin. Now all their eight children, except Joe, were married.

The Baxleys were humble farmers, short on education, but their love and compassion were limitless. Weeping, they put their arms of love around Pearl and little Helen. "Pearl, we know that you will have to give up your company house now. They won't let you live here anymore. We are your mother and father—same as to Ray. Now you and Helen come and live with us."

Pearl, still in shock, had not even realized that the company house could no longer be hers, and that very soon all her money would be gone. She gasped, "But Ma Baxley— you don't have room for two more in your house!"

"Oh yes we do. We've only got Joe there now. We'll change a few things around and you can fit in."

"But I have no money. What shall I do?"

"You can just *live* with us. We love you and Helen and we'll be glad to have a grandchild in the house."

So Pearl, overflowing with grief for Ray and Big Red, and with love and gratitude to his parents, moved back to Herrin, to their house on South 19th Street. Pa put Helen's little bed into a bedroom and gave that room to Pearl. Most of Pearl's things she stored in their barn. Their place was at the edge of town and they had several acres, so they kept chickens, a horse and cow, and made a big garden every year. They never lacked for food. Apple, pear, and cherry trees lined their yard. Pa Baxley said, "When spring comes, we'll put up a swing for Helen out there."

Pearl thought she could not bear the grief she felt, but Ma and Pa Baxley helped her live through it. They put no pressure on her and gradually the shock began to lessen.

Christmas was a very sad day, but Pa decorated a tree and under it were presents for everybody. After a turkey dinner, Pearl lay down in the room she shared with Helen. Gazing at her baby she thought, *If I didn't have Helen in that little bed depending on me, I'd just as soon die right now.* She wept until she couldn't weep any more; then she slept.

When the new year came, money was scarce, and Pearl was restless. She told Ma Baxley, "Ma, I think I ought to try to get a job somewhere and help with expenses."

Not many women worked outside their homes in 1914, so Ma Baxley objected. "Now we ain't starvin', Pearl. We don't have to have any more money and you don't have to work. We got plenty of canned food in the cellar, and we got hams in the smokehouse."

"But, Ma, I've got to do something. We are going to need shoes before long and I don't want you to have to buy them. If I got a job somewhere in town, would you look after Helen during the day? You know she's a quiet little girl and I don't think she'd give you much trouble."

"You know I would. She's no trouble at all. She's so quiet that sometimes I don't hardly know she's in the house."

"Then I'm goin' to try." Pearl made the rounds of stores and shops in the middle of town, and by the last of January she had a job in a laundry. *It's a good thing I know how to iron!*

She walked to work every day, but the work was so hard! She hadn't known so many white shirts existed in Herrin! They had high, detachable collars, and the whole garment was stiffly starched. They had to be turned out on hangers with not a hint of a wrinkle.

For eight to ten hours a day, Pearl stood in the steaming tropics of the laundry, near great hot vats of clothes. Their heavy flat irons were heated on a broad coal stove. As soon as high heat in an iron waned, a new flat, bottom part was attached to the portable iron handle and the cooler one allowed to heat again. Her right wrist and fingers were often burned and cramped, and some days her elbow almost refused to move by the end of the day.

She wore her thick hair piled as tightly and as high on her head as possible to leave her neck free of the heavy, hot mass. In 1914, skirts were long, and shoes uncomfortable for standing all day. But Pearl wouldn't quit. She was very proud to be able to take home her money and pay for her own and Helen's keep.

Little Helen was thriving. She soon seemed to forget her father because she was always with Pa Baxley. She dogged his footsteps constantly, and he talked to her all the time, teaching her. She learned to ride his gentle old horse, and played with the cats and dogs on the place. She scared Pearl nearly to death because before she was two and a half, she was climbing fruit trees which Pa couldn't climb. She picked the apples, pears, and cherries, and threw them down to Pa waiting on the ground with his buckets.

"She'll break her neck or her back!" cried Pearl one evening when she came home from work and found Helen in the top of a cherry tree.

"No I won't, Mama," called Helen's childish voice. "See, Pa told me I always had to hold on with one hand and pick fruit and throw it down with the other."

Pa grinned and said, "Pearl, I think our little Helen is kin to a cat, seein' the way she can climb. She sure is a big help. Wish I could climb like that again but it's been quite a few years since I could get up into that tree!"

Pearl shook her head and went into the house. She couldn't bear to watch her baby that far up in a tree. She had forgotten how she and her brother Bill used to run, chase each other, and climb over the hills and cliffs of Makanda when she was no older than Helen. That seemed like a hundred years ago.

* * *

One evening Pearl dropped wearily onto her bed and closed her eyes, thinking. It had been over a year since Ray died—a hard year, but she was now crying less. *I've been able to appreciate this spring when all the fruit trees were in bloom and Ma's flowers began to open. Thank You, Lord, for helping me through it. I thank You, Lord, for Ma and Pa Baxley—I couldn't have lived without them. Oh, but I still miss Ray!*

Sometimes in the night I wake up suddenly thinking, "Ray's right here with me." Then I feel the emptiness on the other side of the bed. I feel completely bereft then. But I also thank You because those times are becoming fewer. Maybe the worst is over. Ma Baxley said that time would heal the wounds. Please, Lord, let it be true.

CHAPTER TWENTY-THREE
HENRY

On Sundays the whole family went to the Baptist church where Pearl played the organ. But she was still close to Uncle Wallace and Uncle Bev who were Methodist ministers, as well as carpenters. They preached in many evangelistic meetings and sometimes Wallace asked Pearl to go with him to play the organ while Bev played his violin. Pearl looked forward to these meetings.

Wallace was a good preacher, and listening to him, Pearl prayed and opened her heart to God's healing love. She even forgave her father for his drunkenness and ruining her childhood. God's grace had helped her to accept Ray's death and she began to feel new life flowing in her veins.

One day in March, 1915, Wallace came by the laundry to see her. He picked his way through piles of clothes and talked to her over her ironing board. "Pearl, could you come with me tonight? I'm beginning a nightly meeting in Centerfield church and would like you to play the organ for it."

She nodded. "I'd like to, Uncle Wallace. Will you come by and get me at home? I'll get off from work here a little early."

"I'll be at your house about six."

Pearl stopped work at four-thirty that afternoon. She walked home over frozen rutted roads, her coat buttoned tightly around her and her hands thrust up into her sleeves. Helen ran to meet her mother as she came in. Pearl hugged her, "There's my sweet little girl. Are you all right?"

Helen nodded and began to chatter about what she'd done that day. Ma Baxley said, "I know you're tired, Pearl. Supper is nearly ready."

"Uncle Wallace wants me to go to a meeting with him tonight, Ma. Is that all right with you?"

"'Course it is, Pearl."

"Mama, then can grandpa put me to bed?" asked Helen. "He tells me the best stories!"

Pa tweaked her ear. "I've got a dandy one for you tonight. How'd you like a story about a horse who couldn't find his stall?"

Helen scooted her chair close to her Grandpa's.

They sat down to a supper of Ma Baxley's good side pork, home-canned green beans, grits, and biscuits spread with fresh, homemade butter and cherry jam. Then Pearl went to her room, took off her work clothes and washed herself at the big china wash basin. Helen watched her mother dress for church, then comb her long, wavy hair. It sparkled in the lamplight, and she puffed it around her face and twisted it into a smooth knot at the back of her head.

"You're a pretty mama. I hope I'm pretty like you when I grow up."

"You'll be prettier than I am, my sweet baby."

"I like your blouse."

"Thank you, sweetheart. I've been sewing on it when you were sleeping at night."

Pearl wore a flared, ankle-length black skirt, and her many-tucked blouse was white with a lace collar and a tiny red bow. Pearl never wanted frills, but she liked red. All her clothes had to be neat, clean, and practical. Her shoes were black, high with black buttons.

Wallace came for her in his buggy and they rode out of town for about three miles north of Herrin toward Johnston City. Pearl wore a scarf over her head because the wind was strong and cold. Their knees were covered with a heavy wool blanket.

"How's the family, Uncle Wallace? How's Aunt Dora and Taylor and Bill?"

"They're all right. Dora has her hands full with those boys and maybe you know she's expecting again."

"No, I didn't know."

"Dora was very glad to see her brother—her half brother—Henry. He arrived home a few days ago. He's been in California for over two years."

"Oh—that's far away, isn't it? Henry . . . I've heard Dora talk about him. Where did he go to school?"

"To Stotlar School. He quit to work on the farm after about the sixth grade. After a few years, he worked in the mines, then went to California. He's a nice man, Pearl. Maybe you'll meet him."

"What will he do here in Herrin?"

"Right now he's with his mother and dad, Julia and John. They live south of Herrin. Henry says he will work in the mines—he wants to be nearer home."

At the word "mines," Pearl shuddered and pulled the wool blanket closer around herself. "I always hate to think about men working in the mines."

When they arrived at Centerfield, one of the church members had already built a fire in the potbellied stove in the center of the building. Pearl warmed her hands and took off her coat. "Do you want me to play before service starts, Uncle Wallace? While people are coming?"

"Yes, Pearl, that would be nice."

So Pearl fixed the stops and warmed up the organ playing many of the old hymns people loved: *O God, Our Help in Ages Past, O Worship the King, Shall We Gather At The River?*, and a few others. Then Wallace went to the pulpit and announced, "Let us begin the service with another old hymn, *Revive Us Again*."

Pearl began to play the introduction while the door opened to allow some late-comers to enter. The last one came in and hesitated at the door. Pearl lifted her eyes from the music page and looked straight into the eyes of the most handsome man she'd ever seen. He was six-feet-two-inches tall, with black hair, greenish-blue eyes, fair skin, and a square chin with a dimple. He smiled at her and he had the straightest, whitest teeth any man ever had. She looked quickly back at her music but her heart was behaving in the strangest way. It first hesitated a few seconds, then began to thud erratically against her chest.

The stranger sat on the back row during the service, but Pearl knew he was looking at her. After the sermon, Wallace invited anyone who wanted to pray to come down to the altar, and a few came and knelt there. Pearl kept playing the organ softly until they finished their prayers. By then, most of the congregation had left, but the new man was still in his seat.

Pearl was putting on her coat when, with long strides, he was beside her, helping. "My name is Henry Childers—" he said. "I'm Wallace's brother-in-law; his wife, Dora, is my half-sister."

Pearl smiled up at him—way up at him. She was only five-feet-two-inches tall. "I am Pearl Gibbs Baxley. My mother was Wallace's older sister."

Henry nodded. "I know—Wallace told me about you."

"He did? He didn't tell *me* he told you!"

"Well—maybe he's a little foxy that way, because he said to me today, 'Come to Centerfield tonight and meet the prettiest girl in Herrin!' So how could I stay away?"

She smiled. "Uncle Wallace is *your* half brother-in-law, and he is *my* full uncle. Are *we* any kin?"

"I don't think so. Would you *like* to be?"

She blushed.

Wallace came up to them and Henry exclaimed, "You're right, Wallace. She is!"

Pearl blushed again.

Henry asked her then, "Will you be here again tomorrow night?"

Pearl nodded. "Uncle Wallace says the meeting is lasting through next Sunday."

They walked out to Wallace's buggy and Henry helped her up and tipped his hat. "I'll see you tomorrow night." Then he climbed on his horse and rode off—a stalwart, admirable man sitting ramrod straight in his saddle.

Pearl was quiet on the way home. Wallace's horse pulled the buggy over the bumpy, dirt road, jolting them from side to side. The only light was a lamp on each side of the buggy.

Wallace looked at her in flickering dimness. "What did you think of my sermon tonight, Pearl? Did you like it?"

"Uh—sermon? Uh—oh, yes, it was fine."

Wallace chuckled. "What did I preach about, Pearl?"

"Uh—you preached about the prodigal son!" At least she could remember that!

Wallace laughed aloud. "Tonight I preached on the rich young ruler! I think you didn't hear a word I said."

Pearl's laughter joined his. "Well, you got me that time. It's just—I guess I never saw a more handsome man than Henry Childers."

"That he is."

"Is he married?"

"No. I just told him today he ought to settle down."

"How old is he?"

"He'll be twenty-seven in May."

"He's five years older than I am. I'll be twenty-two in April."

Wallace raised his eyebrows and just looked at her.

The next day at work while ironing shirts for the well-to-do of Herrin, she had a mental conversation with herself: *Pearl Baxley, what's the matter with you?*

I don't know. When Ray died I thought I'd never look at another man. But this man seems different.

And you certainly looked at Henry Childers.

Well, he looked at me, too. And he asked if I'd be back tonight.

Wonder if he will come back tonight?

She lifted many irons, connected and disconnected them onto the handle all day long to iron more shirts, ignored the burn on her finger, and at the end of the day she didn't even feel tired.

Henry came back to church that night, talked to her for a while before the service started, and talked again to her afterward. Before he helped her into Wallace's buggy he asked, "Will you come to the service with *me* tomorrow night in *my* buggy?"

Her face flushed but she looked straight at him and said, "Yes, I will," and immediately wondered, *Did I seem in too much of a hurry to be with him?*

He held her hand a little tighter and smiled. "I'll come for you at six. Wallace will tell me where you live."

The next evening after supper, she said to Ma and Pa Baxley, "I met a handsome man at church. He's Uncle Wallace's brother-in-law, Henry Childers. He's coming tonight to take me to the meeting." She thought, *Surely Ma and Pa will be able to hear my heart pounding so loud.*

Ma Baxley rocked for a while in her chair, thinking. Then, "Well, Pearl, I think the time is right. You've been a fine daughter-in-law to us and this is your home as long as you want it to be. But you've been a widow for a year and five months, and you ought not go through life without a husband. You made a good wife to Ray and if you find the right man now, he'll be the lucky one."

"Goodness, Ma! I'm not thinking about getting married! I'm just going to ride to church with him!"

Henry caused Pearl to change her mind. He got a job in Jeffrey mine and worked hard every day. But he not only came to take her to church the rest of the week in the evenings, but came to take her other places at least three times a week after that. The more they were together, the more they fell in love with each other and wanted to be together. Through April, May, and June, Henry took her riding in his buggy time after time.

They talked about everything. Pearl told him about her marriage to Ray and he got acquainted with Helen. They discussed farming about which Henry knew a lot, and Pearl practically nothing. They reviewed the present political situation and Pearl found that Henry was a staunch Republican. She said, "Well, I partly grew up in Makanda and that's a strong Republican town. My pap used to say, "A man's no good if he's a Democrat." So I guess I'm a Republican, too. Do you like to read books?"

Henry hesitated. "I—I went just through the sixth grade at school. Pa needed me on the farm then, so I quit school to help him. I don't like to read books, but I like to read the newspaper so I can keep up with what's goin' on."

"I love books," she said. I like to read just any kind of books you can think about. Maybe I got to like them so much when I was a little girl, because when I was readin' I could forget the bad things at home. I have a good home now with Ma and Pa Baxley—but I still like to read as much as I can."

"I hate it that you are workin' in that laundry, Pearl. I know how hard that is for you."

"Well—I don't particularly love it, but I need the money. I don't like for Ma and Pa Baxley to buy all the things that Helen and I need. I feel better when I can buy them myself. Course, I don't make much, and Ma won't let me give her any money for food."

Henry told her about his family, his time in California, and how happy he was that he'd come home and met her. Pearl knew he was going to ask her to marry him and she also knew that she wanted to do it.

"I have to confess, Henry, that six months ago I would never have believed that I would ever look at another man. But I feel right with you."

"Does that mean you'll marry me, Pearl? I love you and want to marry you. I don't see any use of waiting any longer to ask you."

She looked at him and knew she would love him the rest of her life. "I love you, too, Henry. You realize that you'll be starting married life with a three-year-old child! Can you do that?"

Henry's arms were around her and she was looking up into his face. Her big blue eyes were filled with tears. He nodded and kissed her gently. "Guess I can! When my Ma and Pa were were married, she had a girl five years old, and Pa had *three girls and two boys.* So they started out with *six* kids and then she had seven more! I guess I'll feel natural to start married life with at least one!"

She snuggled her head on his chest and felt totally content.

"Ma wants me to bring you to the farm for dinner next Sunday after church. I told her about you and that I wanted to marry you, so she wants the whole family to meet you. Think you can stand that?"

"Think your ma will like me? Is she easy to get along with?"

"Yes. She's a fine woman. Julia and John Childers will think I found the right girl!"

Pearl nodded. Still—she knew she'd be nervous. But when Henry came to take her and little Helen to church the next Sunday morning, he said, "They're all excited out at the farm."

"I'm nervous," Pearl confessed. "Getting looked over is scary."

"Don't be nervous," Henry assured her. "They'll like you."

When they drove up to Julia and John's back door and Henry lifted her and Helen from his buggy and set them down, she saw only love and acceptance. Henry said to the whole family, "Folks, meet Pearl Baxley. And this is her little girl, Helen. They're both goin' to join our family in July!"

Julia ran down the back steps with her arms wide open to hug Pearl and Helen. She was taller than Pearl, with sparkling brown eyes, black curly hair sprinkled with gray and drawn back to a bun. She had a ruddy skin, high cheekbones, and smiling she showed even white teeth. Pearl immediately knew that Henry's mother was a woman of loving but strong character, and she responded to Julia at once.

John got up to shake her hand, towering over her even taller than Henry. "Welcome to our house, little Pearl Baxley. Been wantin' to meet you—we needed to see the girl Henry's been talkin' about for some months now. And we're surprised to know you're kin to Wallace. We think a lot of him."

"Nice to meet you, Mr. Childers. Yes, Wallace is my uncle—my mother's youngest brother." She smiled at him. "Now I see why Henry is so handsome. He looks just like his Pa."

John grinned and straightened up to stand tall as he could with his six-feet-four inches. "Now that'll get you an extra piece of fried chicken for dinner! Well, here's the rest of the family—my two oldest boys couldn't come today. And my two oldest girls, well, you know that Dora and Wallace are home with a new baby. And Dona is too.

"But here's Eva Jane and her man, Bill," John pointed them out one by one, "George and his wife there, Addie and Dave, her husband, and Ola and Ed. They're the married ones. Here's the ones still at home—Ida, Cena, and Olive. That littlest boy there is Elton—George's son. He lives with us too. His name is Elton, but we call him Mike."

John paused. "Whew—gotta stop and get my breath—most talkin' I've done in a while." He looked around at his family and shook his head. "Women usually do the talkin' 'round here."

Julia smiled at John and put her hand on his arm—a spontaneous, tender gesture. Pearl saw it and the look that passed between them. She smiled. *They love each other dearly—after all these years of married life! I pray that Henry and I will be like that.*

CAST A LONG SHADOW

Book III

An Amended Family

1915 - 1930

CHAPTER TWENTY-FOUR
Wedding

All the Childers and Baxley families, carrying food baskets, trooped into the church grounds at Centerfield that hot Sunday Afternoon, July 18, 1915. Pearl and Henry's wedding day. Wallace's congregation had also been invited and most of them came. They had arrived early and set up saw-horse tables under the trees. Now these tables were loaded with food baskets which would be unpacked after the wedding. They'd also moved the pulpit and seats outside into the shady grove, decorated the area with ferns and flowers, and spread a snowy, white sheet on the ground for the bride and groom to stand on.

Julia helped her girls make their thin, voile dresses, after she had made her own. Hers was light blue, made simply with short sleeves, round collar and a tie belt. The girls were a rainbow of colors. John wore his one dark suit. When they had dressed at home for the wedding, John held Julia's shoulders and stooped to kiss her. "Julia, you'll be the purtiest one there. I was sure lucky when I found you."

"Aw, John, you're the best man I ever saw. If Henry's as good to Pearl as you are to me, then Pearl will be a happy woman." She reached way up to put her arms around his neck, and John held her close for a moment.

Cena, sticking her head into their bedroom door commented, "Hey, ain't you two gettin' purty old to carry on like this?"

Julia laughed. "Never too old to love your man. You'll find out one day, Cena. Come on, everybody—time to go."

Henry stood tall and handsome in a new gray suit and stiff-collared white shirt, his brown hair parted in the middle and slicked down. His face was proud as he smiled down at Pearl.

Though she stood very straight and tall, Pearl came just to Henry's shoulder. She had made her ankle-length wedding dress of white, embroidered eyelet cloth, scalloped at the neck, hem, and three-quarter-length sleeves. She had smocked four rows of the palest pink around her small waist. Her white, pointed-toe shoes had three straps across the instep, fastened with white shoe buttons on the side. A wide, white ribbon, embroidered with pink rosebuds wound around her thick, wavy hair, coiled low on her neck.

Little Helen, dressed in a new ruffled pink dress, sat on a church bench on her Grandpa Baxley's lap. She looked wonderingly at all the dressed-up people—even Ma and Pa Baxley were all dressed up—and at her mother in a new white dress. Her mother had told her that today, after a pretty wedding, Henry Childers would be her new daddy. "Would you like that, Honey?"

"I like him, Mama. Does he have any little girls?"

"No, just you. But some day you might have a little sister or brother. Would you like that?"

Helen nodded. "It'll be like playing with my doll, won't it?"

Pearl smiled. "Well—probably not exactly. But it will be nice. That will be a long time off. Today you will go to the church where Mama plays the organ, and we'll have the wedding outside under the trees. That's why I made you a pretty new dress. After that, we'll both go and live with your new daddy in a new house and you can have your own room to sleep in. We'll take your bed with us."

"You mean I won't sleep with you any more? I like sleeping in your room, Mama."

"I know, honey. But you're getting to be a big girl now and big girls like to have their own rooms. You'll have a bigger place to put your clothes and toys."

"Will Ma and Pa Baxley come to live with us, too?"

"No."

"But won't they be lonesome here when I'm gone?"

"Of course. But they won't forget you—and we'll come to see them often."

Pearl said nothing about the fact that she knew Ma and Pa Baxley would more than miss their little Helen. They would *mourn* for her when she was gone. They idolized this child!

Wallace stood stately and solemn in his black suit, facing the bride and groom, his family, and congregation. "Dearly beloved, we are gathered together here today to join Henry Childers and Pearl Gibbs Baxley in holy wedlock. If any person can show . . ."

"Henry, do you take Pearl . . .?"

"I do."

"Pearl, do you take Henry . . .?"

"I do."

Little Helen's lips quivered and big tears began to roll quietly down her cheeks. She hid her face in Grandpa Baxley's Sunday coat.

He hugged her close, took a folded, white handkerchief from his pocket and gently wiped her face. "Don't cry, little Helen. Your Mama is happy and you mustn't let her see you cry."

"But Mr. Childers said he's gonna take Mama somewhere!"

The old man smiled under his drooping, gray mustache. "Aw—that's just preacher talk. Your Mama will be right here with you. Now set up straight and smile for her. She's had a hard time, but it'll be better for her now and you'll have a good new daddy."

"Will you be close to me too, Pa?"

He nodded. "I'm not goin' anywhere, and neither is your Mama." Helen leaned against him, satisfied.

Herrin's only photographer was there to take some pictures of the wedding party after Uncle Bev played a violin solo. Food baskets were opened and a fancy wedding supper was laid out on the saw-horse tables. Wallace said an extra prayer for the newly married couple before they ate, and then Henry stepped forward. "I'd like to say somethin', Wallace."

Wallace nodded.

"I just want to thank everybody for comin' today to make this the happiest day of my life. I never thought, when I came home from California, I never thought I'd find such a fine girl here—and of all places, I found her right in my own brother-in-law's family. So I thank Wallace for gettin' us together. Before I ever met Pearl, Wallace told me I needed to settle down. When I met Pearl, I agreed with him. So I thank him and I thank you. I hope all you young fellers get a girl as pretty as I got today."

Pearl, standing beside him, didn't make any speech. She just smiled at all of them and said, "Thank you."

* * * *

So much in love and so happy, Henry and Pearl rented a small house on the north side of Herrin. Helen said a tearful goodbye to Ma and Pa Baxley.

"Why don't you just let Helen live with us, Pearl?"

"Why, I can't do that! She's my child. But I'll bring her over often. And you and Pa come to see us, too!"

So it was that after a year and nine months, Pearl again fixed a miner's dinner bucket every day, kissed her husband goodbye, and prayed that he would come home in the evening. She was thankful that now, again, she could stay at home with her daughter—it hadn't been easy walking to town and working ten hours a day.

After her big job in the laundry, to wash her small family's clothes didn't seem like much at all.

She had two large wash tubs, a solid bench (which Henry made for her) to put them on, a big wash board, two flat irons of her own, a fine, strong ironing board, and a six-hole coal stove.

In summer, she put her bench and tubs out under a tree ana heated water in a big black iron pot over an open fire. Once the water was heated, she carried it by bucketfuls and poured it into the tub, washing white clothes first. Then more was heated to boil the whites. She scrubbed them on the board first. It's amazing how clean a shirt collar gets when it's rubbed over with strong bar soap, then rubbed up and down several times on a washboard.

When she finished washing the white things, she carried them over to the pot, and with a sawed-off broomstick, lifted them into the boiling water and poked them down. She let them boil in soapy water for about forty-five minutes—that was called "scalding" the clothes. Then she lifted them out with her stick to an empty tub and carried that back to the bench. Filling the tub of boiled clothes with cold water, she again poked up and down with the stick to rinse them. Then she wrung them out.

There's an art to wringing out a big, wet sheet. She partially lifted it, wet and doubled in half, from the wash water, then whirled it in circle fashion with the bottom edges still in the water. The sheet got twisted several times. Then holding with both hands she wrung it, working her way down from the fold to the edges and wringing in sections. Surprising how much water can be forced out!

In summer, of course, she used the outside clotheslines. Henry put up the lines for her, stretching them tightly over cross arms at each end of the yard. Every week she cleaned the wire, walking up and down, holding a wet cloth around the line. No use spending all that time washing clothes if they'd just get dirty again from sooty clothes lines. And in a coal-burning society, everything got sooty!

But nobody in Herrin ever had a whiter wash than Pearl Childers. She used bars of yellow soap—no powdered soap available. She would cut up half a bar into the boiling water, and use the other half at her washboard. Every Monday morning—one bar of soap. It cost ten cents.

Her big old black boiling pot didn't just sit around the rest of the week. Often in summer, when she didn't want to get the house any hotter than it already was, she'd let the kitchen fire go out and cook her supper outside. She'd put green beans and a ham hock in the pot early in the morning, make a fire under the old pot and cook the beans slowly all day. About an hour before supper time, she'd add potatoes and ears of corn on top of the beans. All the supper in one pot! She would sit in the back yard under her washing tree all afternoon (after the rest of her housework was done) and read books and memorize poetry while the pot simmered and Helen played nearby.

In late summer or early fall, the pot was used to make apple butter. That, too, would cook all day, filling the air with luscious aromas of cinnamon, nutmeg, and apples. Pearl kept a special long-handled wooden spoon which she used for stirring the black pot's contents.

In winter she heated her wash water in a small tub on the coal stove and scrubbed her clothes in the kitchen. Then she had to string up clothes lines in the house and dry her clothes there. Henry had put hooks high in the walls for her lines, and being short, she had to stand on a kitchen chair to tie up the ropes. She always tried to get her clothes on the line early in the day so as to have them dry, and the clothes and lines down before Henry came home from work. Being so tall, he hated to fight his way through a forest of hanging wet clothes.

Pearl was thankful for her sewing machine and now had time to make all of Helen's clothes and her own, to patch the knees of Henry's overalls which wore out so quickly in the mine, and to make their own quilts. Since she sewed a lot, she always had scraps left over to piece her quilts. That she did by the coal-oil lamp when she and Henry rested after supper, and after Helen had been put to bed.

Henry liked to see Pearl take her hair down in the evening. He loved her hair—sparkling, reddish-brown, and waving. She never had tight curls, but her hair was thick, and when it was down, fell into waves the whole length of it. He used to brush it for her and watch it shine in the lamplight. Her hair had grown without cutting ever since she was a child and recovered from typhoid. Now it was so long she could sit on it.

Henry was the head of his household, and saw to it that everything was going right. He was a man Pearl could depend on—strong and trustworthy. He could fix anything that need fixing in the house or yard. She loved him and knew he loved her. But he could never understand her passion for reading. She borrowed books and read all the time she could. But since Henry didn't like to read much besides the newspaper, she managed her time to read during the day so she could talk to him after supper.

Everyday she thanked God for Henry, and for keeping him safe in the coal mine. She couldn't help the nagging fear in the back of her mind every time he went to work. But Henry didn't want her to worry.

Helen seemed to adjust to her new house and new daddy, but she often talked about her Pa and Ma Baxley. "Do you think they are lonesome for me, Mama?"

"I'm sure they are, sweet girl. If you want to, we can walk over to their house this afternoon."

"Yes, I want to go. I want to show them the new dollie you made for me, and my new dress."

One day Pearl confided to Helen, "I have a secret, but I want to tell you. Would you like to know?"

Helen nodded, her eyes round with wondering.

"Well, my secret is that in a few months you are going to have a new baby brother or sister to play with. Would you like that? Of course, the baby won't be able to play with you for a while—it'll be too little."

"Which is it gonna be, Mama?"

"I don't know. We won't know until the baby is here. Which would you rather have?"

"I'd rather have a baby sister. Can I help you take care of her? Can I tell Pa and Ma Baxley about the baby?"

"You can if you want to."

"I'll sing to my new baby sister like I sing to my dollie."

CHAPTER TWENTY-FIVE
Family – A Bird's-Eye View

The next spring after they were married, Pearl and Henry rented a larger house on South 12th Street in Herrin. "We're going to need more room when our baby comes, Henry." Henry agreed. The house they found was just around the corner from a grocery store, and Pearl liked that convenience.

This move put them nearer John and Julia. Henry liked nothing better than a Sunday afternoon when his sisters and brothers could get together at the farm—even the two sisters from West Frankfort and Marion came over often.

Addie and Ola married young. Addie met a handsome man with dark hair named Dave Durham and they were soon married and moved to a farm north of Williamson County—Franklin County. Addie always loved the land. She was beautiful—tall and dark haired, with high cheekbones, and she walked like an Indian princess.

Ola was shorter, with brown wavy hair, gray-green eyes, and a sweet smile. Julia had taught them both to be wonderful cooks, and Ola's homemade bread was out of the ordinary. She had a quiet disposition, which was a good thing, because her husband, Ed Mayer, was a talker.

They lived in Marion. Ed was a small, rather nervous, and very well-read man in history and politics. When Ed and Henry got together, they had some heated debates at election time. After the two of them solved all the political problems of the county, Ed enjoyed talking to Pearl.

Of course, Pearl had studied only a little in high school, but she read all the books she could get her hands on. She read books on politics, history, medicine, philosophy, poetry, novels and essays. And she loved to study the dictionary. Nobody could stump her in spelling, and after crossword puzzles became popular, she worked them as fast as she could write. Life was never dull around either Ed Mayer or Pearl Childers.

Pearl and Henry worked hard for several days settling into their new house, and on Sunday afternoon decided to visit John and Julia on the farm.

Julia saw the horse and buggy drive up and went out to meet them. "Well, come on in—I been thinkin' about you! I wanted to come to town to see your new place, but couldn't get away yet. I jest made some fresh chocolate cake. Come and have some before the kids eat it all up."

"That sounds good, Ma Childers. I bet Helen would like some, too," Pearl said. They all sat down at the kitchen table and Ida and Cena brought them some coffee with rich cream to eat with the cake.

"Got your house all fixed up yet?" asked Julia.

"Just about finished, Ma," answered Henry. I still have to put up the clothesline and fix the door to the coal shed—a few things like that. We hope you come in before long and see it."

"We will," John said, "when we get our garden in."

"After that," said Julia, "we'll come in to town and I'll bring you some canned stuff. I know you didn't get much cannin' done last summer, Pearl."

Cena and Ida were not joining in the conversation. They were just pushing pieces of cake around in their small plates, hardly tasting them, and they kept fidgiting in their chairs. Henry asked, "What's the matter with you two girls? You act like two cats on hot cinders!"

Cena, the boldest squirmed. "Well, Henry, Ida and me, we got somethin' to ask you and Pearl. See, we're ready for high school this comin' fall, and we want to live in town. We've lived on a farm all our lives. Now that our favorite brother, Henry, lives in town, we'd like to ask if we could come and live with you and Pearl and go to high school."

Henry grinned at Pearl, and raised his eyebrows. "Favorite brother, huh?"

"Don't laugh at us, Henry. You are! See, we wouldn't have to walk nearly so far every day if we lived in town. We promise to help Pearl in the house to pay for our keep, and we would be there to help when her new baby comes. Would you let us do it?"

"I don't like that idy one bit!" John declared. "Why didn't you talk to me about this first? I don't like family stuff goin' on behind my back."

"We didn't talk to you because we knew you *wouldn't* like it, Pa," said Ida shaking her head. "But Ma," she begged Julia, "you understand don't you? School is far to walk—and you want us to be educated, don't you? Anyway, we think it would be fun to live in town and meet a lot of kids."

Julia sat thinking for a bit. Then, "You didn't say it, but you probably mean you want to meet boys. Well, I suppose it's about that time in your lives anyhow. It's entirely up to Henry and Pearl. You might make more work for her than you could help her with."

"No, we won't, Ma!" both girls agreed.

Cena said, "We'll do extra work. And Ma, you trained us to work and you know we can. We can help Henry in his garden, too." She looked sideways at Ida, "And we promise not to put seed corn in the corner of his lot. We can milk the cow if he wants us to."

"You think I could trust Old Bossie to you two?" Henry asked, his eyes twinkling. "What do you think, Pearl? You want two feisty girls livin' with us?"

Pearl considered the proposition. "Well, we do have that back room, Henry. We can put a bed in there. They'd probably liven up the place—let 'em come. It'll be nice with a new baby to have help."

"All right then," Henry agreed. "But if I catch you two makin' *more* work for Pearl, I'll send you kitin' home."

Both Ida and Cena jumped up and rushed over to hug Henry and Pearl, their faces glowing. Julia and John didn't look so happy about it. Two more of their children gone! That would leave only Olive and Elton at home. Of course Ida and Cena wouldn't be far away—they'd come to see them often.

So in the fall when it was time for them to start to high school, the girls moved in with Henry and Pearl, and the house wasn't very quiet after that. But their noise didn't bother Pearl at all. And they did spice up the place.

Pearl had forgotten what teenagers were like. Cena and Ida talked incessantly about cute boys, about why they did or didn't like certain dresses, and the kind of shoes they wanted to wear to school. Cena's hair was always curly, and she couldn't fix it to suit herself. Ida's hair was straight and hers wasn't right either. They confided, "Pearl, we sure like livin' with you. You're not so heavy with bossin' us around as Pa is. Guess we better watch Henry, though; he might get just like Pa! When's your baby comin', Pearl? I don't think it'll be very long now—" Cena looked critically at Pearl's bulk.

"No, won't be long now," Pearl answered. "In the middle of December."

The night Ruth was born, Henry pranced around the room holding his newborn daughter at arm's length. "Cena, ain't she the purtiest baby you ever did see?"

"I declare, Henry, I never saw such a crazy man. You'd think nobody ever had a baby before around here," his sister Cena said.

"Well, now I guess maybe they did," Henry admitted, "but this baby is the purtiest." He was walking on air that day. "You sure you can give her a bath all right? If you and Ida work at it together, she ought to get a good bath. Test that water with your elbow and be sure it ain't too hot. Now don't drop her!"

December was rugged in 1916 and Ruth was born at home in the middle of it. A violent snowstorm had arrived before Ruth did, and snow was packed up by the window sills. Henry rode a horse and found the doctor when Pearl began having labor pains. Dr. Murrah had a hard time getting there in his buggy, but he arrived in time and delivered Ruth at home.

"Her name is Ruth," Henry pronounced.

Dr. Murrah must have forgotten about that, if he had ever known her name. The county courthouse was ten miles away, and driving a buggy over to Marion just to register one birth was unthinkable. Evidently Dr. Murrah waited until he had many births to record at the end of winter. By that time he'd forgotten what the Childers baby's name was—so he just made up a name of his own for her. Nothing wrong with his name, it just wasn't the right one!

He must have thought, *Nobody will ever want to look up her birth certificate anyhow, and she looks like Mary Jane material to me.* So he registered Ruth as Mary Jane Childers. Of course, Henry and Pearl didn't know about that—they were calling her Ruth. That's how she started life—with a definite split personality. She didn't know about that either.

Ruth had plenty of people to love her every day—a proud father and mother, two aunts, and a big sister, Helen. So she started life in a happy family.

* * * *

Julia was very lonely for Ida and Cena after they left because they had always been the two noisiest children. But she still had plenty of things to do with John, Olive, and Elton at home.

Mike (he preferred that name instead of Elton), had learned to work like all the other children. At eight, he was small for his age, with an infectious grin and personality. He never knew the word "stingy." He always tried to have a few pennies in his pocket, but they never lasted long—he gave them away. Unusual events seemed to happen when Mike was around, and when he told a story about anything, it was roundly embellished. If nothing had happened, then he'd concoct stories and tell them as if they were real. His cousins were fascinated by him and thought of him as a lovable rascal. He wasn't mean or nasty to anyone, but sometimes his morals, in spite of Julia's constant instructions, had wide open gaps. He could tell a lie and anyone would believe him. So John was very strict with him.

World War I crashed into America and was affecting everybody's life. The girls hadn't been with Pearl and Henry very long before Cena rushed into the house one afternoon. "Ida!" she burbled. "I've met the handsomest boy you ever saw! His name is Arthur, and he likes me too! He's just joined the Army. And he's going to France!"

"How do you know he likes you so fast?"

"The way he smiled at me, and talked to me!"

Ida sniffed. "Don't be so quick to go after him!"

Cena pursed her mouth and shook her head. "I didn't. But I'd like to! He likes farmin', and he's from Franklin County. But he said the army was goin' to send him to France before long. What if he gets killed over there!?" Cena burst into tears.

Arthur Croslin was a slow-spoken, quiet young man and Cena was wild about him. She had always thrown herself one hundred percent into everything she did, and when she fell in love with Arthur, that too was passionate.

Arthur felt the same way. Before he marched off to board the train and ship for France, he easily persuaded Cena to marry him. Desperate war-frightened couples were searching out ministers all over the place. Cena and Arthur were married and spent only a few days together, before Arthur had to leave. Cena came back to Henry's and cried for a week. "I'll be dead before I can ever see him again!"

At that time during the first World War, smallpox was rampant in the United States, and doctors were advising everyone to be vaccinated against it. Cena and Ida took their immunizations and within a few days, the effect of the drug began to overwhelm them. Both of them went down with high fevers, their arms swelled to twice their normal size, and were full of pus. Hundreds of others had the same reactions and almost lost their arms to infection. The scourge was so severe that many people said—and believed—that the Germans had poisoned the vaccine.

Ida and Cena, were sleeping in the same bed at Henry and

Pearl's house, and were sick at the same time. If either of them moved in bed, she risked injuring the other's arm. So tempers were short with each other, and Pearl was hard-pressed to keep the peace between them. As a result of their infections, they bore huge scars on their upper arms for the rest of their lives. Pearl nursed them through the illness even though she was caring for Helen, baby Ruth, and the house.

The war ended in 1918 and, contrary to her dire predictions, Arthur Croslin did come home. Ruth was past two when her aunt Cena greeted her returning husband, with great joy. They moved to West Frankfort and Arthur got a job with the milk company. For many years he drove a beautiful white horse, hitched to a white milk wagon, around town delivering dairy products.

Cena was a fine cook and housekeeper, and took part in everything that went on in West Frankfort. She was never still.

"It's a good thing Cena married a gentle man," Julia remarked to John one day. "If she'd married a fighter, he'd have a war on his hands all his life. Arthur is so quiet. I just wonder if he *will* keep up with Cena—as feisty as she is!"

John leaned back in his chair, thought a minute and answered, "I'll bet he can hold his own with Cena when he has to. He's quiet, but I think he knows it's a sad house when the hen crows and the rooster is silent!"

Before long, Ida fell in love with Ralph Green, a returning soldier, and they were soon married. They moved to St. Louis, and Ralph found a job as a streetcar conductor.

On February 16, 1919, Dr. Murrah made another trip in his buggy through through deep snow to the Childers house on south 12th street. This time it was a son, Pearl and Henry's first and only son. They named him Arthur, for Cena's husband. Of course, nobody ever had as handsome a son, either. Henry strutted like a proud peacock for the second time.

Pearl lay in bed cuddling her new baby. "He really *is* handsome, Henry! He looks just like you."

"I don't know how you could have pleased me any better, Pearl! Not just to have a boy, but to say he looks like me! Yes, I guess he does."

Henry began looking for a house to buy for his family. He was tired of living in rented houses and fixing up someone else's place. He found what he was looking for at 618 South 18th Street. The house had four large rooms, each about fifteen feet square, and a peaked roof. A rear porch about twelve feet wide stretched the whole width of the house. A path behind the house led to the outhouse, sitting with its back to the alley. Once a month, at night, a wagon came through the alley and men shoveled up the contents of the outhouse and took it away. At that time, every house on the street had a privy like it.

The new place cost Henry $400.00—a good price. All the mines were working fulltime, and houses were at a premium. They moved into it the summer after Arthur was born, wagons moving all their household goods.

Ruth was three when they moved and she was excited. "Can I ride in the big wagon, Mama? Can I ride in there with Helen?

Yes, you can."

So Ruth and Helen climbed up into a big farm wagon amongst all the furniture and looked ahead over the backs of two big horses. As the horses clopped slowly up to eighteenth street, she waved to her mother who was pushing Ruth's new baby brother in a go-cart, and to her father walking their cow up the hill. She wished they could all ride with her, but then she giggled thinking of a cow in the wagon alongside her mama's sewing machine.

Henry put up the high hooks inside the house for Pearl's winter clothesline, and strung permanent lines outside. In the long back yard, he also arranged the three huge stones they'd moved with them. These were to set the big black pot on in the middle of the yard. Then Pearl felt at home. Henry also built on a wide, covered front porch and put up a five-foot porch swing. In summer, Pearl swung the children to sleep, and that swing became a focal point of family life. This was Pearl and Henry's last move—this was to be their home for the rest of their lives.

In 1920 summer rains didn't appear, and crops and wells dried up. For years Herrin had limped along with an off-again-on-again city water system, and that year the Herrin lake dried up too. No water at all. Big wagons lumbered around selling water from somewhere—and everybody was buying and saving all the water they could find, in tubs and buckets—whatever they could spare—to hold it. Henry went "water witching" in his back yard, and the switch turned over in his hand at a spot about fifteen feet from the house. So Henry dug a small narrow well, like a bore-hole well and found a stream there.

Pearl said she had never believed in "water witching" but when she saw the switch turn in Henry's hand, and certainly after he drew up water, she believed it. The well wasn't a great source of water, but it helped them over the worst part.

Nevertheless, they still had to conserve every precious drop. Children went barefooted in extra dirty clothes all summer. The children didn't mind—but their mothers were ashamed.

Pearl's kids looked like all the others. She had one special law in her house, however: each kid had his or her turn to wash feet before bedtime. One basin of water served them all. But nobody was going to bed with dirty feet on the sheets that Pearl labored over on washday.

Ever since childhood, Pearl had loved to write funny, rhyming poetry, and she could think up some kind of poem to go along with whatever happened. So, always able to laugh at calamity, Pearl wrote a parody on the then popular tune, *Yes, We Have No Bananas.*

YES, WE HAVE NO CITY WATER

There's a lake outside our town, but it's almost dry.
You needn't be afraid you'll drown, you couldn't wet your eye.
If you want to get a drink, just go to town some day,
Ask, "Have you any water here?" and this is what they'll say:

They'll tell you, "Yes, we have no city water,
We have no city water today.
We have white mule and wine that tastes mighty fine,
And all kinds of drinks and say!
We have old fashioned red whiskey, that makes you quite frisky,
But yes, we have no city water,
We have no city water today!"

Arthur was a year-and-a-half old, Ruth was three-and-a-half, and one day they were playing in the kitchen with Helen who was about eight. That morning Pearl said to Helen, "I have to go over to the store for a few things. You watch Arthur and Ruth for me." Pearl did her "tradin'" at Fears small grocery store next door.

On one side of the kitchen, under the south window, sat a large, old-fashioned trunk which Henry had brought back from California. At one end of the trunk was a big washtub full of water that had just been delivered that day. Helen was playing with her doll when looking up, she saw Arthur crawling on top of the trunk, saw him fall, and heard a splash as he hit the water. She screamed to nobody in particular, "I'll go get Mother!"

Pearl was buying groceries when Helen ran in shouting, "Mother, come quick! Arthur fell in the water!"

Pearl raced home—fortunately only a few steps. Ruth was

sitting in the middle of the kitchen floor singing, "Yes, we have no city water," and Arthur was gurgling in the tub. Ruth must have seen him fall. She was old enough to have sense enough to get him out. But with her split personality—Ruth was too busy singing, and Mary Jane probably didn't like Arthur anyway—she just kept on singing.

Arthur was just about to gurgle his last, when Pearl snatched him out and turned him upside down, smacking his back and bottom. He coughed and vomited and started to cry. Then Pearl put him on his stomach on the floor and pushed and pushed on his back, and all the water he'd swallowed ran out.

Ruth looked up with three-year-old interest at the unusual sight of her mother holding her baby brother upside down by his heels and smacking his back with her hand. That pushing on the floor was interesting, too.

When the crisis was over and Arthur had been comforted, Pearl asked Helen, "Why didn't *you* get Arthur out of that tub?"

Helen's eyes grew wide. "I don't know, Mother. When I saw him fall off the trunk, I got so scared and only thought I ought to run and call you. I just didn't think that *I* could get him out!"

Pearl didn't ask anything of Ruth—that vacant little songbird!

Poor Pearl! She had plenty to cope with—married to a coal miner, no city water, two little idiots, and a deep-sea diver!

Neither Helen nor Ruth could ever remember who put Arthur up on the trunk, or whether he climbed up there by himself. Anyway, he didn't drown.

Olive, the only child of John and Julia left on the farm, would have been a lonesome little girl if it had not been for Mike. As she grew up, she sometimes felt sorry for herself because she thought John gave her a hard time. "Pa, you're just too old-fashioned!" Olive stormed. "You never want me to look beautiful. You think I have to wear extra long dresses and awful lookin' shoes. You just want me to look dowdy! If you'd see all the pretty shoes that I see at school, you'd know why I want some!"

She had bought some pretty "slippers" to wear to school and John had scolded her. With all the walking she had to do, John knew those slippers wouldn't last more than six months.

"You're just wastin' money on things like them fancy shoes. They won't keep your feet dry nor warm either!"

"Oh, Pa! Your notion of a well-dressed girl is just a notion of old 'sensible' clothes and shoes! That idea went out before I was born! Clothes are different now and I want to look nice."

"I want you to buy decent laced-up shoes which will keep your feet dry when you go to school!"

Julia was always in the middle of their disagreements. She sided with Olive for some fancier clothes for her beautiful blond-haired, blue-eyed daughter, yet she tried to be loyal to her husband. Julia, herself, continued to wear long print dresses like she'd always made for herself and worn, even though the style that Olive liked showed much shorter skirts.

When Olive was fifteen, she wrote to Ida, her sister in St. Louis:

"Dear Ida, now that I've graduated from the eighth grade, I am *tired* of going to school and living on the farm. Nobody else is out here except Mike, and I get lonesome. He will soon be leaving to work someplace else, too.

"I'd like to come live with you for a while if you'd let me. I want to find a job and make my own money. I think it would be great to live in a big city and see all the colored lights. We've still got coal-oil lamps back here, you know!"

Ida was not surprised at Olive's letter. She'd heard from her before. She asked Ralph if he'd agree and wrote:

"Dear Olive, Sure you can come up and live with us if you want to. Since Ralph is a streetcar conductor, he meets lots of people. Maybe he can help you find a job."

Of course, John and Julia didn't want Olive to leave because she was very young. But they knew Ida would look after her. The fact that she wanted to go to a big city frightened Julia. *Bad things happen to girls in big cities, especially beautiful girls! Maybe if we were younger and could do more things with her, she wouldn't be anxious to leave. Well—we did have her late! At least we tried to raise her right so now she will have to choose for herself how to behave.*

Olive finally persuaded John to let her go. He bought her a train ticket to St. Louis—but he also bought one for himself. "I won't let you go by yourself, I'm goin' too! I've got to see the kind of place you're goin' to be livin' in. Want to see Ida, anyhow."

Olive, not sure whether she was relieved or sorry that she was not going alone, was as excited about the train trip as she was about going. It was the first train trip for both of them—all the traveling they had done was mostly in Williamson County, and in a wagon or on horseback. Of course she had seen trains in town, but they were so huge they frightened her.

Olive was amazed when they boarded. "Pa! I never dreamed the sittin' places are this big!"

When that mountain of an engine started jerking the train into motion, then sped up fast as it left Herrin, John was nearly scared to death. The feel of such power under his feet made his heart pound, but he didn't want to let Olive know he was afraid. He thought she'd probably be just as scared. After their pulses settled down, they began to enjoy the scenery as they rolled a hundred miles northwest through Illinois to Missouri.

Ida and Ralph met them at the cavernous St. Louis Central Station. Neither Olive nor John had ever seen such a room—looked to them like the whole outdoors was covered over.

Ida and Ralph enjoyed showing John and Olive the city's sights, then they took them to their small home. John felt very out of place in the city. He heard no cows bawlin' to be milked, and couldn't see any grass except little old pocket-handkerchief-sized front yards. He felt stifled by the houses so close together and could see right into Ida's neighbor's house when he went to bed. He didn't like sleepin' with his nose next to the neighbor's, and he didn't like sleepin' without Julia beside him.

John was glad to be heading home two days later. But as he climbed aboard the train again, he grieved to think about his beautiful last child away in such a big place. The scenery outside the train window wasn't very clear because tears kept misting his eyes.

Olive, in St. Louis, took some lessons in hat making, and discovered she had a knack to do that very thing. She soon found a job using those skills. But before long, she fell in love with a charming man and was married when she was very young. Olive never lost her beauty.

One cold November day, Henry came home from work carrying his dinner bucket and wearing his miner's cap as usual. Ruth saw a tiny, squeaky bulge in his big coat pocket. Henry said, "Ruth, Arthur, come here and see what I brought!"

He pulled a fat, squirmy, brown-and-white-spotted puppy from his pocket. "Now here is Jack! He's a pure breed pointer—a real bird dog. I picked him as the best of the litter of nine. I'm going to train him to hunt and he'll be the best bird dog in this town. Now, Pearl, don't *ever* feed him potatoes! That ruins a dog!"

Arthur and Ruth were wild with joy to have a puppy. The night was too cold to put Jack outside, so Henry put him in a box by the kitchen stove. Art and Ruth brought a bunch of old rags to cover him up and keep him warm. But when they all went to bed and the puppy was lonely, he began to whimper.

When Ruth thought her mama and daddy were asleep, she crept to the kitchen, cradled Jack in her long flannel nightgown, climbed back into bed and snuggled Jack down in the big double feather-bed between her brother and herself. That, of course, was before psychologists told parents that a small brother and sister shouldn't sleep together.

When spring came, Jack was all paws, beating tail, and lolling tongue. He was clumsy and uninhibited, loping into everything, but he knew what he was born to do. Instinctively, when he saw a bird in the grass, he'd freeze to a point, one foot raised. He was so easy to train that Henry, with only "A—a—ah, Jack!" could make him obey.

That spring, Henry and his next door neighbor went "halves" on an incubator full of eggs. When the chickens hatched, Henry put his in the outside pen where Jack was. Jack never hurt any of them.

Late in the afternoons, after work, Henry would sit in the back yard and let the chickens out of the pen to wander around in the grass. Henry's neighbors used to do the same. Jack never killed any of Henry's own chickens, nor crossed the dividing line to bother any of the neighbor's flock. Sometimes he would point them, but "A—a—ah, Jack!" from Henry always stopped him instantly.

But one afternoon, one of the neighbor's chickens wandered over into the Childers yard. Before anyone knew what was happening, Jack killed it. The kids never forgot the belting Henry gave Jack. Arthur and Ruth both cried in Pearl's lap. But Henry said, "I don't like whipping Jack. But any bird dog that gets a taste of dead chicken is ruined as a bird dog! Jack is not going to be!" He tied the dead chicken to Jack's neck for two days.

Jack never forgot that incident—he never touched another chicken. But he'd sit on guard at the dividing line between the two yards. Every time the neighbor's chickens came toward their side, Jack was there to nose them right back home. Somehow he knew the difference between the Childers chickens and the neighbor's, although they were all hatched in the same incubator.

Henry was a good, though strict, trainer and Jack did become the best bird dog for miles around. Henry bragged about him. "He's never gun-shy. Not a muscle quivers when the blast goes off above him. You know, Pearl, other dogs blunder in too soon and scare up the birds even before the guns are aimed, and they maul the birds they bring in. But Jack barely touches the birds with his teeth, he finds the ones I shoot, and he drops them neatly into my hand."

Henry was a good hunter; he had hunted for necessary food with his father, John Childers, when he was young. During season he would come home to his own family with his pockets stuffed full of quail, and his hunting skills certainly helped out a coal miner's dwindling budget.

Jack was never allowed to run loose, and Henry trained him to come out of the pen only when *he* told him to. The rest of the family could yell, "Here, Jack, come on, Jack," all day, but he wouldn't come out. Jack knew when it was time for Henry to come home from the mines; he rounded the back corner of the house at five o'clock. Jack had also learned how to put his paw through the slat rails of the fence, lift a wooden bar, and let the gate swing open. About four-thirty every day, he opened the gate. Then he sat right there, not allowing a single chicken to get past his nose and escape. Only when Henry came around the house and called, "All right, Jack, come on out," would he move. Then he became a prancing, leaping, circling tornado.

The night Ruth's baby sister, Irene, was born, her Grandma Julia was there, and Ruth kept hearing strange noises. Ruth asked, "What is that cryin'? What's makin' that noise, Grandma?"

"It's only a cat, Ruthie. Just go on back to sleep."

So Ruth went back to sleep thinking that when daylight came she could play with her new kitty. Imagine her surprise when she found a new tiny, red-faced, baby sister in bed with her mother.

Ruth was five years old when Irene was born, and felt quite sure that she was big enough to help take care of her. "Yes, Ruthie, you can hold the baby and play with her, but remember to watch and hold up the baby's head. Soon she can hold up her own head, but now you have to watch her."

When Irene got bigger and squirmier, Ruth wasn't supposed to walk around with her at all, just play with her on the floor.

One day Pearl told Ruth to take care of Irene *in the house.* She had to go out to the store for a few minutes. Of course, the outdoor summer day was calling Ruth, especially since Arthur was playing under the maple tree in the front yard. Who wanted to stay alone in the house with a baby!

So as soon as her mama walked out of sight, Ruth picked up six-months-old Irene and carried her outside. The baby began to get hot and mad in the sun, and to wriggle in Ruth's arms. Ruth tried to hold her, but the baby leaned over hard toward the ground, and lunged out of Ruth's arms onto the sidewalk.

Of course, she yelled and Ruth was scared to death. To her inexperienced five-year-old eyes, Irene looked perfectly all right, so she picked her up, squirms and all, and beat a hasty retreat to the safety of the front room couch. Irene soon stopped crying when Ruth let her suck on her finger which she licked, then dipped into the sugar bowl. She had to re-dip the finger a few times before all the tears dried up. Did Ruth tell her mama? Certainly not! Not for years!

The Childers family went to church every Sunday and the children sat between Pearl and Henry on the third seat from the front in the middle section of the Herrin, Illinois Methodist Church. The kids knew better than to laugh or play in church. They could not chew gum. They could not sit and read Sunday school papers or work puzzles, make sailboats out of songbook leaves, or spitballs out of collection envelopes. They bowed their heads and closed their eyes during the prayers, listened to the Bible reading and sermon, and joined in the singing. In other words, they *behaved* in church.

One night when Arthur was about three years old, he began acting up in church. Henry warned him once to be quiet. He didn't obey and Henry took him out and spanked him. Then he brought Art back, sniffing and rubbing his eyes, and set him down none too gently. Soon, Art started wiggling and whispering again, and again Henry took him out. Ruth couldn't believe that Arthur wouldn't be still after that—knowing the consequences. But again he started whimpering and making a fuss. The preacher looked hard at him—after all, he was close to the front! Henry took Arthur out the third time and paddled him hard. After that, Arthur always behaved in church. The Childers kids did not disobey their father. They learned it early.

Henry's religion worked through the week—most of the time. It worked when it came to chastising the children for any moral breakdown. It worked in his dealings, and he never deliberately tried to get the best of a trade like some of his "mule-skinnin' friends" did sometimes. Henry loved to trade—anything—pistols and shotguns, or a wheel barrow for a lawn mower. But he never cheated anybody and he would never allow his children to cheat, either. But sometimes he didn't listen to his children as he should.

One day when Arthur was about seven years old, his friend, Archie, stole two oranges from a nearby grocery store. The owner, Mr. Bradley, told Henry that Arthur had also stolen an orange.

When Art and Ruth came in from school that afternoon, Henry said, "Art, come over here. Henry was sitting in Pearl's rocking chair in the kitchen.

"What, Daddy?" Art asked fearfully. Henry sounded mad.

"Did you steal an orange from Bradly's store.?"

"No, Daddy!"

"Mr. Bradley said you did."

"It wasn't me. It was Archie."

Ruth believed Art. Why didn't Daddy believe him?

"If Arthur says he didn't do it, he didn't!" exclaimed Pearl.

"I'm goin' to handle this, Pearl. Mr. Bradley would have no cause to lie about it. Lean over my knees here, Arthur!"

Art was a sensitive little boy and he caught his breath hard and tears rolled before he bent over.

Henry whipped Arthur with his razor strap but Pearl didn't let him do it very long. She took the strap away from him and told Art to go outside. Ruth comforted her little brother under the sweet honeysuckle bush where he sobbed on her shoulder. "It wasn't me, it was Archie. He doesn't have much food at his house."

Ruth despised Mr. Bradley after that, even if he *did* have a store with lots of good things in it. He had lied about Arthur.

Archie, Ruth's brother's dirty-faced little friend, often ate biscuits and gravy with the Childers family after that—Pearl felt sorry for him. His parents didn't get along well together, and at home Archie often had no supper at all. He usually turned up just about supper time which thoroughly irritated Henry. Before feeding him, Pearl always made him blow his nose. She even provided an old rag for the purpose, which she afterward threw into the fire of the coal stove. Then she made him scrub his hands with a small brush. Pearl could never stand dirty hands and dirty noses. It was unfortunate, but Archie had the most permanently runny nose on the street, and a runny nose simply wasn't allowed at the Childers house.

After Olive left the farm, Elton (Mike) was lonesome. The next time Cena visited, he begged her to take him home with her. She said, "You can come for the summer, Mike, but you've got to behave. I'm not goin' to have you cuttin' up and disgracin' us in West Frankfort!"

Mike's eyes twinkled as he promised to mind her. He remembered how it was when Cena was young and lived on the farm with them. Mike had always looked up to Cena because she was so strong and never afraid of anything. He had listened to her when she bossed him around, because Cena was big enough to make the bossin' stick!

When Mike hit West Frankfort at the age of twelve, he

thought of himself as a one-man Chamber of Commerce. He looked around the town and decided that the shoes he saw the inhabitants wearing were doing nothing to improve local morale. He decided to help spruce up the town.

One day he put on his white shirt and white pants, went to the store and bought shoe polish, two brushes and a cardboard container to keep them in. He also took a small wooden box with him, and started on his career. He became the smiling shoe shiner on Main Street in West Frankfort, walking as tall and straight as if he owned half the town.

When he trudged back to Cena's for supper that first day, Mike had a dollar in his pocket. The next day he earned fifty cents more, and did a little tapdance on the sidewalk when a shiny pair of shoes walked away from him. Mike told funny stories to his clients while polishing their shoes, so afterward, they strolled with buoyant steps down the street. For a few weeks, he worked hard and quite eagerly, but wasn't getting as rich as he wanted to be.

Cena made him pay a little for all the food and clean, ironed clothes she provided for him. He began to realize he would never be a millionaire by just shining shoes, so his fertile brain conjured up something else.

One evening he went down into Cena's basement and soon came up with his old dark clothes on. He'd been wearing white, so Cena wondered what he was up to now.

"Mike! What're you doin' with them old clothes on? Goin' out to work in a field somewhere? Kinda late in the day for that, ain't it?"

Mike didn't answer, he just grinned and walked toward the door.

Cena blocked the way. "Mike, I asked you a question. Where're you goin' in them clothes?"

Silence.

"Miiike——?"

He stood up as tall as he could. "I'm goin' to steal me a watermelon."

"To st——— WHAT?!"

He clenched his jaw and looked straight at her. "I'm too big for you to boss any more! I'm goin' out to steal me a watermelon! It's easier than shinin' dirty old shoes all day. It's hot! And I can cut a big juicy watermelon in town and sell it for ten cents a slice. I can make lots of money."

"ELTON CHILDERS! You're not goin' to do any such a

thing!" Cena reached up and grabbed Arthur's razor strap hanging by the kitchen washstand, hooked Mike by the arm and started swinging the strap hard against his legs. "You hear me? You get that idea out of your head right now, Young Man!" Cena was a hefty woman and wasn't afraid to use that strap even if Mike *was* twelve years old! "I've got to make a decent man out of you!"

Mike yelled, and Arthur, coming from work into the kitchen, caught Cena's arm, took the strap away from her, and pushed the boy against the wall.

"Why're you givin' him such a lickin'?" he asked Cena, who was breathing hard.

"Because I'm not goin' to have him stealin' any watermelons and sellin' them in town! That's what he said he was goin' to do!"

"Did you intend to do that?" Arthur asked Mike, shaking him a little.

Mike looked at the floor and his face flushed.

Arthur shook Mike harder and said, "If she hadn't already given you a lickin', I would! Now you sit in that chair for a while and think this over. You'd better decide to behave yourself or you're not goin' to live in this house any more! Cena's been good to you and this is home as long as you act right. But no stealin' anything. You hear me?"

Mike went back to his shoe-shinin' career.

CHAPTER TWENTY-SIX
Julia, 1921
The Hardest of All

To Julia and John it seemed that one day the children were all around them—and the next day they were all gone. And in 1920 since their last child had left home, they simply didn't know what to do with themselves. They talked about it.

They didn't need to raise as much food as they once did. She didn't need to be making new quilts or sweaters, either. She'd had children to take care of ever since 1880, and in 1885 she'd started married life with six!

Now she didn't have to spend so much time in the kitchen any more because she didn't cook over the fireplace. They had an up-to-date wood stove for warmth and cooking in winter, and a coal-oil stove for summer cooking.

But they kept on plowing and planting their small garden, and Julia continued to partly fill her cellar with vegetables, fruits, jams and jellies. She didn't *have* to, but old habits die hard.

As they grew older, they didn't talk much—they didn't need to. They could almost read each other's thoughts. Just *being* together satisfied them. They enjoyed working together in their shrunken garden and sitting on the porch in the evenings during warm weather. John often told her, "Julia, in this lamplight you still look like that purty little girl I married!"

"Oh, John, it's because of you! Love makes ever'thing purty. And you are still handsome—even if your beard is white—and you keep it trimmed so nice."

Julia began to worry because several times John felt so weak and dizzy he had to come in and sit on the porch. He began to tire fast and said, "Don't know what's the matter—just no energy. Got some pains in my heart, too, sometimes."

The heart pains frightened her—that's just the way her mother had been the last year of her life!

She'd bring him a glass of cool well water and sit beside him until he felt better. "Why don't you go and see the doctor, John?" she asked him several times. "Maybe he could give you some tonic. We've got to do something to make you feel better."

"Ain't no use in doin' that, Julia. He'd just tell me I'm a' gettin' old and I know that already. I'll just sit here and rest a spell, then I'll go and finish that row." He'd lean back in his chair and catnap for a while, then say, "I can't set here on the porch in a rockin' chair all day long!"

"Oh, John, don't work so hard. I just couldn't get along without you!"

As the days passed, the thought of having to live without John nagged at her more and more. After all, John was fifteen years older than she. Julia knew all too well the heartache of losing a loved one. As she rocked in her chair in the evenings and thought about all the events of her life, she realized that to face John's death would be the most painful thing she would ever endure. Losing John would be the hardest of all—even harder than her days with Solly.

* * * *

Early in the morning on November 21, 1921, Julia was awakened by a strange sound. She first thought John was dreaming. He had been restless in the night, and he often made little grunting noises when he slept. Then she heard it again—a soft, moaning sound and a kind of gasping.

"John—?"

She sat up in bed and tried to see his face, but the room was too dark. "I'll light the lamp, John."

She quickly crossed to the dresser, struck a match, and turned up the lampwick. Thrusting the light near the bed she looked at him and her strength nearly failed her. John's face was contorted and now a rasping sound of dreadful breathing seemed forced from his throat.

"John!" she cried. "Wake up! I'll get you some water!"

She turned to fetch it, but a new sound came from the bed; a choking sound. John's face was grimaced with pain and his lips moved trying to speak to her. He opened his eyes once, looked at her, and his body grew rigid with an effort to sit up.

"John!" she cried. "John, John!—"

He could not speak. She set the lamp down, then collapsed sobbing as John's body sank back. The silence was more terrifying than the harsh breathing.

"Oh, John, don't leave me," she cried, her head on his still chest. "John, wake up!" Then she lifted her head and clutched his shoulders, trying to shake him, but John did not respond. She leaned over, her hands gripping his shoulders, her face rubbing his. "John, I love you— I can't live without you. Don't leave me—" and her voice trailed off in a shrieking cry.

She sobbed with deep, wracking gasps of breath, her tears soaking into John's nightshirt. She could not believe this was happening so soon.

"John, you've not even had your seventy-first birthday! I wanted to make you a cake! You're too young to die. Your family needs you—I need you. Oh, John—we need to plant our garden in the spring—" *Somehow, if I can keep talking to him, he'll start breathing again,* she thought. "John, how can I—" and she collapsed on his chest again.

Here it is. And I'm not ready—I'd never be ready. This is too soon! This was the third time Julia had been in the shadows when death crept out with someone she loved. But John's death was the most devastating. Part of herself died with him.

At first she couldn't even think what to do. She remembered how she had washed her mother's body when she died. She thought about the time little Ada died and she had to prepare her body for burial. "That's what I must do now," she said aloud. She even started to the kitchen to heat water but stopped halfway there. "What am I thinkin'? I'm supposed to call an undertaker. Oh, will he be gentle with John?" She leaned against the wall for some support. "I'm goin' to do *somethin'* for him!"

Through blinding tears, she stirred up the banked fire in the kitchen stove, put more wood in, filled her teakettle with water and set it back on the stove. She waited, trying not to think. When the water was warm, she took some in a pan with a clean washrag and a towel, into the bedroom. She just *had* to wash John's face and comb his hair. He was always fussy about having his hair combed.

Julia wrung out the rag, folded it carefully and smoothed it over his face. She kissed his cheeks before she patted them dry with a towel. John's comb was on the dresser, where he had put it last night. Julia lovingly combed his thick white hair and his beard. These were the last things she could ever do for him. She even smiled a little. "Oh, John, I'm glad you let your beard grow back that time. You are so handsome, and I love you so much!"

She straightened John's nightshirt, and smoothed the bed covers. Then she sat beside him and told him goodbye. After this she wouldn't be alone with him ever again. "John, I remember when you said, 'Goodbye 'til we meet for our wonderful day.' That was before our wedding. Now I say it to you. 'Goodbye, my dearest John, my love, 'til we meet for our wonderful day.' Remember when the preacher said not long ago, 'Christians never say goodbye forever.' Remember? So this goodbye is only 'til I see you again. Now I have to go and get help to tell the children."

Hardly aware of what she was doing, she put her coat on over her nightgown, threw a scarf over her head and almost at the door, stumbled over her shoes. *Oh, I need my shoes—it's cold outside.*

Putting them on, she walked half a mile, stumbling over hard ruts in the road, to the Martins, her nearest neighbors. The sun was just beginning to peek through cold November mists when she knocked on their door.

One look at her, and Tom and Gertrude Martin knew what must have happened; her distorted, blotched face told them. Gertrude pulled her inside, hugged her, set her down at their table and gave her some coffee to drink—as Martha had done in an hour of need so many years ago.

Her hands and lips trembled so she could hardly drink the coffee. "I just lost John—his heart gave out." They could hardly hear her. " Can you go into Herrin and get Henry?" she asked Tom. "He can get the others."

"I'll be proud to do it for you, Julia."

"And tell the undertaker for me. I have to go back home and stay with John 'til they come."

"I'll come with you," Gertrude said.

"First I'll ride you and Gertrude back to your house in the wagon," said Tom."

"No cause to do that," Julia shook her head. "I can walk back. You better go on in to Herrin."

"No," insisted Tom. "I'm gonna take you back. You've walked enough already."

When the two women climbed from the wagon at Julia's house, Julia walked straight into the bedroom. She stood and looked at John, still not believing the quietness of his body. He looked just as if he were asleep.

Gertrude touched her shoulder. "Can I help you get dressed, Julia?"

Only then did Julia realize she was still in her nightgown and was wearing her shoes but no stockings. She nodded. "Oh—I'll get my clothes on—I'll just stay in here with John."

Gertrude nodded and went to see about the fire.

Dora, Dona, Eva Jane, Henry, George, Ed, and Milt were all there by noon. It would take the others longer to come. As they arrived one by one, they went and stood with Julia in the bedroom to look at John. Surrounding the bed, and through tears they talked about what a good father John had been.

"I've been watchin' Pa lately," Henry said. "I thought he was goin' downhill. Well, we can be thankful he didn't suffer long."

His brothers and sisters nodded.

"Does Addie, Ida, Olive, Cena, and Ola know yet?" Julia asked.

"Yes," Henry answered. "I've sent them all word. They'll probably be here this afternoon. Mike is in Kansas—he won't be able to make it."

Just after noon the undertaker arrived. He said to Dora, "Mrs. Nall, will you please take the women out into another room and close the door? I will ask the men to help me.

Julia was led, helpless and sobbing from John's side. Her girls, weeping, followed.

Henry, George, Milt, and Ed helped the undertaker put John's body into the horse-drawn carriage. The four sons stood with bowed heads, as the horses pulled their father's black, shuttered hearse down the farm lane, away from the place John had loved.

John's body lay in state at the home of Rev. Wallace and Dora Childers Nall, on East Herrin Street in Herrin. Wallace, John's son-in-law, preached the funeral service and the little church was crowded. They buried John in the Boner Cemetery, at West Frankfort, Illinois.

Julia stood by his grave with their sorrowing family, shivering in the cold. Tears almost froze on their cheeks and they couldn't linger there very long. As they walked away with bowed heads, Julia said to herself, *John Childers, beloved of Julia King Childers, how can I ever live without you?"*

When John died, Pearl felt so sorry for Julia because she knew how much love had been between them. They had been apart only a very few nights since they were married. And now that all Julia's children had left home, she would be very lonely.

Pearl was expecting another baby within a month and her house would be filled up. But she put her arms around her mother-in-law, Julia, and said, "Come home with us, Ma Childers. You can always have a home with us."

"Yes, Ma, come and stay with us," Henry echoed. But Julia said, "Henry, I'll come and stay until Pearl has her baby. I know she needs a little help through these days, and I need somethin' to do."

Henry's sisters were satisfied, though they, too, would have liked Julia to be with them. But Julia was with Pearl when on December 29, 1921, baby Irene came into the world. She, too, was born at home. Pearl had never had any complications, and the birth was quick—so quick the doctor barely got there. Henry was just as proud of his new daughter as he was of all the rest of his children. He's the one who named her.

Pearl gazed down at her newest little daughter with the joy she always felt after a birth. Irene was very alert, with big blue eyes and a blond fuzz for hair. Ruth and Arthur stuck their heads around Pearl's bedroom door and asked, "Mommie, can we come in and see the baby now?"

"Sure you can!"

The two children ran in and first hugged Pearl. "When we first heard our new baby cry, we asked Grandma Julia what it was. And Grandma said, 'Oh, it's just a cat!' She sure sounded like a funny cat!" said Ruth. Pearl pulled a small blanket back so the two could see baby Irene.

"Oooh—she's so little!"

"Look, she's holding my finger," exclaimed Art.

"Mommie, now that I'm five years old, can I help you take care of her?" asked Ruth.

"You can both help me," Pearl said. "Taking care of a baby is a big job and I'll need lots of help. Now you can go back into the other room—shut my door and let me rest. And be quiet—the baby needs sleep and I do too."

The children quietly went out and Pearl was already asleep before they could even close the bedroom door.

After Pearl recovered from Irene's birth and was able to do her own work again, Julia said one day, "Pearl, it's time for me to go back home."

"Are you sure you want to go? It'll be so lonesome for you."

"Well, it's home, even though John won't be there." Julia's lips were pressed tight together as she tried not to cry. "Got to go back sometime."

"I'll be sorry to see you go, Ma Childers. I'd love for you to just stay here with us and let your girls break up your house. They could bring the things you wanted here."

Julia was wiping her tears and Pearl went on, "You know, Ma Childers, the Lord really blessed me when he handed out mothers-in-law. He gave me His two best ones! Even if you have to go now, you can come back here any time—we love to have you."

CHAPTER TWENTY-SEVEN
1922, Helen

Before anyone could believe it, the Roaring Twenties were upon them. At the first of it, the mines were working well and Herrin was progressing. By 1922, Williamson County Mine Workers Union was the strongest section of the UMWA in the nation, with 30,000 members. Oldham Paisley, Southern Illinois journalist said, "Men joined the union with more conviction than they joined the church."

Mine workers saw a little progress in making mines safer places to work. They improved mining housing and eliminated the necessity of buying all their povisions from the company store. Now wages were better, but still miners' families lived very close to a ragged edge of poverty. The union stood behind them, so safety improved—but slowly. In spite of improvements, men continued to be killed in coal mines from explosions, gases, or fall-ins. Miners knew their working conditions would never be totally safe, and sometimes bitter fighting broke out between the union and non-union members.

On June 22, 1922, Henry got up early as usual. His mine was on strike so he didn't have to hurry that day. He walked with his milk bucket a block away from their house at 618 South 18th Street, to Hemlock Woods where he kept their cow. He milked her and brought the milk back to Pearl. She strained it through several layers of clean cheese cloth, then set the covered crock in the ice box. The top of the ice box would hold a one-hundred-pound block of ice, and it kept the box cold for about five days.

Pearl nursed baby Irene and put her down for a nap. Then she brought out yesterday's milk, skimmed off the cream for coffee, and poured glasses of milk for Helen, Ruth, and Arthur to drink for breakfast.

Fresh milk is delicious like that with little speckles of cream floating around—and in 1922 it was more delicious because nobody had ever heard of cholesterol. As they sat around the table, Pearl said a prayer, "Lord, we thank Thee for our home. We thank Thee for our children and for this food. Help us to always be thankful, and help us in these times of strike. We thank Thee for our cow and chickens. Bless us all, Amen."

Helen, who was just past ten, giggled. "Mother, do we always have to thank the Lord for a cow and chickens?"

Pearl looked at Helen and drew her mouth sideways. "Well, how would you like to have no milk and no eggs for breakfast, and never have any chicken and dumplin's or fried chicken and gravy?"

Helen knew she'd never like that, so she quietly ate her fried eggs, biscuits, milk gravy, and glass of milk.

"What will you be doin' today, Henry?" Pearl asked.

"Work in the garden. It needs a good weedin'. We'll soon have tomatoes."

"Mother," Helen asked. "Are you going to be sad when I go to Ma and Pa Baxley's?"

"I'm already sad just thinkin' about it. Are you *sure* you want to move over to their house?"

"Yes, I want to go. You have Ruth, Arthur, and Irene here with you, but Ma and Pa Baxley don't have anybody!" She added seriously, "They need me! That's why I ought to go there."

Ruth, age five, asked, "Are you going to see Ma and Pa Baxley today? Can I come with you?"

Helen looked at her little sister. "Not today, Ruth. But in a few days, after Mother can get my things together, I'm going to live with Ma and Pa."

Ruth stopped eating and stared at Helen, her eyes filling with tears. "You mean *live with them all the time? And not live with us?"* Tears rolled down her face.

Helen nodded.

"Why? Don't you love us any more?"

"You're silly! Course I love you!"

"Then don't leave us. Stay here with us all the time!" Ruth wiped tears with the back of her hand.

Arthur, age three, seeing Ruth cry, also started to rub his eyes and sniffle.

"Well, it's not like she's going to fly to the moon," Pearl explained. "Ma and Pa Baxley are Helen's grandparents and all their kids have left home. They love Helen as much as we do. So they want her to come live with them. I'm sad about it, but Helen does love them, too. So I said she could go. If she doesn't like livin' with them, I will bring her home any time she wants to come. She knows we all love her here, don't you, Helen?"

Helen nodded. She was about to cry because Ruth and Arthur were. "You can come over to see us any time. And you can eat dinner with us at noon—Ma Baxley always has lots of food—and you can climb our trees. You can help me pick fruit, too, when it's ripe this summer."

Pearl sat thinking after Henry went out to work in his garden, and the children outside to play. How could she let her first daughter leave? Helen wanted to—she never forgot about living with her grandparents. Pearl sighed. She would certainly have more things there than she and Henry could provide. Pearl knew the Baxleys loved Helen dearly and would take excellent care of her.

Henry worked very hard, but they were barely getting by—just from payday to payday. Often they didn't have enough money to buy shoes when the kids needed them—and it would be worse when they started to school. Pearl would like to have meat on the table more often—something besides bacon. She sighed again.

When the mines were idle—as they often were in summer, Henry found it difficult to pay the light and gas bill. They could have only one light bulb on at a time—and not light the gas oven very often. Pearl was lucky they even *had* a gas stove. They'd just bought it lately—it was far better than cooking on the coal range in summer. They still had the coal range for heating and for cooking in the winter. But when they couldn't light the gas oven, Henry missed the biscuits he loved. He hated "store-bought bread."

The kids were going barefoot all summer—except to church. They were growing so fast she could barely keep up with making their clothes. And even then, she bought the cheapest goods she could find. Yes—Ma and Pa Baxley would feed and clothe Helen well, and Ma had said they'd even send Helen to high school. It was expensive to go to high school! Pearl sighed again—she seemed to be sighing a lot lately—hoping and praying she had made the right decision and that it would be better for Helen.

CHAPTER TWENTY-EIGHT
1922
The Herrin Massacre

Julia saw it before she heard anything. Outside while hanging her work clothes on the line, she spied a thread of dust rising on the main road. *Somebody's ridin' fast!* she thought, and immediately heard a horse galloping full-speed up the lane. Shading her eyes with her hand, she recognized her neighbor Tom Martin.

Tom pulled his horse to a quick stop near Julia and jumped down. "Heard the news about Herrin, Julia?"

"N—no, I've heard nothing. What about Herrin?"

"They's been some killin' in Herrin yesterday, and today the town's gone crazy! More gettin' killed today!"

"Oh, my Lord!" Julia exclaimed. "My family! Who's been killed? Who's doin' the killin'?"

"Don't know who," Tom shook his head. I was in town this mornin' to get supplies and saw people begin to run every which a way. I kept callin' out, 'What's the matter? What's wrong?' but nobody answered. Finally, a man yelled at me, 'Couple of men got shot yesterday, and there's some killin' goin' on out south of town right now!'

"I tried to get him to tell me who was gettin' killed but he just ran to get his horse sayin, 'I don't know! Somethin' to do with the mines.'"

"The mines!" Julia repeated. "Which mine?" A cold chill snaked down her spine despite the warm day. George, Henry, Ed, Milt, and Eva Jane's husband, Bill Scott, worked in different mines. There was a good chance that one of them would be involved in whatever was happening in Herrin!

"I hate the coal mines!" Julia cried. "Always somethin' bad happenin'—somebody gettin' killed. Ever' time I think about Henry and the rest of 'em hunkered over cuttin' coal out of a wall—underground like that—I can't stand it. They'd have been a lot safer on the farm!"

"They would," Tom agreed. "But not everybody can make it a' farmin'."

"You never found out which mine?" Julia asked.

Tom shook his head. "People was runnin' all over. I saw some mobs rushin' on another street two blocks away from me. When I saw that, I started for home. I saw people draggin' their young'uns in off the street and slammin' the doors even if it was ninety degrees in the shade. By the time I was at the edge of town, things seemed awful quiet. Nearly too quiet. Then I heard some shots."

"Is everybody in danger?"

"Don't know. Didn't wait to find out. I don't aim to get in on any Herrin troubles. I knew you'd want to know." He wheeled his horse around. "I'll git on home now and tell Gertrude the news. If she hears it from somebody else, she's liable to think I'm hurt or somethin."

"I'm much obliged to you, Tom, for comin' by."

"Well, Julia, I knowed your boys are there."

Julia watched Tom ride down the lane. Then she stood for a few moments thinking what best to do. "If John was here, he'd know what to do," she said aloud. But she already knew. She simply had to go to Herrin. It might be dangerous, but it wasn't possible for her to stay here while somethin' might be happening to her family in Herrin.

I'll go out and hitch up the buggy. I can do that first. She strode toward the barn, her shoe-top length work dress flapping in the breeze. She straightened her shoulders as if to stand tall against her fear. John had died only seven months ago. She couldn't bear to think of facing the death of one of her children, too.

Ever since John had been gone, Julia had lived alone on the farm. She couldn't leave this house which had meant so much to them both. She did all the work by herself, but now and then Henry and George came out and helped her with the extra hard things. She'd even put in a small garden in the spring.

None of her children wanted her to stay here alone, and probably soon she'd have to listen to them. But working in the garden she felt so close to John. She talked to him just as she used to. She told him about farm things, and lived in memory their years together. Now she said, "John, I got to go to Herrin to see about them." She backed the horse into the buggy shafts.

"I'll take some of that side pork I fried this mornin' and some biscuits and water, and eat on the way in. Don't want Pearl havin' to cook for me. I'll go to Henry's first and see if he's all right. Them mine fights are always bad!"

Julia hurried into the house and changed her dress. "I'll take Pearl some canned sausage and blackberries. She can use some extra." She carried up a few cans of food from her cellar and laid them carefully in the bottom of a basket, adding some fresh churned butter and a jar of jelly. Then she lifted her side pork meat from the skillet in her warming oven and put it into a half-gallon lard bucket. She put in an apple and a couple of biscuits, filled her water bottle, and put them in the basket. She was ready.

On her way out the gate, Julia thought about her cow—she'd ask Tom's grandson to take care of the milkin' tonight and tomorrow. "I ought to be back tomorrow."

Julia's horse, Chestnut, which she and John had owned for many years, seemed happy to be out today. He hadn't had much exercise lately—Julia didn't go to very many places. Julia wiped the sweat from her face as the buggy rolled along. The Twenty-second day of June was a hot day, and she welcomed the breeze in her face. "Thank You, Lord for this fine summer day. It makes the crops grow. I know that rain does, too, but I'm thankful I don't have to get out in the rain today. Please keep my family safe. And bless them families that have lost husbands and fathers today. Be merciful to the ones who done the killin'. I know it makes You sad to have people killin' other people."

Chestnut trotted north along the dusty road toward Herrin. Julia bounced in the buggy and thought about her family. She tried to eat her biscuits and side pork, but wasn't hungry. Nearing Herrin, her tension mounted.

She stopped at Henry's house first and everything seemed peaceful. Ruth and Arthur were playing in the yard. Ruth shouted, "Grandma!"

Julia climbed stiffly down from the buggy, and stooped to be hugged by two small children.

Ruth exclaimed, "Grandma, we didn't know you're comin' today!"

"I didn't know it either, Ruthie. I just decided to come. Is your Daddy at home?"

Ruth nodded and pointed toward the back. "He's out there in the garden. Sometimes he lets us pull weeds. But Arthur's really too little to pull very many weeds. He's only three. I'm five. Helen's inside readin' a book."

Julia said to the Lord, "Thank You. Henry's safe!"

"Is your Mother here?"

Ruth nodded again, her light brown curls sending off reddish sparks in the sun. "Mommie's makin' us a hickor' nut cake. It's Daddy's favorite."

While they were talking, Julia was leading them toward Henry in the garden. Little Arthur was trying to keep up with Grandma Julia's long steps.

Henry, who was keeping an eye on Ruth and Arthur while he worked, straightened up in surprise when he saw Julia. He came striding out of the garden. "Ma! I didn't know you was comin' today!"

"Oh, Henry," Julia hugged him. "Are you all right?"

"Course I'm all right. Been workin' in my garden all day. What's the matter?"

"Well, my neighbor said they's trouble in Herrin. Killin's goin' on. He was in here this mornin' and said there was some men shot yesterday, and this mornin' Herrin was goin crazy—people all runnin' like they was scared to death. They was gettin' in off the streets and takin' their young'uns inside. He come home fast and stopped and told me.

"I just couldn't rest 'til I come in to see if everybody's all right. You heard anything from George, or Ed, Milton, or Eva Jane's Bill? Tom said the killin' had somethin' to do with the mines."

Henry looked surprised. "Killin' today? I never heard a thing. Yesterday, I heard two men had been shot at the Lester strip mines, but I know Bill Scott wasn't in on it. I ain't been to town today. Nobody's been around today to tell us anything." Henry shook his head. "It's sad if it's happenin'."

"I didn't see many people on the streets in this part of town when I come in," remarked Julia. "Maybe everybody's inside. Maybe they're scared."

"If you're that worried, then I better go see what's goin' on," Henry said. "I'll get off these work clothes."

"Well, I'm goin' with you!"

"Now, Ma, I think you better stay here. If there is trouble in town, you'd be safer here."

Henry should have known better. When Julia had her mind made up, it was made! "No, Henry! I come all the way in here to see for myself that my family is all right, and I'm goin' with you! Eva Jane might need me."

They went up the steps of the wide back porch and in the kitchen door. Pearl looked up from her mixing bowl. "Why, Ma Childers! Come in!" She put down her big spoon, dusted the flour off her hands and hugged Julia. "I'm surprised to see you, but I'm glad you came. Are you all right?"

Henry explained quickly. "Pearl, Ma says a neighbor of hers was in Herrin this morning and went back in a hurry. Said there's trouble. Killin's, he said, goin' on somewhere. Ma was worried and came in to see if we're all right. The neighbor said it had somethin' to do with the mines. So we're goin' over to see about Ed and Milt and Bill."

"Oh, Henry, if there's trouble downtown, stay home!"

"Now Pearl, nobody's after me! And if any of 'em are in any trouble, then we can help. You stay here and keep the kids at home. Don't go anywhere."

"All right. I hadn't intended to go anywhere. Ma, why don't you stay with me? Henry can see about them."

"No, Pearl. I feel like I've got to specially see about Eva Jane. Somethin' just tells me she needs me!"

"All right." Pearl went back to mixing her cake. "I'll fix supper for you."

"No, don't. We'll probably eat with Eva Jane."

"Pearl, you know how it is," Henry said. "If there's shootin' on the streets, nobody ought to be out at night. I'll try to get home by supper time, but if I don't, don't worry. If Eva Jane needs us we may not get home."

Pearl nodded and said, "Yes, I've lived in Herrin long enough to know how things are! Ruthie, you and Arthur play here in the kitchen with me while I bake the cake. I don't want you waking up baby Irene."

"Can we lick the bowl?"

"You can. Here are two spoons—wait I'll pour this batter into the pans." Before she could put the pans in the oven she heard Arthur say a soft, "Oh -oh!"

"Arthur dropped some batter on his shirt, Mommie."

"Just a typical afternoon in Herrin," Pearl muttered. "Killing out there and a dirty shirt at home."

* * * *

Henry helped Julia back into her buggy, climbed in and picked up the reins. "Ed lives the closest, so we'll go there first, Ma."

As Julia's neighbor had said, the streets were very quiet. Few women or children could be seen—odd for summer time. They soon pulled up before Ed's rooming house and knocked on his door.

Ed came out wiping his eyes—he looked like he'd been crying. "Why, Henry! Ma! What're you doin' here? Come on in." He stood back looking nervous and shaken, and they went into his small room. It was very untidy.

"You all right, Ed? We heard there's been trouble somewhere in Herrin, and we come to see about you." Henry asked the question before Julia could say anything.

Ed's eyes filled with tears. He started to speak, then broke down in sobs. "Oh, Lord, Henry, this has been an awful day. I should've stayed in Carterville. Nineteen men have been massacred in Herrin today, and not far from here, either!"

Henry was speechless. Finally he managed, "Nineteen men! Where? Who? WHY? How do you know?"

Ed managed to get control of himself. "I'll tell you what I know. Seems it started yesterday at the Lester strip mine—you know where that is, Ma?"

"Henry just told me two men was shot there yesterday."

Henry touched her arm. "Just keep calm, Ma. At least we know now which mine it was and that Milt wasn't in that mine. Let's hear what Ed's got to say; then we'll go over to Eva Jane's."

"I'll come with you," said Ed. "I was tryin' to git myself together and go see about them." Ed slowly let out a long breath as he pulled up a chair. "Here's what I know.

"This mornin' I come out of my room kinda late because all the mines are on strike, you know. I started to walk towards town—didn't have anything special to do. I heard a lot of yellin' in the distance—out in the direction of Power House Woods. Thought I'd just mosey over and see what was goin' on. I wish I'd never went!" Ed buried his face in his hands and mumbled, "I'll never forget that scene as long as I live. It was purely hell out there!"

Julia and Henry waited.

Ed finally raised his head. "Henry, there was a mob out in the Power House Woods, and they had brought all them men out of Lester strip mine. You know that the owner of Lester mine had brought scabs in—Italians from Chicago to work in Lester mine and a whole bunch of gunmen to keep watch. That was after the strike started because union miners wanted more pay.

"Them guards had been shootin' at innocent people on farms around there, and wouldn't let nobody close to the mine. The owner was determined to keep his strip mine workin' with all the scabs and no intention to join the union, neither! He could make a lot more money with scabs.

"What I was told out by Power House Woods was that some union members—radicals of the worst kind—was on a rampage. They was mad because of this union-bustin goin' on at Lester—so mad it was like they had been brought up from hell's pit itself! Yesterday they' blasted some dynamite at the mine and two of their union men got shot. Today they went crazy, and determined to get even.

"They all got guns, went out to the mine and had a war with the armed guards. Mine machinery was blown up. After that, most of the union miners were satisfied that the scabs would leave, since the mine couldn't work any more, they went back home.

"Then the worst thing happened.

"The radicals brought them Italians up from the mine and begin marchin' them them toward Herrin—it's about four miles, you know. They come by Crenshaw Crossin' and Moakes Crossin', marchin' them two-by-two. And all the time on the road, they was beatin' them, breakin' bones, and gun-whippin' them. When I saw that bunch of prisoners, they looked awful. Some was so hurt they couldn't stand up, but the gun-carriers just kept pokin' 'em with their guns and orderin' 'em to stand up like men.

"Well, I couldn't stand up like a man any more, either. I was so weak seein' all that, I couldn't even run away from that awful place. I just fell down in the tall grass. Another feller watchin' with me in the grass said, 'They shot a one-legged man while they's marchin' 'em in, and just left him on the road.'"

Ed wiped his face with his handkerchief. "I didn't want to be seen by that mob! I'm a union man, but I'm not crazy! I'm thankful I didn't know any of 'em. But if the law ever catches 'em and they have a trial, I want to testify in court to what I saw!"

Henry and Julia sat absolutely speechless at this story. Finally, Henry said, taking a deep breath, "Tell us the rest of it, Ed. We'll have to know sometime."

Ed just kept shaking his head and closing his eyes. "Henry, I hope you never find yourself in anything like that. Out in the woods, they's a long, barbed wire fence. The mob—the ones that had guns—was between fifty and seventy-five men. They lined all them Italians up before that barbed wire fence and told them they had a chance to stay alive. They was to run as fast as they could and maybe they'd live.

"Of course, whoever could run tried to. But it was just a sport to them radicals. They acted like they was practicing shootin' at squirrels or birds. They waited 'til the men moved, then just shot 'em down. I think eleven was killed at the fence. Then they took off and caught three more who had made it near to the Harrison farm—and shot them, too. And Ma, the worst part of it was that there was some *women* out there eggin' their men on! They was screamin' at them poor Italians.

"When them Italians left Chicago for Herrin, they shorely didn't know what they was gettin' into. They was bein' cussed at and shouted at that there'd never be another scab in Herrin—never!" Ed stopped, and silence hung heavy in the stuffy room.

"What'd you do then, Ed?" Julia asked softly.

"If Pa'd been there, he'd have been as sick as I was. We seen animals killed all our lives. But we ain't seen men killed. It ain't the same. I remember when our little Ada died and you and Pa talked about the soul goin' up to Heaven. Well I hope them fellers believed in God, because I prayed they'd be killed soon and got out of their misery.

"After them union radicals killed the eleven at the fence, I got so sick to my stomach that I just turned around and puked. Couldn't help it! Me and that other feller sat in that tall grass and shut our eyes, cryin' like babies!

"That mob then jabbed the five or six prisoners who was still livin, and made 'em take most of their clothes off. They made 'em then walk barefooted over the brick road toward the cemetery. Most could barely walk—they just kept fallin' down and then they was jabbed with guns again and had to get up. I laid in the grass and cried and said, 'Oh, my God, that mob ain't men, they's animals—*worse* 'n any animals I ever knowed about!' I waited there 'til the crowd had gone toward the cemetery with the last of their prisoners, then I sneaked back home.

"I didn't know what happened at the cemetery, but a buddy of mine told me just a little while ago. He said them union radicals made the rest of the men dig their own graves, then tied 'em together with ropes around their necks, and shot 'em. Even if one wasn't dead, he fell with the others. Then somebody come along to see if they was all dead. When one or two groaned, they just grabbed their hair and pulled back their heads and slit their throats!"

Ed couldn't go on for a while. In the silence, Julia felt her heart pound. Lester was Bill's mines! He wouldn't have been in on the killin'. But sometimes men go out of their heads. Would the mob go after a *union* man who *didn't* join with them?

Ed broke the silence. "Herrin will be a stink in the nose of the whole country over this." He leaned back in his chair with his eyes closed, shaking all over.

Tears ran down Julia's cheeks. Ed looked terrible. "You had anything to eat today, Ed?" she asked him.

Ed shook his head. "Can't eat anything yet."

Henry sat with his head bowed, trying to believe what he'd just heard. He knew that some in Herrin's population counted life cheap. But this was a massacre! And Herrin would have to live with it. For years ahead, he now realized, when a man had to admit he came from Herrin, Illinois, he would be judged worse than a jungle animal. "Oh, God, don't turn your back on us," he prayed. "We'd better go see about Eva Jane," Henry said in a voice rough with emotion. "Come with us, Ed. At least we can get you some coffee over there."

He helped Ed out of his chair and held on to his arm while walking to the buggy. Ed could barely stand. Julia came after them, wiping her eyes. It was a quiet shock to realize that the sun was still shining hot in Herrin, but none of them could shake the chill in their hearts.

Henry urged the horse across town on side streets, avoiding the business section. They rode in silence, praying that all would be normal at Eva Jane's house.

As they walked across her porch, the front door was flung open and Eva Jane fell into Julia's arms. "Oh, Mama! How did you know to come just when I needed you?!" She began to cry great sobs on Julia's shoulder.

Oh, Lord, he's dead! Julia thought. *Bill must be dead.* She and Henry held Eva Jane up until her sobs lessened enough to allow them all to go inside and sit down.

Ed started to shake all over again at seeing Eva Jane so upset. *Could Bill have been in that crowd without my seeing him?*

Eva Jane wiped her face. "I'm so glad you're all here. I'm so worried I—"

"Where's Bill?" asked Henry, fearing the worst.

"I don't know!" cried Eva Jane. "He's been gone all day and didn't come home to supper! After dinner at noon when Bill hadn't come home, I took the children and we went for a walk towards town. It was a strange thing that hardly anybody was around—seemed like the streets were all deserted. So I went to see a friend—she has some kids that plays with mine—and I said the town seemed kinda funny today. She said it looked that way to her, too—she'd been home by herself all day.

"Then her husband came home and he sent the children all to another room to play. And he told us that Herrin had a lot of trouble today and that some men from Lester mine were killed." She caught her breath and looked at the three of her family, gesturing helplessly. "Well, that scared me to death. He said he'd walk home with me and he did. But he hurried back to be with his own family. And Bill ain't come home yet!"

"I saw some killin', Eva Jane," Ed said in a near whisper. "It wasn't Lester men who was killed, it was the men who come in to work during the strike. I didn't see Bill in that bunch at all."

Eva Jane stared wide-eyed at him. "How — what else did you see, Ed?"

"Eva Jane," Julia broke in, "Ed hasn't had a bite to eat today and tellin' his story is hard. Can you fix him somethin' to eat first?" Julia's eyes met Ed's and they exchanged an understanding look. Eva Jane need not be told all the details.

Eva Jane jerked herself back to reality. She realized she'd offered her family no hospitality whatever. Her own children had not been fed, either, and now it was seven o'clock. "Oh, Ma. Of course I can get you all some supper. I didn't think once about eatin'. But please tell me what you know while I get it." She got up and headed for the kitchen—they could see her legs shaking.

Henry rose and followed her. *She doesn't need to know what all Ed saw today!* "Where did Bill go today?"

"He went to a farm out by Moakes Crossing."

"What did he go out there for?"

"Well, he knows a farmer out that way, who owns a bunch of hogs. Every year we buy one, and then in the fall his friend kills it and dresses it for us. It gives us good winter eatin—farm sausage and ribs and things. And since the union is on strike and he's not workin' he just went today to buy one. Said if the strike gets over, maybe he wouldn't have time, once the mines started again."

Henry nodded. "What time did he leave home?"

"He was walkin' so he left early—about six. I thought he'd be back by noon. Tell me what Ed saw, Henry."

"Well—he *didn't* see Bill. He saw some of the strike breakers from Lester mine bein' shot—out close to Power House Woods. That's a ways from Moakes Crossing. So don't worry, Eva Jane. Bill may have had to lay low if he saw that mob. He wouldn't be any part of it—he ought to be home soon." Henry put his arm around Eva Jane and hugged her. For a moment she relaxed against his shoulder.

For all of Eva Jane's worry, she put a fine meal of ham, boiled potatoes, green beans and cornbread on the table. Julia had taught her well. When they all sat down, she motioned for Henry to ask the blessing. After the prayer, she looked less worried and said, "I realize I'm hungry too! Come on, everybody, help yourselves." And she filled her children's plates and passed the food around.

During supper, Henry and Julia and Ed avoided each other's eyes, lest each see the others' worry and Eva Jane might see it, too. Ed said very little, but he did eat a few bites and drank two cups of coffee. His trembling stopped and some color reappeared in his cheeks.

By the time they finished supper, it was dark, and Eva Jane sent her children to bed in spite of their objections. "No, you can't stay up any more. Go on! Wash your feet before you get into bed, too. You been goin' barefooted all day." Then she said to Julia, "Mom, I can't believe I'm forty-two years old and have three kids! Seems like no time at all that we moved back close to Herrin!"

Julia nodded. "You're just the age now that I was when Olive was born!"

"I know, but I don't want any more kids at this age! Eva Jane frowned as she looked out of a window at the falling darkness. Suddenly she was worried again. *It's bedtime,* she thought. *Bill wouldn't still be gone unless he was in trouble.* Her lips began to tremble again, "Ma—" she said softly, turning back toward Julia who saw her tears.

"I know, Eva Jane." Julia hugged her first daughter. "But I think your Bill's goin' to be all right."

They washed up the dishes and again sat in the living room with Ed and Henry. Nothing to do now but wait.

* * *

Was it only this morning that Bill Scott had left Eva Jane and his children at home, anticipating a peaceful day in the country?

He'd left home early, and began to walk toward his friend's farm out by Moakes Crossing. He was in no hurry— he wanted to enjoy the long walk—hadn't been out here since a year ago. And he had all day. So he ambled along, looking at fields, crops, and woods as he passed alongside them on the road out of Herrin.

Bill was almost at Moakes Crossing, when down the road about a half mile, he saw a big bunch of people approaching. It looked like some of them were marching, and most of them were following behind the marchers, carrying rifles and shotguns and yelling. As the crowd neared him, Bill stepped off to the side of the road to let them go by. And he couldn't believe his eyes when he saw the condition of the men in front.

Nearly every one of them had blood streaming——either from his head, or hands, or soaking through his shirt. The prisoners of the mob were supposed to be marching two-by-two, it seemed to Bill, but they could barely stand, let alone march. Some of them obviously had broken bones. One of the men had a wooden leg, and was bleeding from many wounds.

Who were these wounded men, and who were those following with guns? Suddenly, Bill recognized two, men he worked with at Lester! Before he could get over his shock, the man he recognized called out, "Hey, Bill. Come on! We got an extra gun. Git over here and help us!"

Bill was stunned, but tried not to show it. "Don't look like you need any help," he drawled. "What you doin' to these men?"

"These ain't *men!*" the leader spat out. "These'er *SCABS!* They come down here to work our mine and ruin our union! We're gonna show 'em what we do to scabs."

He turned and gave orders to a couple of men. "Git that one-legged man over there to them woods and shoot him!" Looking at Bill again, he yelled, "Come on!"

Bill watched openmouthed, while two gun-carrying radicals grabbed the man with the artificial leg and half dragged, half carried him off the road into some foliage. Two shots rang out.

"Come on Bill! You're a union man!"

Bill stepped further back from the road. He didn't like the tone of voice nor what he saw. He shook his head.

Bill's mine buddy—or he used to think of him so— then stepped out from the clamoring men and snarled in Bill's face. "Who do you think you are? Are you on the side of them scabs? Are you agin' our union?"

Again Bill shook his head.

"Well, if you ain't agin' us, then come on!"

Bill tried to be calm. "I can't do that. It ain't right."

Before he could say another word, Bill heard a sharp crack of a near rifle, and at the same instant felt a searing pain on the side of his head. He fell to the grass and that was the last he knew for a while. He did vaguely feel someone kicking him, and a voice—like a million miles away—snarling, "Let him be. He's gone anyway. He's hit in the head—ain't nothin' but a traitor and they're bad as scabs." Then more shouting, "Get on there! March like men!" Blackness closed in on Bill and he lay motionless in the grass beside the road.

He didn't know how long he lay unconscious. But slowly he began to wake up. Moving his shaking hand to his face and temple, he felt half-dried blood all over that side. The bullet must have just grazed his head. At least he was still alive, but the danger was real. If any union radicals from that mob should come back to see about him, they'd kill him for sure. He'd seen them all, and now his life was worth nothing. Lying in the afternoon sun, he kept his eyes closed and listened. But no sound broke the silence.

He remembered that just before he met that hellish procession, he had passed a barn close to the road. Maybe he could crawl to it and hide there. *I don't dare try to go home in the daylight—those men are on their way toward Herrin, and may come back.* Cautiously he raised his head and looked through the grass until he spotted the barn. *I can make that! Hope nobody comes by on the road.*

Bill rolled over on his hands and knees and slowly began crawling through the grass toward the barn. Pain beat a tattoo in his brain. Hearing a horse in the distance, he dropped flat, hoping the rider wouldn't notice any disturbance in the grass. The horse trotted on by. When they were out of sight, he resumed his journey. He was dizzy and several times had to lie panting on the ground.

The hardest part, he knew, would be making it across the barren barn lot. Nothing to cover him there! He lay low for at least fifteen minutes more, watching the barn. It seemed empty. He saw no one go in or come out. *Maybe I'm lucky,* Then, *Yes! Lucky with a bullet-grazed head!*

Luck *was* with him. The cows were out in the meadow, and he could see the farmer way across the field with his back to his barn, hoeing. Inch by inch, Bill wormed his way from the road, across the barn lot, and through the barn door. Not even a dog was visible, and the barn cat that ran in front of him would never tell.

He finally covered the distance inside the barn to a large stack of hay in one corner. He burrowed under it so far that even if the farmer did fork any out, Bill would still be covered. Pushing some hay away from his nose far enough to allow him some breathing space, he gave in to faintness again. *What'll they do to all the men?*

Hours later, Bill Scott woke up lying on his face in a dark barn, nearly smothered by a haystack. For a moment he couldn't remember where he was.

He raised his head and listened. All he could hear were farm night sounds—frogs croaking in a pond and cattle munching nearby.

It must have been dark for some time for he could see the moon high in the sky through some slats in the barn. "I gotta get home!" he whispered to himself as memories of the day flooded his mind. "Eva Jane will be awful upset."

He hunched his shoulders, lifting some hay off his back and dragged his knees up to a crawling position. Listening again but hearing nothing, he inched out from under the hay, slowly and silently, heading toward the barn door. But he felt faint and sick and twice had to stop and lower his head because of its hard throbbing.

When he finally reached the door, he pushed it open carefully, afraid a squeak might be overheard by someone. Once out of the barn, Bill crawled toward the road, which shimmered in the pale moonlight. When his knees became too sore to crawl, he stood shakily to his feet, stooping low to move forward in an awkward shuffle. There! He was finally out of the barnlot! Just before he reached the road, he sank down to rest in a ditch full of high grass. Bill felt hot, and sweat ran down his face.

He reached into his hip pocket for a handkerchief, and wiped it across his face. Beginning to fold it up again, he glanced at it. What in the world was on his face that made his handkerchief so dirty?"

Even in half moonlight, he could see that his handkerchief was covered with blood. To be sure, he smelled it. Dried blood! When he touched the side of his head, he winced with pain.

Once again the scene of that morning seemed to dance before his eyes, and in spite of the heat of the night, Bill shivered. All the day's sequences arranged themselves in his brain, in order, as he lay beside the road in the high grass. *It's nearly the middle of the night. Now I must get home—can I ever make it home?*

He looked down the deserted road toward Herrin. *Maybe somebody will come along and give me a ride in a wagon. But that isn't likely. Wagons don't usually roll at night.*

Bill pulled himself to a standing position by holding on to a fence, and took a few practice steps. No more dizziness, but his knees felt like rubber. Once on the road, through sheer force of will, he commanded his legs to take him nearly three miles to his house in Herrin. Bill knew it would be a much harder walk than when he had started out this morning! But maybe by resting sometimes and holding on to fences, he could make it home.

Henry, Ed, Julia, and Eva Jane had sat for a long time in silence. Eva Jane cried quietly much of the time, but now all her tears were dried up. The night wore on, the clock striking each half hour. Not even any street noises to be heard.

At a quarter past three, they heard something fall on the porch. Eva Jane jerked up stiffly. "What's that?"

"I'll go see," Henry jumped up. He turned on the dim porch light and peered out. There was Bill—lying on his back, covered with dust, dried blood, and sweat. "Eva Jane—" Henry called.

Eva Jane pushed past Henry through the door. When she saw her husband, dried blood streaking his face, she cried out, "Bill! Bill! Oh, Bill, wake up! Oh, Henry, is he dead?"

Henry knelt beside Bill to feel his pulse. Bill's eyes fluttered open.

"No, Eva Jane," his voice croaked. "I ain't dead, but I need some water real bad."

Eva Jane fetched the water in one minute. Bill took three gulps and fell sound asleep with his head on her arm, water running from the corner of his mouth. He didn't even wake up when they put him to bed and washed his face, nor when Henry cleaned his wound and put medicine and a bandage on his head.

"He'll be all right," Henry said. "Ma, you want to stay here?"

"Yes," Julia answered. "I'll stay with Eva Jane. You take my buggy and go on back to Pearl. She'll be worried."

The next day Henry and his neighbor, Ed Misker, talked about all the killing. "I *saw* them prisoners before they was killed," Misker said. "Me and my brother Alvin and a couple of other men was at Crenshaw Crossing, and we saw this mob a' comin' so we hid in tall grass beside the road. Them Italians was a sorry lookin' lot—some had been so beat up and bloody they could hardly walk. I felt bad for them, but I couldn't do anything agin' all that mob with guns."

"Did you recognize any of the men carryin' the guns?"

"Lord, yes! I know some of 'em. Only I don't think I'm gonna know 'em after this. I can't forget what their faces looked like in that mob. And later they killed nineteen men—it was a real massacre."

Henry sat silent for a while. "That's just what my brother Ed told Ma and me. He saw what happened in Power House Woods. That means a lot of trouble for Herrin—won't be long before the whole country knows about Herrin's killin'. You know, Power House Woods is close to where we lived on South 12th Street. I'm sure glad we moved to South 18th.

* * * *

In succeeding days, newspapers all over the country blasted Herrin as "Bloody Herrin, in Bloody Williamson County." Pearl read the newspapers and cried. And as bad as the killings were, when those who did them were finally put on trial, they were judged "NOT GUILTY." So Herrin suffered the double blow. It was for naught that brave men who saw it happen did testify against the mob. Ed Misker and his brother were two who did. All those who testified for the prosecution were said to be as brave as soldiers who fought the Germans in France.

People in other towns shunned Herrin, afraid to come, and afraid of anyone from Herrin. Men from Herrin who tried to get a hotel room in other cities were denied.

The whole area suffered from shame.

CHAPTER TWENTY-NINE
Julia–Without Him

For Julia on the farm, life returned to "normal," although to her, the days weren't *really* normal—not without John. Nothing would ever be normal again. Day after day, Julia rose alone to do her chores. She ate in the morning, alone, in the evening she rested, and at bedtime, she slept—all alone.

No, nothing was normal—John was gone. But his work clothes hung behind the kitchen door, Sunday shoes in the bedroom closet. His longlegged underwear was in the dresser drawer, his comb on top, shaving things on the kitchen wash-up table, his leather strap hung above. She talked to him often and it seemed natural to her.

One day at noon she was eating her meal of sausage, canned corn, and biscuits, when Henry came in the kitchen door with a letter in his hand.

"How're you doin', Ma?"

"Jest tolerable, I guess. Git awful lonesome. Seems like I ought to wait for John to come in from the field before I eat. It's all I can do to keep from ringin' the dinner bell to call him."

"I don't like it for you to be here by yourself, either. You ought to come and live with us—or some of the other kids. No call for you to stay here."

"Your family all right?"

"They're all fine. That little baby, Irene, don't want to sleep very much, though. Keeps the whole family awake with cryin' half the night. Sometimes in the mine I get so sleepy I just lean up agin' a coal wall and sleep a little."

"I know all about bein' sleepy with young'uns. Had plenty of practice. What's the letter you got in your hand?"

"Well, Ma, it came to me," Henry said, turning the letter over and looking at it. "But when I opened it, 'twas really for you. Somebody in Creal wantin' to know if you'd like to have a job?"

"A job? In Creal? Read it to me, Henry. "

He opened the letter. "Dear Julia, We heard about the death of John, your husband. And we been thinkin' that you might be lonesome livin' by yourself now. You had a good man and we are sorry to hear about his goin'. We've knowed him nearly all his life.

"Now that he is gone, we thought you might like to take a job livin' with us. My Mary is poorly and can't do the work she used to. We need somebody to live with us and do for us. Would you like to take the job? We got a good bedroom you can have, and we'd pay you five dollars a week. Of course, all your livin' is free. We remember what a good housekeeper you are, and thought you might like to live back in Creal for a spell. Let us know.

Your good friends, Mary and Frank Allen"

Julia sat thinking. "The Allens. Of course I remember them. They was good friends to us." She laughed at a memory. "I'll never forget one time when Frank came over to see John. It was February and John was a'fixin' harnesses in the kitchen, and about five of you kids was playin in there. I was sittin' in my rockin' chair knittin' heavy winter sox for John. Frank Allen talked to John about buyin' a calf, but Frank was watchin' me knit. He said to John, 'You got a gold mine there! Yep, you got a gold mine there in Julia!'

"John said, 'Well, I agree, but why do you say that now?'

"Frank said, 'Well, just look at all the stuff she's doin'. She's knitted nearly one whole sock jist while I been sittin' here! I wish my wife could knit like that. I seen your young'uns in church—did Julia knit all them sweaters?'

"John nodded. 'She did. She keeps us all warm with her socks and sweaters. If you want your wife to learn, why don't you send her over here? Julia'll teach her.'

"Frank shook his head and his mouth turned down in a funny way. 'That'd never work,' He said. 'She'd tell me not to buy any more socks because she was gonna knit 'em fer me. But before she could ever do that, my feet would jist freeze right off.'"

Henry and Julia laughed together and Henry thought, *That's the first time I heard her laugh like that since Pa died!* "Well, Ma, what do you think about this letter? What kind of answer do you want me to send 'em?"

"I'd have to break up my home here—but it would be a chance for me to earn some money. I need to save some. Maybe that's what I ought to do. I can take care of their house and them, and at the same time have company in a house. Guess I'd rather keep busy and have somethin' to do. And I ought to earn my own way." In memory she heard herself saying nearly the same words when she was fourteen. *I'll never change. I still need to be independent!*

"Go ahead, Henry, tell the Allens I'll come. It'll take me a couple of weeks to get this place cleaned out, but I think I'd like to do that. It'll be nice to be back in Creal—it'll make me think of old times. Come on, Henry get a plate there and have some corn and sausage and biscuits with me."

After Henry went back home, Julia talked to John a little.

John, I'm goin' to leave our home. I don't want to do it, but I can't live here without you and be alone. No sense to it! I remember these people in Creal—it is a job for me and I can make some money. I have a feelin' you'd say it was the right thing to do.

It meant breaking up her home, and it was a sorrowful time. She thought she could never do it—too many memories swirled about her. But finally with Ola and Cena's help, she sold a few things, and gave most of the rest away to her family.

Selling her horse, Chestnut, was the hardest. Her friends Tom and Gertrude Martin wanted to buy him, and also Julia's buggy. They knew he was a good gentle horse, and that's what Gertrude needed to drive. Julia could barely get up the courage to part with him, because John had loved that horse and it had been a member of their family for a long time.

The morning Tom was coming for Chestnut, Julia went out to the barn and rubbed him down. Then she leaned her head against his sleek side and whispered, "Chestnut, I hate to see you go. I'll miss you, and I think you will miss me. But I can't take as good care of you as John did. You've been good to me and I was never afraid when I drove you out. You always brought me home safe. Now you be good to Gertrude, too." Her tears made a big, dark, wet spot on his smooth, brown coat.

When Tom drove Chestnut out of the barn lot an hour later, Julia thought about the day so many years ago when she went to live with the Crawfords. That barn lot had died. Now, so had this one.

She divided all her canned goods between her girls and soon the house she'd lived in so long was just a shell.

"Cena, I'm gonna keep my chair—that was my ma's chair and I can't bear to part with it. I'll probably die sittin' in that rockin' chair! That and some sheets, towels and special things I want, will you take 'em home with you and keep 'em for me?"

"You know I will, Ma."

"Some day I'll come back to your place and get 'em. But now I can work for a while. It's hard to believe that I'll be goin' back to Creal Springs."

* * * *

"George, I'm so sorry to be cryin' like this." Julia wiped her eyes on her pocket handkerchief. "But travelin' on this road—you just don't know what it does to me! The first time I ever went over this road was on horseback. Me and your uncle Joe went this way and I got a job in the Creal Springs hotel. Course, I met your pa there. And the first time I went with John this way, we had six young'uns in the back of the wagon with some trunks, and tied on top was my rockin' chair!"

This was an old story to her son, George, who was driving her back to Creal in his new car. Yes, he'd heard it many times, but he knew his mother liked to talk about her memories.

Now, thirty-seven years later and around every curve, memories flooded Julia's heart and eyes. They went south, down through those unchanging Ozark hills. But other things had changed. This time she was speeding in a car so fast! This was 1923 and women on the road were wearing very short dresses and bobbed hair.

Homes had radios now, and whole families could hear music and laughing and talking from that little box! Marion was a big town—one could get lost there. Many things had changed. But Julia didn't feel she had changed much, even though she was fifty-eight. She didn't feel fifty-eight. In memory she saw again her beloved John and herself in that new wagon with her oak chest, six children, and her chair rocking gently on top of the chest.

When they reached Creal, she couldn't believe they were there so soon. They passed the old hotel place, and memories again overwhelmed her. She'd met John there and had begun to live again. She sobbed and said to George, "I think you better stop 'til I can git over this cryin' spell and wipe my face before I see the Allens. I jist never thought comin' back to Creal would do this to me!"

"Yes, I know, Ma. This trip brings back lots of memories to me, too. I remember when I was a little boy here and it doesn't seem long ago when me and Henry played 'round here."

The Allens, welcomed her with smiles and handshakes. They *did* look old and they did need help!

CHAPTER THIRTY
The 1920s–Life After the Massacre

Before the massacre was cold news, Williamson County had to acknowledge another problem. After Prohibition was passed in 1920, illegal but prominent roadhouses and booze joints began to thrive all over the county. At first nobody wanted to talk about it or admit it. But gangsters and bootleggers, owners of rival roadhouses, began to fight and kill one another in order to be kingpin. Some brave people said it was as bad as in Chicago, 300 miles to the north, where Al Capone and other gangs fought and killed each other. Williamson County was smaller and everyone knew everyone else. But the Shelton gang, the Charlie Birger gang, and "Jardown" (Blacky) Armes' men and others fought just as bitterly.

Since Pearl read everything, she knew about Herrin and Williamson County's national and international reputation. Pearl also knew that in Herrin and Marion each, more than 100 road houses and "soft drink parlors" ran wide open. Whiskey, gambling, and prostitutes were always available. Every election day brought more bullets flying between different factions.

Like so many other Christian people in the county, she believed that only God's Spirit in the hearts of prople could clean up the place. In spite of so much gang warfare around Herrin, Pearl and Henry were loyal church members and tried to keep God's Spirit in their own hearts. They raised their children by Christian principles, and Pearl memorized Scripture and repeated it to the family often. Her children memorized it, too.

Pearl was proud of Henry. He always carried himself yard-stick straight, looked nice in his clothes, and took good care of his one dress-up suit which he wore for several years. He was not afraid of anything, and although she did not like guns, Pearl had to admit she felt safer because Henry knew how to use them.

He was extremely hardworking and proud of all his family. He was a man of his word and was thoughtful of Pearl. He never left the house without telling her where he was going and when to expect him back. She could absolutely depend on him. And of course, he was so very handsome—still the most handsome man she'd ever seen. She was thankful to have him, even though he was quite bossy and wanted to handle all the money himself.

But that was not nearly as bad as having the kind of husband she knew some women had. Some men spent all the money they made on drink, and frequented roadhouses with fancy women.

Henry often bought things from the company store. He knew it wasn't mandatory any more, but he was caught in the system, so often his pay was very small. Sometimes they argued about it.

"Henry, if you'd give me enough food money at the start of a week, I could get things cheaper at other stores. But because you want to handle all the money all the time, we have less. That company store just holds you up!"

"I know it, Pearl, but sometimes I ain't got it to give you."

"Credit at that company store is an awful thing! We're on a merry-go-round of buying on credit, then no pay at pay time. How can we ever do anything different?"

Henry sighed, "I don't know, Pearl. Wish I did."

Helen's life was easier with her grandparents because they were not quite so poor.

One day in 1924, great excitement reigned in the 600 block on South 18th Street, at the Childers' house. The family heard a loud honking out in front and ran out to see what was going on. HELEN stepped out from the driver's seat of a Model T Ford! The car was black, had four doors, open sides, a wide running board, and was sparkling new. Helen was dressed in a new outfit.

Pearl gasped, "Helen! Did *you* drive that car over here?"

Helen smiled, very sure of herself. "Yes, I did, Mother. Uncle Joe Baxley taught me to drive it. It's his car."

"But—you're only twelve years old!"

"Well, if I can pedal a sewing machine and make a dress, I can drive a car. It's not hard."

"You'll have a wreck. Did you make your new dress? I can just see you in a wreck and that new car all smashed to bits. You'd ruin your dress." Pearl shook her head. "What am I talkin' about? I'm so surprised I don't know what to say!"

Ruth and Arthur first stood with their mouths open, then started jumping up and down. "Mommie, can we go for a ride? Helen, will you take us for a ride?" To get a ride in a car was the peak of a dream. Henry had no car; few people did. And if they did, women didn't drive them. Helen had to be the smartest big sister that ever was.

After some reassurance from Helen that she wouldn't wreck them, that she'd been keeping secret the fact that she was learning to drive and had lots of practice, the whole family climbed in. Yep, she *could* drive it. Henry sat in the front seat with his hands clenched knuckle-white the whole time. Pearl, sitting with the kids, gripped the edge of the back seat. Helen drove them up and down the streets, the children not at all afraid and sticking their heads out to catch the cool breeze. In 1924, very few cars were on the roads, so even if she wobbled a little in her steering, it didn't matter. And no policeman stopped her to ask any questions, because nobody had ever heard of a driver's license.

* * * *

One night at the supper table when Ruth was about nine years old, Pearl said, "Ruth, what in the world is the matter with you? You've been scratching ever since you got home from school."

"I *itch,* Mama."

"I do too, Mama," Arther chimed in.

"Don't see how they could get chiggers in the wintertime," Henry remarked.

"Did you ever itch a lot like this, Mama?"

"Oh, I probably did when I was a kid, but I don't remember it." Pearl passed Ruth another biscuit.

Ruth took it, spread butter and apple jelly on it and said, "Well, maybe you didn't, but I itch! I can't help it, Mama, I just want to scratch all the time!"

"I'll have to have a look at you kids after supper," Pearl promised.

Anybody who's ever had scabies will never forget it. And anybody who's ever tried to scratch an itch inside of long winter underwear knows what it's like. It didn't last just a day or a week, they scratched all winter. The only known cure was lots of baths, scrubbing with a hard washrag, then smearing on vile-smelling yellow sulphur salve. Ruth and Arthur had to stand naked near the stove after putting on the salve, to allow the heat of the warm bath and warm air to drive the medicinal effects into the skin.

Pearl always hung their home-sewn pajamas over the line behind the stove so they'd be toasty warm at bedtime. When the kids put them on, even with the itch, they felt good.

The kids must have caught scabies at school. Pearl had no

idea how many at school had itch, because it was an un-talked-about matter. But surreptitious wiggling and skin-rubbing went on every day in practically every room and in every seat. Who knows—maybe even the teacher scratched!

But Pearl was ashamed and told nobody about *her* kids. They had to scratch in private!

* * * *

Summer rolled around again. Art and Ruth were sitting on the back steps. "What can we do, Art?"

"I don't know."

Ruth thought for a while. "How'd you like to dig a big hole?"

"What for?"

"Well—I've heard China is down there. But if we miss China maybe we could find Hell."

"What will Daddy say?"

"I don't know. Anyway, he's at work and Irene is asleep and Mama has gone to the library, so we can get a lot done before they get back."

The two children ran to the tool shed, got two of Henry's shovels and started to dig in a corner of the garden. Old Jack lay and watched, his nose on his paws. Though the day was hot and the shovels were heavy, they had a small mound of dirt piled up by the time Pearl got home from the library.

"What in the world are you kids doing?"

"Just digging a hole, Mama."

"What for?"

"We heard that China or Hell is down there."

Pearl smiled. "I don't really think you'll find either one, and when Daddy comes home he will probably make you fill it all up." She went into the house with a load of books under her arm. But she was on their side!

Jack heard Henry coming before the diggers did, and when Henry said, "Come on, Jack!" he tore out of the gate. Henry came on around the house with his dinner bucket under his arm, his carbide lamp on his cap, and Jack capering around his feet. He stopped and just stood tall looking down at his offspring. "What are you kids doin'?" he asked gruffly.

"Don't be mad, Daddy. We just want to dig a hole."

"Looks like you already did. Don't you know you're messin' up my yard?"

"Please, Daddy, don't make us fill it up. When we finish playing in it, we promise to fill it all up. We want to find China now, and it might take us a long time." They were afraid to tell him they were also looking for Hell. He might not be as sympathetic to their hellish desires as their mama was.

He watched his children dig a bit more with his heavy shovels and finally decided. "Them shovels are pretty big for you? All right, you can dig all you want to. But you have to put all that dirt back just like it was when you're finished. And if it is a big hole, you'll have to plant some more grass on top for me."

"Yowee!" Their foreign realms visas were guaranteed!

The hole got deeper and bigger, so one day they had to dig some steps in the side to go up and down so they could carry the dirt out in a scrub bucket. They'd tried to throw it out lately, but most of it fell back and landed in their hair. Their pillow cases got dirty at night, and Pearl didn't like that.

Then, of course, they had to dig niches in the sides to keep some cold biscuits and jelly and water for refreshment while they worked.

News of the big hole at 618 South 18th Street began to sweep the neighborhood. Some of their bored friends peered down.

"Hey, Ruth, whatcha doin' down there?"

"Just diggin'."

"We ain't got nothin' to do. Can we help you dig?"

"Well—go home and get your shovels and your own biscuits and jelly."

"Our Mama don't make biscuits."

"Then get your own store-bought bread."

"Okay. We'll be back soon."

Since their friends were so interested, Ruth and Art began to get plenty of free labor. She and Art sat on the grass beside the Hole, lined friends up and directed them all to take turns digging. Bighearted Ruth and Arthur did bring out cold water for them to drink, and gave them permission to use the Childers privy. But Ruth and Arthur were *Bosses of the Hole!* The other kids did what they said!

When rain poured down, their platoon had more fun. The cave was so deep they waded knee-high in the water and thought they might be close enough to Hell that the rain might seep down and put out the fires! Ruth would order, "Now everybody be quiet and listen for the sizzle!"

That hole took up most of their time that summer, and

before school started they had to fill it all up again. Henry came to think of it as a good ploy to keep all the neighborhood kids out of trouble. He even planted the grass.

* * * *

"Pull up your stockin's, Ruth, and get the wrinkles out of your ankles!" ordered Henry.

Ruth often heard that command in the winter time, because though they were poor, they could never be sloppy and so labled "poor white trash." They grew up without a bathroom in the house, so took their baths in the kitchen in a round, tin washtub. Every Saturday in the winter, the tub was set in front of the coal stove's open oven door. Warmth! Ruth felt she was transported to the orbit of luxury when it was her turn.

Her Mama shut the kitchen doors and ordered the other kids to stay out while she had her bath. Pearl filled the tub half full of very warm water, and Ruth sat cross-legged in front of the stove with water up to her chest. Oh! the joy of washing clean, Mama powdering her all over, then helping her slide into a pair of clean, white, tight-fitting, long-sleeved, long-legged cotton underwear, buttoned down the front with a drop seat.

When she first slithered into it on Saturday afternoon, the legs were snug, and where they fitted down into her long, brown stockings, scarcely a nodule was visible. On Sunday they still looked smooth, but by Monday when she got ready to go to school, they had stretched somewhat and the underwear lapped on the outside of her legs. On Tuesday, Wednesday, and Thursday, each day the knobs grew larger, and by Friday she wore a voluminous bulge on the outside of both legs. Then her stockings had a definite tendency to sag, and the garter rolls above her knees were so thick that they rubbed each other when she walked.

In those days of scarce water supply, cold weather, her Mama washing clothes on a board in the house and drying them on lines above their heads, nobody ever thought of changing underwear in the middle of the week.

None of the other kids changed theirs, either. Ruth knew because she used to watch legs at school. Some kids' dad's hadn't taught them how to lap the underwear legs over neatly, they just pushed them down into their stockings any old way. So they had blobs all around their ankles. But whether they lapped or blobbed, as the week wore on, everybody's legs got bigger and bigger bulges.

Even the richest girl who could play the piano had them. Ruth used to watch her blobs when her foot pedaled the piano in class as they sang "The Star-Spangled Banner."

* * * *

Every spring they couldn't wait for Pearl to let them go barefoot. One of Ruth's clearest memories is of her Mama putting her hand on the ground, then shaking her head. The ground was too cold. But finally, the magic day always came. Off went winter underwear, shoes, and long stockings. Tender, whitened feet mincing on new grass; every blade tingled. Toes wiggled in sheer joy. Trees were easier to climb because bare feet were made for trees. They stubbed ant hills with exploring big toes, and splashed flat-footed through mud puddles. Does anything feel better to bare feet than soft, squishing mud?

When cold weather came, they played in the kitchen where Pearl's rocking chair was. Of course they could have played in the other three rooms, but they seemed frigid and empty because their mama was in the kitchen. They did most of their living there—especially in winter. Because Pearl cooked on a coal range, the kitchen was always warm and smelled good. Pearl baked a lot of her own bread because Henry didn't like "store-bought bread."

Pearl was a wonderful cook, and sometimes she had plenty of supplies to cook with. Chili, spaghetti, chicken and dumplings, pork roast, or roast beef with brown gravy, biscuits, cookies, chicken pies—they were all the greatest in the world. But sometimes when times were hard, they might have only bacon, biscuits and milk gravy for a meal. Whatever they had, they thought their Mama could make it better than anyone else.

Ruth sobbed when Helen went to live at Ma Baxley's house. Helen's moving and leaving was, for Ruth, probably the most traumatic event of her early childhood. She missed Helen!
But she and Arthur often went to see Helen at Ma Baxley's.

"Mommie, can Arthur and me go to see Helen?"

"Arthur and *I*."

Ruth nodded. "Yeah, Arthur and I. Can *we* go over to see Helen?"

Pearl looked at the sky. "Well, it doesn't look like rain today so I reckon you can. But play outside over there. I know Ma Baxley doesn't want you in the house all the time."

"We will. I wish Helen lived here."

Pearl nodded. "So do I. I miss her. Comb your hair, Ruth."

"Okay, Mama, but it pulls!"

Ruth gave a token try at raking the comb through her curly, reddish-brown hair.

Art brushed his hair also. Pearl looked at him critically. "I think you better change your shirt, Arthur. Looks like you and Edward wrestled too much. And, Ruth, take this jar of apple butter to Ma Baxley. I don't know whether she has made any yet this year."

Art and Ruth skipped down the street, Ruth carried the apple butter, and they both jumped over cracks in the sidewalk. "Don't step on a crack, it'll break your mother's back!"

They loved to go over to Helen's, and they loved to be together. Ruth felt very protective of her little brother, but secretly she felt he was a great protection to her. After all, *he* was a boy!

The mile walk seemed long, but they had fun when they got there. Helen, though she was five years older than Ruth, played with them. They climbed fruit trees and ran all over the barn lot. Helen showed them the smokehouse—to them a very scary place. Pa Baxley had lots of things stored up there—spooky things. And always above their heads hung hams, all sewed up in cloth sacks. "Poor little pigs!" Ruth said to Art, as they looked up at the silent hams.

They ran out of the smokehouse and saw Pa Baxley working in his garden. He seemed too old to be doing that hard job. He wiped sweat with his shirt sleeve, and sweat even dripped off his drooping, white moustache.

Ruth and Arthur thought that Ma and Pa Baxley were rich, because they had given Helen a room to herself and her own sewing machine. She was already making clothes for herself.

* * *

Ruth and Henry were two members of a mutual admiration society. Ruth's handsome father was thin, muscular, and a tall six-feet-two with a dimple in his square chin. He had straight, coal black hair, greenish-gray eyes, and absolutely perfect teeth. In fact they were so flawless, that once before an emergency appendectomy, a nurse ordered him to remove his dentures. Though doubled up in pain, he gallently tried to get them out for her.

Henry was very strict, but they knew he loved them and would always take care of them. Ruth was afraid of him sometimes—but only when she knew she had misbehaved. He commanded his children to walk tall and straight, do right, and to make up their minds that they could accomplish anything they really wanted to. He wasn't afraid of anyone. Though his education was not as good as that of many other people, he never felt inferior.

"Anybody ready to go to town with me?"

Saturday afternoons in the summer were special. If Art and Ruth were cleaned up, hair combed and shoes shined, they could walk to town with their daddy. Irene was too little to go. They'd go into a cool, tiled-floor drugstore, where a big ceiling fan blew Ruth's curls all around. They could wrap their ankles around the wire legs of a Coca-Cola chair and have an ice cream cone. They knew that their father was proud to show off his two well-behaved children. Ruth *always* behaved then, because she wanted him to be proud of her.

One-eighth Indian, Henry was bossy and bullheaded, each night sleeping in the surity that he was Master in his own house. But their mama, who was always happy and cheerful even if they had only bread and sorghum to eat when times were hard, had a mind of her own. They were so different—and the kids adored them both. Pearl was smart enough to let Henry think he was boss, but she would do anything she wanted to do bad enough. (That's exactly the philosophy he always taught his kids, anyway.)

Henry loved Pearl's thick, wavy, long reddish-brown hair. It was her most beautiful feature. But it got to be the summer when all the ladies were "bobbing." Pearl would see them in church with pert, short hair, creamy-white necks suddenly emerging from under the burden of curls and braids, and she longed for a bob. Pearl could easily sit on her hair, it was so long. Ruth used to watch her sitting in the yard in the sun drying her hair, while it cascaded in glittering brown over the back of the chair and brushed the ground. Ruth liked to comb it for her while she dried it.

One evening at supper Pearl made a little speech. She must have been practicing it all day to work up her courage. She knew the reception it would call forth. "Henry, all the women are getting their hair bobbed. It looks nice and so easy to take care of. Is it all right with you if I get my hair cut?"

Henry looked at her as if she had suddenly suggested that she wanted to feed her kids to the wolves, and he bellowed, "No, Woman!" Then he added, "I don't want to hear no more about it!"

"But, Henry, it's too hot!"

He was still roaring. "You've had that hair for thirty years! Ain't no hotter now than it ever was. You're not going to cut it and that's final!"

"Well, it's *my* hair!"

He banged his fist on the table and all the dishes jumped. So did his kids. "I don't aim to sleep with no bald-headed woman! You cut your hair and I'll leave this house!"

Ruth and Arthur believed every word he said. Ruth prayed that her mama wouldn't cut her lovely hair, though she did feel sorry for her when she saw her wiping sweat over the hot stove in summer.

One scorching afternoon while Henry was at work, Pearl went to town leaving Ruth to watch her little brother and baby sister. When Pearl came back she carried all her glistening brown waves in a sack, and her neck looked long and bare. Her hair was snipped just under her ears. Ruth stared in terror, and Art and Ruth both began to shake because they thought they'd not have a Daddy when he saw Mama.

When he came home from work, Pearl was turning bacon in a skillet, cooking supper. She just stood there and didn't say a word. Arthur and Ruth held on to each other behind the kitchen door. Henry took one horrified look at her, slammed his bucket down on the kitchen table and thundered, "God, Woman, you look like the devil!"

Though Pearl probably thought it was the truth, she answered calmly, "Even if I do, quit swearing in front of the kids!"

Black clouds rumbled, but he didn't leave home.

* * * *

Everybody knew in the 1920s that Herrin, Illinois was the scene of bloody mine riots and gangster wars. The Childers kids grew up in the middle of it. They were all proud of their daddy, because they knew he was one of the good guys. Their town, Herrin, was full of bootleggers; several gangs romped in Herrin, terrorizing decent people and warring on rival gangs. Sometimes Charlie Birger visited there.

For a time Henry was a deputy sheriff trying to help rid the town of gangs and bootleggers. Pearl and the others in the family were terrified when Henry and Pastor Glotfelty were shot at and almost killed in broad daylight.

It happened on an afternoon when Henry was talking to the pastor on his front porch. He and Glotfelty were discussing the dangerous situation in Herrin. Henry was facing south when he suddenly spied a long, black, open sedan car screeching in a turn onto 16th street and heading north. As the automobile roared toward the parsonage, Henry saw a snub-nosed machine gun poking out the side from the back seat. He just had time to shove the pastor to the porch floor and fall on top of him before the machine gun opened up and spat a line of bullets about a foot above them. He had recognized the car. He knew the men in it hated Glotfelty because of his preaching against the wide-open booze joints, the prostitution, and the gang wars.

In Herrin, men had been killed in street gun battles, in hotel lobbies, and in illegal bars blaring wide open in spite of the law. Fires were set, and a grocery store was bombed.

Pearl was afraid, mostly for Henry. Like most other men in Herrin, Henry carried a "Colt 45" all the time and he was an expert marksman. That gun was under his pillow every night, too, in spite of Pearl's objections.

"I ain't doin' anything that Pastor P.R. Glotfelty don't do. He preaches with a "45" in his pulpit every Sunday. Look what they tried to do to him!"

Pearl wanted Henry to keep out of the whole thing and stay at home. But in Herrin at that time, a man couldn't hide behind his wife's skirts. He had to take a side and defend it. Then trouble came close to home.

Harry Walker, their neighbor directly across the street, was reported to be a follower of the Shelton gang. Harry was gunned down one evening, and his friends brought his body home. His wife, Kit, was grief-stricken; she shrieked and cried all night, the chilling sounds carrying all over the 600 block on South Eighteenth.

Henry and Pearl were tense. Henry hated the Shelton gang and its hangers on, yet members of that gang were practically staring him in the face on that hot Sunday night late in August, 1926. They were all over the front porch and in the house directly across the narrow street. Too close for comfort.

Henry told Pearl, "I heard some of that outfit talking when they brought Harry's body home. I heard them say, 'They might have got Harry, but we'll get Childers.'"

Pearl threw her arms around Henry. "But you didn't have anything to do with Harry's getting shot!"

"No, I had nothin' to do with him gettin' shot. But when one of their gang dies, they take it out on somebody else. They just don't like anybody who's agin' bootleggin' and they know I am!

Pearl's face went white and she felt like the world was closing in on her. "Henry! Don't *do* anything. It won't help any of us if you get yourself killed. We got three kids to raise, and I don't see how

I could ever do it without you!"

He stroked her hair. "Now Pearl, if they don't bother me, I won't bother them. But I am goin' to be on watch all night. I want you and the kids to sleep in that back room. I'm gonna lay behind the big honeysuckle bush all night and if they roar by here shootin' up this house, at least I'll get one of 'em!"

She cried on his shirt (she couldn't reach up to his shoulder), pulled a handkerchief from her pocket and wiped her face. "That'd be no comfort to me if you died."

Ruth never forgot the night that Harry Walker was killed. She was almost ten years old when the night chill crawled up her spine as she heard Mrs. Walker keening in anguish. Ruth had never heard anybody cry like that before.

She began to shake when her father said he was going to stay under the honeysuckle bush and keep a lookout. Under that bush was one of Ruth and Arthur's favorite hide-and-seek, places. All afternoon the two children watched their daddy clean and oil his shotgun and pistol. His shotgun was an L.C. Smith 12-guage double-barreled, with thirty-inch full choke. He was very proud of that gun and was a crack shot with it. Ruth was wiping tears with the bottom of her dress when Henry went into his hideout.

"Don't cry, Ruthie, I'll be all right."

"But they might shoot you, Daddy!"

"Well, Ruthie, dying is not the worst thing in the world. I have to die sometime, and living under gangsters would be worse. Don't you worry, if one of them gets me, I'll take him with me."

"But Daddy, that doesn't make me feel better! Thinking about you dying is terrible!" She tried to stay awake in her bed to watch with her daddy. She liked the bush hiding place, but shivered as she thought about how awful it would be to stay under the bush all night by herself. She could almost smell the honeysuckles that her daddy was smelling. Every time her eyes closed, she felt guilty because her daddy was watching to keep them safe, and *he* wasn't able to sleep. So she shouldn't either! But sleep crept up in spite of her guilt.

Henry did watch all night behind the bush and he kept both his pistol and shotgun ready. Pearl, nearly sick with worry, didn't sleep a wink. Even with her hearing loss, she could hear Kit Walker's grief. She knew how Kit felt, losing her husband, no matter what the cause.

Though many other killings happened in the town, none unsettled the Childers family as deeply as did Harry Walker's death.

Through countless, sleepless hours Pearl shuddered and wondered whether Henry would be next. Henry carried a gun for years afterward because bootleggers and gang wars lasted a long time and nobody felt safe in Herrin.

* * * *

Until the depression shut them all down, Henry worked in the coal mines. All the years Ruth was little, she lived in terror of the mines. She thought a lot about Helen's father, and was always afraid when she saw her father go to work. She used to get up at four o'clock in the morning just to spend a few minutes with him before a truck picked him up to go to work.

Popular in those days was a phonograph song about a little girl who told her daddy goodbye one morning when he went to work in the mines. He was killed that day. It was called, "The Song of the Miner's Daughter," and it used to haunt Ruth. She listened over and over again with sweet agony to the little girl on the record crying for her daddy.

Sometimes Ruth and Arthur would walk a mile-and-a-half over to their Uncle Milton's house. He lived across town beyond the high school, by the big overhead bridge. They used to love to play on that bridge and under it, and Uncle Milt had wonderful trees in his yard which were just right for climbing.

One day Art and Ruth spent the morning there. They had enjoyed their noon dinner with their cousins, and were out in a tree pretending to be big apes when Uncle Milt came out and called them down. He said, "Arthur and Ruth, I'm goin' to walk home with you now. I heard your Daddy has been hurt in the mines."

All that long way home Ruth and Art cried and worried about their dad. Pearl met them at the door with her finger on her lips and they heard groaning sounds coming from their bedroom. "Daddy got hurt in the mines today—some coal fell on him, Ruthie, and he has several broken ribs. He hurts a lot, so you and Arthur and Irene play outside and don't bother him nor make any noise."

"Can't we just see him?"

Pearl nodded. They tiptoed into the bedroom.

Their Daddy was lying spread out on his fancy iron double bed, his face twisted in pain. He was groaning with every breath and they could see wide bands of tape wound tightly around his chest. He hardly looked like their Daddy for he was not very clean. Coal dust darkened his fingernails and black was all around his ears and his hairline where the print of his miner's cap was visible. They could smell the odor of his carbide lamp on his hair. He opened his eyes a little. Ruth wanted to throw herself on his chest—she couldn't stand to see her big, handsome, strong father lying helpless and moaning.

"Oh, Daddy, I feel so bad because you're hurt. Can I get anything to help you?"

"Put a cold rag on my head, Ruthie."

During the next two months while his bones healed, they all waited on Henry, bringing trays to his bed and trying to make him comfortable. It was summertime and the house was hot. Ruth often stood and fanned him and brought him ice water.

Many of their friends from church came to visit Henry when he was feeling better and able to talk to them. All the men were miners, and nearly all of them had, at one time or another, been hurt in some mine accident. So they sat around his bed and swapped stories. Their wives often brought some dish of fancy cooking which they thought Henry would like and Pearl would also appreciate. They knew the Childers kids would.

* * * *

One of Pearl's dearest friends was Mrs. Shoemaker. If it had been at the time when women wore pants, people might have thought Mrs. Shoemaker was a man. She stood tall and broad for a woman, with a thatch of white hair. Her hair was long and thick and she wore it twisted around the top of her head. Ruth thought it sort of looked like a bird's nest up there, but she never told her mother she thought that. She really loved Mrs. Shoemaker very much.

Mrs. Shoemaker had a big nose with an over-and-down curve like a sheik from Araby. Her arms were thick and her hands work-worn. Her eyes, though, were like violets sparkling in the dew, and when she looked at Ruth, Ruth felt loved.

Sometimes Mrs. Shoemaker came to Pearl's house to visit, and Pearl often took her children to visit Mrs. Shoemaker, to spend the morning talking, and have lunch. They both enjoyed that.

One summer day Mrs. Shoemaker set her table with many good things like fried chicken, green beans, corn on the cob, hot biscuits, and iced tea. Ruth and Arthur were there, smelling all those goodies cooking while they played on the front porch. They could hardly wait until noon. When they were all seated, Mrs. Shoemaker asked the Lord to bless the food, and then proceeded to pass the dishes around. Ruth and Arthur were happily chewing on a chicken leg when Mrs. Shoemaker said, "Little Irene, aren't you eating anything today? What would you like to have? Some chicken?"

Irene, about three years old and sitting in Mrs. Shomaker's ancient high-chair, shook her head.

"Some green beans and a biscuit?"

Again she shook her head.

Ruth exclaimed, "Irene, this is good!"

Another head shake.

"Then tell me what you want, Irene." Mrs. Shoemaker was puzzled. "Don't you like any of the things we have here today? If you don't, what do you like?"

Irene, in the high chair, looked down at her empty plate. "I only want a biegy. Fice me a biegy."

"Oh, Irene!" Pearl was embarrassed. "We've got plenty here. You don't need that!"

"Fice me a biegy."

Ruth was disgusted and interpreted for their hostess. "That silly little kid only wants a fried egg. That's what she means!"

"Mrs. Shoemaker rose from her chair at the head of the table. "If that little girl wants a ficed biegy, that's what she's going to get." And she soon came back with two fried eggs, which she put down in front of happy little nitwit Irene.

Mrs. Shoemaker had cooked the eggs "over easy," and Irene stared at them for a minute and then looked up at Pearl. "Mommie, she ficed it on the wong side!"

Pearl said sternly, "Irene, you eat those eggs!"

She did.

Ruth and Art ate all the chicken and biscuits they could hold.

In the midweek prayer services at the church, Mrs. Shoemaker attended as regularly as did the Childers family. When it came time for testimonies, she always said the same five-word sentence. Her speech was clipped—she wasted no words. "I'm on the Lord's side!"

And everyone knew she was.

She made the best fudge in southern Illinois, cooking it in an iron skillet in her coal grate. Sometimes she asked Ruth to spend the night with her, and she always made fudge. She held the heavy black skillet, set over hot coals, with her left hand, stirring with a big wooden spoon with her right. To test when the fudge was nearly done, she dropped spoonfuls of the brown bubbles into a cup of cold water and gave it into Ruth's grubby little hands.

One winter night Ruth was there, enjoyed the fudge, and at bedtime plunged deep into a big featherbed with a heavy comforter up to her chin. Mrs. Shoemaker came in, saw that Ruth was tucked in, then the floor rumbled when she got down on her well worn knees to pray beside the other feather bed. Among her thanksgivings she also thanked the Lord for the Childers family.

Ruth thought, *She's too old and too heavy to get on her knees to pray on that cold floor. I don't pray on my knees, and mine are young and bony.*

Then Ruth felt guilty because she knew her good friend Mrs. Shoemaker was closer to God than she was.

CHAPTER THIRTY-ONE
1920s–Economy Slows

Pearl and Henry were thankful that Henry was still working. He could feed his family, and plenty of love and discipline were top priority in the Childers household. None of the children ever felt deprived or inferior to anyone else.

Henry often said to them: "Stand up tall! I don't ever want to see you slouch like a dog with its tail between its legs. Stand up! Be clean. Be proud of yourself. You got plenty of brains—now use them right! You can do anything you make up your mind to do and you are as good as anybody! But you have to work!"

Every evening at 5:30, Henry stepped out on the back porch to hear his mine whistle. The family had to be silent while he listened for Old Jeffrey's instructions. Only then could he know whether he would work the next day. Three long whistles meant work. One long and one short whistle meant it "blew out," as the miners say—no work the next day.

On March 19, 1925, Henry didn't have to work. That morning at breakfast Pearl said, "Henry, that old clock we have is going to make you miss your ride to work some day. It starts and stops all the time. Don't you think you'd better get a new one—one we can trust its alarm to go off?"

"Yes, I reckon so, Pearl. I'll go downtown and see about it this morning."

Henry came home at noon with "Old Ben," the large, round-faced, spraddle-legged Big Ben wind-up alarm clock that sat on the kitchen shelf every day the rest of their lives. As a ritual each night, Henry wound the clock, set the alarm, took it into the bedroom and put it on the dresser. Every morning the clock went back to the kitchen shelf. Old Ben's tick was loud and determined, as if to say, "It's up to me to get this Childers family going on time." And it did the job well for thirty-nine years, surviving many repairs and cleanings. Before long, Old Ben wasn't just an "it", but a "he." and he ticked so loud even Pearl could hear him.

On the afternoon of the March day when Old Ben joined the family, suddenly a black cloud came up out of the west and a terrible tornado struck "Little Egypt," killing 500 people. It demolished Murphysboro. Many houses in Herrin were undamaged, including Pearl and Henry's house, but the yard and roads were blocked with huge, fallen trees. Old Ben sat on his kitchen shelf and ticked, unafraid and unharmed through it all.

But the Childers family always remembered Old Ben's birthday. The radio was calling for workers to volunteer to go to Murphysboro, about twenty-five miles west of Herrin—to pick up the injured and dead, and to help clean up the town. Henry went with many others and they stayed for several days, helping Murphysboro get itself together.

Henry had always been interested in first aid, and after the tornado he took a long course and earned a certificate of proficiency in first aid. When anyone felt faint or was in an accident, Henry was always ready. He carried a little vial of spirits of ammonia in his pocket to revive people. He was very good at bandaging sprains or making splints for broken bones.

All his first aid equipment was kept in a built-in corner cupboard in the kitchen, which was a kitchen/dining/family room. Henry liked their big, comfortable kitchen.

Heavy work shoes and small school shoes were cleaned and polished for the next day and kept by the back door. On one side of the room sat the ice box, capable of holding a 100-pound block of ice. About every four days a strong man wearing rubber boots and a rubber apron carried in the 100-pound cube, held in huge tongs. Using his apron-covered knee, he steadied the ice, pushing it into the big top door of the box. He always had a perfect fit.

Ruth and Arthur, like every other kid in the neighborhood at one time or another, raided the ice wagon for small chipped-off pieces. When the ice carrier came from the back of any house, the kids would scatter in all directions.

At mealtimes something funny usually happened, and they were sure that lots of laughing and racket helped the food digest. Pearl often wondered what the neighbors thought about their noisy, laughing Childers family.

The kitchen table was sturdy oak, covered with a red-and-white checked oilcloth, and its three leaves could expand for lots of company. Straight-backed chairs sat around it. After supper the table became a desk, where three children memorized new spelling words, learned to read and tried to understand arithmetic problems. The table was battleground for many anagram games. It was also the place where the big Sunday crossword puzzle was spread out and worked by quick-thinking Pearl. Ruth and Arthur learned to play Ping-Pong on that stretched-out table. That was where dressmaking took place, with material unfolded and patterns pushed, turned around and scooted enough to make a new dress.

Ruth's dresses were cut down for Irene. Ruth was lucky enough to inherit Helen's dresses when she was finished with them, and the two girls were enough the same size that very little alteration was needed.

That same family room was the wash-up room at the small sink, and Henry always cautioned the family not to put anything down it to stop up the pipe. On cold winter nights, the room often smelled of popcorn, and cocoa with a big, fat marshmallow floating on top. Summertime treats were ice cream or watermelon.

The kitchen was also the place to get a haircut, in winter to wash clothes, and to take a bath in the same round tubs. The most delicious pies, chicken and dumplings, chocolate cake, fried chicken, stews, soups, chilis, and homemade bread in all of Herrin could be found there, because Pearl was a great cook. While cooking, Pearl was always making up a rhyme and laughing about something. In spite of the scary things going on in Herrin, Pearl and Henry's was the happiest house anywhere, and many other children loved to come over and be part of the Childers fun.

But the economy began to sag. In September 1925, Ruth and Arthur walked home at noon on the first day of school. They found Pearl washing clothes under the grapevine, which had finally grown into an arbor large enough and thick enough to shelter her from the sun. Clothes were boiling in the big black kettle set on three stones in the middle of the yard. She was vigorously scrubbing her children's clothes on the washboard. "You're home early?"

"They let us out early—it was too hot in school."

"Well, go in and take off your school clothes and shoes. There's some bread and peanut butter and jelly on the table. Put on something old to play in."

"Mommie, my new teacher said we had to have a special kind of tablet and pencils and crayons."

"Mine did too, Mommie," Ruth agreed. "And I have to have a new kind of reading book. Can't get a secondhand one anywhere, 'cause it's a new kind of book."

Pearl stopped rubbing Arthur's shirt on the washboard and leaned on her tubs. Sweat was running down her face and she was tired. She wasn't even smiling today. Mine work had slacked off, and the money didn't go far enough. They had no savings at all—they lived only from week to week on what they had from last week's pay. Ruth had a rush of sympathy for her mother because she worked so hard and had so little money.

"I'm sorry, Mommie. I wish we didn't have to buy all that new stuff. I know it costs a lot of money."

Pearl sighed and rubbed her arm over her forehead. "It isn't your fault, Ruthie. We'll find the money for your things somewhere." She thought, *It's the same thing every school year—the kids needing things and so little money to buy with. We have to buy goods for clothes, and shoes—oh, the shoes! How fast they wear out. How many cardboard soles I've cut to slip inside small shoes! I wonder if times can get any worse.*

But she knew they could. Sometimes she felt guilty because she had allowed Helen to stay with Ma and Pa Baxley. But now that the mines were slowing down and there was less money, she was glad that Helen was with the Baxleys. They could buy all the things Helen needed.

* * * *

One night in the fall of 1926, the family was eating a supper of bacon, biscuits and milk gravy. Pearl spoke up. "Henry, I think I can get a job—for at least two days a week. Ruth and Arthur are in school now and it will give me something else to do, as well as make a little money."

"What kind of job?"

"I can help Mrs. Glotfelty in her house—I've heard she's looking for some help. Housework I can do best. And I am sure she wouldn't mind if I brought Irene with me when I work there."

"I don't want you working in other people's houses!"

"I know. But the kids need clothes and shoes, and the mines don't work enough. If it's all right with you, I'll go see about it tomorrow. You know we need money."

Henry picked up the newspaper to hide his emotion. Pearl stared a long time at the newsprint wall which hid him. She knew his pride was hurting. She longed to comfort him—but she couldn't buy necessities with comfort. She really didn't want to work anywhere else but in her own home, but decided to make light of it. So she said, "Silence. Well, I guess silence gives consent. I'll go tomorrow."

Henry couldn't say anything.

Mrs. Glotfelty was a short, softly heavy German woman with

a mania for cleanliness. She had white hair drawn back tightly into a knot at the back of her head. Her skin was very fair, she had a small smiling mouth, and her light blue eyes twinkled behind tiny, octagonal-shaped rimless glasses. She and Pearl had been friends ever since Rev. Glotfelty had been appointed pastor of the Methodist Church in Herrin. Pearl said that Mrs. Glotfelty made the most delicious tiny, delicate biscuits she ever ate. Those biscuits probably wouldn't have satisfied Henry, because he liked his large enough to make several mouthfuls.

Mrs. Glotfelty welcomed Pearl with open arms when she applied for the job. And she didn't mind that Pearl wanted to bring Irene with her—Irene was a very quiet child.

So Pearl began to work in the parsonage and for many years helped that parsonage first lady and succeeding Methodist pastors' wives. She also got one more housework job—helping Mrs. Storme, the undertaker's wife, in her big house. Besides that, Pearl often did ironing for people at home. Nobody could iron like Pearl. In the hot summer, she used to get up at 4:00 a.m. (dawn), put her ironing board out on the front porch and iron clothes while taking advantage of the coolest part of the day.

Irene, always an early riser, usually got up shortly after Pearl did, and after eating her fried egg, would sit and talk to her mother while she ironed.

Pearl actually enjoyed working in the parsonage and with Mrs. Storme. She loved these ladies and they loved her happy way of working and never feeling sorry for herself because she had to work. She made about $2.00 a day—two days a week. Once, after a day's work at Mrs. Storme's—washing dishes, sweeping and scrubbing floors, and cleaning some silver—she left her this note on the kitchen cabinet:

> I cleaned your floor down on my knees–
> Your humble servant aims to please.
> I know when Heaven I finally make,
> A dusting cloth with me I'll take.
> And if you're lucky and get there, too,
> I'll dust a golden chair for you,
> String up your harp, and shine your crown.
> And then perhaps I shall sit down
> And rest a thousand years or so–
> THAT part of Heaven YOU'D like, I know!

* * * *

In the middle of the town's turmoil, music brought joy to the Childers' house. Irene, grown beyond her "ficed biegy" stage, wanted to learn to play the piano. Since the Childers family was in church every time the doors were opened, they heard hundreds of hymns played and sung.

For a while, Pearl and Henry had kept a piano for a neighboring family while they were away. Pearl had often relaxed by playing hymns—of course she could read music. The family sang at the piano with her and she taught them many, many church songs. They learned all the songs by memory, and while they had the neighbors' piano, Ruth learned to play somewhat by picking out the chords which sounded right. But they never had any money for music lessons.

When the neighbors took their piano home, that big empty corner glared at all of them. Pearl often said, "Henry, I really miss a piano. Maybe we could get a secondhand one somewhere."

One day Henry came home and called Arthur. "Come with me, Art—we'll go down the block." Then he said to Pearl, "In ten minutes get the door open, move that chair, and make a way to the piano corner!"

"What in the world—? You got a *piano?*"

Irene and Ruth yelled for joy and excitedly helped Pearl scoot Henry's big chair out of the path. They watched wide-eyed as Arthur and his daddy walked south down the street and went into a house in the next block. After a few minutes, with some neighbors helping, they moved a piano out of that front door and *rolled it up the sidewalk* to the Childers house!

"I can't believe it!" Pearl exclaimed.

The men grunted, lifted the heavy piano up two steps to the porch, and soon an almost new shining, black piano stood in the corner of the living room. And it belonged to them!

Pearl was ecstatic. "Oh, Henry—it's so pretty! How did you happen to buy it from those folks?"

Henry tried not to show how proud he was of himself. "Well—you been wantin' a piano, ain't you?"

She hugged him. "You *know* I have! But where did you get the money for it? How did you find it?"

"Oh, I been askin' 'round town—and here it was close to us all the time! The feller it belonged to said his kids used to play this thing but now they're all married and gone. It was just takin' up room in his house."

"I'm so happy! But Henry, how did you pay for it?"

"Uh—now, Pearl, don't ask me that. You know better'n to look a gift horse in the mouth."

Pearl was still waiting for an answer.

"Well, if you must know—I traded my gold watch for it."

Pearl's big blue eyes widened. "Oh, Henry! That fine watch you got in California? But you loved that watch!"

Henry shrugged. "Well, I don't need such a fancy one—I can get a cheaper one. And that feller down the street took a shine to it. So we just made a trade."

The kids wondered why their mama was crying when she had just said she was so happy.

Immediately all three kids started to "break in" their new piano. Henry sighed, "No more peace around here, I bet."

Pearl smiled at him. "You big old softie! You knew it would be noisy and yet you gave up your beautiful watch." She hugged him. "I'll miss that fancy gold chain draped across your stomach!"

No truer words were ever uttered than Henry's words about "no peace." Somebody was "pounding on the piano" all the time.

When Irene was about ten years old, she took lessons from a friend of hers who charged her five cents a lesson. Pearl and Henry had no money to buy any music, so Irene memorized her friend's pieces and learned to read notes. The next year she paid another friend ten cents for each lesson. She practiced faithfully—in fact, all the time, and began to play sometimes at church in her Junior League and in the "little" Sunday school. *Bringing in the Sheaves* was the first song she played for church. She said it was easy—no sharps, no flats.

During the next few years she made deals with music teachers. She cleaned their houses and baby-sat their kids in exchange for lessons. Ruth's little sister was as stubborn about learning to play the piano as she used to be about wanting to eat ficed biegys.

* * * *

In 1927, when Ruth was ten years old, she had one of the greatest thrills of her life. Charles Lindbergh had just made his famous solo flight to Paris, France, and came back to a tumultuous parade in St. Louis.

Just before that, Ruth's Aunt Ida had visited their house, and invited Ruth to go back with her for a two-week stay. Of course,

Ruth was wild to go—she'd never been to such a big place as St. Louis. While she was there, "Lucky Lindy" came home. Aunt Ida took Ruth downtown for the parade, and though thousands of people lined the streets, she had a front line place to stand.

She could almost have touched him. His tiny plane, *The Spirit of St. Louis,* in which he made his flight, was mounted on a small truck. Ruth *did* touch the truck! And when "Lindy" came straight in front of her, he looked at her and smiled. Now that was the greatest thing that had ever happened—Charles Lindbergh *smiled* at her! She bragged to everybody about it, adding, "I'm sure if he ever saw me again, he would remember me!"

* * * *

Having grown up on a farm, Henry loved to make a garden every summer—his corn patch was the envy of the neighborhood. Most of their summer eating came from his garden, but Pearl didn't know much about growing things—she just knew how to cook them.

Henry was sitting on the porch swing late one afternoon, resting after his day in the mine, and Pearl was in the back yard. Soon she came through the house, and sat down by Henry in the swing, wiping sweat with a well-worn washrag. "Henry, I don't know what you're going to do. The wild onions are just taking that back section. It took me more than an hour to pull 'em out of there!"

Henry glared at her in unbelief. "It took you— WHAT?" he bawled. "Pearl, when it comes to a garden, you're the craziest woman I ever saw! Them AIN'T wild onions! I PLANTED them onions!"

Art, Irene and Ruth were on the porch too, and at Henry's roar, their mouths fell open. Then they shot around the corner of the house where they could roll on the ground and laugh in private.

Pearl never lived that down. Henry was so mad it took two years before he could laugh about it.

Never having finished his education beyond the sixth grade, Henry read slowly. He read only newspapers. And he often resented the way Pearl could completely lose herself in a book.

"Always got her nose stuck in a book!" he sometimes snorted. But when it came to a church program where Pearl was the star performer, he was very proud. She often "gave readings"—without any trouble she could memorize long passages. She could answer the preacher's question about a cross-word puzzle word, win an anagrams game, or write a funny poem. Yes, he was proud of her.

Pearl walked nine blocks to the library at least once a week, returning four books and bringing home four new books at a time. She was pretty and joyous, and wasn't above sitting down on the kitchen floor with her kids for a game of jacks. But she could never finish the hand of "knock the devil off the stump" in a jacks game.

* * * *

One October day when Ruth and Arthur were in grade school, a virtual deluge of rain began. It poured in wide streams down the windows of the schoolroom, and clouds grew so dark that the teacher turned on the lights. Thunder rolled and it was hard to hear anything else. Ruth began to dread going home for lunch, and she was sure many other kids dreaded it, too. This was a cold rain and Ruth had worn only a short jacket that morning.

About eleven o'clock they heard a firm knocking on the schoolroom door. The teacher opened the door and there stood Ruth's daddy! He was wearing his long overcoat and carrying an umbrella, but still, water was running off him. He held a wax-paper-wrapped packet in his hand. He looked beyond the teacher and his eyes searched the class until he saw Ruth. He nodded his head to her, staring wide-eyed at him, and then said a few words to the teacher. He handed her the umbrella and package.

Ruth couldn't believe her eyes! Her daddy *never* came to school. But he had walked in that awful rain bringing lunches to her and Arthur. And he left his umbrella for them too, which meant he splashed back home getting wetter than he already was.

If Ruth had ever doubted that her father loved her, the sight of him standing at her classroom door, drenched to the skin, convinced her she was wrong. She hunched her shoulders, hugged herself, and shivered in joy. Nobody ever had a finer father! Many of her friends walked home for lunch in the downpour.

* * * *

Henry could be stern and gruff—and often was. But he was a very good father. Twelve kids within two blocks on South Eighteenth Street played together, and they usually played in the Childers yard. Their yard was no bigger than any other, but Henry wanted his kids at home. So the other kids came there.

Their favorite game was Andy Over. That was when they divided up into two sides and threw a ball over the house, where somebody on the other team caught it. Then that whole team would run around the house, the one who caught the ball tagging those on the other side. They played with a hard rubber ball, which of course, bounced on the roof and knocked shingles loose. Many evenings after work, Henry climbed onto his roof and mended shingles broken by Andy Over. Sometimes their ball would land in the square groove around the chimney and Henry would grumble up the ladder to rescue it for them.

When it was too hot to run, they sat on the Childers back steps and played Dip. That was one crazy game.

One person was the "teacher" and the rest were "pupils." The teacher stood in front of the pupils with a cup of water and a teaspoon. Omniscient, the teacher would ask a question with only one tiny clue as to the answer. For example, "I am thinking of an animal. What is it?"

A hand would go up.

"Yes, Gladys, what is the animal I'm thinking about?"

"A tiger!"

"No, Gladys, you are wrong. You must be punished." The teacher would throw a teaspoon of water in Gladys's face. (A towel was also provided.) If the answer was right, then Gladys got to be the teacher.

If they ran out of water from wrong answers, they filled the cup again. Sometimes, in very hot weather, they used a tablespoon instead of a teaspoon. That kept them cooler.

* * * *

Root beer was a very popular drink in the 1920s, and all the Childers family liked it. Summers were hot, and sometimes just plain old water didn't satisfy. A company sent Art a sample with directions for making root beer at home. He made it, they tried it, and they were all hooked. This brew was not really a brew like "home brew" which had alcohol. Pearl would never have countenanced anything like that! Root beer she permitted.

Art often stirred up his mixture and poured the dark liquid into quart jars, and screwed on the lids. Sometimes he kept those jars in the icebox, but if they didn't drink it up fast enough or the jars took up too much room, Pearl had to remove them to keep the food cold. Once Art said, "We drink that stuff up so fast I'm gonna make a double recipe. So he stirred up his concoction and stashed the jars in the clothes closet which was built into the corner of the room where the kids slept.

Several days went by and the root beer was ready to be drunk. First, though, they had to finish what was in the icebox, never considering that the cache in the closet wouldn't be safe.

But one evening they were eating supper when a sudden, loud BANG exploded from the closet. They all jumped up and raced to see. Art stuck his head in the closet door and said, "Oh, oh! Too hot I guess. It must have soured!"

Henry said in a tight voice, "Let *me* see in there!" And pushing Arthur aside, stuck *his* head in. When he withdrew it, his face was red and angry. "Arthur! Get that mess out of this closet! Right now before any more of 'em explodes!"

"Okay, Daddy. Don't be mad! I never thought they'd be dangerous."

Pearl looked at all of her kids' dripping, smelly clothes hanging there and made her usual comment, "That does very well! We'll have an extra washday tomorrow!"

The next day, all three kids had to help do the washing, which probably hurt Art's manly pride. Boys weren't supposed to do washing or hang out clothes. They just blew up things.

* * * *

In Williamson County, the Roaring Twenties finally began to grind down to a gasp with Charlie Birger's hanging in Benton on April 19, 1928. Hundreds of men, including Henry, went to Benton to witness the hanging. Pearl said, "I can't understand why you'd want to go up and watch that man being hanged! I know he's killed lots of people and had others killed, but to watch it——" she shuddered.

Henry couldn't understand her objections. "When Charlie Birger and some of the others get what's comin' to them, this is goin' to be a better county!"

Some of the others involved in gang murders were found, arrested, and sentenced. Most people in Williamson County hoped and prayed that peace would reign supreme after years of fear and violence, and that now, people could rest a little and just be happy.

But that wasn't to be. For Herrin and Williamson County—along with the rest of the country—were hit hard with another calamity. This, too, would go down in history.

CHAPTER THIRTY-TWO
Economy Hits Bottom

Julia lived for several years with the Allens, keeping their house, cooking, washing and ironing. She even went out in spring and hoed up a little vegetable patch. They all took pleasure in working a little in the garden.

When Mr. Allen became feeble, she took care of him. When he died, Julia was a great source of comfort to Mrs. Allen. But Mrs. Allen didn't live long after her husband died—she didn't want to.

Julia looked for another household which needed somebody to "do" for them, and she didn't have to look long. Creal Springs was becoming a place where many older people moved in to spend their last days. Julia liked the feeling of still being able to work. She also liked saving the money she earned. All her expenses were part of her pay and besides that, she earned five dollars a week. She felt that was a very good salary.

She saved at least half of the money in her trunk until George could come in his car and take it to the Marion bank and deposit it for her. Julia still had a horror of ever "bein' beholdin'" to anybody and she liked the feeling of having a bank account. To her it seemed a fortune—and it meant security.

Her children Addie, Cena, Ola, and Eva Jane came to see her often. Almost every weekend in good weather, a carload of her children and grandchildren would pull into the yard. The couples she stayed with didn't see many people, so to have company come, and children too, was a treat.

But Addie began to weaken, and soon she wasn't able to come any more. Julia worried about her. The doctor told the family that Addie had tuberculosis.

Addie was just wasting away. Julia took a few days off and Cena took her up to see Addie. Julia was so grieved to see her lovely daughter, who, she always said, "looked and walked like an Indian princess." She was just a shadow of her former self, and she couldn't get out of bed any more.

In 1927, Addie died at the age of thirty-five. Dave Durham, her husband, was left to be both father and mother to their three boys and a girl. George brought Julia up from Creal Springs in his car for Addie's funeral. All the family came. Everyone loved sweet Addie. Julia thought that no sorrow was as hard to bear as having to bury a husband and a child.

* * * *

During the first years of the 1920s, the peak number of coal mines in any area of the whole United States, was a hundred mines in the three Illinois counties of Williamson, Franklin, and Saline. They hoisted coal every day. But during the last years of the 1920s, the count of working mines fell to sixty, then to fifty. Mining coal was the lifeblood of Herrin and Southern Illinois. But the newspapers said that the fear of a stock market crash was rumbling all over the country.

Men who worked below in the coal mines knew nothing about the stock market, nor did they understand how it could affect them. But they could see it. Coal demand began to slip. Some mines began to work on part-time basis and others closed. Tipples rusted and men no longer stepped out onto porches to hear their whistles in the evenings. Jeffrey, Henry's mine, worked longer than some, but Henry wondered how much longer it would last. He was working maybe two days a week.

The stock market crash of October 24, 1929 did not wipe out Pearl and Henry's bank account—they had none. Henry, reading the paper the next day, exclaimed, "What's going to happen to our country now?"

Pearl looked up from stirring chili on the stove. "Oh, I reckon it'll go on as it always has before. The only good thing for us was that we had no money to lose."

"Yep," agreed Henry. "I guess lots of people all over the country now will be poor—just like us."

Ruth, setting the table for supper said, "The paper says people are committing suicide because they lost all their money. I'd rather not ever have money than to have Daddy do that! We get along just fine!" She went over to hug Henry. "Daddy, do you want me to give you a facial after supper?" She liked to do things for her Dad. Henry loved to have Ruth comb his hair and put cream and lotion on his face. It was almost a nightly ritual. She'd massage his face and tell him she was rubbing out all the wrinkles. She hurt to see her dad and mom getting older. Her Dad had grieved deeply when he lost his sister Addie.

That Christmas was always remembered by the whole family. Arthur got a sled. It took Henry a long time before Christmas to scrape together enough money to buy it.

Art's face shone like a candle when he saw his new sled under the tree. "Daddy, can I go out in the snow right after breakfast? I'll ask Edward to come play with me and my new sled!" Arthur hurried, put on his overshoes and went next door to his best friend's house. Before long, the two boys were pulling the sled up and sliding down the hill, taking turns pushing each other. Arthur was pushing Edward when the accident happened.

The front of the sled runner hit a rock hidden in the snow, the sled front tilted down and the back runner went high into the air. Art was pushing fast, and when the back of the sled went up, the runner pierced his heavy overalls and thrust deep into his thigh, making a large, half-moon wound. It didn't bleed much and though it hurt a lot, he tried not to cry. Edward pulled him home and Art came limping into the house.

"Daddy, I hurt my leg!"

Henry pulled down Art's overalls, looked at the laceration and knew it was more serious than he could deal with. Henry never owned a car, so Ed Misker took Henry and Arthur to Dr. Duncan, who'd taken care of the family for many years after Dr. Murrah's death. Dr. Duncan carefully cleansed the open tear in Art's upper thigh, pulling threads of cloth out of it, and sewed up the incision. Art was in a lot of pain that evening.

"Daddy, is Art going to be all right?"

"I think so, Ruthie. Doc fixed him up just fine."

But a few days later, Art's temperature shot up, his neck began to stiffen and his teeth clenched together—lockjaw! Henry called Dr. Duncan at the first sign of it that day, and the doctor came out. He gave Art a tetanus shot, praying it wasn't too late.

Nobody in the family ever forgot that bedside vigil. Dr. Duncan sat there the whole day watching Arthur. Ruth, thirteen years old, cried all the way to school because she was afraid he wouldn't be living when she came home. Eight-year-old Irene feared she'd not have a big brother. Edward was very much afraid he would lose his buddy. Pearl and Henry were almost beside themselves because they thought they were going to lose their only son. Lockjaw usually killed people.

Old Ben ticked the minutes away as the morning and afternoon dragged on. Pearl cooked a meal, but none of the three felt like eating. Art seemed to be in a coma.

Pearl, Henry, and Dr. Duncan did not move from Art's bed.

After school, Ruth and Irene raced home, wanting to be there, yet afraid of what they might find. Tiptoeing into the room, they searched their mother's face for a sign of improvement, but Pearl silently shook her head as she wiped tears away.

Another three hours passed before a definite answer came. About six o'clock, Dr. Duncan, who had been staring at Arthur's face for hours, reached over and began to feel his face and neck. A slight smile twitched the corner of his mouth and he stood up stiffly. "Well, Henry," he said quietly, "your boy's going to be all right. The muscles have begun to relax now. Thank God!"

Pearl sobbed in relief, and tears of joy ran down Henry's cheeks. The children had never seen their father cry. Even Dr. Duncan wept. God had answered their prayers!

Nobody at 618 South 18th Street ever forgot that sled!

* * * *

And nobody would ever forget about the stock market crash and how it affected the whole United States. At the Watch-Night service on New Year's Eve, December 31, 1929, fervent prayers ascended from every church in the country for God's care and protection for the coming year.

Julia had heard on the radio about the stock market crash in New York City, and how, because of it, once-rich men were finding many ways to commit suicide. But she knew nothing about the stock market, and New York was far away from Creal Springs, Illinois, in Williamson County.

After a few days, frantic men on the radio said that many banks were also going broke. Julia didn't understand how banks could be related to each other so much that if one went broke, they all went broke. It sounded to her like John's three little girls in bed—if one turned over, they all had to turn!

Her money was safe, she knew. Julia wasn't worried, because the stock market crash—whatever that was—had nothing at all to do with Marion, Illinois. New York was too far away for citizens of Marion and Creal Springs to worry about. George had told her to keep her money in the Marion bank because it would be safe there, and George had been putting her money there all along. Her money—a fortune for her—now had increased to about eight hundred dollars. Because it was her habit to deny herself things unless they were absolutely necessary, she'd been living frugally.

Citizens of Williamson County found it hard to believe the whole country was poor. Of course, the miners knew they were—they always had been. But now, the situation was getting worse. In February, 1930, some who had a little money were still trusting it to banks for safekeeping, but then in Hurst, near Herrin, the first area bank closed.

Still, Williamson County people believed their county could ride out other bank closings. But April 14, 1930, the Marion Trust and Savings Bank closed after $145,000 was withdrawn in a run. Those who took out their money that day were lucky!

The next morning, April 15, 1930—Julia would never forget it—George drove his Ford car out from Marion with great speed, tore into her Creal Springs yard, and screeched to a stop. He raced up the steps. "Ma, Ma!" he gasped, "have you heard the news? All the banks have gone broke—the Marion bank too! Our money is all gone—all the money I had in the bank and yours is all gone too, Ma!"

Julia stood stock still in the kitchen, her knees beginning to quiver. "Gone? Gone?" she echoed stupidly. "How is it gone? Where is it gone? Who took it?"

George, his hands trembling, shook his head. "Don't know! They say banks all over the country've gone broke and closed. Everybody's going to be poor, looks like, Ma!"

"George, did you go to the bank and try to get our money out? It couldn't just go away!"

"Ma, the bank doors are locked and barred. Nobody can get in to get any money! They just tell us it's all gone."

Julia sank down into a rocking chair in the kitchen door, the same as Ellie Crawford had done long ago in 1879. For the first time Julia felt beaten and old and tired. She had worked for eight years and saved that money.

"I don't have anything at all. Nothin' put by to keep me in my old age. All this time workin' and savin' and it's all gone." She sat rocking and shaking her head, trembling, rolling and unrolling a handkerchief.

She had been thrifty before, but now Julia became a penny-pinching miser. She refused to buy anything for herself, saving every cent of her salary. She hid it all in the toe of an old stocking, buried in the corner of her trunk. It eased her mind to see the cache grow a little each month. She *could not* become a burden to anybody before she died!

Julia continued to wait on old people who couldn't feed themselves very well and spilled food on their clothes. She helped them to dress and take their baths. She cooked their food, washed their dishes, and carried out their chamber pots when they couldn't get to the outhouse.

The economy continued to decline. The Herrin State Bank closed, and the city's delinquent tax list was the largest ever published in southern Illinois to that date.

Kit Carson, their postman, brought a letter one day which Pearl read and then began to tremble. "Henry! Look at this! They say that if we don't pay our taxes, they're going to sell our house to collect what we owe. Henry, we'll be out on the street! What are we going to do?"

"Let me see that letter!" Henry tried not to show his despair, but Pearl knew how he felt. They were sitting in the porch swing at noon time in the summer—they'd just had their lunch of tomato soup and bread, and the two younger kids were playing under the trees in the back yard. Ruth was washing dishes in the kitchen. Henry read the letter, his face fell, and his arm slowly relaxed until the letter lay on his lap. His voice sounded muffled. "Only one thing I can think of, Pearl. We'll have to borrow the money somewhere! We can't have our kids on the street!"

"Who in the world would loan us that much money? Two hundred dollars is a fortune! How many years have we not paid taxes to add up to that much?"

"Don't know how long," answered Henry, shaking his head. "It's been a long time since I paid any taxes. I just couldn't do it. Even if I'd have known at the time that we might be put out on the street, I guess I couldn't have done anything about it."

"Henry, what about our friend in Metropolis? Maybe he would loan it to us."

"Yes, I guess he's the only one who would have it. I'll write to him. Lord, I hate to ask anybody for a loan!"

Henry wrote his letter, the friend *was* a friend, and their house was saved. But with work at the mines so sporatic, Henry's loan payments were very small. Two years passed before the full loan was repaid. Every time they read the paper, Henry and Pearl were sad, because they found other families' homes were being sold for taxes. What would their friends do? Where would they sleep?

Many businesses closed but some managed to squeak by. Items in stores were cheap, but many people still found necessities hard to buy. A man could get a new suit for $10, or his wife could buy a cloth coat with a fur trim for about $5.00. But *who* could spend a whole $15.00 on *clothes!*? Bread was 8 cents a loaf, eggs were 10 cents a dozen, and bacon about 25 cents a pound. Boys' bib overalls were about $1.00, and a man's overalls cost $2.00. One could buy four thin pork chops for 25 cents, or a meal at a restaurant for 50 cents. Not many could afford a restaurant meal.

A few mines were working two days a week, but after a while they closed altogether and Henry, like thousands of others, was totally out of a job. He joined the Hodcarriers Union, and from then on could work in any kind of construction or building repair. Henry was never afraid of hard work. Every morning of the week would find him downtown on the [closed] bank corner by 6:30. That was when superintendents who had any job at all needing man-power came to choose whoever they wanted to work for them. Henry could do just about any kind of work, so he often got jobs on a day-to-day basis. Some seasons were fairly good, but in winter, jobs were hard to find.

Henry's willingness to do any kind of work and Pearl's constant upbeat attitude held the Childers family together. Pearl never grouched about having less to cook—she just tried new ways of making food go further. And the more bare their pantry shelves became, the more Pearl's Pollyanna attitude came forth, and the more she found to write funny rhymes about. When her brother Bill was hospitalized, she tickled his funnybone with this:

They took me to the hospital–I was in awful pain.
The doctors cut my head right off, and stuck it back again.
They tried their best to find my brain–it was a hopeless task–
I could have told them, "I'se insane" but no one thought to ask!
They stuck me with a needle, and they shot me with a gun.
I thought, *They're surely finished,* but they had just begun.
They cracked my knees and pinched my ears
And sat upon my chest.
The nurses urged them on with cheers,
They wouldn't let me rest.
But something seems now to be amiss–
My toes ain't where they b'long.
I wonder if it could be this–they put my head back wrong!

Bill wrote to Pearl, "Little sister, you are the only one who understands me. I think I'll come to your house and let you take care of me. Being in the hospital is nearly as bad as you described it. I know you could give me better care." But he didn't come.

Friends came to the Childers' house and went home cheered up because they always found something funny there to laugh about.

President Roosevelt started the Works Progress Administration. Those workers built new-fangled WPA outdoor privies all over town—privies set in concrete, no less, replacing the old-fashioned, leaning-with-age kind. Lately when Pearl had gone into her old one, she always hoped it would keep standing until she got finished that time! The Childers family was lucky enough to get a new fashioned fancy one.

Pearl said, "Well, I'm glad these new toilets are set in concrete. They're strong and the wind doesn't whistle up so much when you're sittin' there. The sides are put together better, the door shuts tight, the roof doesn't leak, and the Sears Catalogs don't get wet when it rains!" Nobody ever heard of buying toilet paper.

Pearl made all of her own and her children's clothes. She wasn't the greatest seamstress in the world, but she turned out many well-done outfits on her New Home pedal sewing machine. She taught Ruth and Irene to sew. During the summer time, often some of Henry's sisters' children came to stay for a while. Pearl also sewed for them.

Thursday was Quilting Day at the church. Each lady interested in helping world missions, went to the church basement with a dish of something for lunch, and her favorite thimble and needle. Under-school-age children, and in summer all girls who wanted to learn to quilt, tagged along. The smaller children played in some Sunday School rooms during the morning, but the older girls sat around the long, stretched-out quilt frame and learned to make very small stitches. At least four women would sit on each side of the quilt and one or two at each end. Each one sewed with one hand under her stitching place to guide the needle. About every hour, they rolled the long quilt under on its frame one more turn, and clamped the ends down. Finally, the two long rolls met in the middle for the finishing looping and knotting of thread. And as they stitched, they talked and cheered each other up, and tried to solve all the problems of the church, the bootleggers, and the depression.

At noon, quilters, cramped from sitting all morning, stood up and walked stiffly to the table. They laid out their plates and forks, and opened up their bowls of green beans, corn, turnip greens, and sometimes chicken and dumplings, ham, or pork chops. Somebody always brought corn bread, and sometimes a chocolate cake appeared.

"Come to dinner, kids!"

The noon meal was the only thing the kids had been waiting for all morning. The choice of good things to eat on Quilting Day was so much greater than they had at home. This church fellowship helped many near-poverty families weather the depth of the depression. Hope was always there. God was real, He was worshiped, and spirits were lifted.

CAST A LONG SHADOW

Book IV

PEARL'S FAMILY

1930s - 1940s

CHAPTER THIRTY-THREE
Depression

"Mom, do you know of any other family that has more fun than we do? I go to other kids' houses and they don't seem to be very happy."

"Ruthie, did you ever think it was because we might be a little crazy and not bothered by it?"

"Yeah, maybe so—but I'd take our family any day."

Pearl was always writing funny poetry and they could laugh about anything. During the depression after the 1929 stock market crash, it was either laugh or die.

In July one year the thermometer panted upward until it reached 112 degrees for several days. One man in Johnston City claimed that although his setting hen had deserted her nest, the eggs hatched all by themselves. Some people saved their gas and fried eggs on the sidewalk.

Living was easier in summer because Henry made a garden and grew their own vegetables. They still had chickens and that helped with meals, though the kids didn't like to see Henry wring the neck of a chicken.

The $2.00 Pearl made each day she worked helped too. Sometimes Henry found work and they always had *something* to eat and wear, though later Pearl couldn't remember how they did it. Lean years stalked by, their children grew taller, and Pearl and Henry wondered what kind of world they would inherit.

In the middle of a hardship summer, Ruth's friend Sue came to stay with them for a while. Sue's father was very ill in a hospital for a long time, and her mother was in a rest home. Sue had no one to live with, so Pearl asked her to come and live with them.

Pearl had no extra bed and Sue knew she'd have to sleep on the floor. But Ruth couldn't bear for her to sleep on the floor alone, and neither could Art and Irene. So every night that summer, all four of the kids slept on the floor near the front door to catch a breeze. Of course, they used to talk and giggle, and Henry couldn't sleep with all the racket, so he fussed at them. Because Pearl's hearing was not so keen, their noise never did bother her; she just turned over and fanned herself to sleep.

When all four kids would finally settle down, Henry would drop off to sleep and start to snore. Suddenly he'd wake himself up with one grand snort, pop up in bed and yell, "You kids be quiet in there and let me get some sleep!"

Shrieking laughter would start again.

The Depression was real. Food was scarce and jobs hard to find. Henry walked to town every day to pick up any job at all from the few businessmen who hired workers off the street. Their small, four-room house was always clean and the children were too, even if they had only crowder peas or pinto beans and cornbread with bacon drippings to eat, and could barely pay the small light bill. Maybe they had fried eggs and biscuits and canned-milk gravy (after they had sold the cow), or sweet potatoes. Anyway, Pearl and Henry often fed friends who had less. And any beggar who came to the door was also fed something. During the Depression, lots of beggars made the rounds. The Childers family went to church every Sunday and thanked God that they had each other and their own house.

Once after a lesson in nutrition at school, Ruth's teacher asked, "How many had an orange for breakfast? Hold up your hands."

Ruth held up her hand because she didn't want anybody to think her Mama and Daddy didn't feed her enough. And she prayed all the time that her Daddy wouldn't ever find out she told her teacher a lie. But they had oranges only at Christmas time—one in the toe of each stocking on Christmas morning. Pearl used to peel each one's orange, slice it thin and sprinkle sugar over it. What a treat!

At school, children could buy a half-pint of milk to drink at recess. The school newspaper, *The Bell,* each week published the number of half-pints of milk that were sold to students. Ruth always wished they had enough money so she could drink milk at recess. She seldom did.

Once in a while the kids could buy their lunch at a lunchroom near the school. They never had more than 15 cents, but that was enough. For 5 cents they could buy a hamburger with a pickle, for 5 cents some potato chips, and the last 5 cents went for a glass of Coca-Cola. Now that *was* a treat. Sometimes they had to choose between a drink and an ice cream cone. Hard decisions!

Deprivation—Ruth didn't know what the word meant. But when they lost Jack, she knew.

Jack was a much loved dog. They had depended on him to watch their new chickens every spring. Then work in the mines began to slack off, and Henry's dinner bucket and carbide lamp and cap gathered dust on the top pantry shelf. Pearl could buy five pork chops for a quarter then. Sometimes, they could afford them. Ruth often wished that some day her Mama would miscount, and she could have two pork chops instead of just one—but they didn't have even one apiece very often.

One by one they ate their chickens because they stopped laying. The chickens felt the heat and probably felt the depression too. Late one summer Ruth overheard Henry say something to Pearl which made her blood congeal. Her parents were talking quietly.

"I'd sure hate to have you do that, Henry," her Mama said.

"It kills me to think about it," her Daddy answered, "but thirty-five dollars is a mighty big price for a dog, and Jack's the best dog for miles around. That fellow really wants to buy him. He wants my gun, too."

Ruth was stunned. She ran stiff-kneed with shock into the next room and yelled at them. "No! You're *not* going to sell Jack. You can't sell him!" She dissolved in tears.

Her father soothed her hair. "Ruthie, if we can figure any other way to get along, I'll not sell him. But we can't even feed him enough."

Fear stalked the Childers kids. How could they ever live and not have Jack to play with? Nothing would seem right. Finally in the fall when Jack was about six years old and they had no more money and no more chickens, her Daddy sold Jack—and his shotgun, too. And he grieved all fall.

The back yard died. Would Ruth, Arthur, or Irene ever forget how it was? That waiting pen and no welcome bark. A sagging gate, and no wagging tail. Meaningless mornings and mourning children.

Many times Arthur and Ruth walked a long way across town to see Jack in the strange pen. He went crazy when he saw his family, and of course didn't understand why he couldn't come home with them. They petted his wet nose and hugged him through the rail fence. They talked to him and told him that when Daddy got enough money, they would buy him back. Then they cried all the way home.

Of course they never could buy him back. He died before the Depression was over.

Years later they took in a little stray brown dog and named him Buster. Buster had no fancy pedigree like Jack, but he loved the family and kept the yard cleared of neighborhood hounds.

One evening after supper they all heard a fearful growling and gnashing of teeth in the back yard where Buster had challenged an unwary visitor. Pearl and Irene were washing dishes, but Pearl ran out of the house to try to separate the dogs. Ruth and Arthur ran after her. Irene, who was about nine, had read, "If you throw water on fighting dogs, they will break up the fight." So Irene rushed out the back door with the dishpan of water and threw it in the dogs' direction.

Henry, resting on the front porch heard the commotion, jumped up and rounded the back corner of the house just as Irene hurled the water. He got it full in the face!

At his bellow of rage, the dogs let go of each other's throat, escaped and hid under the house. Pearl carried in the dishpan. Art and Ruth staggered around to the other side of the house and rolled in the grass, holding their sides in laughter. Irene tottered toward the privy. Henry forgot his religion long enough to cuss a little and without another word he tramped inside, pushed Pearl away from the kitchen sink, and washed his face. Buster didn't show up all night.

* * * *

"Mommie, I got the job!" Ruth's eyes were shining as she bounded into the front room one day in 1935. "I start to work tomorrow."

"Oh, I'm so glad for you, Ruthie." Pearl hugged her. "It's been hard for you to just to sit around since you graduated from high school. I guess you're pretty lucky to find a job—lots of kids don't. Think you'll like working at Woolworth?"

"I'd rather have a typing job some place, but couldn't find one." Ruth shrugged. "Anyway, I'll make the big sum of a dollar and sixty-seven cents a day and that's ten dollars and two cents a week. Sounds a lot better than nothing. Course, since they just started something called Social Security, I will have to pay a little out of that to the government. It's still better than nothing! But I'll get to see a lot of people I know—everybody comes to Woolworth's sometime or other."

Ruth worked hard at Woolworth, and gave Pearl some of her pay to help buy food. Soon Arthur began working a few hours after school, and he helped some too. At that time, everybody was contributing whatever they could to the family budget. They used to tease Irene and tell her that even though she was little, she could scrub floors, so they were looking for a job for her. Irene was more interested in learning to play the piano than she was scrubbing anybody's floors.

Ruth saw a dress in a shop window, and the price was $5.00. She tried it on and it fitted her so into the layaway it went. She didn't mind that it was nearly a month before she could get it all paid for. Now, at least, she had one new dress to wear the next time she saw her boyfriend, Jerry.

They sat together as a family in church—always in the same pew. Pearl would go in first, then the kids, and Henry on the end. Henry usually came in *just* before the service started; he talked to his friends outside for a while.

Naturally, Henry thought that no young man alive was ever good enough for Ruth, and he didn't appreciate any fellows hanging around. When Ruth was fourteen, her daddy said she was too young to date. But he didn't know about the great crush Ruth had on Jerry. Jerry was six-feet-four and Ruth was five-feet-four. She had to look way up to Jerry. Jerry often came over and they took walks together, sometimes went to the 10-cent movie, or went to get ice cream. Henry usually didn't know about that.

One Sunday night Jerry got bold enough to ask Pearl if Ruth could sit in church with him. Pearl nodded okay, so they sat on the back pew. Ruth scrunched down beside Jerry when Henry walked by to his usual seat, never noticing her. He hadn't expected her to be back there.

When Ruth's daddy sat with his family, he was King of the Pew. That night he looked down the line of his children and the oldest was missing. Over bobbing heads of the singing crowd, Ruth saw him lean across two kids and whisper to Pearl. She couldn't hear a word, but true as if she did, he asked, "Where's Ruth?"

Pearl smiled at him (to squelch his anger). Whatever she said, Ruth saw her father's dark head begin to swivel and his eyes begin to search. She bent way down to rub a spot off her white shoe. But she couldn't stay close to the floor forever, and Henry finally spotted her sitting next to her boyfriend, who was taller than he was. Her father glared holes through her. But after he got used to the idea that Jerry was a decent young man, it was easier for Ruth to go places with Jerry. Henry still wished Ruth would wait until she was about thirty-five years old to go out with any man.

One Sunday afternoon, Jerry came to see Ruth when Henry and Pearl had gone to visit some friends. Henry had a favorite rocking chair with wide, flat rockers which had been in their house as long as Ruth could remember. No one else ever sat in it when Henry was at home because it was his! That Sunday afternoon Jerry sat in it, laughingly pulled Ruth down on his lap and rocked her. Well, he was too energetic and rocked back too far. They heard a sharp crack, and the chair, Jerry, and Ruth all fell over sideways. They'd broken her father's chair!

Ruth knew they didn't have any money to buy him a new rocking chair, and she couldn't imagine their house without it. She was so scared that she didn't even enjoy Jerry's company any more, and told him to go home because there would be an explosion when her father walked in and saw his chair.

No explosion, but she lived with guilt.

The experience was so traumatic for Ruth, that afterward she honestly couldn't remember whether she told her daddy a lie or the truth. She did know that he wouldn't like it if he knew she sat in Jerry's lap! The chair was too old and too badly broken to be repaired, and Ruth had to live with the guilty knowledge that her daddy was never as comfortable in any other chair.

Bang, bang, bang! went Henry's hammer on a July morning in the mid 1930s. The day before, the lumberyard truck had brought, and Henry had helped unload, boards—two-by-fours and two-by-sixes, flooring, and wall boarding. Then he got out his hammer, saws, and drills, and began to measure and cut. His neighbor, Ed Misker ambled over. "What are you doin', Henry? Looks like you intend to build on a new room here."

"That's what it is, Ed. Ma has been workin in Creal now for over fourteen years and she's beginnin' to slow down. I told her I'd build a room onto my house for her and she could come here and live. Gonna put in a bathroom too. Been usin' that outdoor privy long enough."

"Think your ma will come? I remember she likes bein' independent."

"Yeah, she does. But she's gettin' old and I don't want her tryin' to live by herself any more. I think I've about convinced her to come. By the time I get this room finished, I think she will. My sisters all want her to."

Henry worked on the room the rest of the summer. It was a large one, about fourteen feet square, with its own outside entrance at the back. Another door led from the back bedroom of Henry's house. "There! Ma can come and go as she wants to. She can come through our house, or go out her own back door."

Knowing what she liked, Henry put in a small wood stove for her to cook on in winter, and a coal-oil stove for her summer cooking.

Finally the time came that Julia decided, after working nearly fifteen years, that she wasn't strong any more. Not strong enough to lift people older than she was. And she was too tired to constantly be at someone's beck and call. She began to feel weak and wanted to rest more than she ever had in her life. Though hard to admit it to herself, she realized her working days were over.

Ida wanted her to stay with her for a while, so in the fall, Julia left Creal for the last time, and visited Ida. She enjoyed being with Ida and Ralph and their only child, Juanita, but she was homesick for southern Illinois. Ida called Henry and told him, "Well, I can't get her to stay any longer. We'll be bringin' her down next Saturday, Henry."

So Julia came. Henry and Pearl had her room all ready. Cena had brought all her mother's own things from storage: her own bed and sheets and quilts, her old rocking chair and a footstool. Cena also brought a kitchen cabinet, a small eating table and a cook table, and they all easily fitted into the room. It was a cozy, attractive place.

When Julia saw her own things scattered around in the nice new room Henry had built for her, her lips quivered and tears spilled over. If she couldn't live with John, then living with their son, Henry, was good.

Pearl hugged her. "Ma Childers, I'm so glad to have you here. Now I want you to feel at home. I know you're an independent lady, but we'd all like you to eat with us most of the time. You're used to cooking for people and you know it's no more trouble for me to cook for one more. We are all are happy you're here."

Julia walked around touching her own things which she hadn't seen in fifteen years. Her rocking chair! How she had missed that. She sat down and savored the moment with closed eyes. "Henry, you done a good job. Thank you for this room—I know it was a heap of work for you. And you got me my own cook stove, too—you knowed I'd like that. No, Pearl, I appreciate your welcome, but I'd just like to cook for myself for a while. It'll feel good to be quiet. I'll come and eat with you sometime though. It's just good to be here and it's also good to be with my family."

Julia passed her days doing her own housework, listening to a small radio, and going to church on Sundays when she was able. She loved to sit on the front porch when the weather was warm enough, listen to children playing, watch neighbors work in their yards, and talk to them.

She received a little money each month from the state old age pension, so she always waited for the mailman to bring it. Sometimes he also brought her letters from her children, which she asked one of the family to read to her.

Julia would never trust another bank. Her bank was still her old black sock in the trunk's corner. She had enough to buy her own groceries (which she insisted on), and her other needs were minimal.

But she was achingly lonely. She missed being on a farm. She missed the fields. She missed her old home. It had been home to her even though they had never owned it. They had rented it for years. Now, more and more she began to rest and doze in her chair, and her thoughts were of John and their lives together.

CHAPTER THIRTY-FOUR
Love Sings in a Tent

Early in June, 1936, the Childers family gathered around the noon dinner table. "What do you think about Preacher Phillips' announcement?" Henry asked.

"You mean the tent meeting?" Pearl helped herself to some biscuits and green beans. "I think it's a good idea. I like camp meetings—we haven't had anything like that in town for a long time."

"Do we have to go every night?" Arthur asked.

"We'll go as much as we can. Tommy Harper's going to be the evangelist and he's a good preacher."

"I'll tell you what I think is great," Ruth broke in. "That quartet from Asbury College. Just think, four new guys in town for two weeks, and just the right age for my friends and me too! We're talking about trying to have a party or something for them after the service one night."

"What about your boyfriends that live here?" Art teased.

"What boyfriends? Right now I don't have any. I'd like to meet some new faces around here."

Their church had always been important in the Childers family's life, both socially and spiritually. But Henry and Pearl never dreamed the change that a single church service would make in Ruth's life.

Ruth said to Katie, her friend, "I'm not very interested in the revival, but what the pastor said about *four young men* sounds like good reason to come and see them."

"Yeah, let's see what the others think," said Katie. "Maybe we can each hook a quartet member and have some fun."

All four agreed. "Sure! We're good, church-goin' girls, and maybe we can liven up things around Herrin for a while."

"About time," said Ruth. "Nothin's happened here since our dads ran the bootleggers out of town in the late Twenties! Remember—it's 'choir front and center' on opening night!"

In the middle of the next week the girls heard the sad news that ONE of the quartet members was married. That dampened their spirits a bit, but they said, "Oh, well, let the three best women win!"

Ruth later thought that the Lord ought to have made an inner intuition or at least some kind of pre-awareness that "Today is a fateful day." But nothing warned her. So the beginning of the end of her life dawned bright and shining.

On the evening of Sunday, June 28, four prettied-up young women sat on the front row in the choir. The meeting was held in a big tent outside on the church lawn, and the choir was divided so that women sat on one side of the platform and men on the other.

That electric moment came and the quartet filed in from the back of the tent and came toward the front. While whispering something to Katherine, Ruth just lifted her eyes and froze in her chair. She was staring straight into the blue eyes of the red-haired bass singer. Her heart suddenly skipped about a half-dozen beats and then pounded. She tried to swallow but her throat was too dry. Her first thought was, *That's the man I want to marry!* Her next thought was, *That's the craziest thought I've ever had! They're here for only two weeks!* So, her thoughts whirling, Ruth just couldn't stop looking at him, and he kept staring at her, too.

She didn't hear anything of the sermon that evening, or what Katherine said to her, or what she said to Katherine. Ruth was conscious of only one man in the whole tent, and that was the basso.

When the quartet got up to sing their first song, Ruth nearly fainted at his marvelous voice—very low, but melodious and sweet. She also saw that he had freckles on his neck. After their song she looked over at him again, and his eyes were on her. Every time she looked throughout the whole service, their glances met.

Ruth forgot all about hooking a boyfriend for two weeks. After the service was over, Katie nudged her and said, "Come on, let's go meet them!"

In a trance, Ruth said, "I'm not interested in meeting *them!* I'm—Katie, I just want to meet the bass guy. Hands off—he's mine!"

Ruth had never ever been shy—always the opposite—but that Sunday night her knees were knocking together. She did some mental exercises to inflate her courage, went straight to him and said, "My name is Ruth Childers. I'm a member here and we're very happy to have you in our church."

She didn't know what she expected—but the guy was tongue-tied. He didn't say a thing—just stood there holding her hand and looking at her with those vivid blue eyes. The two of them were on a desert island in a sea of murmuring Methodists.

Ruth couldn't think of anything else to say, so they just looked at each other. She finally remembered her mother was waiting, so she retrieved her hand and floated—yes, floated through that sea and out of the tent. Turning around for a last glance, she saw the basso, J.T., still standing there, dumb, still staring after her. He was paying no attention at all to the congregation who had come up to shake hands with him.

When Ruth drifted onto the bed that night and looked out the back window, the world was bathed in an eerie, bright glow. The barn, the coal shed, and the W.P.A. privy were encircled in halos—and she knew she didn't have glaucoma!

When she walked into the grounds the second night of the tent meeting, a special friend of Katie's said, "You know, Ruth, that basso, J.T. Seamands, is very interested in you. Would you like to go riding tonight after the service with Katherine and me? He would like you to come."

"Would I?!"

So after the second sermon which Ruth didn't hear, Clarence brought his car around and Katherine was with him, and J.T. was too. Ruth thought it strange that J.T. opened the back door of the car and got in first, leaving her to climb in behind him and shut the door. The idea struck her that J.T. didn't have very good manners. She thought, *Well, he can't talk, he doesn't have good manners, so what am I doing here?*

When his tongue came untied she heard him speak with a beautiful accent she'd never heard before. It sounded partly Scottish and partly English. With his cadence and musical deep bass voice, she was entranced and had goose bumps within five seconds. She was so enamored that she barely listened to what he actually said. She just wanted to hear his voice.

She finally listened. He said he and his younger brother had grown up in India where his parents were missionaries, and he had been in the United States for only three years. Then Ruth realized that having come from India, his manners were different. She had read that in India, men always came first and the women came trailing behind. But she quickly figured she could always teach him some American etiquette!

They had a date every night after that when the service was finished. He walked her home (the long way) and they sat on a small concrete railing of a bridge and talked for hours. J.T. was very serious. "I fell in love with you the minute I saw you in the tent, Ruth. I never felt this way before."

Ruth sighed. "I confess it's the same with me. And I never expected to fall in love like this! Maybe I should be coy and have a guy chase me for a while. But I want you to know right now!"

"And I want to know right now. We won't be here very long, and at the end of the summer the quartet will be gone for a whole year. We're going on an evangelistic tour around the world—to many countries. We already have our tickets."

Ruth was stunned. "For a whole *year*? How can we do that?"

"I'm beginning to wonder. But I can't drop out now. We'll just have to live through it—I guess it'll be a real test of love. If you want to date someone else while I'm gone, go ahead. But please don't forget me!"

"I could never do that."

"When I come back if we still feel the same way about each other, we'll be engaged then. But it isn't fair for me to ask you to promise anything. You are too beautiful to sit around for a whole year—lots of guys will want to date you."

"Maybe they will. But then maybe you'll find some other girl somewhere in the world that you'd rather have than me."

"No danger of that."

"Well, it seems like it's a dangerous possibility. We fell in love so fast—maybe when you have time to think about it more, you'll change your mind. But I hope not!"

"Don't worry about that."

"Okay. Let's cheer up and not waste the time you are here. I work at Woolworth, as I told you, and every day I have half an hour break at 10:30 each morning. Would you like to come downtown then?"

"I'll be there."

For the next two weeks, J.T. waited at the door for her to come on her break, and after standing on her feet for hours—what did they do with the next half hour? They walked.

Ruth's job at Woolworth that summer was selling ice cream cones. Clerks in the store were not allowed to stand around and talk to customers unless they were buying something. So J.T. came in every afternoon and bought one ice cream cone after another, and stood near Ruth while he ate them. Her boss often walked by, with a quizzical look, wondering who the ice cream nut was. During the two weeks he was in Herrin, J.T. ate more ice cream than anybody else in town ate all summer long. And he had good manners—just different from those she was used to. After all, he had been raised in a "men first" culture.

Sunday morning after one week of the special meetings, Ruth jumped out of bed at the unusual hour of 6:30. Pearl was making breakfast—coffee and scrambled eggs.

"Mom, is it okay if J.T. comes to dinner after church this morning?"

"Sure, Ruthie, but we don't have anything special."

"What are you going to have?"

"Oh, same thing we've had often enough—some more pinto beans and biscuits. Not too much choice, I guess."

Ruth made a face. "Ugh! We've had pinto beans ever since last summer when Daddy helped Uncle Arthur on his farm and got paid in pinto beans! And we still have bushels more stashed under the bed!"

"Yes we have," her mother answered. "And thankful we ought to be. Many people don't even have beans these days. Pintos aren't so bad. They're good for you, even if they are poor people's food!"

"I tell you, when these are gone, like maybe in 1950, I'll never eat another pinto bean in my whole life! Butter beans are better.

"Anyway, Mom, I have a little money left from my Woolworth pay. If I go over to Mrs. Meneese's house and buy two chickens, will you help me clean and fry'em? Wish we still had our own chickens! But if I can get them, we can have mashed potatoes—we've got potatoes? And you can make some biscuits and gravy. I want to make a great impression on J.T., and nobody can fry chicken like you can!"

Pearl's blue eyes crinkled and she beamed at the praise. "Yes—and you can sure pour on the flattery! If you want to go get chickens, just hike out!"

Ruth put on an old pair of slacks and shirt, took fifty cents from her purse, borrowed Art's bicycle from the front porch, and rode a mile across town enjoying the early Sunday morning quiet.

Mrs. Meneese, a friend from church, was drinking her morning coffee when Ruth knocked at the door. "Well, hi, Ruth. Aren't you out kinda early this morning?"

"Yeah, but I'd like to buy a couple of chickens, Mrs. Meneese, if you'd sell them to me on Sunday. I know you don't usually sell on Sunday—but this is special. I want to ask J.T. Seamands from the quartet to come home to eat Sunday dinner with us." She was breathless and it wasn't just because of the bicycle ride.

Mrs. Meneese smiled and nodded. "Uh huh—I've seen you and J.T. Seamands walk out of that tent every night after service! I'll be glad to sell the chickens for such a good cause, even on Sunday." She finished her coffee and said cheerfully, "Come on outside. "We'll have to catch 'em first!"

They chased her fryers around the big lot until they caught two. Then they tied the chickens' legs together and draped them, squawking, over the bicycle's handlebars. Ruth paid her the fifty cents and rode home.

Pearl had heated water to scalding, and Henry, grumbling a little, mumbling something like "no sense in bringing that boy home," came out and wrung the chickens' necks. Soon they were plucked and cut up and ready to be fried as only Pearl could fry them. Then Ruth took an hour-and-a-half beautifying herself for the Sunday morning encounter with J.T. When J.T. came for noon dinner (ecstatic at being asked), he was so moon-eyed looking at Ruth that he didn't know whether he was eating fried chicken or pinto beans. And Ruth was so googly-eyed looking at him that she just automatically, without any protest, began to wash the dishes afterward. Watching them, Pearl knew her little girl was in love.

Ruth had gone to church all her life, and considered herself a Christian. But Tommy Harper's good sermons every night made her listen and think. Some of the preaching soaked in. One night she asked herself, *What am I headed for? What am I worth to God?*

She answered her own question. *I'm worth everything to God. He died for me—he loves me.*

Next question: *But what am I worth <u>for</u> God?*

Answer, *Not much! That is, not much in comparison to some other people.*

Ruth looked at the quartet—those four fellows, all with beautiful voices—who had dedicated themselves to service for Jesus Christ. They could have been making much more money singing on radio—they were that good. But they had chosen the best. And here she was, not ever giving anything back to God in return for His blessings.

So the last night when the sermon made her face up to herself, she walked to the altar and prayed earnestly. In prayer she surrendered her life to Christ. She asked God to use her in some way, though she had no idea how He would do that. But she felt so much better.

She felt even better later, because J.T. kissed her for the first time. She was so happy she was ready to die—anytime.

J.T. and his brother, David, were living with their grandmother in Wilmore, Kentucky, while their parents were still missionaries in India. J.T. had just finished his junior year in college, and David was in high school.

J.T. had written to his grandmother, Mrs. Shields, from Herrin telling her about Ruth. She immediately sent Ruth an invitation to come and visit her in Wilmore. Ruth knew she was going to get "looked over." And she was scared!

J.T. and Ruth both cried when the quartet left Herrin. J.T. wiped her tears away and told her, "This time apart won't be very long. I'll come back after our next meeting in Ohio and take you down to see my grandmother. I can't wait for you two to meet each other—I love you both so much! I hope your father will give you permission to go to Wilmore with me."

"Oh, he'll grumble, but he'll give permission."

Ruth didn't know what she expected his Grandma Shields to be like, thinking she might be something like her Grandma Julia. But they were totally different.

Her house was marvelous—Ruth had never seen anything like it. Mrs. Shields had traveled all over the world and collected things. She had Persian rugs all over the floors, carved tables, exotic lamps, wall hangings, and everything was so rich looking and in such good taste. She showed Ruth some of the embroideries, silver, and tables which J.T. would inherit, and Ruth was bowled over. She had been thinking that J.T. came from a very poor missionary family—and he was as poor as the Childers family. Ruth thought all missionaries were poor. But his grandmother wasn't.

Then Ruth was more scared. She knew that Mrs. Shields could tell from her clothes that her family was in the middle of a depression in Illinois. And she thought Mrs. Shields would decide that this girl was certainly not high enough on the social scale for her grandson.

But Grandma Shields had no such reaction. She was a delightful person—Pennsylvania Dutch, tall and stout, with very definite ideas about things, and a wonderful cook. Her two grandsons were her whole life. As soon as Ruth arrived, she treated her like a granddaughter, so Ruth supposed J.T. had told her that she was the girl he wanted to marry.

With all those Persian rugs and everything so grand, Ruth walked around on tiptoe—afraid she'd ruin her reputation—and the first night she nearly did. Since they arrived very late from Herrin, Mrs. Shields soon showed Ruth up to her guest room and stayed talking for a while. A small, armless "slipper chair" was placed by the bed, beautifully upholstered, and Ruth was tired. She intended to take off her shoes.

She plopped down, and the whole bottom fell out of the chair! Ruth was so shocked she didn't know what to do—but couldn't do anything because she had fallen through the frame of the chair and was stuck tight. Her legs were hanging over the edge of the hole—but the rest of her was wedged in.

Grandma Shields' mouth fell open when she fell through, but the next minute they both were screaming with laughter. J.T. heard them and rushed in to see what was going on. He found his beloved stuck in a most undignified pose, making her first impression on Grandma!

Ruth wrote a letter to her mother the next day: "If I can last out the week without disgracing myself in any other way such as spilling ink on a Persian rug, or breaking some of her finest china, perhaps she will be able to stand the sight of me."

One day while in Wilmore, J.T. and Ruth were strolling around the Asbury College campus which was only half a block from Grandma Shields' house. Ruth asked him, "J.T., what are you going to do when you finish college?"

Without hesitation he said, "I'm going to be a music teacher, but my college major is speech."

Ruth was satisfied with that—he had plenty of musical talents. He played trombone, piano, and organ, and could accompany himself when he sang solos. And whatever made him happy made Ruth happy. Every morning since she had been visiting in Wilmore, he woke her up playing love songs on their baby grand piano. What a delightful way to wake up!

During the rest of the summer, the quartet had meetings in churches and Christian camps around the country. Ruth and J.T. were able to be together another two or three times—she thought she could have been called a "camp follower." But she enjoyed the camps very much, the high spot being always to hear the quartet sing. She dreaded the day in September when they would leave for Great Britain and begin their year-long tour. How could they ever stand to be apart for a year?

But the parting day came and J.T. left, both of them in tears. Ruth knew they wouldn't see each other for a whole year—a test of faith, courage, and love. They first went to England, Scotland, Ireland, and Wales for about three months, with engagements in many churches and town halls; then they sailed for South Africa.

Mail ships were carrying extra cargo those days, because they wrote love letters to each other nearly every day.

The most important letter Ruth ever wrote in her life, she wrote in January, 1937. She had struggled with the decision whether to tell J.T. about this incident, because she didn't want him to think that she was taking *his* future into her hands. She didn't know how he would accept such news.

The quartet was in South Africa for about four months, so this letter was addressed to J.T. there:

Herrin, Illinois January 7, 1937

My Dearest J.T.

This letter will come as a surprise to you, and no doubt you will think I am a little weird. I hate to think that I will have to wait two months for an answer, but since you are so far away and ships are so slow, I know I will.

Now for the strange thing that has happened. Last night Mom and I went to prayer meeting at the church, and arriving a little early, I found some folders on the table, picked up one, sat down by myself and started to read it. Mom sat with some of her friends. As I was reading, I was surprised to see that the folder was written by your father in India, and it was about the missionary work there. Suddenly, in the middle of a paragraph, God spoke to me as clearly as my mother does, and said, "Ruth, if I call J.T. to India to be a missionary for Me, will you be willing to go with him?"

Now, I thought that was the craziest thing I ever heard, that God–for it must have been God because nobody else was near me–would ask me to go to India with you. My first thought was that my mind was just overinfluenced by what I had been reading about India, so I started to read again and ignored the Voice. But again, that clear Voice, "Ruth, would you be willing to go to India with J.T.?"

I have never believed that God really talked to people like that in these days, but when the Voice came a second time, I answered Him. I bowed my head, closed my eyes and prayed, "Lord, You know more about me than I know about myself. You probably realize that I'd be a very poor missionary. But if You want me to go to India with J.T., then I will go, if he wants me to. Lord, you'll probably have to help. I've never thought of myself as missionary material."

That was all. I do not in the least understand it. Why would the Lord ask me such a question? I know that Voice was not imagination! And God knows you aren't going to be a missionary–you told me in Wilmore that you are going to be a music teacher. So if you think I'm crazy, maybe I am. But I feel at peace tonight.

First I wrote you another letter and didn't tell you of this incident, for fear you might think I am trying to direct your life. Somehow, I could not mail that letter; I had to tell you this. I am *not* trying to direct you–but I'll go wherever you go. My name is Ruth–and "Whither thou goest, I will go." Another Ruth said that a very long time ago–not, of course, to her sweetheart, but to her mother-in-law (of all people!). These beautiful words are my answer, too. It doesn't matter to me what you do or where you go–I'll be there if you want me. Music teacher, or missionary–if you love me, that's what counts.

Your Ruth

All their letters had to be sent by ship in 1937. Ruth knew it would take one month for her letter to reach J.T. in South Africa, and another month to get his answer. So she sat back to wait for the two months to creep past. She spent many anxious hours that first month wondering what he thought about that special letter. But she didn't have to wait the SECOND month! In exactly *one month* she received the following letter, written by J.T. in Capetown, South Africa at the same time she had written to him:

Capetown, South Africa

January 7, 1937

My Darling:

This letter may seem strange to you, but I must tell you of a decision which I had to make, the background, and why I had to make it.

When I was about fourteen years old, and a junior in high school in South India, my roommate and I once got up from our beds about midnight and went out into the streets in Kodaikanal, South India, to witness a noisy religious procession that takes place there annually. It was a Catholic demonstration, but it had all the characteristics of a Hindu ceremony.

There were several wooden "holy carts" being drawn through the streets by pious devotees. Each cart carried an image, one of Joseph, one of Jesus, and one of the Virgin Mary. The cart with the image of Mary was the largest and most important, and attracted more attention than either of the others.

Following the carts was a long line of people carrying smaller images on their heads–images of numerous Catholic saints. Throngs of people threw rice and flowers upon the carts and images as a token of their devotion. Leading the procession were musicians, beating out loudly on their tom-toms, to the accompaniment of shrill Indian clarinets. Now and then someone shot off a small rocket or firecracker to add to the din of the procession; others danced enthusiastically before the images. The only difference between this Catholic and any other Hindu procession would be that the latter would have Hindu idols rather than Catholic images.

As I stood and gazed at this ceremony during that night hour, the thought came to me, "Is this true Christianity? Is this the message that God intended for India?" To say the least, I was horribly shocked by the display of Christian idolatry (if we can call it that) and by the utterly false impression it was giving the Indian people.

Then suddenly, above the din and confusion, I heard a still, small voice within me say, "I have chosen you as My messenger in India. I want you to come back and carry the true Gospel to these people." The inner impression was so simple, and yet so strong, that I felt it was a definite call from God. I have never been able to get away from it since that night.

After I returned to the United States, in spite of the fine influence of Asbury College, the change from Indian life to American life had an adverse effect on me. My consecration began to slip. I felt it would be all right for me to be a preacher at home without going ten thousand miles away to India. But then later, I changed my mind altogether and wasn't even willing to preach. But with the quartet, I still seemed to be a committed Christian.

When I fell in love with you, I was afraid to mention God's call on me to go to India as a missionary, for I thought you would have nothing more to do with me. That day when you asked what I was going to be, I said, "A music teacher."

Now, this morning, while I was dressing, the Spirit of the Lord suddenly began to talk to me. The Voice said, "J.T., how long, how long must I strive with you? I have called you to be My servant in India. You were once willing, but now have gone back on your word. What is your final decision?"

My heart was miserable, my life defeated. I had fought long enough. I fell on my knees, wept tears of repentance, and prayed to the Lord with my whole heart, "If Your will for me is India, to India I will go and gladly!"

Immediately I felt the joy and victory that once I had known, return to my heart. The burden of disobedience was lifted. But the Spirit of God wasn't through dealing with me. The Voice went on to say, "What about that girl in Herrin, Illinois? You are in love with her. She doesn't know about your call to the mission field. Suppose she is not willing to go with you to India? What then? Will you reject My call and marry this girl? Or are you willing to follow Me, *whatever the cost,* even if it means giving up Ruth?"

Now this was, indeed, a difficult question! For a while I was staggered by the alternative that faced me. But I am in dead earnest. I have promised the Lord that I will obey Him, WHATEVER THE COST.

So now I am writing this to you. I feel I *must* do what the Lord wants me to do. I don't know what you will think about it, but if you are not willing to go to India with me, then our relationship as sweethearts must cease. I love you and I hope you will be willing to come with me.

- Yours forever, Jaytee

With tears pouring down her cheeks, Ruth hugged J.T.'s letter to her breast. "Thank You, Lord! I thought I'd have to wait another whole month for the answer to my letter. And *he* thought he'd have to wait an extra month for his. Now we must be getting them about the same time. You had it all planned. Thank You, Jesus."

That's the way it was! That's the way J.T. and Ruth knew for certain that they were meant to be together. In His marvelous timetable, God had it all planned out. They met at the right time, fell in love at just the right time, and He called them both at the same time. From that moment on, they both knew that whatever else happened throughout their lives, they belonged to each other forever.

When Grandma Shields heard about how this happened, she said, "Mission boards want college-trained people. That's where I can help—I'll send Ruth to college if she needs my help. She can come down when J.T. gets home from this world tour—that way she can finish college when J.T. finishes seminary. Perfect!"

* * *

"Ruthie, I see you got another letter from J.T. in South Africa. Pretty stamps! Looks like you two are keeping the sea-mail ships busy these days." Pearl was commenting during a family supper on a cold day in the middle of February, 1937.

"Yeah, you're right, Mom. It sure is hard to be in love with somebody who's halfway around the world!"

"You're sure it's real love?" Irene asked Ruth. She loved a love story.

Ruth sighed. "I don't know what else to call it. "I can't think about anybody else—other guys seem insignificant compared to J.T. And when I get a letter, I read it over fifteen times before I can put it down. You think that's love, Mom?"

"Must be." Pearl buttered her cornbread.

"Are you engaged?" Art wanted to know.

Henry snorted and choked on his coffee.

"We're sort of unofficially engaged," Ruth answered as if she didn't know Henry was trying to drown his disapproval in his coffee cup. "If we both still feel the same way when he comes home in September, we'll make it official."

"You're too young to get engaged!" Henry set his cup down hard. "Ought to wait 'til you're twenty-five!"

The whole family laughed at him.

"Mom, weren't you twenty-five when you had me?" Ruth asked. "And hadn't you already been married a year-and-a-half?"

Pearl took a bite of cornbread. "Well, you know what the trouble is, Ruthie. Henry thinks there's not a man on earth that's good enough for you! He'd probably like to keep you at least until your fortieth birthday."

"Make it forty-five." Henry knew when he was outnumbered.

The month of March dragged by. One evening about the first of April, the family was at supper, and this time Grandma Julia had joined them. Trying to be casual during the talk, Ruth said, "Grandma Julia, Mom, Dad, Art, Irene, I want to tell you all something. This is going to shock you." She paused and swallowed. "Yes, you'll probably be shocked, but J.T. and I feel that God has called us to go to India as missionaries."

The family sat in stunned silence. Then, "Go—go to *India?*" Pearl found her voice first.

Ruth nodded.

"To *India?* You'd die with some awful disease in India," Henry pronounced. "I don't want you to go anywhere. But to *India!* It's crazy. It's too far away!"

"Well, Daddy, J.T.'s parents have lived there as missionaries for a long time and they haven't died of any disease yet."

"But I don't want *you* to go there and that's final!" her father said. He was used to being obeyed, and this was a desperate order. But Ruth was now twenty years old and he knew she would live her own life. He still tried. "Anyway, how could you go? What do you have to do to be a missionary? I never saw one."

Grandma's gentle voice asked, "How can you get to be a missionary, Ruthie?"

"First, I have to go to college."

"You mean go to school some more?" she asked.

"How in the world could you do that?" Henry asked, more amazed with every revelation.

Now Ruth had a new surprise. "You remember last fall, before he went on his trip, J.T. took me to Kentucky to meet his grandmother? She lives in Wilmore, right by Asbury College. Well, J.T. has written to her that he is going to be a missionary and that I have agreed to go with him. First thing she said was, 'Well, we'll have to send Ruth to college. We can do that.'

"So when J.T. comes home in August, I'll be going with him back to Asbury College. His grandmother will pay for it. Just think of it! ME in college!" Ruth sat back and looked at her silent, stunned family. Nobody had ever expected this.

Finally Henry's voice choked, "I don't want to think of it." He looked straight at Ruth, his eyes a little dimmed with tears.

Ruth jumped up and hugged her father. "Don't be sad, Daddy. Be glad for me! We've got a wonderful plan and we hope you will agree. We won't get married right away—his grandmother doesn't want us to either. But after my first year in college, we'll get married in June of the next year—that's long enough to wait.

"Then I will finish college as a married lady and he will finish seminary. We can't go to India until we get through with college and seminary. It's hard to believe all this can really happen. But it can. So all of you, please be happy for me." She looked at each beloved face around the table.

"Grandma Julia's lips were trembling. "We'll pray for you, Ruthie. I don't even know where India is, but it must be very far away. Must take a long time to get there."

Ruth nodded and patted Grandma's arm.

"Yeah, we're happy, for you," agreed Arthur and Irene. "But we don't want you to go so far away."

"Well, one of these days you kids will be leaving home too," Ruth prophesied.

Pearl looked down at her plate to hide her tears. "Don't even talk about that time." Then she smiled. "Why, it'll be awful! When you all go off, Henry and I will only have each other to fuss at!"

Henry ate a piece of cornbread in silence. Then, "I thought you told me that J.T. was going to teach music when he got out of college."

Ruth nodded. "That's what he said at first. But the Lord changed his mind. He told me later that he knew all the time God wanted him to be a missionary. As far as I'm concerned, it's something I never thought about before in my whole life. But I know the Lord spoke to me at prayer meeting last month. Going to India is not just something I thought up all by myself, Daddy. So if you're going to fuss at anybody about me being a missionary, then fuss at God. It's His idea."

"Then I suppose J.T. will have to study to be a preacher, won't he? Is that what he will learn in seminary?"

"Yes, that's it. See, he has one more year of college first. Then he will go to Asbury Seminary, which is just across the street from the college. They train preachers there. We plan to go to summer schools and he will finish seminary in two years instead of three. I will make college in three years instead of four. We'll come out even and be ready to go to India in 1940."

Henry said nothing more, he just shook his head, stood up and bumbled out of the room. Both he and Pearl knew they were facing long, lonely years ahead.

They both accepted this projected future in their typical ways. Henry began to worry about all the bad things that could happen, and Pearl began to see the bright side of everything. She had always greatly respected preachers, and now she would have one for a son-in-law. That made her proud. Still, she knew, preachers were just like other people and some of them did dumb things sometimes. One day she heard about a preacher who went hunting with disastrous results. Of course, she wrote a poem about it:

A preacher from the city went out to hunt some game.
He shot a "striped kitty," now wasn't that a shame!
His wife took just one sniff and cried,

"Oh, what a stink!"
She opened the dog house, pushed him in,
And left him there to think.

The dog barked out, "Stay 'way from me!
Your perfume I resents.
You'd think a guy with a Ph.D.
Would 've surely had more sense!"

* * * *

The long year finally passed and September came, bringing J.T. home from his world tour. Ruth was beside herself in anticipation. A friend drove her up to Mount Vernon, Illinois to meet his train.

When they returned to Herrin late that afternoon and Pearl took one look at J.T. and Ruth together, she knew it was settled. The year apart had done nothing to dampen their love for each other. Ruth couldn't quit smiling and she was wearing a diamond engagement ring. J.T. was beaming with joy and he couldn't quit playing the piano and singing love songs to her. The house was pure bedlam. Henry went out for a walk.

Quiet descended when a few days later they left by train for Asbury College, promising to come back at Christmas time. Henry and Pearl said, "It's not so bad to have you only 300 miles away in school. You could always come home if you wanted to." They determined not to think about the other, long, impending separation. That was three years away!

Grandma Shields bought J.T. a new car and gave them a beautiful engagement party when they arrived in Wilmore.

It had been four years since Ruth had graduated from high school, so she had to study hard to get her brain working for academic achievement. She didn't make perfect grades, but was often on the dean's list, sometimes making a straight A average for the quarter. Concentrating on college courses was difficult that first year because she and J.T. were so much in love they only wanted to be together.

The cold winter months passed slowly for Pearl and Henry, Arthur and Irene. They all missed Ruth. Then one day in the middle of April 1938, she called home. "Mom! I'm so excited I can hardly talk! I feel like I'm going to faint or just float away with joy or something like that.—"

"Ruthie! What's happened?"

"Well—I bet you won't believe this. You know at Christmas time we were planning our wedding. You also know I've always wanted a church wedding—but I knew Daddy couldn't afford it for me. J.T. said not to worry a bit about it, he would pay for everything. But that didn't seem right to me, and I was kind of mourning about that. I knew Helen would make a beautiful dress for me, but I didn't even have any money to pay for the cloth! The Lord must have felt sorry for me, because He sure fixed things up—I still can't believe it."

"Ruthie! What are you talking about?"

Henry put his newspaper down, and Julia came out of her room to see what Pearl was talking about on the phone. They said, "What? . . ." but Pearl shushed them and said to Ruth, "Both Henry and Grandma want to know what's the matter, so tell me quick—"

"Mom, I'm just jumping up and down. I've told you that I am working here at Asbury College in the radio office—I pay off my room rent like that. Well, yesterday a letter was delivered to me here in the office from an insurance company in Missouri which I had never heard of. I nearly fell in a dead faint when I read it. Listen, Mom, I'll read it to you.

"It says, 'When you were a baby, your parents took out an endowment policy on you; they paid on it for a little while, then they allowed the policy to lapse. Now that you have passed your twenty-first birthday, the policy has matured, and we are sending you the amount due to you—the amount your parents paid, plus the interest. Enclosed, please find a check for $55.95.'"

Pearl gasped, and her mouth dropped open. Henry and Julia crowded close, trying to overhear.

"Mom, when I read that letter I thought somebody was playing a joke on me. You know that much money is worth about eight weeks of working at Woolworth! Then I tore into my boss' office and asked him to read the letter and to tell me if the check was genuine. He read it and said, 'Looks real to me. Go cash the check and find out.'"

Henry was saying, "Pearl, what in the world is she talking about?"

Pearl asked, "Ruthie—was it a good check?"

Ruth screamed into the phone, "Yeeesss! I'm a millionaire! I've got plenty of money to buy my dress goods and ice cream and cake and all the rest! Can you believe all that? Whether you do or not, just tell Preacher Phillips that the church wedding is really ON and I can pay for it!"

"Oh, Ruth—I had totally forgotten about that insurance policy. We just couldn't pay on it very long."

"Well, Mom, you sure paid on it long enough to pay for my wedding——"

Henry was tired of waiting. He yelled into the phone, "Ruth, what is the matter? You sick?"

"Oh, no, Daddy, but I can't repeat all that over again. Mom will tell you, but I will say now, THANKS for paying for an insurance policy on me when I was a baby. I'm rich now because of it! I've got $55.95! See, you paid for my wedding after all and I love you. Bye, Daddy. If I sound crazy, I am. I'm crazy happy!"

On June 4, the kitchen at 618 South 18th Street in Herrin was being readied for a wedding dinner. Pearl made all the food. She had to make a lot, because all Henry's sisters and their families had promised to come. That was quite a crowd! Pearl, as usual, sang in the kitchen while she made chicken salad, pies and a wedding cake. Helen, Irene, and Art were there to help, but Ruth was certainly no help. All she could do was wander around with a smile and a vacant look on her face, while J.T. played the piano and sang love songs to anybody who would listen.

The confusion was so great that Pearl finally guided J.T. and Ruth through the back door and told them to go sit in the shade of the grape arbor. Julia came out her back door and sat with them. "Ruthie, I have a new dress to wear to your wedding."

Ruth hugged her. "Oh, Grandma, you and Mom will be the two prettiest ladies there. Does all this confusion remind you in any way of when you and Grandpa got married?"

"Julia smiled. "Yes, it does in a way. I got married in my brother Joe's house. His wife, Martha, and me—well we worked for days gettin' ready for it. When John arrived with his five kids—well, I thought, 'How can I be a good mother to all them kids? That's a lot of family to start married life with!'"

"Was Grandpa a good husband?"

"He shore was, Ruthie. He made his kids mind, and we all worked together. I think we raised a good family—altogether we raised thirteen children."

"No wonder you're tired, Grandma. I don't think we'll ever have that many kids."

* * * *

On Sunday afternoon, June 5, 1938, Henry walked proudly down the aisle with Ruth on his arm, and gave her away to a red-haired bass singer. Julia and Pearl, sitting on the front row of the packed church, tried not to cry into their favorite handkerchiefs. As Ruth and J.T., that enraptured couple, came out the door of the church, a colored movie was being made to send to J.T.'s parents in India. They hadn't met their new daughter-in-law.

Ruth said, "I don't know how the Lord does it. Two years ago I didn't have much. Now I have a beautiful wedding and a wonderful husband. It's like God gave me the moon with a fence around it and a couple of suns thrown in!"

* * * *

The next two years flew by—they were marvelously happy. Grandma Shields paid for Ruth's college. J.T. traveled every weekend with the quartet, and usually made enough for them to live on. They lived close to the college in a three-room apartment, budgeted $25.00 for rent and $25.00 for food each month. They gave tithe of ten percent to the church. Usually, not much was left over. Wilmore was a small town, so most of the time they walked to school. No doubt Ruth was still poor—but she had been all her life, so how could she think about being poor when she was so happy?

Ruth washed their clothes in the bathtub on a washboard and hung them on wooden racks in their apartment. She ironed clothes at night after finishing college assignments for the next day, and cooked on a two-burner coal-oil (kerosene) stove.

Usually Ruth's classes were so arranged that she was able to go home to fix their lunch. But one quarter she had a class which met from 11:00 to 12:00, so J.T. learned to cook a little during that quarter. They ate an awful lot of fried eggs and toast, and no doubt their cholesterol sizzled!

The next summer the quartet had many meetings. At one time, J.T. had been gone for a week and because of summer school, Ruth had to stay at home. She missed J.T. so much and thought the week would never end. When she heard the quartet car in the driveway, and heard him whistle for her with his special whistle, she was electrified! She tore down the stairs and threw herself into his arms with such abandonment that his glasses went flying through the air—landing on the third step and breaking both lenses. J.T. looked askance at his glasses, hugged and kissed Ruth and murmured, "The female of the species is always the most ferocious!"

That week he had made a grand sum of money—just enough to pay for new glasses! They cheerfully ate some more eggs and toast.

J.T. was a wonderful, sweet man. He was not as exuberant as Ruth, and he was very absentminded. Every once in a while he drove the car over to the college, and by evening had forgotten he took it, so he walked home. When Ruth reminded him it was time to put the car in the garage for the night, he discovered it wasn't at home. Then he had to walk back over to the school looking for it, for by that time he had forgotten where he parked it!

One day they planned to go shopping together, and he told Ruth to wait out in front of the house while he got the car. She stood waiting for him on the sidewalk, and suddenly heard a crash and a tinkle of falling glass. She ran around back to see what had happened. There was J.T., down on his hands and knees in front of the garage doors picking up broken glass. He had a most sheepish expression on his face. He had gone in the side door of the garage, started the car, and began to back out. But he had forgotten to open the garage doors.

During their last semester at school, one weekend they went home to Herrin for a visit and to get Ruth's birth certificate. She needed it to apply for her passport.

Of course, she didn't know about her split personality! When she and J.T. went to Marion, the county seat, to get the certificate, the clerk began looking for her name in the birth register for 1916.

"I'm sorry, Mrs. Seamands. But we have no birth registered for Ruth Childers for the date you said you were born. The only one on your birth date is one Mary Jane Childers."

"Mary Jane Childers? Could she be a cousin that I don't know? Who are Mary Jane Childers' parents registered there?"

"Let me see—they are Henry and Pearl Childers."

"What! Henry and Pearl Childers? But they're *my* parents, and I'm the only child they had on my birthday. As far as I know I didn't have a twin sister."

"Well, Mary Jane is here and you're not. Have you ever changed your name?"

"Only the last one—when I got married I changed it from Childers to Seamands. What can I do? I've got to have a passport."

"Where are you going that you need a passport?"

"We're going to India in a few months."

"The only thing you can do, Mrs. Seamands, is to go back to Herrin and get your father and mother. They will have to find three witnesses who have known you all your life. They must sign an affidavit stating that your name is not Mary Jane Childers, that when you were born you were named Ruth Childers. It must be that the doctor registered your birth with the wrong name."

Ruth turned to J.T. "Well, what do you think of that? Looks like you've married the wrong woman. Mary Jane's been here all these years, but I was never heard of."

J.T. grinned. "I don't care what your name is, honey, I love you anyhow. But, yeah, it does feel strange to be married to the wrong woman."

So her father and friends brought Ruth to life. They swore before a Notary Public that Henry Childers' daughter's name was Ruth, and not Mary Jane.

Finally receiving her passport with the name Ruth Childers Seamands stamped inside, at last fused her personality. She'd been split for twenty-four years!

* * * *

The 1930s closed with the Depression ten years old and beginning to lessen. Hitler was making loud noises and big problems in Europe, and some people were beginning to worry about the Japanese in the Far East.

At home, other problems mounted. Pearl was beginning to have very painful arthritic spasms in her wrists and fingers. But she always tried to make light of it.

CHAPTER THIRTY-FIVE
World War II – the 1940s

Pearl and Henry celebrated their twenty-fifth wedding anniversary on July 18, 1940. Ruth didn't get home, but Art and Rene were with them to celebrate. Helen was married to Everett Brown and living in Cincinnati, so she was missed, too.

"Gonna make me my favorite cake today, Pearl? A hickornut cake?" Henry asked at breakfast.

"Well, guess I'll have to do that. If you'll crack the hickory nuts and pick 'em out, I will."

Irene looked critically at Henry. "Look at you, Daddy! Been married all this time and still you don't have any gray hair. You look so young!"

Pearl laughed, "Yeah, but look what living with him has done to me! Look at my white streak!"

"That just makes you look distinguished, Mom," Art grinned at her.

"Just so you don't say I look EXtinguished!" Pearl laughed at herself. "Henry, I just had to write a poem for you especially for today. I'll read it to you. Now this poem is what I think YOU think about today:

SILVER WEDDING MEDITATIONS — 1940

Henry says,

Twenty-five years ago today,
The preacher had some words to say;
He took away my liberty,
Oh what a fatal day for me!

No more do I step out with the boys.
Forsaking all my bachelor joys,
My erring feet no more may roam,
But take the narrow path back home.

Still I am satisfied with life,
I have a good and faithful wife;
And though my roving days are gone,
She keeps my buttons all sewed on!

While they were eating their anniversary dinner that evening, the phone rang. It was Ruth calling from Wilmore, Kentucky.

"Hi, Mom, is Daddy home today? He'd better be!"

"He's here. He's eating his favorite cake—"

"Hickory nut?"

"Yes. I can't believe we've been married for twenty-five years. Seems just like yesterday that you were a towheaded kid running around here!"

"Yeah—time can sure go fast! And J.T. and I've been married two years! I'm sorry we can't be home for your anniversary, but it won't be long until summer school is finished. Then we are going to break up our apartment here and come home to stay with you until we start for India. Think you can stand us for three months?"

"You know we can! But to talk about going to India so soon—I can't get used to the idea that I won't see you for six or seven years! I—" she choked a little and wiped her eyes.

Ruth could almost see through the telephone. "Now, Mom—I know it'll be hard. But I KNOW you. You'll write a funny poem and cheer yourself up. I just hope Daddy will be cheered up!"

"So do I. How's J.T.?"

"He's fine—he's not here just now, he's in class— making all A's. And by the way, I'm making quite a few myself. Now, Mom, I want to ask you something."

"Okay. What, Honey?"

"I'm sending you an anniversary present. But I want you and Daddy to give me a present, too. I want you both to go down to the studio there in town and have a good picture made of the two of you. I want to take it with me to India and I'll keep it forever. Will you get Daddy to do that? Tell him it's what I want most before we go—a really GOOD photograph of you both."

"We haven't had a studio photograph taken since you were a baby! I'll tell him. Oh, it'll be so nice to have you home for three months! This house is lonesome without you!"

"I know—I love you, too. Well,I gotta go to class, Mom. Let me talk to Daddy for just a minute before I go."

Pearl handed the phone to Henry who had finished his cake and was hovering over her shoulder.

"Hello, Ruthie. Everything all right?"

"Everything's wonderful, Daddy. Happy Anniversary! Wish I could be there for some of that cake."

"Yeah. Even though we've been married all this time, Pearl can still make the best cake and biscuits, and—"

"You're right. Daddy, I just have to go to class or I'll be late. Let Mom tell you what I want you to do for me—it'll be a wonderful present. Next time I'll talk to you the longest. I love you."

Henry hung up the phone and sat down again at the table. Now he was satisfied; he knew Ruth would call. "She sounded fine, didn't she?"

"I wanted to talk to her," Art said.

"Me, too," echoed Irene.

"She's almost late for class," Pearl informed them. "Henry, she's sending us a present and she wants you and me to have a good studio picture made of us—an anniversary photograph. Wants to take it to India with her."

Henry pushed back his chair, got up from the table, went down the back steps and stood looking at his garden.

"That's something he simply cannot stand to think about," Pearl said to Arthur and Irene. "And neither can I!"

* * * *

Ruth and J.T. came home after they were graduated in August. How great it was for Pearl to have her kids together again at home! They were all there except Helen, and as they gathered around the supper table, the talk and laughter was like hundreds of other nights in the Childers household. Except now they also had J.T. who added his wit to the conversation.

The next three months passed as if it were only three weeks, and December 15—Ruth's twenty-fourth birthday dawned. Pearl made a big birthday dinner for Ruth and they all tried to forget this was the last birthday she would be at home for a long time.

"I wish Helen could have come today," said Ruth. "But the doctor thought she ought not to travel when she's pregnant. What do you think about being a grandma, Mom? You and Daddy are sure fine lookin' grandparents! Who knows—maybe we'll make you grandparents of some little redheads someday!"

Pearl looked up and pretended to consider a weighty decision. "Well, yes, I think we would like that. Helen and Brownie will definitely have fine children, and you and J.T. ought to have at least one quite sensible child!"

After supper, Ruth and J.T. cleared the table and washed and dried the dishes. Then they went across town to see some friends, Irene went out on a date, and Arthur left for work. He was a cook in a hamburger shop.

Pearl and Henry kept on sitting at the kitchen table, just resting, Henry's long legs stretched out under the table. Pearl sighed, "Well, I guess this is the last time we'll have Ruthie on her birthday for a while." She sniffed. "I don't know how I'm going to stand it when she leaves. Our first baby! But we have to think of their call to India. Can you imagine *our* daughter going all the way to India as a *missionary?"*

Henry rubbed his chin. "No, I can't. I don't want to think about it, and I don't want her to go, either. All kinds of sickness over there—who knows what'll happen to her?"

"We'll just have to trust the Lord about her. At least Art and Irene are still with us." She sighed. "This house is going to be so lonesome with Ruth gone—she's so much fun to have around. And that J.T. can make anybody laugh!" Pearl reached over and rubbed Henry's hand. "Can you believe we've been married for twenty-five years and our kids are all grown up? It just seems impossible!" She smiled at him. "You're still handsome though, and I love you. Not a bit of gray in your hair! But there is in mine. Yes—I'd marry you again if I had the chance!"

Henry winked at her. "And here I am married for twenty-five years to a good-lookin' lady. Now she's got a white streak in her hair, but that don't spoil her. Did we eat all them biscuits?"

Pearl laughed. "You are sure romantic! Yes, we still have some biscuits warm in the oven, and somebody once said something about the way to a man's heart being through his stomach!" She opened the oven door and put two biscuits on a clean plate. Then she got out butter and molasses. Henry put a big chunk of butter on his plate, poured some transparent amber sorghum molasses on it, stirred the two together with his knife and spread the thick mixture on the two sliced-open biscuits. "Ummmmm—" He savored the delight. "You might be an old lady with white hair, but you can still make good biscuits! Any more coffee in that pot?"

The next day the available ones of the Childers clan gathered at Cena's. They wanted to see Ruth and J.T. before they left for India. No one in the family had ever been that far away. During World War I, her Uncle Arthur was in France, but that was only about halfway to India. So it might be a long time before they could get together again. Ruth was especially close to her Aunts Cena, Ida, Ola, Olive, and Grandma Julia.

They had a grand feast—the table piled high with fried chicken, ham, roasts, vegetables and desserts—as only the Childers women can all cook. When everything was ready, Cena announced as she always did, "Well come on—we don't have much, but I hope you can all make out on this!"

They still sat at the table even though they couldn't eat any more and remembered family incidents. Henry retold the story about the red-and-white checked gingham shirts the boys had to wear to school one year. Ola talked about Ida and Cena pouring a quart of seed corn in a corner of Pa's field. Ida remembered Cena grabbing Julia's hen and wringing its neck only because it irritated Henry. Cena reminisced about backing Ida against a wall and jerking out her loose tooth, and how Ida yelled, though nobody believed it hurt a bit.

Julia recollected her honeymoon ride with six kids in the wagon and her chair rocking all the way to Creal. They'd all heard the stories before, but time made them precious. They laughed and cried with the remembering.

And then they told Ruth and J.T. goodbye. Leaving was painful.

December 20 dawned and Pearl didn't even want to get up. This was Ruthie's leaving day. She and J.T. had to drive to California, attend some meetings for a few days, and then board a ship for India on December 30th. All week before they left, J.T. had been doing silly things to make Pearl laugh so she'd forget how sad she was. Once he put on Pearl's frilly apron, got out the dust cloth and meticulously dusted a kitchen chair, sat down and started playing silly songs on his accordian. His mouth twisted in such a way that the whole family exploded in laughter. Henry didn't say much, he just went around with a long face.

But now the time had come. Their car was finally loaded and the whole family stood around in the cold December wind, not able to think of anything else to say. They held onto Ruth as if they could never let her go, but finally she and J.T. climbed into the car. Tears were rolling down all their faces. Pearl, Henry, Irene, and Art watched the car as it went north down Eighteenth Street, as far as they could see it, then they slowly turned and stumbled into the already lonely house.

For days they all tried to put on brave fronts for each other.

Pearl made a fine Christmas turkey dinner, but nothing was the same. Everybody was sad.

Pearl and Henry hadn't spoken to Ruth about it, but they were worried about Art who worked fourteen hours a day in a smoky hamburger joint. They had been noticing for some time how thin and tired he looked. And recently he had begun to have night sweats.

Pearl's arthritis was bothering her constantly and she suffered excruciating pain in her hands and wrists. Henry was doing more of the housework for her and lifting things. He even learned to iron clothes.

When 1940 closed, the Depression was eleven years old but not so severe. Hitler was making more problems in Europe, and people were worrying more about what the Japanese might do.

New Year's Day, 1941, brought a shock. Arthur fell on a wet, slippery driveway, and began spitting up blood.

Dr. Duncan took X rays. "Well, Arthur, it looks like you've developed a blister on your lungs. When you fell, the blister broke and caused this bleeding."

"But is he going to be okay, Doc?" asked Henry. He and Pearl waited anxiously for the answer.

"Yes, Henry, but I want him to stay in bed for at least a week. Then, you know, Henry, he's been working too hard. All that smoke and fumes frying hamburgers all these years. How long you been working, Arthur?"

"Oh—since 1936. I did work for a while in a drugstore, but went back to the diner."

"How many hours are you working a week?"

Art looked very thin and tired as he answered, "I work seventy-two hours every week and I make $17.50."

"Seventy-two hours over that fryer? No wonder you got a blister on your lungs! Now Art, I've doctored you since you were little, and I want you to be well. You've got to think about quitting this job and going to a warmer climate—like southern California. I know it's hard to give up any job in these days, but your health comes first. Your lungs don't look good."

Pearl sat down hard in her chair. Ruth in India, and now Arthur had to go to California! At least California was this side of the Pacific ocean!

Art lay back on the pillow and closed his eyes. He was so tired! Pearl looked at him with tears. He was so handsome—yet so thin. He was twenty-two years old and weighed only 117 pounds. How could they not have seen that he was working too hard? He'd have to rest and eat plenty of good food to gain his proper weight!

Ruth and J.T. began their journey on New Year's Eve, 1940 and had hardly cleared land when they were in the middle of a big storm at sea. The ship rolled, pitched, and glided down into great valleys of water, only to then be lifted over another mountain of water. Furniture which was not screwed to the floor slid from one side of the room to another. Walking around was hard, going up and down stairs nerve-wracking. After a few days the seas became a little more calm.

One day J.T. said, "Honey, you know I think you better begin to learn to cut my hair. We don't know where we'll be sent in India—we may even live way out in some village where there is no barber. You always cut your own hair—do you think you could do mine?"

Ruth, with a lifetime of experience of cutting her own hair, was cocky and sure she could do it. Her father had always told his children they could do anything they made up their minds to do. So she answered, "Course I can do it. I packed a barber comb, scissors and clippers in my suitcase. You mean you want me to cut your hair now?"

"Well, we're on this ship for a month or more, so we're not going anywhere else. Now is as good a time as any."

She pulled out a straight chair into the middle of their cabin, and told him to sit there. Her ego told her she could do it, but she had forgotten that the sea was still very rough. Her clippers were the old-fashioned squeeze kind—the faster you squeezed them in your hand, the faster they would clip. So she started on the right side of the back of J.T.'s neck, squeezing hard and moving fast. Suddenly, the ship gave a big lurch toward her, and her speed with the clippers took them up J.T.'s neck and snip, snip, snip up and over. She looked in surprise at the swath they left over the top of his head.

Saying nothing to J.T. but to herself, *I better even it up,* she started up the left side of his neck. With more experience in sailing, she would have realized that if one time the ship yaws to the right, its next yaw will be to the left. So the first thing she knew, her squeezing hand had taken the clippers again over the top of J.T.'s head—in the opposition direction. X marked the spot on top!

Nothing she could do now except simply clean off his neck. When she finished, without saying anything about the disaster, she took the towel from around his neck and shook it over the wastebasket. He got up from the chair and looked in the mirror. He probably couldn't believe what he saw, so he put his glasses back on and looked closer. Then he turned slightly green, said he was feeling seasick, and went to bed until his hair grew out. He missed several meals. Ruth, who never felt seasick, staggered through the ship to every meal and enjoyed every bite.

When J.T. was well enough to trust her again, Ruth did learn to cut his hair. She did a good job, and J.T. often remarked, "I like you to cut my hair because I like kissing my barber."

They wrote letters from the ship and mailed them from all the strange sounding places that Ruth never dreamed she'd see. She hadn't even known how to pronounce them right.

The first letter from Ruth and J.T. to Pearl and Henry was postmarked Honolulu, January 8, 1941, where their ship had put in for a few days. Ruth wrote:

> Dear Mom and Dad, the mission board decided that we will live in Bangalore, South India, for the first year and study language there. We'll rent a small house and start having a baby while we study language!
>
> When I got to Honolulu I received your letter telling about Art. We were sitting at our table on the ship at lunch, and they brought the mail on board. I started to cry, and couldn't eat any more. I just wanted to turn right around and come back home, I can't stand to think about Art so sick! I know how bad you all felt – especially with us so far away.
>
> But we have our work cut out for us, so I have to put personal feelings aside. I know God will take care of Art and that he will be all right in a while.

Ruth's next letter was from Singapore, then from Penang, and Ceylon. The Childers family had to look on the big world map to see where all those places were. Finally the great news came from Bombay that they'd landed safely. Enclosed were pictures of them with J.T.'s parents who had met them at the dock. They looked so proud at having their son back in India. And they loved Ruth!

In April, Ruth wrote that she was pregnant, they'd rented a small house, and had bought a small dog. Kanarese language study had to be their first priority—lessons for eight hours each day. They took walks in the evenings, getting acquainted with their neighbohood, and already found another new missionary couple who were also expecting a baby. Ruth wrote, "The other girl and I take walks together sometimes, both of us pushing our stomachs ahead of us! We attend church, go to prayer meetings, and we hosted a big birthday party for J.T.'s father's 50th birthday. He is a wonderful man—that E.A. Seamands—and I'm lucky to have him for a father-in-law.

"I'm learning to like the hot, spicy Indian curry and rice and their breads too. I learn something new everyday in this very old country. My baby is due about Christmas time."

DECEMBER 7, 1941! No one living at that time will ever forget the shock on Sunday, Pearl Harbor Day! The Japanese bombed and destroyed many American lives and ships in Pearl Harbor.

Henry and Pearl Childers sat in front of their radio, stunned. When they heard President Roosevelt's speech about this day living in infamy, and that the United States was now at war with Japan, their first thought was, "Ruth!? How will this affect her?"

On the day after Christmas, Henry and Pearl received the following cablegram:

BEAUTIFUL BABY GIRL. BABY & RUTH FINE.
— J.T. Seamands

A week later, Ruth wrote to Henry and Pearl:

Our American government wants all Americans to evacuate India and go home–we've been getting letters from our U.S. Consul ever since the baby was born. I may have to bring the baby and come. Our little Sylvia is so beautiful and I couldn't bear it if anything happened to her, so I must do what I can to protect her. The government officials wrote to us that if we didn't accept this order to take the ship to the U.S.A., they could not be responsible for our safety. This is an awful decision because it would mean leaving J.T. He feels he must stay here because he is ready to start a Bible school.

Fear is prevalent here that the Japanese may try to take over India. They have bombed Ceylon–not far away, and some of the Andaman Islands off the east coast. I'm not trying to worry you, but these things you must have read in the newspapers. J.T. says if the Japanese do come, he can disappear into a village and live like an Indian. He has the language well, and is used to the food. But not for me. No proper care for the baby. It's an awful decision.

We have orders from the Indian Government to dig slit bomb-trenches in our yard, and we've all had a hand at digging. They are called zigzag trenches because they are shaped like a Z, and they must be seven feet deep and four feet wide. It's quite a job. I started our gardener digging yesterday and went out after an hour expecting to see something accomplished, but he had done practically nothing. When I scolded him, he held out his skinny arms and said, "No power, Madam, no power." I decided I had more power than he did, so I dug for an hour. He just sat and watched me.

Twice a week we have air-raid drills too, and every light must be blacked out at night.

Our friends have had many hours of conversation with us concerning the decision whether to go back to America. They have decided to stay in India. But none of them have babies who might be in danger. This decision is driving me crazy, because I feel that I may be secretly criticized because I am thinking of evacuating.

I hope the Japanese don't bomb Bangalore as they have been threatening to do. Not only for our sakes. Bangalore is a very beautiful city–it is called the Garden City of India. Parks and beautiful gardens are everywhere, with walks and flowering trees, and benches in the cool shade. But this is also a very busy city with lots of manufacture. Now an airplane factory is here and that might be a threat to the Japanese.

We have prayed a lot for guidance, but it looks like the Lord is going to let us make up our own minds. I suppose that is because we will have to live with whatever decision we make. Help us pray. Love, Ruth.

P.S. Now it is a month later; I have made the decision and it has just about killed me to do it. I am now in scorching Bombay, waiting for the ship home. J.T. feels he should stay in India and it is breaking both our hearts, but I feel I must come home for Sylvia's sake. I would never leave J.T. otherwise. Because of censorship and dangers of war travel, I cannot tell you when we sail, nor on what ship, but I will telegraph you when we land in New York. Pray for our safe journey. . . .

With great sorrow between them, J.T. took Ruth and his beautiful baby to Bombay to put them on the ship. They had no idea that they would be separated nearly three years by the war.

She stood with six-month-old Sylvia in her arms on the deck of the ship, the S.S. Brazil, as it was pushed away from the Bombay docks and J.T. Her heart was like stone. Standing with her were hundreds of women with children who had made the same decision—to go home, while lining the dock were husbands and fathers who had made the same decision J.T. did—to stay in India and continue preaching the Gospel. People were crying all around her. She felt in that moment she was leaving the biggest part of her body in India and that she would never be whole again.

The S.S. *Brazil* had been a massive American luxury liner, but was recently converted into a troop transport, carrying 5,000 people. No luxury now! No comforts on board now; only the plainest of food, and they lined up for it for every meal. What a jam of people!

She hadn't been that near to so many people in her whole life. She felt like she couldn't breathe. But it got worse.

In the cabin to which Ruth was assigned were fourteen bunks. Before, this cabin had been for officers, with two comfortable beds. Now, *fourteen* women crowded in, with only one bathroom. Bunks were in tiers of three, with two extra. They could not sit on their bunks, they had to bend over and roll into them. If they sat up, they banged their heads on either the bunk above or the ceiling.

Before leaving Bombay, J.T. and Ruth had found in the bazaar a small, old iron cradle-bed swinging in its stand, for little Sylvia. The stand fitted exactly between two tiers of bunks right beside Ruth who was in a lower bunk. Sylvia made the fifteenth person in that one small cabin.

Each night before dusk, a sailor came in and with a big tool, screwed their portholes closed—locked and sealed them—thus shutting out every bit of light and air. Their flashlights were confiscated, so no lights in the cabin or the bathroom. Only a faint red light glowed in the halls, barely showing anyone the way to the bathroom. In those days of no air conditioning, they sweltered through every night. Above Sylvia's little bed was a tiny air vent through which outside air was pumped. The baby got most of the benefit, but that didn't keep her from quickly being covered with prickly heat. Ruth had been able to find one small can of baby powder.

Passengers were told that their portholes were closed and flashlights confiscated because the faintest speck of light can be seen for forty miles on the ocean. And the enemy was there, waiting with torpedoes for American ships! So nobody smoked on deck, either. Those who smoked, congregated in the halls outside the cabins, polluting what little air they *did* have to breathe.

Twice a week a shrill whistle through loud speakers nearly burst the earsdrums of every passenger as they were called to assembly. They were given orders to wear their life jackets at all times, and they listened to lectures on how to abandon ship. There was one cardinal rule: The Captain said, "No matter what else you lose, don't ever lose your shoes! Many people who are eventually rescued lose their feet because of extended exposure to salt water."

No life jacket was small enough for a six-month-old baby, so Ruth had to tie Sylvia in her own jacket with her. Only one other small baby was on board, the rest were able to walk. If they had been bombed and thrown into the water, those two mothers could not have kept their babies alive. To tie a squirming baby into a heavy, restraining life jacket and then climb flights of stairs to an upper deck, took all the strength Ruth had. Yet, she had to go upstairs several times a day because the dining room was not on her deck. And much time must be spent in open air instead of the crammed sleeping quarters.

Because of the way their lives had been so upset, Sylvia was nervous and cried a lot, waking in the night twice for feedings. She was probably not getting enough milk from Ruth, but they both were lucky she was not a bottle baby. No baby formula aboard a troop transport!

It was so black in the cabin from sunset until dawn that they could not see their hands in front of their faces. Each night Ruth kept powder and diapers within reach, and when Sylvia woke up, she changed and fed her without ever being able to see her. She had to feel all over the baby and her bed to be sure everything was all right.

Their route was south through the Indian Ocean, sailing down and around Africa, and the heat in the cabins was unbearable. They crossed the equator with no air conditioning, and fifteen people in Ruth's cabin. Some larger sleeping quarters held many more.

The first night out was so ghastly that everyone had the same idea. Ruth made three trips to a topside deck (up three floors), carrying bedding, life jacket, and baby, to find a place to sleep in the open air. The ship was completely blacked out, so she felt around, spread out a blanket and lay down with Sylvia beside her to try to sleep on the hard deck. During the night, she knew that other people came out and lay down near her, but she couldn't see anything. At daybreak, she woke up with her face right beside the face of a strange man. He was somebody or other's husband and Ruth said, "Good morning. Did you sleep here all last night?"

His wife on the other side of him said, "Well, I didn't know who he was sleeping beside, but I was right here!"

They had just finished that intellectual conversation, when two sailors came out to hose down the deck. Finding it jammed with sleeping people and bedding, they just stood there with hands on hips and cussed. That wasn't so intellectual, but was extremely descriptive! That day orders came down from the Captain that no more sleeping on decks was allowed. So back to the stinky cabins they went.

Their course continued to be south until they rounded the tip of South Africa, then north up on the other side. They zigzagged constantly the whole way home, for six weeks. About seven minutes they went southeast, seven minutes southwest, all the way to South Africa. Then after that, seven minutes northeast, seven minutes northwest, and so on and on, day after tense day, and night after stifling night, as they crossed the equator twice.

The Captain told them in one of his briefings: "We zigzag like that so an enemy vessel cannot get a 'fix on us' and torpedo us. The least time in which they could do that is a little more than seven minutes. So every seven minutes we change our course." It made sense to his passengers—they hoped it made sense to the enemy.

During the awful nights with their portholes closed, sleep was almost impossible. They had been warned not to undress at night during the most dangerous part of the journey, so like everyone else, Ruth slept in her clothes, and even shoes for many nights.

The air was filled with constant tension because they knew that on the east side of Africa, the sea was full of Japanese submarines. One evening they met a convoy of six American ships going north. *Brazil's* passengers waved wildly at American troops in the convoy. Within half an hour of passing them, the Captain received an S.O.S. that three of those American ships had been torpedoed and sunk—in the same place his ship had just sailed over! They begged for help to come back and pick up survivors. But the Captain of the S.S. *Brazil* answered that his was a refugee ship, with mostly women and children aboard and he could not turn back. The news swept through the passengers and they broke into tears. They had just waved goodbye to lost American boys.

One night about two weeks after sailing, Ruth woke up feeling very ill and managed to roll out of bed in the blackness to fumble her way to the bathroom. Once there, she lost consciousness and fell on the floor. Her cabinmates heard her fall, pulled aside the door curtain to let in the faint red glow from the hall, and managed to identify her and drag her back to bed. But they didn't know what was wrong with her.

When the sailor came in the next morning and opened up the porthole, they could see that Ruth was very sick with a raging fever. Sylvia was screaming to be fed, and Ruth was unable to respond to the baby. So her roommates just laid her beside Ruth and she nursed. Then they took Sylvia on deck for a walk and called for the old missionary doctor on board—Dr. Corpron. Ruth was shaking with chills and fever and Dr. Corpron, who had treated many cases, said it was a bad case of malaria.

Ruth really thought she would die for a while. For two weeks she was flat in bed, unconscious part of the time. Her cabinmates took complete care of baby Sylvia. Ruth was so weak that she couldn't do anything for her. They just put her beside Ruth and she nursed by herself, then they took her away. Fortunately, in spite of her mother's high fever and chills, the baby lost no weight—but then she didn't gain any either. Ruth lost fourteen pounds.

Their ship rounded Capetown, South Africa, and put into port for a day. Some of the people got off to walk around a bit, but Ruth was too weak to do anything. Finally she began to be able to walk, but on very wobbly sea legs. Dr. Corpron had been giving her quinine, the only cure for malaria, and her skin had a definite yellow color. At least she was alive and very thankful to God. During the trip when she was able, Ruth read over and over in the Bible the Book of Psalms. The promises of God's sustaining grace gave her hope that they would reach home safely.

A short time after she was able to be up, she heard the shocking news that Dr. Corpron himself was very ill. He had acute appendicitis and needed surgery.

For more than a week as they approached South Africa, the sea had been very rough. Many people were extremely seasick and couldn't get up. Everything not tied down on board shifted from one side of a room to the other, and staircase climbing or descending was prohibited. Food was brought downstairs by the crew.

One other missionary doctor, Dr. White, was on board. When he examined Dr. Corpron he said, "He must have surgery, but with this kind of sea, I cannot operate." So he called a group of the missionaries together and said, "We must pray for Dr. Corpron. I can delay the surgery until 10:00 o'clock tomorrow, but then I must do it. If I don't, he will probably die. So let's pray both for him and that God will still the sea."

Dr. White reminded the missionaries that Jesus had stilled the waters when He was on earth. He read to them Luke 8:24: *And they came to Him and awoke him saying, Master, Master, we perish. Then He arose, and rebuked the wind and the raging of the water: and they ceased, and there was a calm.*

A prayer vigil went on all night for Dr. Corpron, but the storm continued. At 9:00 o'clock the next morning the ocean was still too rough, and Dr. White shook his head. But suddenly, by 10:00 o'clock, a calm! It was as if their ship had suddenly sailed into a sea of glass.

Dr. White said, "Thank You, Lord," rushed Dr. Corpron into the ship's surgery, and successfully completed the operation. Almost as soon as Dr. Corpron was safely back in his own bunk and strapped in, the storm was raging again. But Dr. Corpron's life was saved. Christians all over the ship praised the Lord.

After they left Capetown South Africa, they zigzagged north through the Atlantic ocean, and moved into more dangerous territory. On the west side of Africa, German submarines were everywhere. They had already sunk several ships in the area. The *Brazil* had orders to stop at Bermuda, southeast of U.S.A., and take on two hundred soldiers and sailors who had been on American ships which had been torpedoed and sunk. They had either floated by lifeboats into Bermuda, or had been picked up and brought there by some other vessel.

Many of *Brazil's* passengers lined the rail and watched as those tattered servicemen climbed up the outside stairs. Ruth, holding baby Sylvia, was watching as they stumbled up. One big man bellowed, "Well, I've just had two ships sunk under me, and I don't expect to reach America on this one!" His lips curled open wide and showed a mouth empty of everything but a tongue and gums. He announced he had been taking a shower, with his false teeth on a shower stall shelf, when his last ship was blown apart. The passengers clapped for him.

But that remark did nothing for *Brazil's* passengers and their already low morale! From Bermuda on to New York, because of the danger of German U-boats, the ship was granted the protection of an American destroyer to go before them, and two airplanes as escorts, flying around before and after their ship.

Those last days turned out to be an unending nightmare, and nobody slept. Measles had broken out among many of the children below decks, and everyone could smell the disease. The odor was so vile it almost made people vomit just to walk by the stairs.

The day after they took on the escort in Bermuda, Ruth was lying down with baby Sylvia in the cabin, when suddenly the ship shook with some sort of explosion, then immediately another one. At once the sirens on the ship wailed, and the Captain's voice shrilled over the crackling radios, "All passengers to their lifeboat positions! All passengers to the lifeboat decks!"

Ruth grabbed up her baby, tied her in the life jacket with her, and snatched up a small bag which she had kept ready for emergency. In it was the only can of powdered milk she owned—she had bought it in Bombay—two diapers and a dress.

Everyone was on deck almost immediately, standing in line and ready to get into the lifeboats. Some of the older missionary couples going home to retire refused to be separated by the "women and children first" rule. The women hung back and said if they had to die, they would die with their husbands; they would not be separated. Tears flowed freely after that decision!

Passengers stood and waited there for nearly an hour, but nothing else happened. Finally, the "all clear" was given and they were dismissed. The emergency had been created because their destroyer escort had spotted a German submarine lying in wait. The destroyer had fired two torpedoes, at the sub, and the *Brazil* was so close to the destroyer that they thought their own ship had been hit. They kept looking around and saw some oil appear on the water near their ship. The Captain put on full speed, and they got away—still zigzagging.

After dismissal Ruth started back down to the cabin, but she was so scared, and still so weak from malaria she simply couldn't go. Her knees would hold her up no longer. She sank down on a deck chair, shaking, and nearly fainting. Sylvia, screaming to get out of the tight life jacket, brought her to her senses.

The next midnight quiet was suddenly shattered by cries and screams from the upper decks, and the ship began to tremble as if in sudden convulsions. The chaotic sounds and quaking rolled Ruth out of bed, but she couldn't leave Sylvia, and wouldn't disturb her unless it was necessary. She had not been able to sleep—the next day they were to land in New York, and six weeks of nightmare would be over. She had been lying there just thanking the Lord that they were near home. Now this! *Oh, Lord, are we really going to be on American ground tomorrow? Please protect us from whatever is out there!*

One of Ruth's roommates rushed upstairs to see what was going on, and soon came back and told a scary, incredible story. She said, "About three or four hundred people were sitting on the top deck, and many on other decks. They were going to sit there all night to see New York appear. All was pitch blackness around them. No moon, and not a speck of light anywhere. They thought there was only our dark, camouflaged ship zigzagging through a black ocean, with two planes flying overhead.

"Suddenly, one of the planes dropped a flare directly in front of the prow of our ship. Right there in our ocean path loomed up another huge ship—an American minesweeper! Both vessels had been traveling in complete, soundless blackout and we almost had a head-on collision.

"The pilot of the plane overhead could see the phosporescent glow of the ocean water which each of our ships churned up. He could see the glow of our troop transport sailing nearer and nearer to the minesweeper, and the only way—but a very dangerous way—to save a crash, was to drop a flare directly between us. When suddenly in the blinding light, people on both vessels saw another bearing down on them, pandemonium broke out. Immediately our engines were crashed into reverse, the ship shuddered and shook, but we missed the smashup—by a very few feet. We were so close to each other's ship that a mighty wave was created between us. That's part of what we felt." Nobody in Ruth's cabin slept that night!

The next morning about seven, everybody was out on the deck as the skyline of New York appeared. Women, children, soldiers and sailors wept unashamedly, as they passed the Statue of Liberty. They were all singing "Praise God from Whom All Blessings Flow" with shaky voices and tears streaming down their faces. Ruth felt like kissing the ground because it was American ground. Sometimes during the awful six weeks, she had doubted she would ever see it again.

During the voyage Ruth had met a very sweet, middle-aged missionary woman who had come out of Burma. Her husband had insisted she leave ahead of him, he wanted to stay one more day and destroy all mission papers before the Japanese captured their Burmese town. He had told his wife, "If I can't get to Bombay, then I'll catch another ship and meet you in New York." So she had walked the torturous road out of Burma for many days, with many others who finally struggled over the "hump" into India. She had looked for her husband on the Bombay docks, but he wasn't there.

All through the trip home on the *Brazil* she was sure her husband had found some other ship going to America, and would meet her when she landed. The morning they docked, she leaned over the railing, searching every face she could distinguish. She saw some friends from her mission board there and waved to them.

Many friends on the *Brazil* stood back allowing her to go off first. They watched as she ran down the gangplank to see her board members and get news of her husband. They knew what her first question was. They saw her reaction. Her face changed from happy expectancy to total shock. Then she threw up her hands and shrieked, "Oh, NO! It can't be!"

Her husband had been captured and killed by the Japanese, the day after she had left her mission compound in Burma.

After her ship docked, Ruth sat on her suitcase all day in the customs shed (no seats were provided), waiting for her one big trunk to come up out of the hold. She had to take care of Sylvia, of course, but sometimes she just put her down on the suitcase to sleep and sat on the floor beside her. She also had to nurse her in public, but having lived in India, that didn't bother her too much. A diaper over her shoulder helped.

Finally at 4:00 o'clock in the afternoon, her trunk came up and with a sigh of relief she hoisted her baby and dragged her suitcase to the customs official. He was a redheaded Irishman (she loved redheads) and he said, "Young lady, I've been watching you all day sitting there with your baby. Haven't you got a husband?"

"Of course. I have a perfectly wonderful husband! But he stayed in India."

The Irishman cussed a little and answered, "Well, I think it's a damn shame he let you come by youself. I hear you had one hell of a trip. Where are you going now?"

"To my parents' home in Southern Illinois."

"Well, I know your train leaves soon, so I won't search your trunk like I've been doing the others all day. I don't believe you even thought about bringing in any contraband. I'll put this seal on it—there, get home fast. You look sick!"

"I'm just getting over malaria," Ruth said. But what she really wanted to do was to kiss him because he was so blustering kind.

* * * *

That six weeks had been the worst of Henry and Pearl's lives. They knew Ruth was on the ocean *somewhere,* dodging Japanese and German submarines. Every day the newspapers listed ships sunk and how many people perished. They knew she had left India the first part of June and that the journey would be long if she DID get home. All they could do was pray. Their church was praying with them for Ruth's safe return, and many other friends called to say they were very concerned for Ruth and her baby.

Pearl sat on the porch swing night after night and watched Henry pace up and down the sidewalk. Usually they went to bed early, but sleep was impossible. Neighbors on their porches spoke with sympathy, asking Henry if he'd heard any news. His voice was muffled even to his own ears when he tried to speak and say, "No, not yet."

Finally, toward the last of July, came the phone call and the marvelous sound of Ruth's voice. She and baby Sylvia had landed in New York and would be home on the train the next day!

Henry and Pearl both dissolved in tears. Thank God! She was safe! "I hope we never have to live another six weeks like the last six have been."

They met Ruth and little Sylvia in Carbondale and were so shocked when they saw Ruth that they could hardly speak. Ruth was skin and bones and barely able to lift her baby. Her face had a sallow color, and she swayed on her feet. The baby was beautiful.

"Oh, Ruthie! What in the world is the matter with you?! Are you sick?"

"Oh, I'm a lot better now. But I had a terrible case of malaria on the way home and was unconscious part of the time. Awful chills and fever."

Henry took the baby from her arms. "Oh! She sure is purty! Seven-and-a-half months old and fat as butter! How in the world did you take care of this baby when you were so sick?"

"I'll tell you all about it later, Daddy. I'm still weak and know I must look awful. Haven't had any decent bath or washed my hair for six weeks. Have no idea how much weight I lost."

"You lost too much!" declared Henry. "Oh, Ruthie it's so good to have you home."

Pearl hugged her and she could feel Ruth trembling from weakness. "The last year and a half you've been gone seems like a lifetime. Let's get you home and put you to bed."

"You mean in a *real* bed? Where, if I sit up in it, I won't bang my head on a bed above me? That sounds like heaven!"

The day after Ruth arrived home, baby Sylvia came down with measles. Ruth had to rest a lot, so Pearl and Henry were needed again. Slowly Ruth began to regain her strength as the baby also recovered. And while Ruth recuperated, little by little, she told her mother and father about her trip home.

CHAPTER THIRTY-SIX
Realities of Change

"Grandma Julia, I'm glad you're here with Mom and Dad." Ruth sat with her grandmother, watching baby Sylvia crawling around on the floor.

Julia smiled. "Watching your baby takes me back a long time to when I used to watch my own, Ruthie."

"You had a lot to watch, didn't you, Grandma?"

"Yes, I did. And I think your little Sylvia is the prettiest baby I ever did see. She's smart, too. Wonder what she'll turn out to be?"

"I guess only the Lord knows the answer to that, Grandma."

Pearl's arthritis continued to make her life miserable. Unrelenting pain hit her wrists and hands. To pick up the baby was excruciating. To lift a heavy skillet from the stove took both hands, and then sometimes Henry had to do it for her. The doctor said, "We don't know what to do for arthritis except take aspirin for the pain. Far as we know now, nothing can cure arthritis.

"But I've been reading about a new drug that's called cortisone. It shows some promise to help arthritic patients. We can try it if you want to, Pearl."

"Give me anything that will stop some of this pain and let me live a little easier."

Pearl was one of the first people in Herrin to take cortisone—she became a guinea pig for it. Ruth cried sometimes watching her mother suffer. Pearl would soak her hands and arms in warm water and try not to cry, but sometimes the pain was too much. Then Ruth would remember the many years that Pearl washed their clothes in the big round tubs, carrying water, scrubbing all those clothes and wringing them by hand. Heavy wet sheets and so many pairs of underwear and overalls! No wonder arthritis had hit her hands!

Ruth's in-laws, Arnett and Yvonne Seamands, had been aboard a Dutch ship, sailing to America for a regular furlough, when the Japanese struck Pearl Harbor. The rest of their trip was, like

Ruth's, a harrowing six-week experience, but at last they had arrived home and were living in Wilmore. They invited Ruth and the baby to come and live with them. They wrote that if Ruth came down, they would help with the baby if she wanted to take some seminary classes.

Ruth had another hard decision. Arthur was in California, so he wasn't at home to help take care of their mother. Irene had recently been married and was in a home of her own, so she couldn't help much. But Henry said, "Ruthie, this is a good chance for you to get some more schooling, if that's what you want. I can take care of Pearl."

Ruth pondered. If she stayed in Herrin, she could help her mother. But when the baby cried, and Pearl was in great pain, Ruth could see that her situation was worsened. She hated to leave her mother, but she felt that it would be better for Pearl and Henry if she did leave. They were simply not used to having a baby around, though they loved her dearly.

By the first of September Ruth was feeling stronger, so she went to Wilmore and registered for some seminary classes. Grandmother Shields, Mother and Dad Seamands together helped with the baby. Never was a baby more loved or better cared for than was baby Sylvia. The only one missing was her beloved J.T.

"This house is awful quiet now that Ruth and the baby are gone," Julia said to Henry and Pearl. "Seems like I never get tired of being with a baby."

"It's too quiet," Pearl agreed. "I wish I could have held the baby more. Maybe this cortisone will work and let me do things like I used to. Ma Childers, I'd like to be able to help you more, too. I know it's hard for you to do your own work and cooking." Even with her own pain, Pearl could see that Julia was not very strong.

But the main thing was that Julia couldn't see things as she had before. Sometimes when she bumped into furniture she'd make light of it; she'd laugh at herself and say, "Now why couldn't I see that big chair?"

Cena and her youngest daughter, Shirley, came down from West Frankfort at least once a week to see Julia and Henry and Pearl.

"Shirley, do you want a lemon drop?" Julia asked her young granddaughter during one of their visits. "I always keep some for you. It's my favorite candy, too."

"I know you do, Grandma. Sure, I'll take some."

Julia handed her the jar of candy and Shirley cried, "Oh, Mama, they're all covered with ants!"

"Ants?" exclaimed Julia. "I don't see any ants!"

Cena held the jar closer to Julia. "Mom, don't you see all those ants running around in there? You been eating these things and never noticed that?"

"Well—guess my eyes ain't good as they used to be." Julia shook her head. "No, I jist can't see 'em."

Cena shook her head. "Well Mom, now it's time. I'm takin' you home with me—this just makes me more determined. If you can't see all those ants, who knows what you're liable to eat here when you're cookin' for yourself? You just got to come. Anyway, Pearl is in a lot of pain most of the time, Henry says, and she would want to help you if you needed it, but she couldn't. I'm younger than Pearl and I have no arthritis like she has, and I can help you."

Julia sighed. "Well, Cena, I guess you're right. I been thinkin' about that. Pearl is awful good to me—she tries to get me to eat with them. But—" Julia sat down in her rocking chair, thought a bit and sighed again. "It would be nice to spend my last days on a farm. I'll never get the love of land out of my bones. I've been in this room long enough to feel at home now—I'm used to livin' here and I like it. But Pearl does suffer a lot and I don't want to make any more trouble for her."

"You know what our farm is like," Cena said. "You'd feel right at home. You get yourself together, and tomorrow I'll send Arthur down with the truck. We'll bring all your things up to our house. It's plenty big, as you know. Our other girls are gone—only Shirley is at home, and you can have the whole upstairs."

Like Ruth, Julia also hated to leave Henry and Pearl, but she knew it was for the best. Maybe they would be able to come to West Frankfort and see her sometimes. Henry wasn't as young as he used to be either, and it was hard for him to work and take care of Pearl, and Julia didn't want to be trouble to him. Anticipating living on a farm again made her heart feel warm and comfortable.

The next day Cena's husband, Arthur, came and he and Henry loaded Julia's belongings onto his truck. "I'm gonna miss you, Ma," Henry choked. "It's hard to see you leave here. I like you to be here."

Julia tearfully hugged him. "I like bein' here, too, Henry. You made a nice place for me and I'm much obliged. But if I got sick, it'd be too hard for you to have two sick women on your hands."

* * * *

Of course, Ruth kept in close touch with Pearl and Henry by phone. Soon after Julia left, Pearl began to have trouble with her teeth and gums. The cortisone eased her arthritis, but now this! Pearl and Henry were both shocked to hear the dentist say, "Mrs. Childers, I think these teeth must be pulled. They're almost falling out by themselves, you know."

Pearl gasped, *"All of them?"*

The dentist nodded. "Yes, all of them. Your gums have been diseased for some time. I know this is bad news, but we can make you nice new teeth, and you'll get used to them."

The ordeal of all her teeth being pulled was bad enough, but it seemed to Pearl that afterwards, her arthritis became worse. She believed that all the infection which centered in her gums, now spread all over her body, scattering pain everywhere. Even with Pearl's sunny disposition, living was difficult. Arthritis alone was enough, but now she had to get used to false teeth! Of course, she wrote a poem about it—when she could think straight.

MY NEW STORE TEETH

My teeth are shiny, new and bright;
They, like the stars, come out at night.
I cannot chew, nor even speak–
For want of food I'm getting weak.

The winning smiles that used to chase
Like sunbeams o'er my lovely (?) face
Are gone – alas! I know not where,
And in their place a haunting fear
Lest I, on some unlucky day
Will yawn too wide, and then away
Will go that pesky lower plate,
I could not dream a sadder fate!

My disposition, once serene,
Is growing surly, cross and mean.
I think I'll seek some lonely glen,
Far, far away from haunts of men,
And live alone a year or two–
Until a pork chop I can chew!

* * * *

After a couple of months, Pearl began to feel better. The cortisone was suppressing her pain and she could function quite well. Even though she was gaining some weight (because of the drug, the doctor said), she was again doing her housework with minimum difficulty. Cortisone seemed like a miracle to her.

One day Henry came home from town all excited. "Pearl, I heard some news today. I can get a job if I want it. It would be the best job I've had since the mines shut down. Because of this war, the government sent out word that they need men in California to work in the shipyards."

"In California!"

"Yes, California. I know that's a long ways off, but I would be close to Arthur. They are making ships out there and they need lots more men. We've got to double up manpower and make more ships if we intend to win this war."

"How would you get there? You don't have the money."

"The government will pay the way of any man or woman who wants to go there and work. I'd go on the train. I would like to take the job, but I'm worried about you—you couldn't go with me—housing is scarce. I'll have to live in a boarding house. Would you be all right here? Should I go?"

Pearl's heart sank, but she knew many wives were without their men because the country was at war. "Well, I don't know what else could happen to me that hasn't already happened. I can get a boy to cut wood for me, and the grocery would bring things—"

"I hate to leave you, Pearl, but this is good money. I could save a lot and we sure do need to save some. I would send you money every two weeks."

"How long do you think this job would last?"

"Until the war is about over—who knows?"

"Well," she was suffering inside but couldn't say so, "we ought to be as patriotic as everybody else. Ruth is without J.T.; she will drive here often to see me. In the summer, she'll come for a longer time. Oh, Henry, how will I ever do without you? I've never been without you since we've been married! Now—" She hugged him, buried her face in his chest and her tears wet his shirt.

"I know it won't be easy for either one of us but—" Henry couldn't let Pearl see how near to tears he was. "At least we have telephones."

For the second time in his life, Henry rumbled by train to California. This train was jammed with traveling servicemen and their families.

Hardly believing the silence, Pearl stayed home and literally kept the home fires burning. Without Henry for the first time in twenty-eight years, she wrote a poem for him:

For My Man in California

My dear, the house is clean and neat,
(Since you are gone with your big feet),
No overalls hanging behind the door,
No black tar marks upon the floor.

But the stovepipe doesn't look just right
(In fact, it fell the other night!).
The garden weeds would hide a bear,
I have no one, my jokes to share.

And when I'm sick and cry and groan–
Then it's no fun to live alone.
When winter winds begin to roar,
And snow creeps in around the door,
And white frost on the windows form–
WHO'S GONNA KEEP MY COLD FEET WARM?

Anyone who lived through World War II is not likely to forget the day-to-day round of war bonds, rolling bandages, walking instead of riding (to save gasoline), lists in newspapers of ships sunk, planes shot down, and local boys lost. Stars appeared in many windows signifying that a boy from that home had been killed.

Ruth and J.T. suffered, too. Separated nearly three years, their letters were always censored. Often lines were cut out of letters which the receiver could only guess about. Sometimes Ruth was in dispair, she wanted to be with him so much. She had to tell herself, *Look here, many other women are without their husbands. And the Japanese didn't invade India, so J.T. is safe. Other women are not so lucky; their husbands are dead. So count your blessings, study and get all the education you can in the seminary, and keep busy. Yes, of course, Sylvia keeps three people busy!*

Of less importance was the constant rationing of meat, butter, sugar and other things, and the black market that sprang up.

* * * *

J.T.'s Grandmother Shields suffered a severe heart attack in November, 1943. She was recouperating at home and the family thought she was going to be all right. One day she sat up in bed and asked for a pen and paper. She wrote this short letter to J.T. in India:

> Dear Darling J.T., This is goodbye. I am going up
> to live with Jesus. Be a good boy. Your little
> Sylvia is so sweet. Always stick to the Old Book
> and meet me in Heaven. Love from Grandma.

Grandma Shields died the next week. They all grieved, but little Sylvia seemed to miss her great grandmother the most. They had been together every day for more than a year.

Grandma's letter was delivered to J.T. in India weeks after he had received the cablegram about her death. That letter was very precious to him; he preserved it in the family Bible.

Irene's first baby, Jack Arthur, was born Valentine's Day, 1944. After Pearl paid Irene and her baby a visit in the Herrin hospital, she wrote this for Irene:

THE LITTLE STRANGER

A dear little stranger, one cold winter day,
From the playground of Heaven, happened to stray.
A careless angel when it was too late,
Remembered to fasten a tiny gate.
The little boy in his earthward flight,
From the wondering angel was soon lost to sight.
And then without pausing for slumber or rest,
As a homing pigeon returns to its nest,
Straight to our open doorway he flew–
Without any luggage–not even a shoe.
We welcomed him gladly and asked him to stay.
He's just what we wanted on Valentine's Day.

The dreadful war rumbled on. In the middle of November, 1944, Ruth called Pearl. Her voice was an octave higher than usual and she was crying with joy. "Mom! Guess what! I had a cablegram from J.T. in Bombay. He's on his way home! He's on the ocean now, headed this way! He finally got permission to come on a troop transport! Oh, I don't know how I'm gonna wait for six weeks!"

"Ruthie! That's the best news I've heard since *you* got home! Think he will be home by Christmas?"

"That's just about the time he will get home. Sylvia will be three on Christmas, and maybe he can make it for her birthday! We'll come up afterwards soon as we can."

Pearl said, "I've got news, too. Henry phoned and said his job seems to be winding down. They're laying off some men and he thinks he will be home before too long. Looks like our families are finally going to get together again."

In the middle of Christmas Day, Pearl's phone rang. A beautiful bass voice said, "Is this Pearlie Childers?"

"Oh, J.T., I'd know your voice anywhere! Are you in Wilmore?"

"I just got in last night. It's so great to be at home. And I'd never have known my little Sylvia—she's grown so!"

"Welcome home! What did Sylvia say to you?"

"Well, of course, Ruth has been showing her my picture all the time, and telling her that her Daddy was coming home. This morning when she got up I was here, so I lay down on the floor in front of the Christmas tree to get acquainted with her."

"I bet you enjoyed that."

"Yes, I did. She crawled all over me and looked me up and down. Finally she said to Ruth in a sort of bored voice, 'Mommie, is *this* the only Daddy I've got?'"

Pearl laughed. "That sounds just like her! You've sure got a brilliant little girl!"

"When is Pop Henry coming home from California?"

"Soon, I hope! Looks like the Japanese are getting licked good and it can't happen too quick for me! I hope all you Seamands people have a real happy Christmas!"

"You too, Mom. Ruth says you're having lots of trouble with arthritis. Is it any better?"

"I'll never be cured, but cortisone helps me stand the pain. I just have to live with it. Bye, J.T. So glad you're back."

In 1945 World War II was finally over and Henry came home. For Pearl, it was wonderful to have him at home to take charge again. Before long he found a full-time job in the Herrin Water Company. The work was hard—often digging up water mains when the ground was frozen solid, but the pay was good. He and

Pearl finally had come to the point where they didn't have to pinch every penny twice before they spent it.

* * * *

Early in January, 1946, Pearl's phone rang. It was Ruth calling from Hartford, Connecticut where she and J.T. had been in graduate school since the summer of 1945. "Hi, Mom. Is everything all right?"

"Everything's fine."

"Is Daddy all right? It must be tough outside digging in frozen ground for broken pipes! Is it too much for him?"

"Well—of course it is hard when the ground is so frozen—but so far he's doing fine."

"And how is your arthritis?"

"Okay, I guess. If my hands didn't pain, my back didn't hurt, and my knees didn't ache, I'd be in fairly good shape!"

Ruth laughed, "I see it hasn't changed your disposition any. Mom, the doctor says my baby will come the last week of January. Do you think it would be possible for you to come up here and stay a couple of weeks with me? Would Daddy mind too much?"

"I think Henry could probably stay alone that long—"

"Well, Sylvia is lively, you know, and J.T. is in school every day, and I will need a little help. I hope Daddy won't be mad at me for taking you away—"

"He lived alone for two years in California—I guess he can stay alone for two weeks at home."

"Sylvia is anxious to see Grandma Childers again—"

"I'm anxious to see her, too. Let me know when to come. I'll be on the next train."

"Thanks, Mom, that relieves my mind a lot. We'll call you. Love you both!"

Ruth's second baby, Sheila, was born the last day of January 1946, and Pearl was there to welcome her. Sheila was a beautiful little red-haired baby with a quiet disposition—just the opposite of rowdy Sylvia. To Sylvia, the appearance of a baby sister was both a threat and fun.

Pearl knew that J.T.'s work at Hartford was only a prelude to his and Ruth's return to India. She could barely stand to think about that. Henry said, "It's crazy for them to go back to India after all the trouble they had before."

"Now Henry, you know she couldn't help the war."

At the end of the summer of 1946, Ruth and J.T. and the two children came home for a visit before returning to India. This parting was as hard, maybe harder than the first time, only this time Pearl and Henry had to say goodbye to two grandchildren. They realized that the next time they saw them, the children would be half grown. In the 1940s, missionary terms lasted between six and seven years!

Yes, for Pearl, and Henry, 1946 was a year of excitement and then loneliness. Ruth and J.T. and their two daughters left in September for India. And Irene and Jack with their two sons left for Colorado the next January. All the children were really gone—the nest was vacant.

One day an old friend she hadn't seen for quite a while visited Pearl. "Well, Beulah! Come on in, you're a sight for sore eyes! I've just been sittin' here feelin' sorry for myself because my kids are all living somewhere else."

"I thought you might be—heard that Ruth had gone back to India, and that Irene just went to Colorado." Beulah was a big woman with a loud, happy voice. "I just took a chance you'd be at home today, Pearl. It's been too long since we had a good visit! Is Henry workin'?"

"Yes—he's on the water-main crew. He took his lunch. We can gab all day!"

Pearl and Beulah had known each other ever since Pearl had moved to Herrin as a young girl. They reminisced and laughed the rest of the morning. Pearl cooked pork chops, mashed potatoes, gravy and biscuits for lunch, and for dessert they ate chocolate cake. A good old-fashioned dinner guaranteed to put on three pounds.

They sat at the table for two hours giggling about their grade school and their growing-up days. They remembered the clothes they wore, and the hair-dos they used to think were so flattering. They sniggered about childhood crushes on boyfriends, and the trials of old age. Pearl dug out old faded photos and they laughed some more.

"Pearl, where has the afternoon gone? It's four o'clock. I have to go home."

Beulah and Pearl hugged each other. "I'm so glad you came!"

"Let's do this again. You come to my house next time, Pearl! Today made me feel young again!"

"Yeah, it even helped me forget about my arthritis. Now that you're leaving, I can feel it again!"

After Beulah left Pearl sat down at the kitchen table and wrote a poem which she dedicated to Beulah:

WHEN YOU AND I WERE YOUNG

I'm thinking of the "Good Old Days," of which we love to sing,
When Ma and Pa knew nothing–but WE KNEW EVERYTHING!
We never heard of calories, our teeth were all our own,
We bit the corn right off the cob, and chewed a chicken bone!

We walked to church on a board sidewalk,
our steps were strong and free.
In our high-top shoes and trailing skirts–we were a sight to see!
Our hair puffed out around our face on a smelly, itchy "rat,"
And oh, how proud when we could wear a "Merry Widow" hat!

The preacher rambled on and on–not a word we heard him say,
Our thoughts were on our best friend's "beau,"
we'd like to steal away.
But now we're old and fat and gray, with bunions on our feet,
We talk of aches and pains all day–and "What are we gonna eat?"

We go to bed and park our teeth in a little plastic cup,
And hook bifocals on our nose as soon as we get up.
But we thank the Lord for what we have–
we still can use our tongue,
And talk about the "Good Old Days," when you and I were young!

At age fifty, Pearl had taught herself to type. That was a good thing, because when arthritis began to cripple her hands, writing was difficult. She could still peck out her letters and poetry on her little portable typewriter. She put together a poetry notebook for each of her children, and also for some friends.

One day she began thinking about their clock—Old Ben. Henry had brought the clock home on the day the big cyclone struck Southern Illinois in 1925. Old Ben had ticked every day since then. Henry faithfully wound it every night, and during the day it occupied the same small kitchen shelf. Pearl loved to hear the tick of Old Ben as she sat in her chair. She told Henry that Old Ben was company for her, and that some day she was going to write a poem about him.

Often one of the children would ask, "When are you going to write about Old Ben, Grandma?"

She finally did, and it was one of her favorite poems.

A TRIBUTE TO OLD BEN ON HIS BIRTHDAY

My faithful Old Ben is now twenty-two
  He is tarnished and aged and gray:
He runs on his back, but still goes right on
  Doing his duty each day!
In storm or power failure, in thunder or rain–
  Electric clocks aren't worth a dime.
Old Ben stays serene and calmly ticks on–
  And keeps us right up with the time.

His alarm wakes us up from a beautiful dream–
  Don't think we can have a short snooze–
He keeps up his clamor as though trying to say,
  "Wake up or your job you will lose."
The children are grown with homes of their own.
  The grandchildren come back to see
If Ben is still here, and, "Grandma," they say,
  "How old will Old Ben get to be?"

Now that, I don't know, but I'm dreading the day
  When I put him away off his shelf
Among old relics of a long ago day–
  It will seem I've lost part of myself.
His ticking I hear when I can't get to sleep,
  It comforts me all the night through.
I hope I can keep you for many a year–
  Old Ben, is my tribute to you.

Irene lived a hectic life in the wild plains of Colorado with her husband, Jack, and their three children.

Ruth's unique life in India unrolled to Pearl and Henry in many letters. Ruth wrote of crows, cobras, and kraits in their yard, rats in the storeroom, civet cats in the attic, monkeys looking in their skylight windows, and dozens of other extraordinary happenings.

Every strange experience that any of Pearl's four encountered became a topic of a poem. When Pearl's fertile brain could think up a poem, she was happy.

CHAPTER THIRTY-SEVEN
JULIA - 1943 - 1948
Almost Home

When Julia worked in Creal Springs she somehow felt closer to John there. It was so easy to remember all the years they had lived on their farm in Creal. She had now moved to Cena's, and living again on a farm, once again she felt close to John.

Arthur was a skilled farmer and kept his cows and horses and buildings in good shape. Arthur was a gentle, kind man, and in the evenings he often sat and talked to Julia about farming, asking how she and John did this and that. Arthur's friendliness made her feel right at home. "You make yourself at home, Ma Childers. If you feel like goin' out to the garden, you do it. Or if you just feel like sittin', then you do that."

Sometimes Julia did feel good enough to walk in the garden and pull some tomatoes, pick a few green beans for dinner, or hoe out a few weeds. When she did, she thanked the Lord for good land.

One day when she and Arthur were sitting on the porch talking, she thought of something John had once said and she began to laugh.

"What's so funny, Ma?" Arthur asked.

"I was just thinkin' about Cena and how naughty she used to be. She was always into everything, not afraid of anything, and she tried everything. I often thought she'd probably kill herself tryin' to do some outlandish deed—used to worry me nearly to death. And when she grew up and met you, she was still mighty feisty. When you two got married, one day I said to John, 'I wonder how Arthur will get along with Cena—he's so quiet!'

"And John said, 'I think Arthur knows that it's a sad house when the hen crows and the rooster is silent. He can handle Cena!'"

"What's that about a hen crowin'?" Cena stuck her head out the door. "I heard the last of that and it sounds just like somethin' Pa would say!"

Julia and Arthur just laughed.

Most of the time Julia was content to sit on the back porch and look at the rolling countryside, to hear the cattle lowing as they came in to the barn in the evenings, and to see the crops grow. She loved to hear the rhythmic thump of Cena's churn, and longed to once more get out and feel soft, moist earth between her bare toes. *Wouldn't it be nice,* she thought, *to be able to give John a cool drink at the end of a planted row? How I still miss John!*

"Cena, I have no doubtin' that this'll be my last move. I feel good to be back on a farm. I started my days on a farm and I'll end 'em on a farm. What could give me more joy than that?"

In the evenings she and Cena spent many hours together on the porch. One balmy evening when Arthur had gone back to the fields for a while after supper, Julia called, "Cena—"

"Yes, Mom. I'm washin' up the dishes."

"Let 'em go for a while. Come on out here on the porch and set a spell. I want to talk to you."

That was unusual for her mother to ask her to stop in the middle of any job, being the worker she was. But Cena came out wiping her hands on her apron. Cena was a very pretty woman, tall and heavy with curly brown hair and twinkling hazel eyes. She was as feisty as when she was a child, and always found something to laugh about. But she wasn't laughing today because she was worried about her mother. She could see Julia was rapidly failing. "Yes, Mom—? What's on your mind today?"

Julia looked out over the land. Her hands were shaking and she rolled and unrolled a handkerchief "It's purty here . . . a restful place to end my days. I—I want to tell you somethin', Cena, been thinkin' about it for a long time now. It's hard for me to tell it, and maybe it'd be better just to die without the tellin'."

She sighed. "I've never told any of the rest of the young'uns. John knew about it, of course, but we agreed that the young'uns didn't need to know. But I've made up my mind, and I want to tell you."

"It sounds serious, Ma. What is it?"

"It's about your sister Eva Jane's daddy. Eva Jane never knew about this before she died—" Julia wiped her eyes. She still grieved over Eva Jane's death. "And I don't think her young'uns ever ought to know either. It'll only bring 'em grief. Of course, all my brothers knowed about all this goin' on, but they didn't mention it to anybody. For years before they died, they never mentioned it to me anymore, either."

"Ma—if it's somethin' that's gonna upset you so much, maybe you just ought to forget about it. I don't like anything to upset you now, it isn't good for you."

"No, Cena, I feel I want to tell you this now." Julia had difficulty beginning her story, but though her lips were trembling, she went on.

"When I was fourteen years old my ma died and I wanted to make my own way. So I went to live with a neighbor man and wife—I was goin' to earn my keep on their farm. . ."

Cena sat in great astonishment and tears as Julia poured out the story of her life with Ellie and Solly Crawford, and the pain and sorrow before she married John. Her mind was very clear, and she was crying and shaking with remembering. Some of the words were hard to say.

"Oh, Mom—! I can see why you didn't want us to know! I can't believe that awful man did all those things to you! Didn't his wife know? How could she not know what was going on? She must've been awful dumb not to have caught on to something!"

Julia shook her head. "I don't know how she couldn't think that somethin' was wrong but——"

"Oh, Mom—" Cena wept, "I feel so sorry for what that man did to you and what you had to go through— How in the world did you ever keep that secret all these years? It must've tore you up to have to keep it all inside. Did you and Dad ever talk about it?"

"No. Not much after the first time I talked to him about it. John knew it weren't my fault. He just couldn't stand to think about it so we never mentioned it anymore. I was surprised that he would want to marry me after he knew—I thought I wasn't good enough for him."

"But of course he thought you *were* good. He *knew* you were good! Nothing of that was your fault!"

"Even though it was such a long time ago, Cena, sometimes I think of it and feel some of the things all over again. I just got to thinkin' now that because the whole community where I come from knew about it—somebody might say somethin' to you sometime. It's not so far from here, you know. It's a wonder nobody ever mentioned it."

"No, Mom. Nobody ever said a single word about you at all. I'd 've been sure to hear it."

Julia nodded. "I'm thankful for that. But I wanted you to know. You've been takin' such good care of me and I didn't want to die without all the truth bein' told to you. Now I can rest easy about it all."

Julia leaned back in her chair exhausted. She had done it, and by telling Cena, she relaxed. "I don't feel like I'll be here much longer, Cena. I'm old and I'm tired, and my days are spent. Soon I'm goin' to Heaven to be with your Pa. It won't be long—the Lord is so good."

So after more than half a century, Julia and her daughter wept together for the sorrow that young Julia had endured. And they thanked God that He had kept Julia; that His grace had been sufficient—even bountiful.

When they fell silent, shadows had lengthened on the porch and soon Arthur came in. Julia and Cena were glad that Arthur couldn't see their tears.

CHAPTER THIRTY-EIGHT
OUR WONDERFUL DAY

The day came on June 15, 1948, when Julia seemed to slip from reality in Cena's bedroom and enter a half-and-half world. Her body was on the bed, but moments, bright and sad, were dancing in her mind—whirling, like a kaleidoscope with all the minute colors blending into one another . . .

She didn't want anybody to find her. A great heaviness crushed her chest because her mother had died and now she was alone in the old haymow. Her brothers were calling her but she didn't want to go out because she heard the sound of nails being hammered into a box. She struggled, but it was no more than a faint jerk of her hand and a tightening of her breath. Strange that she should hear Cena's voice saying, "I think she's going, Arthur."

Suddenly Julia was afraid, rigid with fear. She shivered and Cena drew another blanket over her frail form. But the blanket was too heavy, it was pressing her down. Somebody was rustling paper—but to Julia it was corn harvest time and she was down in Mr. Crawford's south field among the rustling corn. And Mr. Crawford's face was evil.

Then she was working in a hotel room—she was putting something away in a dresser and a man named John was thanking her—

"John said, ''til we meet for our wonderful day. . .'" She murmured. "That's what John said."

"What did she say, Arthur?" Cena asked softly.

"Something about 'a wonderful day'—"

Moments—fusing—blending. Somebody said, "She seems to be rallying a little—her pulse is stronger than it has been for some time."

Julia's eyes were closed, but a faint smile hovered around her wrinkled mouth. Of course her pulse was strong! Wasn't she twenty-one years old and hadn't she just married her John—the man she loved? She was feeding their children chicken and wedding cake. Strange that a chair would be rocking on top of a trunk.

Moments—spinning—swirling. Then the kaleidoscope stopped dancing, and moments—bright and dark of all her years—began to merge into gray shadows and recede from her. Julia could now see a hill and a faint light.

"Julia! Julia!" John's voice! John was calling her! She hadn't heard his voice for twenty-seven years, but she was making no mistake. A great, suffocating happiness swept over her and her heart pounded wildly against her ribs.

Cena was holding her hand and felt Julia catch her breath.

John was calling her! Julia stepped lightly, joyfully, young and beloved from her wrinkled, white-haired shell on the bed, and started running toward John's voice. Her hair tumbled out of its pins, the way John liked to see it, fell in a mass of black curls down her back and streamed out in the wind as she ran.

"Julia! Julia!"

"I'm comin', John!" There! She could see him—tall, young, handsome—just a little farther up the hill. The light grew brighter behind him. Everything else fell away. Shadows—they were only shadows behind her.

Childhood, sorrow; girlhood, sorrow; marriage, all the hard but happy years with John; sorrow, and lonely mists at the last. They were nothing but shadows. Her whole life was only a prelude to the supreme joy of this immortal morning. Floating, laughing, beautiful, lithe of body and perfect in love, Julia reached up and John caught her hand. They stood gazing at each other, drinking in the moment, knowing they had an eternity of moments like this to come. With their arms around each other, they turned and walked up the hill.

Precious
in the sight of the Lord
is the
death of His saints.

CAST A LONG SHADOW

Book V

RUTH

1946 - 1960

CHAPTER THIRTY-NINE
Back to India

Ruth and J.T. were sent to live and work in Belgaum, a medium-sized city about 300 miles south of Bombay. Belgaum is a bilingual area, on the border of Kanarese and Marathi languages. They both accepted this assigment with joy.

J.T. had first been taken to India by his missionary parents when he was three years old and they lived in a remote area. His playmates were the servants' children. While his father was out preaching in villages, the cook was entertaining little J.T. with tales of the *devva (devils)*. He early learned to love Indian legends and history, and the Indian people. So it was natural that God called him as a missionary, back to his people. Many of them had heard little if anything about Jesus.

He spoke Kanarese language beautifully—many Indians said he spoke it better than they did. After just a few months of study, while Ruth was in America during the war, he successfully passed all three extremely difficult Kanarese exams—an accomplishment never achieved before or since by any foreigner.

Immediately he began to write Christian lyrics—in Indian style music. In English songs, words rhyme at the end of the line *if* they rhyme. But in Kanarese, poetry rhymes at the beginning of the line. J.T. rhymed his Christian lyrics *both* at the beginning and end of the lines, and the people thought he was a genius. His lyrics were put into books, and wherever Ruth and J.T. went to visit villages, they could hear the congregations singing his songs.

In Belgaum, Ruth began learning Kanarese again. But the children learned both Kanarese and Marathi, because they played with Indian children from both sections. By the time Sheila was three years old she was proficient. If a villager came to the door, Ruth could usually tell by the way he was dressed and his turban was tied which language he spoke. If she decided it was Marathi, she would send Sheila to the door. Ruth could understand some Marathi, but couldn't speak it—it is totally different from Kanarese.

Sheila, without being told, seldom missed her cue. She'd look at the person, and then ask him in his language what he wanted.

Sometimes the man wanted some help from her father, sometimes to be taken to the government hospital, perhaps some worm medicine for his children, his children to be admitted to the mission school, or some other need.

Sheila would then translate for her mother.

J.T. was appointed as district superintendent of *two* adjacent districts. That meant hundreds of miles to travel in his jeep, many village churches and schools to oversee, and dozens of pastors and teachers to lead and nurture. The church in India at that time was not very self-sufficient; the district superintendent was looked to for everything. Village preachers often had little education, and church building programs lagged. There were few government schools in villages, so mission schools were imperative.

Together Ruth and J.T. wrote hundreds of letters to raise money from folks back home to dig village wells, and either build or improve village churches, clinics, schools, parsonages, and teachers' houses. J.T. also helped village economy by starting Christian cooperative societies. Indian Christians were mostly from the outcaste section, and usually worked for very poor wages for the high caste people. J.T. acquired loans from government for them to buy raw materials so that Christians could start their own small businesses. Some farmed, some worked with leather (only outcaste people will touch a dead cow), some made rope, mats, brooms, wove everyday saris, and some kept village stores.

J.T.'s preaching kept him away from home a great deal—often for two or three weeks at a time. It was unthinkable to come home every night—the roads were too bad and he was too far away. Many villages were off main roads, so the jeep was essential.

J.T. spied one village on top of a very steep hill. No missionary had ever visited it before and J.T. was determined to go up. When he finally roared to the top in low-four-wheel-drive, the villagers met him wide-eyed. They exclaimed, "Since the day of creation a wheel has never been able to climb this hill. We don't even have bullock carts up here."

J.T. usually took with him a cook boy, food supplies, camp cot and bedding, and prepared to stay awhile. That's the only way he felt he could do a good job of preaching or helping, to stay with the people and get to know them. Ruth stayed on the mission compound, overseeing her seventy-five village boys in their hostel.

Every time J.T. returned home, a long line of people waited to see him. The word spread in minutes, "Sahib's home!" and they sat on the porch while he unpacked the jeep. Each one had a need.

But after coming from dusty villages, J.T. always took a bath before seeing anyone. And that was about the only time in the day when Ruth could talk to him. Other people's problems seemed too pressing.

A bucket of hot water from the reservoir in the kitchen wood stove was hurried to the bathroom (running water). The only way Ruth could talk to him was to supervise his bath! As he stood and soaped himself, then poured quart-cups of rinse water over himself, he would tell Ruth all the news of the preachers, teachers, and village life.

She'd tell him about all the happenings of the compound, especially house problems. "Honey, the rats chewed more labels off some food cans in the storeroom, and yesterday a horde of monkeys played on the roof again, leaving broken tiles. We'll have to fix that roof before the monsoons in June."

And J.T. would say, "Well, my darling, that's better than having cobras. I'm glad you can take it!"

But the rats did upset her. Great rats running all over their house every night. "Honey, they chase each other snickering around my bed, knowing I can't sleep. Every night they get into my tall flour can on the kitchen table—I didn't see how they get that tight lid off. But last night I heard a familiar scratching. I stood in the kitchen door in the bright moonlight and watched a big rat stand on his hind legs and push the lid of the flour can with his nose until the lid clattered onto the floor."

"Really? What did you do?"

"It's what *he* did. In a second that rat was down in my flour. If I could have caught him, I'd have dusted him off, for American flour is so precious here in India. But when I swooped down, he escaped, like a white ghost running across the floor."

"Tonight I'll kill some with my hockey stick."

"I hope you do. Every night I'm awakened by their thumping around in the storeroom—sounds like a robber invasion."

Rats eat anything. They ate their toilet paper which is an expensive luxury item in India. They ate holes in the tents which were stacked on a side verandah, awaiting camp meeting time. They got into the table drawer of the kitchen and chewed on the handles of knives and ate half of Ruth's rubber scraper. That was the last American scraper she had, so she got mad.

She got a Siamese cat and kept it inside. That cat slunk around at night, and those rats suddenly got quiet as mice. They kept the cat every night in our house by the banyan tree, and began to enjoy some nights of unbroken sleep . . . until then they suddenly discovered they were jumping. In fact, the whole place was jumping. Fleas. Fleas! Everywhere! Ruth's family jumped at odd moments and scratched in odd spots. Then they shooed the cat out the door.

They squirted DDT everywhere, but the fleas loved it. They still hopped, and the Seamands family still jumped and scratched. And with the cat gone, the rats came back—they didn't mind the fleas. They were used to them.

Ruth said, "Maybe we have to make a choice. I don't know whether to take the rats without cats and without fleas, or to take the cats and fleas without the rats. Maybe we have no choice."

It really wasn't her choice. The cat had kittens, new fleas hopped into being by the thousands, the rats had little ratlets, and it was all Ruth could do to keep from having the screaming meamies.

Having a tame cat and kittens on the doorstep wasn't enough. Wild cats invaded their attic. Several wild cats, or civet cats, came to take the place of the first one they shot. Those civet cats ran and howled and fought all night on the ceiling over their heads. So she then had cats on the doorstep, civet cats in the attic, fleas in her bed, rats everywhere, and bats in her belfry.

She wished she could read a nice, calm American newspaper!

* * * *

Sylvia and Sheila of course didn't like the rats—they wanted something they could pet. So in the beginning they had a couple of love birds, an Irish setter, two cocker spaniels and a horse of an unknown breed. But one day the headman of a village, a good friend of J.T.'s, sent a messenger to say that he had captured two small deer in the jungle and wanted to give them to Sylvia and Sheila.

Of course the two kids were wild to get two baby deer. Ruth and J.T. stood there with the village messenger discussing whether to accept them.

J.T. was a pushover. The next day they all drove to the village in their jeep and returned with the two deer in the back. Sheila sat with them, holding the male deer's head on her lap. She didn't want them to be frightened.

They needed more room for a zoo. They had to keep the jeep outside, and tie the two deer in one corner of the garage and the horse in the other. Ruth said one day, "Next, we'll have to move out of the bungalow and add an elephant. Of course, we need a parrot too."

That village headman must have been psychic! The next day somebody called Ruth to the front door, and there stood the same man who had given them the deer. He hadn't brought a baby elephant, to Ruth's surprise. He brought a parrot.

They put the parrot, which they named Popeye, into an old cage. Sylvia gave Popeye half a banana and he ate it right out of her hand without taking half a finger off. Sheila fed slices of bread to the deer whom they called Bambie and Flower. Their birds' names were Goldie and Chirpie; the dogs were called Blackie, Lucky, and Rosie; the horse's name was Rusty.

Sheila also had a guinea hen who slept on the roof every night in outright defiance of the civet cats and snakes. But the guinea hen made so much noise that Ruth once said, "If that hen doesn't simmer down, she's going to simmer in a stew some day!"

"Mother! You wouldn't do that to my hen, would you?"

"I come from a long line of farmers, and we eat lots of chicken," Ruth told her horrified daughter. "And I'm stunned at the size of our zoo. How can we feed them on a missionary's salary?"

"Mommie, some of them will eat grass."

They had some "naturals" which they didn't feed, but which joined the zoo anyhow. They were the big black-faced, white-whiskered monkeys which jumped on the roof continually, breaking tiles so that every monsoon season they had to buy more buckets to catch the leaks.

Ever-present cobras slid around the grounds, so the children could never play in tall grass. Striped kraits—tiny, deadly snakes—adored the coolness of their bathroom's stone floors. Scorpions sometimes were seen—fortunately, not too many. Of course, they could never forget the jungle cats which occupied their attic and fought with the rats which occupied the whole house.

Out in the yard lived a small family of mongoose which killed the snakes. They were beloved! Sometimes the Seamands family looked up into their eight skylight windows high above the living room, and in every window they could see monkey faces peering down at them. It was the opposite of most zoos—there monkeys are the ones in cages and people peer at them. Here the monkeys were free and the Seamands family sometimes had eerie feelings!

Any house rocks with children, but their place hummed, cawed, whinnied, barked, whistled, and shrieked.

* * * *

On June 20, 1948, Ruth received this cablegram from her parents:

> GRANDMA JULIA DIED AT CENA'S. SHE WAS BURIED IN BONER CEMETERY BESIDE GRANDPA JOHN. WE MISS YOU AND LOVE YOU — MOM AND DAD.

Ruth mourned for Grandma Julia. *Grandma was so good for us. Though she had a hard life, she showed us how to live. She has cast a long and blessed shadow over all our lives. Without her I would not be here. Thank you, Lord Jesus, for Your grace through her to all of us.*

CHAPTER FORTY
Python and Praise

Camp meeting time rolled around. J.T. called coolies to help unpack all the mission tents from the side verandah, nearly a hundred of them, and hired coolie women to spread them out on the grass over their fourteen-acre compound. Then the women set to work mending holes caused by rats during the past year of storage. While the women worked, their babies crawled all over the tents, dressed only in shirts and wool caps. Village babies never wear diapers; consequently, the Seamandses often had stinky tents.

With an accumulation of patches acquired over several years, the tents looked like the forty-year wilderness tents of the Children of Israel. But the Christian campers paid no attention to the patches at camp meeting. They moved into the tents and hoped the snakes would stay outside or down by the river.

One evening before they went off to camp, Ruth and J.T. were invited to dinner at the home of an army captain who lived across town. As they neared his house they had to cross a bridge, and Ruth noticed a small blue light burning under the bridge.

"Why is a blue light burning under the bridge at the side of your house?" asked Ruth, as they entered the captain's house.

Their host answered, "A very large python about eighteen feet long lives under that bridge. Some Hindus nearby worship the snake. Every night one of them lights the blue light and puts eggs and milk there for the python to eat. It is well fed, never leaves its bridge home, so it doesn't eat up any dogs, cats, rabbits, or children."

"You must be scared to live so close to that snake all the time. And you don't even have any screens on your house! I wouldn't sleep a wink if I knew a big python was that close to me!"

He laughed, "Aw, I'm not afraid of this snake. A python is not dangerous unless it is hungry. We've lived here two years, and that light has been on every night. That's the sign to everybody that the snake has been fed, so children can freely play around."

During dinner Ruth kept her feet up on the rung of her chair, as if that would have helped any with a hungry python around, and she kept looking at the shadowed, open doorway behind her.

Even though conveniences were few, Ruth and J.T. always enjoyed camp meeting. Ruth and Joseph, her cook, went out two days before camp started, unloaded supplies and got their camping kitchen in order.

J.T. took out a work detail at the same time, and set up their tent. Then he and his coolies began to dig long slit trenches to be used as latrines by the village people. Ruth and J.T. had their own little private trench in their own little private latrine tent. Ruth simply could not use a community one.

When the preaching meetings started, one of the standard announcements at *every* service was that every person must *be sure* to use the dug latrines, and help keep the campgrounds clean. With 500 people on the grounds, if people went to the toilet anywhere they wanted to, as people do in villages, living would become difficult within a few days.

Many times American visitors came to their camp meetings, and of course they could not understand what was being said, since it was being said in the Kanarese language. Ruth always sat by them to translate. Everytime she had to translate the latrine announcement, they usually got so tickled they were almost hysterical, especially with the final instruction, "After doing your job there, rake some dirt into the trench to cover it up!" What an announcement for a church meeting!

Two days before their 1948 camp, while J.T. was doggedly digging with sweat pouring down his face, Ruth said, "Honey, somebody should award you a Ph.D. of B.L.D., that is a Ph.D. of Better Latrine Digging."

He wasn't impressed, just wiped the sweat and said, "This is one job they didn't tell me about in seminary. If I ever teach mission classes, I'll teach this, but I'll give it a fancy name I'll call it Techniques to Tropical Ministry, or How to Make a Toilet for 500."

The physical side of life took second place during camp meeting time. Village Christians came to worship and went home with their spirits revived. Many came to hear the Gospel for the first time. Some were converted and became Christians, in spite of the persecution they knew they would have to face when they went home to their villages.

Not only poor villagers came, but also many middle class people from nearby towns. Teachers, lawyers, bankers, businessmen of all kinds came, some out of curiosity.

J.T. started that camp meeting when they first went to Belgaum. His father, an old hand at jungle camp meetings, came to help him. They were able to rent a few acres of land by the Khanapur River and were thankful because there they had plenty of water and firewood. Every year their jungle camp meeting grew.

Singing was spirited and a big part of the meetings, because Indian people like to sing. Many brought their drums, horns, cymbals; the rest clapped their hands in time with the music. Sometimes they sang all night. Sleeping was difficult.

Preaching there is different than in America. Indian people feel they haven't even heard a sermon if it lasts less than an hour and a half; they will sit for a very long time. So the minister preaches for a while, then bursts into song, and the congregation joins in. People get up and stretch and sing a while, then sit down cross-legged on the mats again and the preacher goes on.

Sometimes a meeting lasts three hours. If babies get hungry, mothers nurse them there. It is their custom, and nobody is embarrassed. Mothers don't want to miss a word. If older children get tired, the mother unrolls some Indian bread from a handkerchief; they eat it, lie down and go to sleep.

Meetings are held under the trees, where a large tent-roof (pandal) has been raised. The camp "walks" (or happens) in the month of February, for that is the dry season.

This seven-day meeting fulfills a great need for Indian Christians. Living in a country which is so predominantly Hindu, with Hindu customs and holidays being celebrated all the time, Christians must have a substitute. This camp makes them feel that Christians are not just a small isolated group missing all the fun of religious celebrations.

Many of the songs they like to sing are those which J.T. wrote. The Bible speaks of many gifts, but God must have thought up an extra one for J.T. The ability to write Christian lyrics in the Kanarese language is a special gift to Christians in the Belgaum area.

One night at camp when it was J.T.'s turn to preach, he changed the order of the service. After the singing he said to the audience, "We are in a courtroom tonight. I am going to call to the witness stand four witnesses. I will appoint three judges to bring in a verdict. I am appointing my father, one village preacher, and the third a village layman, as judges. After they hear all the witnesses, they must bring in a verdict about Christ. Now I call the first witness. He is to tell us what Christ has done for him."

The first witness was a simple villager, uneducated, dressed in a dhoti and turban, with a long-tailed shirt hanging down under his coat. He spoke in poor Kanarese, but with great sincerity. He said, "Friends, I was born an untouchable in the Hindu religion, but I heard of Christ through missionary J.T. Seamands. It took a while, but I decided to give up my idols and put my trust in this Christ. I was an untouchable, but God touched me. I was an outcaste, but God took me in. I was born in lowly circumstances, but God lifted me up and made me His child. Now I am following Him."

When he finished, the whole audience shouted, "Jaya Christ!" Victory to Christ.

The second witness was called. He was better dressed, spoke in high-class Kanarese, obviously was well educated. He addressed the audience, "My friends, I was born a high caste (Brahmin) in the Hindu religion. I was proud like the Pharisees of the New Testament. I very carefully observed the ceremonies prescribed by my religion, such as a daily bath, the daily worship of the gods, recitation of my sacred scriptures and slokas. I wanted to find peace, but I could not find it in my religion.

"Then I heard of Christ Jesus and accepted Him as my Savior. He pulled me down from my self-righteousness, and He humbled me. I used to despise the untouchables, and would have nothing to do with them whatever but now I can accept them and love them as my brothers. I am now a disciple of Christ."

Another wave of "Jaya Christ!" from the congregation.

The third witness was called to the platform. He too was well dressed. He said, "Friends, I was born a Muslim and followed the prophet Mohammed. I was very religious. I memorized portions of the Koran and carefully kept the rules of my religion. I prayed five times a day and gave alms to the poor. I observed faithfully the Ramzan fasts—one of our most important occasions. During Ramzan month, no true Mohammedan will eat or drink anything during the hours of daylight. We get up at three o'clock in the morning and cook a big meal and eat. Then nothing else touches our lips until after dark. We are not even supposed to swallow saliva. I prayed much, denied myself pleasure with my wife, but nothing ever gave me peace in heart and mind.

"Then I began to read the New Testament, and I saw my sins and I saw my Savior. When I came to the words of Jesus, 'I am the way the truth and the life,' I felt my search was at an end. I saw that Jesus was more than just a prophet like Mohammed. He was the Redeemer. So I trusted Him and became His disciple. I was cast out of my home and disinherited by my father, but God took me into His kingdom and made me His son. I used to despise these Hindus because they worshiped idols, but now God helps me to love them."

"Jaya Christ!" rose from every throat.

Then J.T. called the fourth witness. He was educated and well dressed. He began his witness. "Friends, I was born a high caste Hindu, but during my youth I became disgusted with the old-fashioned ideas and idolatry of my religion. I knew those idols could not answer prayer. I decided that religion was all useless.

"I got in contact with some Communists and was attracted by their promises of a better way of life for our country. So I joined them and became a Communist. But when they started to teach me to lie, to destroy, and even to kill if need be, for the Communist causes, I began to see that Communism is not the answer to a good way of life. I had no stomach for killing.

"One day somebody gave me a New Testament and I began to read it carefully. I decided that this is true religion, and that Jesus Christ alone can uplift the world. So I decided to follow Him and I became a Christian. Now I am striving to help establish His Kingdom upon the earth. They say Communism is revolutionary, but Christianity is the world's most revolutionary force!"

Another "Jaya Christ!"

After the four men had finished speaking, J.T. stepped between them, the former untouchable and high caste on his right, the former Muslim and Communist on his left. Then he said to the audience, "I am a man from the West. The same Christ that these friends found here in India, I found in America. When I put my trust in Him, He changed my life and made me His child. Now I feel that I am a brother to these four witnesses."

Then he put his arms around all four of them and asked the three judges for their verdict concerning Jesus Christ.

The judges went into a huddle while the congregation sang a triumphant Kanarese song. When the song ended, the Indian pastor stepped forward as spokesman for the judges. He said, "Friends in this congregation, having heard the witness of these four, and how Christ has redeemed them, our verdict as judges is: Christ can save people of all castes, creeds, and countries. He can save people from East and West. He is Savior of *all* who believe on Him."

By this time the congregation could sit still no longer. They stood and, with arms raised high, shouted in unison, "Yesu Masih Maharajah Ki Jai!" Victory to Jesus the Messiah!

No one present at that celebration will ever forget that camp meeting.

CHAPTER FORTY-ONE
A Morning in the Mission House

Their low, rambling, laterite-stone house squatted under spreading banyan branches. Long banyan trailers, propelled by Indian sun, searched for secure places to spring into life as new trees. But they found no anchor on the red roof tiles. In frustration they groped over the eaves, then cascaded down the ruddy stone sides.

In the trees, twenty-pound langur monkeys courted and played tag, jumping from limb to roof, thumping open cracks in the tile. From the kitchen below, charcoal smoke, blending with pungent odors of curry and dhal, drifted up, seeping heavenward through every fracture.

Inside the house Ruth heard their doorbell. Not a *real* doorbell—someone coughed on the porch. Through the open door, she saw three strangers standing there.

"Salaam, Mem-sahib," the tonga driver softly put his palms together in greeting and nodded, his nine-yard turban bouncing forward a little on his head. "I brought you some guests from the station, Madam." He spoke in the Kanarese language.

Ruth was surprised. "Station? I . . ."

A portly American stepped forward, taking command of the situation, holding out his big hand to shake Ruth's. "You're Mrs. Seamands," he told her.

She looked up and nodded. She already knew that.

"I am Congressman Charles Crow and this is my wife, Susan."

"Oh, Congressman! I am so sorry. I would have met you at the station, but I thought you were coming tomorrow."

Mr. Crow brushed aside her apology. "It isn't your fault. We got an earlier plane."

"Well—come in—come in." Ruth turned, her eyes darting here and there to see if the living room was in order. She also wished she was wearing something better than a housedress, bobby sox, and saddle shoes. But raising one eyebrow and making the best of it, she looked down at the shoes, stuck out her foot and bravely remarked, "I hear these are all the rage for fourteen-year-olds in America."

The Congressman's little wife nodded and smiled.

"It's so nice to have Americans visit us out here. We get lonely for home folks." Ruth paid the tonga *walla* and dismissed him. "Now, please sit here in the living room—your room is not quite ready. I was just about to make up your beds, but my ayah can do it. I'll bring you some tea and biscuits."

They sat quietly in low conversation with each other as Ruth brought in the tea tray. Strong Indian tea, boiled with milk and sugar and a pinch of ground cardamom. "Estation tea" they called it, because that's what they always drank when they traveled on trains and stopped at stations. "Here you are. One needs liquids often here—the heat, you know. And try some of these biscuits, uh, cookies. I made them this morning."

"You call them biscuits here?" Susan asked.

"Oh, the British call them that. What we call biscuits, the British call scones. These are just plain old American oatmeal cookies."

They drank thirstily. "This is very good tea—and I love the cookies," exclaimed Susan. "I didn't expect oatmeal cookies in India." They put their cups back on the tray.

Ruth was just pouring more tea into their cups when a large, black-faced, white-whiskered langur monkey loped from the guest room, through the corner of her vast living room, and out the front door. Susan Crow, eyes bulging, screamed, quickly covered her mouth with one hand, and held both feet up off the floor. Then she asked, "D—do they live here with you?"

"Well," Ruth answered, "not with my permission." She tried to calm Susan. "Don't worry about that monkey—he's probably afraid of you, too. Because we don't have any screens yet, they sneak into the bath rooms when they find the outside doors open. They like to eat the soap."

"Eat the *soap?"* They echoed in unison—their cultural horizons widening with every passing second.

Ruth shrugged. "I guess that's because they don't have any toothpaste!"

Charles Crow boomed—if a crow *can* boom. "Eat the *soap?* I thought that monkey had *rabies!* He was foaming at the mouth!"

"No—they just like soap. Sorry—you'll probably find their teeth prints on your new bar—it's the last one I have. Just keep your outside bathroom door closed."

Susan quavered, "M—maybe this isn't a good time for us to visit India, Charles."

He patted her shoulder and whispered in her ear, "We'll face it together, Dear."

Ruth smiled at them. She remembered how she felt when first in India. "Don't worry—it's a good time. Drink your tea. This is really a nice, quiet place most of the time. Of course, when the children are all here, then it's a different story . . ."

Before she could finish her friendly defense of their living quarters, they heard a great crash and yell coming from the wall. That was followed by a series of heavy whacking sounds and more shouts. Susan whimpered, drew her feet up on the couch and sat cross-legged. "C—Char—les? . . ."

The rotund VIP, used to taking charge, jumped straight up. "WHAT was THAT?"

Ruth sighed. "That's just my noisy husband. He's in that storeroom—" she pointed to two small double doors on the far side of the room. "He's killing rats in there with a hockey stick."

Two heads swiveled. Susan squealed, "RATS? You—you mean *big* ones?"

Ruth nodded, and Susan shivered, her shoulders hunched up to her ears.

Charles' mouth fell open. Repeating after Ruth like a child in kindergarten, he quoted, "He's killing rats in that storeroom with a hockey stick." He looked dazed.

Ruth couldn't help but giggle. "He's pretty good, too. They can't get away from his flying arm fast enough. We can't keep rats out of the storeroom—they drive us batty rattling cans all the time."

"Cans? What kind of cans?"

"Big cans. We have them made in the bazaar—with tight lids."

"What's in the cans?"

"Oh—food like cheese, flour, sugar, and also pantie hose, slips, bras, silk and nylon things—lots of things. We can them because rats will eat anything. They love nylon." Ruth kept talking to try to make her guests feel at home. "Those rats eat all the labels off of food cans, too, and sometimes we don't know what we're going to eat for supper. Whatever we open is our supper surprise. Sometimes it's gulosh with meat, and sometimes it's a can of jelly. But I always make bread to go with it."

The VIP and Susan sat stunned, allowing their tea to get cold.

After a minute of reverent silence, the storeroom doors banged open and J.T. came out grinning, carrying his hockey stick. "Got six that time!" He noticed his flabbergasted guests. "Oh—I didn't know we have company."

Ruth said, "I didn't think you heard our guests come in—you couldn't hear anything over the noise of your war with the elements!" She turned. "This is Congressman and Mrs. Crow. Charles and Susan."

"I'm sorry. Welcome! Nice to have Americans out here. Please excuse me a minute—I'll get a basket for the dead. *Molli*—" he called.

"Yes, Sahib?" answered the gardener from outside the back door.

"Bring in that big basket. We have more dead rats to dispose of." Then turning to Ruth he said, "I'll wash my hands and then I'd like some tea." He exited toward their bathroom, carrying his hockey stick.

Susan covered her eyes with a dainty, lace-edged handkerchief and leaned her head back against the couch.

Their barefoot, wizened gardener appeared. He wore a bright red turban on his head, and a once-white *dothi* tied around his skinny hips and bowed legs. He carried an oversized round basket. Bits of grass and banyan leaves clung to its insides. He disappeared into the storeroom and they heard some thuds. The molli soon re-appeared, lifting the basket to the top of his turban, as he quietly padded from the room.

Susan missed the tableau, but Charles watched, his eyes rolling and following the molli's every move. His face showed no expression.

J.T. came back, and Ruth poured a cup of tea for him. He sipped his tea and munched on an oatmeal cookie.

Stout-hearted American Crow gulped, cleared his throat, searched for and finally found his voice. "W—wha—what will he do with those rats? Bury them?"

J.T. shrugged. "No, we don't bother to bury them. We believe in nature's own disposition."

Stalwart American Crow, curious, asked, "How does nature do that?"

"We just throw them out——the crows eat them."

Susan moaned and quietly fainted.

Honorable American Crow turned white.

CHAPTER FORTY-TWO
Rajah's Wedding

Many things about missionary life were hard and lonely. J.T. and Ruth missed family and friends at home, and having them see their children grow up. They missed American food.

In India after World War II, items like sugar, rice, and wheat were rationed for ten more years. They never had enough.

For ten years Pearl and Henry sent Ruth box after box of flour, sugar, cake and bread and soup mixes of all kinds—and things they could not find in Belgaum, like tissues. One special box gave the whole family much pleasure. From good friends, the Mercers, at Christmas time they received two cases—one of Baby Ruth candy bars and one of soft toilet paper. Happy days!

No hotels were nearby, so travelers often came to the mission house asking for a place to stay. Ruth and J.T. hosted VIPs, many ordinary people of different races, and once three rabid European communists. Of course, Ruth didn't know they were rabid communists—even if she had, she'd not have turned them down.

They arrived at 9:00 p.m., their big noisy van stirring up dust under the portico. "Can we stay with you? Someone said you take in travelers. We've driven from the northern border of India." They spoke in stilted English. "Actually, we've driven all across Europe."

They looked like it. Their clothing must have been slept in and traveled in for many days. A slight breeze wafted odors proclaiming they desperately needed a bath.

"Have you had any dinner?" Ruth asked, as they stiffly climbed down from their van.

"No, we found no place. We had some cheese and bread with us at noon."

"Come in," Ruth's hospitable soul urged them. "The fire is out in my wood stove and the servants have gone home. You can stay, but you'll have to wait while I build a new fire and cook something for you. The stove will also heat bath water."

The three visitors lolled on wicker chairs, drank some water, tried to talk to J.T. and keep from dozing at the same time.

Within an hour Ruth made a fire, heated four bowls of left-over soup, sliced a whole loaf of her homemade bread, buttered it and made oven toast. Nine fried eggs accompanied the toast, with fresh oranges and bananas for dessert. She called them to the table.

They wolfed every bit of food she had provided, washed it down with Indian tea, and burped loudly. During the meal J.T. and Ruth sat with them hoping their bath water would soon be hot.

With his belly full, one of the men asked, "This is a mission house? What kind of mission work do you do?"

J.T. thought they were really interested in Christian work. He answered sincerely, "Well, I go out and preach in villages, help to build churches, establish schools and clinics, teach Bible truths, try to help people with their everyday lives and show them how to find God. That keeps me quite busy."

The biggest smart aleck of the two retorted, "Well, I think it's stupid for you to spend your life here preaching to these people. Can't you see that Christianity has failed the world? It's in an awful mess. Only Communism can bring order out of this chaos!"

Ruth's spine instantly stiffened, but she remembered just in time she ought to show a Christian spirit. Right then her spirit didn't feel very Christian. She could barely keep from reminding them, "You idiots are enjoying hospitality, a meal, hot water for a bath, and you will have a bed tonight. That's *because* this is a mission house and we are here to preach the Gospel. Why didn't Communism provide you with all that?"

She was so upset she had a hard time sleeping that night, especially with fanatical nitwits sleeping in her guest rooms.

Missionary life was not all loneliness, crises, and hard work. Sometimes something unusual happened. Ever since they arrived in Belgaum, two of their best friends were His Highness, the Rajah of Sawantwadi, and his mother, Her Highness, the Rani. The Rajah was twenty-five years old, a strikingly handsome young man. He had the rank of a Lieutenant Colonel of the Maratha Light Infantry. For two years he was engaged to his own first cousin, the third daughter of the Maharajah of Baroda, and the wedding date finally rolled around.

The word *maharajah* refers to a more powerful ruler than just a plain rajah. The Rani of Sawantwadi was a sister of the Maharajah of Baroda and marriage is allowed in India between a sister's son and a brother's daughter. It's not allowed between a sister's daughter and a brother's son. So the sister and brother of

Sawantwadi and Baroda had decided their children should marry. The bride was ten years younger than her cousin, so he had to wait until she grew up.

A week before the wedding, the Rajah invited Ruth and J.T. to a garden party at his villa in Belgaum. Though their real palace was in Sawantwadi, they preferred to live near Belgaum. Three days before the wedding, the Rajah and Rani gave a special dinner to which Ruth and J.T. were also invited. Ruth dressed up in her best Indian silk sari. J.T. said, "Honey, you look like a rani yourself."

They ate Indian style (though the Raji and Rani did not usually eat this way in their home), sitting cross-legged on the floor, with small wooden tables about six inches high. On top of each table was a big silver plate about sixteen inches across, with many different kinds of food, and around the plate were small silver bowls containing more food and spices. They ate Indian style with their right hands, and afterward servants came around and poured warm water over their hands from a large silver urn. Catching the dirty water was another big silver bowl.

In the place of honor, of course, sat the Rajah, in a gold brocade coat, with a red and gold turban on his head. He sat on a low chair crafted in silver and upholstered in red velvet, and he ate from solid gold dishes and drank from a gold glass.

On the day before the wedding, at his invitation, J.T. and Ruth drove with the Rajah in his Packard convertible, to Poona, where the ceremony was to be performed—about 200 miles. Part of the time he was driving eighty-five miles an hour, and they were scared. It's one thing to go eighty-five miles an hour in America, on superhighways, but it is quite another to go that fast in India, where the road is narrow, not even paved, and where around any bend may be a string of bullock carts, or monkeys, or cows, and from any side road a donkey or a person may wander.

For snacking on the trip, Ruth took along some cucumber sandwiches and homemade glazed doughnuts. The Rajah and Rani especially liked the doughnuts. They'd never tasted them before Ruth arrived on the scene in Belgaum.

The last ceremony for the Rajah before the wedding was a ceremonial bath, performed again by his married sisters, his aunt, and the married sisters of the bride.

Wearing a *dhoti* (straight piece of cloth tied around him pants-fashion) the Rajah was seated on a low silver table with his feet on a silver footstool. Around the table were five brass vessels of water, and around these vessels, and enclosing them and the table into one small space, was a saffron cord wound around seven times. One at a time, each married lady of his family took off her sandals and stepped into the sacred space. She dipped her right forefinger into red powder and touched his forehead, feet, and ears; then with almond paste did the same thing. Then she poured five small brass vessels of water over his head.

When his sisters and cousins had finished, the Rajah surprised Ruth by saying, "Ruth, you come here and get into this picture too. Pour some water over my head."

Shades of Christian ethics! What should she do? Should she take part in a Hindu ceremony, or insult a good friend by refusing? Deciding instantly for friendship, she took off her sandals, stepped barefooted into the enclosure, and poured two *chumboos* of water over his head. Then the cord was taken from the chumboos and carefully lifted up over his head. Everyone was careful not to touch him—that would have been bad luck for him.

A delicious curry and rice meal was served to all his guests that evening, and then they were shown to beautiful rooms in the houses of some of the Rajah's relatives. Ruth and J.T. slept fine in such unaccustomed luxury.

The next day, December 8, at exactly 5:56 p.m.—the auspicious hour according to the horoscope of the bride and groom, the wedding ceremony began. Guests were seated outside under a huge *pandal* (canopy) which was hung with orange and yellow curtains and strung with varicolored lights. The wedding procession was led by a twenty-five-piece police band. Then came the bridegroom in his Packard convertible, which looked different than it had the day before when the Rajah, J.T. and Ruth were speeding through dusty roads and villages. The car was completely washed, and covered with a blanket of roses. His chauffeur was driving.

The bridegroom, a descendant of the the famous warrior king of Indian history, Shivaji, looked like a figure out of a fairy tale himself, as he stepped down from his car and entered the canopy.

He was dressed in a gold brocade coat made like a frock coat, with no buttons, and tied at the side with a gold cord. Across his shoulders and back was solid gold-wire embroidery, intricately made with red satin to form the shape of a peacock—a fowl sacred to the Hindus. Hems of both his sleeves and the bottom of the coat were heavy with the same gold embroidery with red-velvet flowers.

He wore a Marathi *pugaree* (turban) of spun silk whose fibers had been dipped in melted gold. Over this was a gold crown set with diamonds and rubies, with gold tassels hanging down on either side of his face. He wore aiguillettes, because of his rank in the army, medals on his chest, five rows of precious pearls, and a big ruby ring. The jewels he wore were worth many thousands of dollars.

He carried a *dupartha* (jeweled sword), tied to his side with a golden chiffon sash. He wore soft shoes of gold brocade to match his coat, and the toes of the shoes curled up and over. These shoes were taken off when he entered the canopy. He wore the customary long white trousers, tight below the knee, big above with a drawstring in the waist, to afford ease when sitting cross-legged on the floor.

In the middle of the pandal was a platform of bricks, all decorated with flowers, and to this the groom made his way. Since J.T. and Ruth were his guests, they were on his side of the pandal, and did not see the bride enter.

She came from the opposite side, and as they both approached the platform, a red and gold curtain was held between them while four Hindu priests, chanted in Sanskrit. The guests stood, and on cue threw handfuls of rice on the couple while the chanting went on. After about ten minutes of this, with a burst of applause from the crowd and a blast of music from the band, the curtain between them dropped and they had their first look at one another for many months. She could see his face through her heavy veil, but he could not see hers, for in Hindu weddings the bride's face is totally covered at the start.

She was most gorgeous in a pink and gold sari, and wore strings of beautiful pearls and diamonds. The bride and groom then sat facing each other on the platform, seated on silk cushions, while the priests continued to chant in Sanskrit—and neither the bride nor the groom understood the Sanskrit language.

The Maharajah of Baroda, the bride's father, and his aides then came around garlanding everyone with flowers. Then they poured perfume, dipped from a silver bowl with tiny silver spoons, on the backs of their guests' hands.

After this the couple sat down on the platform again, but so many rajahs were milling around wishing them good luck that Ruth and J.T. couldn't see the bridal pair at all. They just had a good look at all the rajahs.

They had met, a rajah or two at some special functions, but here they were overwhelmed with pomp and glitter. Present were the Rajahs of Dhar, Dewas Jr., Gwalior, Kolhapur, Baroda, Joth, Akalot, Jamkhindi, Ramdurg, and Jewar—all in their own gold and jewels. Their families also wore their crown jewels. Nothing is better than a royal wedding to bring out the best everybody owns!

They could see stately Sikhs in purple or red, with jeweled swords at their sides, their long beards caught up in nets, rolled under and tucked up under beautifully fitted turbans. The servants standing around the pandal were also a harmony of color, in blue uniforms with orange and silver breastplates and wide gold bands about their waists, wearing turbans to match. Nearly 1,000 people had come to this wedding and were all milling about, talking to each other in many Indian languages.

About this time Ruth's friend, Rani Sahib, the groom's mother, saw that Ruth was lost behind so many rajahs. So she sent a servant to bring Ruth from the guest section to sit with her in the place of honor on a gold couch, just beside the platform where the ceremony was going on. From there Ruth watched the whole ceremony with no hindrance. Poor J.T. just had to fend for himself.

Now Ruth was in the women's section, and there was real beauty, unbelievable beauty of face, clothing, and jewels. Lovely, fair women, ranis and princesses, wearing saris of every hue of the rainbow, with wide, wide gold borders, gold tissue blouses, crown jewels, necklaces and bracelets of emeralds, diamonds and rubies, heavy earrings pulling down their ears, and their foreheads decorated with small glittering stars of red, blue, silver, and gold. Ruth was totally dazzled by this fairy tale display, and amazed to be right in the middle of it.

When the noise of talking quieted down somewhat, and when she could tear her eyes away from the lovely women, Ruth looked again at the continuing wedding ceremony. At that time the bride's father and mother, the Maharajah and Maharani of Baroda, were sitting beside the bride and groom while the chanting of the priests continued. This was the time when they officially gave their daughter in marriage.

After they stepped down, a cotton cord was passed around the bride and groom seven times, binding them together. The cord was then cut in half and twisted, and the groom tied his part around her wrist, and she tied her part around his wrist. The two married sisters of the groom put four gold toe-rings on the bride's toes and then raised her veil to tie the wedding *tali* around her neck.

Now the bride could really see her handsome groom and he could see her. She was certainly a dazzling fifteen-year-old. A golden crown, beautifully set with rubies and diamonds and matching his, was put on the bride's head, fitted over the band of pearls which was holding her now-raised veil in place.

At this point, questions were asked of the groom and then of the bride, and he, answering "Yes," poured a little rice on the bride's head and she did the same—each five times. He touched her forehead with flowers, and they put garlands on each other.

The bride and groom moved to a smaller platform and this time they sat together on the same silk cushion. The end of her sari was tied to the scarf around his sword. In front of them, the four priests chanting in unison built up a sacred fire. (Before this, the priests had been chanting by turns, each priest trying to outdo the others.) This sacred fire was made with wood, *ghee,* (liquid butter), honey, milk, curds, and oil. Now actual vows were said in Sanskrit by the priests; then the groom arose and walked around the fire seven times. Only after this was done were they considered officially married. This whole ceremony had taken two and one-half hours.

By then it was dark outside, and colored lights and floodlights made all the gold and jewels seem to come alive. The pandal became a vital, pulsating fairyland.

From the beginning to the end of that afternoon, Ruth had been scribbling in her notebook. Knowing she'd probably never find herself in any other situation so exotic, she wanted to describe everything. She giggled as she thought, *In my old age I can revel in memories of great past glory. I don't want to forget anything—not a friend, not a rajah, nor a jewel.* Descending from such a glittering mountaintop was difficult.

Reaching home in Belgaum the next day, they were back into their chosen work with poor village people who lived next door to all those riches, yet never saw them. But sometimes in dirty villages they caught glimpses of real beauty. Now and then an extraordinarily bewitching child would peek out from behind a mother's greasy sari and stare at J.T. and Ruth, those peculiar foreigners, with winsome brown eyes. And often when a tiny baby was brought for baptism, the hope and joy and love in the parents' faces flooded the hearts and eyes of the missionaries.

CHAPTER FORTY-THREE
Of Smiles and Sorrow, Cashew Nuts and God's Care

Ruth often wore a sari, that beautiful, flowing Indian dress. Besides being graceful, a sari hides a multitude of figure faults.

One evening she and J.T. were attending a dinner party at the Belgaum Club, and Ruth was seated alone at a small table waiting for J.T. to join her. An Indian gentleman, a good friend of theirs, strolled up.

"Good evening, Mr. Desai," Ruth greeted him. "Won't you sit here and talk to me for a while? J.T. will be coming in a few minutes."

"Yes, thank you. How are you, Ruth?"

"Oh, just fine. I haven't seen you for a long, long time."

"No, you haven't been out for tennis lately with J.T., have you?"

"No," Ruth answered. "I've been busy. You look as if you had lost a great deal of weight, Mr. Desai. Have you been dieting?"

"Yes, I feel a hundred percent better. I've lost twenty pounds."

"Twenty pounds! That *is* dieting. You've lost your stomach."

He eyed Ruth. "You look as if you had put on some weight this last while. Why don't you go on a diet too? It is really quite painless, you know."

"Tell me about your diet," Ruth encouraged.

"Well, I think you would like it. I must say I think you looked better the last time I saw you." Bluntness was one of Mr. Desai's sterling characteristics. "You've gained a little too much, you know. Now this diet is simply diet plus exercise. First thing in the morning you get up and drink one glass of *nimbu pani.*"

"You mean just plain limeade?" Ruth asked.

"Yes. Then after that you must do half an hour of exercise."

"What kind of exercise?"

"Oh, all kinds—bending, kicking your legs, swiveling your hips—all that. Then the only breakfast you have is one cup of coffee, without sugar."

"I don't like coffee."

"Well, one cup of tea then. Don't overeat for lunch or dinner; just eat a normal amount. But every evening, there must be more exercise. Now I like tennis, because that exercises all the muscles. Really, Ruth, you would feel a lot better if you took off some weight. I can give you moral support. Why don't you come out and play a game of tennis with me tomorrow?"

"Oh, I'm not a good tennis player. That's why I don't play with my husband—or rather, why he won't play with me. I spoil his game."

"I'm not such a good player either, but I just play to run. Keeps me limbered up. If you decide to join me, I'll be glad to play you two sets tomorrow. If you lose a few pounds, I promise you'll feel much better."

"I have no doubt of it," Ruth said. "I always feel better when I lose these extra pounds. It won't take me long to lose them, once I start."

Mrs. Desai had come up in time to hear the last of their conversation, and she firmly took her husband by the arm and led him over to a corner, where she whispered something in his ear.

Ruth watched, and smiled at him, as he first looked startled, then incredulous. Ruth got up and walked over to tell him he was forgiven. He saw then that what his wife had just said was true—even though Ruth wore a sari, anyone could tell she was nearly eight months pregnant.

Cablegram from Miraj, India, to:
Mr. Henry Childers, Herrin, Illinois, U.S.A.
September 1, 1950

ANOTHER BEAUTIFUL RED-HAIRED
GIRL. SANDRA JOAN.
— J.T. Seamands

Dear Mom and Dad:

Well, who'd have thought that we would have *two* redheads? Everyone who comes to see little Sandra Joan remarks how like Sheila she is, for she has a red fuzz all over her head, exactly the color of Sheila's. She is really a darling, and of course will be called Sandy.

I had a rather hard time again, and my *ayah,* Jothi, was with me for most of it. After Sandy was born, Jothi sat on the floor all night long and held

Sandy on her lap. Two or three times I woke up and saw her sitting there and told her to put the baby down and go to bed. But she said, "No, Memsahib, the baby might choke. I will sit and hold her till morning."

She thinks the baby is wonderful, and I think *she's wonderful!*

My bad news is that now I've developed an infected hip from an injection I had in Kodai three months ago, and must have surgery on it. The doctor tells me I must stay here at least ten days. I have time to write you a long letter while I am just lying here, so I'm going to tell you about our latest encounter with snakes in Belgaum. Here goes.

Shortly before I came to the hospital, the *moli* (the gardener) was sweeping the floor, all bent over with one of those short brooms they use. He suddenly drew back and shouted, "*Havu! Havu!*" (Snake! Snake!)

There was a krait, over by the side door in the living room. I had no stick handy, so fast as I could with my extra weight, I jerked off my saddle oxford and killed it just as J.T. came racing down the steps from the office. He bawled me out for killing that snake with such a *small* thing as my shoe. Imagine! I should have had a stick at least three feet long he said, because kraits jump!

One morning we heard the cook in the kitchen saying, "*Ayyo*, come and see the big snake!" We ran out and saw that a coolie had brought a half-grown six-foot python which he had killed near the back of our compound, near the small Mohammedan cemetary. We don't often see pythons in Belgaum, but we are near the big jungle, and we have lots of foliage which affords good hiding places. Not every missionary family kills snakes–many tell us that they never see one on their compound, and others see them only rarely. Who knows–maybe they like me?

My scariest experience took place in the dead of night, at 2:00 a.m., when I was going through the small dressing room to the bathroom. I had not turned on any lights, but was carrying a flashlight. From a low rafter, some dirt and small stones fell down on my head. Thinking a rat was on the rafter, I turned the light up, and there was a krait stretched out just over my head. In the light of the flashlight, it glided back into a hole in the rafter. J.T. was away as usual, Sylvia in school in Kodai, so I was alone with Sheila.

I looked for something to kill the snake with, but all I could see was the Bissel carpet sweeper, so I quickly unscrewed the handle. Thinking I could drive the snake out of the rafter and then kill it, I whacked the rafter a few quick blows. Then I stood still in horror, because part of the rafter collapsed and fell to the floor practically on top of me. It was completely hollow.

White ants had eaten all the middle out, just leaving a paper-thin exterior. I was afraid there might be a whole nest of snakes there because snakes don't like living alone. What in the world would I do if they all fell down on my head at once? I stopped thumping that rafter in a hurry and went back to bed. Confidentially, I wiggled all night.

The next morning my cook brought some coolies, and we stood with sticks and stones ready while they took down that rotten rafter, but no nest of kraits, not even one snake. That meant that there was at least one krait hiding somewhere in the roof, and we have no ceilings, just tiles over our heads! The whole roof had been leaking so badly that we'd already bought tiles to replace it. So I told the coolies to take the whole roof off.

I went to the bazaar while they worked, and when I returned I asked them, "Did you find any snakes anywhere in the roof tiles?"

"*Howdo, Memsahib.* We found a nest with three kraits in it."

"Did you kill them?"

"*Howdo, Memsahib.* We killed two, and we will probably find the other."

I took their word for it, though I wondered. The next day they told me they had found and killed the third one.

"Where did you throw the dead snake?"

"Out under the mango trees, Memsahib, in the tall grass."

Well, I had a hunch they hadn't killed it, because Hindus don't kill any kind of creature if they can help it. So I said, "Show me where you threw it."

"But Memsahib, there may be others in that tall grass!"

"Well, I have my bamboo pole with me–just show me that dead snake."

Trembling, they guided me out to a spot in the compound where the grass was waist high because the milkman had not yet led his buffaloes to that spot. Acting like a hunter on an African safari (in India), I parted the tall grass with my bamboo pole and looked. Sure enough, one small krait was very much alive and was trying to find his way back to his rooftop paradise. I made short work of him!

Other snake stories I could tell you, true ones, too–but after all, a missionary does other things besides fight snakes and monkeys. Besides, if I told you any more, you'd cable me to come home.

I think J.T. is just baffled by our third daughter! Our Indian preachers tell him he has bad *karma*, but it looks to me like we're stuck in a rut! Sandy is so cute though–who would ever want to exchange her?

Love, your female producer of females, Ruthie

God's care for His children is never-ending. He said, "Lo, I am with you alway . . ." and J.T. and Ruth had occasion to prove this over and over. Sometimes it seemed that God went "way out in left field" to help them. They knew He expected them to ask for help—they were His children.

The infected hip Ruth mentioned in her letter was serious. It had been caused by a nonsterile injection, given three months before, not by Dr. Evans, Ruth's doctor, but by another. Dr. Evans in Miraj hospital saw the swollen, red lump when Sandy was born, and said that Ruth must have surgery on that wound and allow it to drain. So he operated, excised the infected tissue, and put in a drainage tube. That was the beginning of two years of constant pain.

Ruth took her new baby home—100 miles from the hospital, certain that her hip would heal. Pain was incessant, as the wound *almost* healed. She couldn't sit straight, lie on her right side, drive the jeep, walk, or do anything without pain.

When Sandy was three months old, Ruth had to return to the mission hospital for a second operation on the wound. The doctor cut deeply into the large abscess, and again, instead of sewing it up, packed it full of gauze to absorb infection. Now her pain was so great that she had to have an anesthetic to even change the gauze and bandages. She could barely walk, sitting was practically impossible, and driving the jeep was agony. Of course, she was nursing Sandy at the same time.

Returning from the hospital the second time, she tried to relax for a few days, but fate had something else in store. Into Ruth's haze of suffering came her good friend, Sylvia Culver, to visit her and her new baby. Sylvia, for whom Ruth had named her first daughter, was also from the Herrin Methodist Church, and was a missionary whose station was about eighty miles south of Belgaum. She was pregnant, and on her way to the Miraj Hospital for a seven month check-up. She hadn't seen Ruth for a while and wanted to stop for a couple of days.

"Oh, Sylvia, how good to see you!" Ruth hugged her friend sideways, because her pregnancy looked very advanced. "Is your baby nearly due?"

"No," answered Sylvia. "I'm only seven months pregnant."

"Seven months! Are you sure?"

"I'm sure."

"Well, you've probably heard this before, but you look further along than that."

Sylvia sighed. "That's what everybody says. I just wonder what size I'll be at the end of the next two months! To tell you the truth, this is a hard pregnancy and I feel bad most of the time."

"Well, sit here and rest. We're in the same boat—sort of," Ruth said. "I'm not pregnant, but I'm in pain all the time with a hip infection, so you can just sit here and I'll just lean sideways and we can talk and feel sorry for each other. I'll get us some tea."

Over the tea they caught up with each other's lives. "J.T. is gone way up to North India," Ruth told Sylvia, "so I'm the 'missionary in residence' on this compound. People come to me for everything, and I don't feel like doing anything for them. It's all I can do to just nurse Sandy. But my Ayah is a jewel and helps me."

"I know what you mean. Weldon is staying at home with our two boys. I've not been much help to people lately either. And 'help' is what we're supposed to be here for. I'll be glad when my baby comes. You sure do have a little cutie in your red-haired baby, Sandy. I hope I get a girl."

Ruth cuddled her baby. "She's a good baby, too. Well this is three girls for us!"

"Yes, I want a girl this time," Sylvia was wistful. My two boys are handfuls. If I do get a girl, I'll name her after you."

"Oh! That would be nice."

In the middle of the next morning, suddenly Sylvia went into labor. The water broke, so Ruth was sure the labor was genuine. She said to herself, *I thought Sylvia looked like she was nine months along!* But she was worried because Sylvia's doctor was 100 miles away, and they could never make that trip with her in labor.

Ruth's Rani friend just happened to stop by at that time and when she heard what was happening, she said to Sylvia, "I know a lady doctor and her husband who run a natal clinic. It's down the hill toward the bazaar, about a mile from here. It's probably the best place for you. I can take you there if you want me to."

Ruth said, "Sylvia, that's probably the wisest thing to do. I know I couldn't do a good job of delivering your baby. And no doubt this lady doctor has had plenty of experience."

Sylvia, in distress, nodded agreement.

So Rani Sahib took Sylvia in her German car, and Ruth, leaving her baby with the ayah, climbed into her jeep and followed. She would have to come home and nurse her baby in another three hours but she was worried because Sylvia's own doctor was not on the scene. She knew it would be hard for Sylvia in a perfectly strange place with a strange doctor.

The small clinic was meant only for delivering babies. Many village women and also town women came there to give birth. But the amenities were few and the lady doctor had no equipment for babies or mothers with any special kind of problem. Nothing for premature babies.

When Rani Sahib explained Sylvia's problem, the doctor welcomed Sylvia graciously and said, "Of course, we will help her. That's what we are here for!"

Rani Sahib expressed her thanks and concern for Sylvia, then she left to go back home.

They had arrived about 11:00 o'clock in the morning, and Sylvia's labor was on in earnest. Ruth stayed as long as she could, but at two o'clock in the afternoon she had to go back home to nurse her baby. She ate some lunch, then about 3:00 o'clock again left her baby with the ayah and went back to the clinic. Her friend was still on the delivery table.

Ruth walked in to a sight she would never forget as long as she lived. Sylvia had just delivered a miniature baby boy, but it was dead. The baby was lying uncovered on a steel folding chair beside the table, and Sylvia was lying undraped, looking at it. The doctor had her hands full with Sylvia, and had not been able to even cover the baby. For Sylvia was again in labor—she had been carrying twins and not known it!

Ruth's tears for her friend were swift. She leaned over Sylvia and stroked her hair saying, "I'm so sorry. . ."

Tears were rolling from Sylvia's big, brown eyes and back into her hair. Ruth gripped Sylvia's hand as another wave of pain washed over her, and a second tiny boy was born. Identical twins. Looking at the baby, Ruth knew that it, too, would soon slip away. But for a time it was breathing, and the doctor's husband, her helper, took the baby into another room and wrapped it tightly.

While the doctor was caring for Sylvia then, Ruth looked into another room, found a bath towel and wrapped the tiny stillborn in it and carried it into the other room, out of Sylvia's sight. She grieved that no incubator or any modern facilities were available. Later that evening the second baby died.

By that time though, Sylvia was in a state of psychological shock. She seemed not to be able to speak, or react or even sleep. She could not eat or drink. She was put into a bed and simply lay there with her eyes open and staring.

All night Ruth stayed beside her, talking to her, stroking her hair and face, reading some Scripture, even singing some Christian hymns, but Sylvia showed no reaction at all. She seemed to be in another world, far detached from the sorrow of this one.

At 6:00 p.m., 10:00 p.m., 2:00 a.m., Ruth had to climb up into the high jeep, and in great pain bump up the hill to the mission compound. No matter what else happened, little Baby Sandy had to be fed. But every time she went home and came back, the trip was worse. She had no rest the whole night, and in her wound the throbbing increased until her whole right side was a hot, searing jagged sword of pain. But she knew she must be beside her friend—even if Sylvia didn't seem to know that she was there.

When daylight came Sylvia showed no change. She was still awake, with no response to anyone or anything. It was 6:00 o'clock and Ruth must go home again, eat some breakfast and feed her baby. How much longer could she go on like this?

Again she clumped down the outside stairs to her jeep parked in front of the little clinic, and was barely able to hoist herself up into the high jeep seat. She started to turn on the ignition, but couldn't even see it for the tears that flooded her eyes.

Ruth put her head down on the steering wheel and cried, "Oh, God, *please* send somebody to help me! I can't do all this by myself. I *cannot* go up and down this hill driving this bumpy jeep any more, but I *have* to.

"Lord, you know I have to go down to the carpenter's shop in the bazaar and order a little coffin made for these babies. I must find a cemetery secretary, buy a lot and find someone to dig a grave. One of our preachers should arrange for a little service for them. I have to send a telegram to Sylvia's husband, he doesn't know anything about this! Besides all that, I *have* to stay with Sylvia. I'm the only person she knows here. Help me, Lord. Please send somebody!"

Ruth didn't know how she expected the Lord to answer her desperate cry, but she was sure He would. If the Lord had spoken to her audibly, He might have said, "All right, Ruth, I'll send somebody to help you. What kind of person do you want?"

And if Ruth had wanted to test the Lord, she might have answered, "Well, Lord, I don't know any Mormons. So why don't You send me a Mormon from Salt Lake City? Why don't You have him out here in India on some crazy mission—like maybe, getting the worms out of cashew nuts?"

No, in her wildest imagination, she would never have thought of that. She just asked for help and then said, "Thank You Lord, bless Sylvia and help me to help her—but *please* send somebody to help me! Thank You, Amen."

She wiped her tears away, and bumped home. Every time the jeep jolted, she groaned. She fed her baby, ate breakfast, and limped back to the jeep. No help yet. Sylvia still looked as if she were sound asleep, with her eyes wide open. Nothing seemed to penetrate her mind at all.

At 10:00 a.m. again Ruth, now almost in shock herself, steered the jeep back up the hill to the mission house, fed her baby, and back down again. Her side was ablaze, and her eyes almost refused to stay open. Again she sat beside her friend, talking, trying to get some response.

About 11:30 she was still sitting there, trying to keep awake, when she heard someone call in the reception room, "Is there a Mrs. Seamands here?"

It was a strange voice, an American voice. She hobbled out and there stood a young, handsome, American man she had never seen before. "Yes, I am Mrs. Seamands," she said. "What can I do for you?" No matter what state she was in, she was still supposed to help people.

The tall, blond, American seemed to fill up the tiny reception room. He shook hands with her. "Mrs. Seamands, My name is Tom Akers. Can I stay with you for a while? I've been told that you often take people in at the mission compound."

Her eyes filled with tears. "Tom Akers, can you drive a jeep?"

Like any other American he shrugged, "Of course I can drive a jeep."

"Why are you out here in Belgaum, India, asking me for a place to stay?"

Tom smiled. "Well, you see, I am a Mormon. I come from Salt Lake City, and I'm out here in India giving three years of my life for my church. I'm an etymologist—some people call me a 'bugologist'. I'm here to show the Indian government how to get the worms out of the middle of cashew nuts." He said it as if his mission were the simplest thing in the world.

Ruth must have heard wrong. And her brain was not properly processing what her ears heard. Or else this young man must be stupid in spite of his American good looks. Her eyes widened, "Worms? Worms in the middle of cashew nuts? I eat cashew nuts every day. Am I eating worms?"

Tom didn't seem to want to answer that question. "Does your servant cook those cashew nuts before you eat them?"

Ruth nodded. "Yes, he fries them in butter."

"Well, then," grinned Tom, "don't worry about eating them. You need all the protein you can get."

Ruth was horrified. "Just go on and eat them—now that I know? I never saw any worms. Are you just making all this up? Cashew nuts grow all around here—do they *all* have worms?"

Tom's voice was soothing. "I know they grow all around here. For some time now, the American government will not allow cashew nuts from India to be imported into the USA, because of the worms. And India is losing a lot of money. So I'm trying to help the Indian government get rid of them. *That's* the reason I'm here."

Ruth couldn't take it all in. Bugs and worms and cashew nuts and governments—who cared about them? She was a mass of pain and needed help and sleep. She simply dissolved into tears and Tom handed her a large white handkerchief. Between sobs she told him, "No! That's not the reason you're here. At 6:00 o'clock this morning I asked God to send somebody to help me . . ." and she poured out all that had happened to her friend, Sylvia, her two dead babies, and all the things she now needed help with.

She wiped her eyes on his handkerchief and said, "Tom Akers, you can stay with me forever if you will just drive this jeep for me and help me get all the things done that must be done. I thank the Lord because I know He sent you."

Tom took Ruth down to the bazaar where they gave a carpenter the order for a small wooden coffin. It was finished within four hours. Her telegram brought Sylvia's husband on the first train from the south. A gravesite was bought and grave diggers hired.

An Indian minister had a service for the babies as soon as Sylvia's husband arrived. In deep sorrow Weldon walked with some Belgaum friends to the small Christian cemetery behind the mission compound. Through it all Tom Akers helped Ruth, then Weldon. While Weldon was at the cemetery, Ruth stayed with Sylvia. Though it was late afternoon by then, Sylvia still showed no reaction. *Surely with Weldon here, she will begin to respond,* Ruth thought.

Weldon stayed with Sylvia that night and Ruth could finally sleep. She first showed Tom to the guest room, and asked her cook to give him something to eat. Until her own baby Sandy demanded to be nursed, Ruth practically collapsed.

On the third day Sylvia had improved enough to go home with Ruth. When she asked for a drink of water, the household gave thanks.

Weldon had to go back to his own station and his two boys, but Sylvia continued to stay with Ruth for ten more days. It was a time of healing. Ruth told Sylvia how she'd asked God for help, and He had sent Tom just when she needed him the most. Ruth's own pain from her hip wound plagued her for a long time.

Tom made the mission compound his home base for several months, with daily trips to the cashew nut orchards. There he worked with the orchard tenders, teaching them how to properly grow and pack the cashew nuts.

Yes, God's special sent-one helped Ruth and Sylvia, and also helped the nut growers with their worms.

It's true. God really goes way out sometimes.

CHAPTER FORTY-FOUR
CRISES

After two years and four surgeries, Ruth's hip wound finally healed. That hip looked a little lopsided, but at least her pain was gone.

Sandy was a beautiful little red-haired girl who loved to play with all the pets on the compound and to read books. Ruth enjoyed teaching her to read and write—Sandy simply couldn't wait to go to school.

One day when Sandy was five she got a fever, then a chill. Her temperature began to climb higher and higher with chills at the same time. Malaria! They had to get to the mission hospital 100 miles away.

The monsoon season was on, but J.T. readied the jeep. Ruth made a bed in the back seat, put Sandy into it and sat on the floor beside her, keeping a cool cloth on Sandy's head as the jeep plowed through muddy roads and forded small streams. It took nearly six hours to go the hundred miles to Miraj hospital where Sandy was born. Little Sandy was unconscious part of the time.

They arrived at the hospital in the middle of the night, in pouring rain, and knocked at Dr. Evans' door. The doctor rushed Sandy into the hospital and began treatment immediately.

Those were anxious hours. Sometimes Sandy didn't know her father and mother. But slowly she began to be aware of her surroundings, and within a few days they saw a change. Sandy suddenly opened her eyes and said, "Mommy, I'm hungry! I want an egg and a banana and some milk."

Ruth cried with joy. *Thank You, Lord, for better medicines than I had when I had malaria thirteen years ago.*

During the next year, Sandy told her mother several times that she had a secret. Finally she said one day, "Mommie, my secret is that I am praying for a baby sister. Sylvia had a baby sister and Sheila had ME for a baby sister. Now I want one! Are we ever going to have a baby?"

Some months later Sandy's prayer was about to be answered.

Sylvia and Sheila were in boarding school, down in the tip of South India, 800 miles away. A month before Ruth's baby was due, J.T. again readied the jeep. Monsoon season was on and they knew the roads would be difficult.

J.T. was writing a book, by hand, in the Kanarese language, and he could keep on writing while they waited in Miraj the last month. No such thing as waiting until the baby was due and then starting for the hospital. The doctor had given Ruth orders that she must come and stay there during the ninth month.

They stayed in Dr. and Mrs. Evans' home, and Ruth tried to make herself useful. She was kept busy typing letters and working in the hospital supply room, and J.T. claimed a secluded corner of a big porch where he could write. Sandy found another missionary's child to play with and that made her very happy. Back at home in Belgaum there were no other missionary children.

For most of the month, J.T. sat on the verandah sheltered from blowing rain, and laboriously wrote his book. The days of the last month before birth were dragging for Ruth. Would that baby *never* come?

One day two letters arrived. They were from Sylvia and Sheila in the boarding school. Sheila was eight years old and Sylvia was twelve. Ruth opened Sheila's letter first:

> Dear Mommy and Daddy:
>
> I am glad it is almost time for our new baby to come. I hope you are enjoying waiting there in Miraj hospital. I am having a good time here in boarding school, but yesterday I had an accident. I was playing ball and ran into a boy's back and now I have a broken nose. It hurt at first but not now. I look funny with it all lopsided, and when I wiggle it, it squishes. No more news now. Love, Sheila

Beginning to be in shock, Ruth opened Sylvia's letter:

> Dear Mother and Daddy:
>
> Yesterday Sheila broke her nose and we had a hard time getting the blood stopped. We finally did, and she says it doesn't hurt any more. At first the doctor and nurse said it was broken, and now they say it isn't. Even as dumb as I am, I *know* it is broken. It is smashed clear over on the side of her face, and when wiggled, you can hear the bones grate together. She looks awful and nobody seems to be doing anything about it.
>
> When Sheila saw the doctor, he asked her if she would go down to Vellore and get her nose set at the hospital there. I wanted her to do it.

But Sheila was so scared she said, "No, don't bother about it. I always did have a crooked nose."

Imagine that! Well, I told the doctor she most certainly did *not*. I personally hope they do send her down to Vellore, for I don't want my sister going through life with a nose squashed sideways. What shall I do about it?

Last week I went out hiking by myself and killed a snake. It isn't going to be the last one I kill, so just prepare yourself. Nothing else has happened this week. Love, Sylvia.

Ruth's first thought was that if anything else *had* happened that week, she'd have a heart attack! Then she did the best thing she could do under the circumstances—she practically went into hysterics. That letter had been on its way to them for seven days, and all this time her lovely, red-haired daughter Sheila was going through life with her nose squashed sideways. Not only that, but her brave dark-haired, daring daughter Sylvia might be killed by snakes while hiking alone over the Palni mountains.

The doctor calmed Ruth down and said, "J.T., you must go and get Sheila down off that mountain and into the Vellore hospital. Go and stay with her. If the baby comes before you get back, we'll take care of the baby and Ruth."

Ruth moaned and mopped tears and the baby kicked her for such disturbing behavior. "Give Sylvia a good paddling for hiking and killing snakes alone. She knows very well hiking alone is against the rules."

J.T. rushed to get his suitcase, bedding roll, and water jug ready for the long trip. He also gathered his writing materials and his notes. He didn't want to just sit with nothing to do.

Ruth sat weeping and mumbling to herself. "It took that letter so long to get here that there's no telling what condition that lopsided nose is in now. Sheila might look like an idiot forever!"

The journey by train from Miraj to Vellore takes thirty-three hours. J.T. was nearly beside himself with worry, though he hadn't wanted Ruth to see that he was upset. Even then, he arrived shortly before Sheila. He had telegraphed the school and asked them to send Sheila with a woman servant down the hill to the Vellore Hospital. The doctor there took one look at Sheila and rushed her onto the operating table. The break was eight days old, the nose was broken in two places, and Sheila looked awful.

J.T. stayed with her through a week of breathing through her mouth while her nose was stuffed and taped. J.T. worked on his own manuscript, and Sheila read many books from the hospital library. When the bandages were removed, Sheila heard the doctor say these sad words, "I'm very sorry, Sheila, but your nose is not straight; we have to do it all over again."

Eight-year-old Sheila suffered through another operation and another week of healing before getting an okay from the doctor to go back to school.

J.T. kept Ruth, back in Miraj, informed through telegrams. At first Ruth thought all the upset would cause an early birth, but after the fuss the baby obligingly settled down and waited for her father's return to Miraj. So he was there and one of the first to welcome their fourth daughter into the world. Another beautiful redhaired girl! Sandy was ecstatic!

Ruth and J.T. had a Sylvia, Sheila, and Sandra, but they couldn't agree on another name beginning with "S". So they compromised and named her Linda.

Cablegram to Henry and Pearl Childers Oct. 5, 1956:

SURPRISE! ANOTHER BEAUTIFUL RED-HAIRED GIRL. LINDA HELEN — J.T. Seamands

If J.T. had been baffled by a third daughter, he was stunned by the fourth. Some of the Indian preachers told him, "Sahib, something must have happened—you have bad karma. But you are good to us, so maybe God will be good to you yet!"

Four girls for Ruth and J.T! The thought of all those dowries staggered them!

CHAPTER FORTY-FIVE
A Day With The Angels

Everyone knows that Heaven isn't Heaven without the angels, and for nine months out of every year, two of Ruth and J.T.'s four angels had to be sent 800 miles away to boarding school. It was the only way to insure them an education in the English language and in American subjects. So when their children reached the age of seven, they had to go. That was by far the most difficult part of missionary life—being separated from their kids.

When she had to part with *her* children, Ruth knew how Pearl and Henry felt when their family left home.

The most difficult part was sending Sylvia first. Sylvia never wanted to be separated from her mother, and every time she had to go, they both suffered. Sheila was different. After Sheila's seventh birthday, she was anxious to go because she had her big sister there. Sandy was five years behind Sheila, so for several years Ruth had two in boarding school and one at home.

Each year, in April or May, after lonely months of work on the hot plains of south India, J.T., Sandy, and Ruth went up to the Palni mountains, up 7,000 feet to the Kodaikanal School. There they took Sylvia and Sheila out of boarding school and kept them in their apartment and sent them to day school. This was Ruth and J.T's vacation. Of course this year they also had Baby Linda to take with them. What fun!

As usual, after three months without Sylvia and Sheila, they had to get acquainted all over again. They both exclaimed over Sandy's growth, how much she knew, and how smart their baby was to whistle so early. Their apartment rocked with the furor.

Every time Ruth arrived in Kodai, she saw that her two school age angels needed repairs. This time was no different. Sleeves were outgrown, hems were scalloped up with safety pins, bangs below eyelash level, socks mismatched, and shoes full of holes. Ruth was a a missionary, yes, but she was a Mama first, and being with her children—even with so many repairs to make—meant happiness for her.

Sylvia had always said she wanted to become a doctor, and

after she studied one year of biology, she knew a great deal about the human body. From then on Ruth had to be very explicit when describing any symptoms to her. This year on their second day with them, Sylvia had a pain in her midsection, and Ruth remarked, "You probably have worms. They're very prevalent here!"

"No," she replied thoughtfully. "I think I have a valve spasm, and I'm not sure that roast goat appeals to me."

Ruth was putting lunch on the table. After dormitory food for four months, Sylvia and Sheila had requested three four-course meals every day. They were never filled up.

Ruth called the rest of the family to lunch. J.T. is brilliant, of course, and Ruth felt lucky to have him as the father of her children. But he could never remember where he put the jeep keys and many other necessary things. While they were eating lunch on the day of Sylvia's valve spasm, J.T. was expounding to his family a lecture on Theistic Evolution, at the same time he was eating a roast goat sandwich. Oh yes, they ate mutton in India most all the time, only it usually turned out to be goat. Anyway, Sandy thought the sandwich looked good and said, "Daddy, make me a sandwich like yours."

Between snatches of discourse on deep theological truths, in simple English, he piled on a piece of bread two juicy slices of goat meat, some mustard—to temper the strong taste, homemade pickles, a slice of tomato, and a lettuce leaf. He was still deep in thought and logic when Sandy's plaintive voice broke in. "Daddy! You made that sandwich for me and now you've eaten it all up!"

A twist of bread crust, a curl of lettuce, and a few drops of pickle juice dripped from his dedicated fingers. His ears turned red in embarrassment.

Sheila and Sylvia, valve spasm and all, went back to school and two Indian children came in to play with Sandy. Ruth told them to play in the front bedroom so they wouldn't wake up Baby Linda. In a few minutes Sandy came in and said sternly, "Mommy, you told us to play in that room. Well, in that room there is a devil, in the living room there is a ghost, on the verandah there is a naughty girl, and in the tree there is a cobra. Now where shall we play?"

What an imagination! What a question! Ruth supposed the devil might be easier to handle than the ghost, the naughty girl, or the cobra. So she said, "Go back and tell that devil he's in the wrong house!"

Sandy marched with her little Indian friends back to the door of the bedroom and yelled in the Kanarese language, "Hey, devil!

Get out of here. This is a missionary's house and we're going to play church."

Evidently the devil understood Kanarese and left for more hospitable surroundings. In a few minutes the children were playing happily in the bedroom.

Ruth liked fried chicken for supper. She liked it better when it was served with stimulating conversation. Their chicken that night was excellent—or it started out to be.

While Ruth was enjoying a tasty morsel of crispy white meat, doused liberally with high-calorie gravy, Sylvia said, "Mother, I had a super time in biology today. I anesthetized a frog and cut it open while its heart was still beating. I studied especially its heart and lungs. Did you ever see the inside of a frog?"

Ruth's stomach lurched. "No, I didn't! Please change the subject and let me enjoy this chicken, though it's now lost its flavor. Sheila, would you like a leg?"

"Speaking of chicken and frogs and things, Mother," Sheila answered, "do you know how a duck-billed platypus feeds its young?"

Ruth swallowed some gravy again, mentally quieted her queasy stomach, and wondered why her children always had to be geniuses when she was eating. "No, how? Like every other animal, I suppose."

"A platypus is not an animal; it's a mammal." Sheila glowed with knowledge. "It hatches eggs though, by carrying them around under its tail. To feed the young, it secretes milk in little pouch-like parts, and the young lap it up like dogs. Please pass another chicken leg. You sure do know how to fry chicken, Mom."

"Thank you for the compliment, Sheila. But I am *tired* of frogs' hearts and platypuses' pouches. Now change the subject to something calm and digestive, and let me enjoy this chicken!"

"Something digestive, hmm," mused Sylvia with naughty eyes. "Something perhaps like gastric juices, bile, and acids. Mother—" she broke off, "don't eat so much of that gravy. It's too fattening and I don't want a fat mother! I often look around and see girls with fat mothers and I feel sorry for—"

Ruth looked straight at her oldest brilliant daughter. "You stick to your gastric juices and frogs' hearts," she muttered, "and I'll take care of this gravy!"

"Mother," asked Sheila between bites of crispy chicken, "will you pop some corn tonight?"

Ruth sighed, thinking of how she'd like to read in bed. "I still have a lot of work to do. If I'm not too tired, maybe."

"Please say yes. Just pop a little, please?"

"Well, if I feel like it."

Rolling her eyes Heavenward, Sheila sought higher help, intoning, "Oh, Lord, let her feel like it!" Back to earth she said sadly, "Today is my last day as president of my class. Miss Liddle says I'm just the type to be president."

"Too bad you can't be president of the United States," her father said.

"Why not, Daddy? Oh yes, because I'm a girl. Well, maybe by the time I grow up, a woman can be president. I hate to give up my presidency here." She shrugged. "Oh well, I've had a good reign!"

Sheila took Baby Linda down and put her on the potty-chair. The other children wandered off, and J.T. and Ruth sat and smiled at each other over dirty dishes and piled-up chicken bones. He held her hand for a minute, and she thought he was thinking the same thing she was. She was thinking of how they met, what a wonderful family they now had, and how proud he must be to be the father and husband of such a clan. Then he smiled at her again and asked softly, "Have you paid the electric bill yet?"

Does romance die so quickly? After only twenty years? Before Ruth could answer, a crash and a yell brought them both to their feet. Baby Linda had fallen off the potty-chair and turned it over on herself! After bathing and settling her down for the night, Ruth answered some letters. One was to a publisher, and she sent him the signed contract which hooked him into publishing her book.

Altogether, it had been a rare day in Heaven. Nothing boring about a day filled with bangs, hems, lectures, platypusses, presidents, devils, ghosts, naughty girls, cobras, potty-chairs and publisher's contracts.

The house creaked and settled for the night and so did Ruth. She lay there thinking, *I'm an ordinary mama, I guess, with ordinary reddish-brown hair, ordinary green eyes, the usual number of wrinkles for my age. I'm medium tall, medium fat (hmmm—well maybe a little more than medium), and I have medium-sized feet. But I'm really in a class by myself after all, because I'm the mother of four adorable angels—three of them redheads. So I don't feel one bit ordinary!*

Before the children went to bed, she had popped the corn and Sheila was fervently grateful. "Thank You, Thank You, Lord, for letting her feel like it!"

Sylvia's future medical fingers probed her middle and she

remarked, "I'm glad you're here, Mom. We must see about this valve spasm."

Little six-year-old Sandy hugged her mother tight and said, "You're beautiful, Mommy. I hope I'm a good mommy like you some day."

Baby Linda whistled in her sleep.

Stars hung low, moonlight shimmered through the window, pungent odor of eucalpytus trees filled the night, and J.T.'s sleepy arms encircled her.

Living with angels was heavenly.

CHAPTER FORTY-SIX
To Sea in a Ship

Ruth and J.T. had been in India nearly seven years during their last term of service. They were homesick—and now, in the middle of 1959, furlough time finally arrived. Ruth wanted to see her mother and dad, Helen, Art, and Irene. J.T. wanted to see his parents who had retired from India, and the children wanted to see all of them—plus America.

The Seamands family arrived early in the morning at the Bombay docks to board ship. Ruth could hardly wait. She was as homesick for her country as she was for her relatives. She had always been incurably patriotic; no one could imagine what happened inside her when she saw an American flag. She always choked and blinked, knowing that all the people who live in America really do not appreciate their wonderful land. To Ruth, the American flag is the most beautiful in the whole world, and anyone who ever scorns that flag should never be allowed to live under its protection.

That day their family of six lined up with twelve pieces of hand luggage, and sat on their suitcases waiting until their passports and health papers were checked. They watched the commotion of others arriving, and of huge cranes lifting luggage and supplies into the hold. After a three-hour delay they were waved onto the ship.

J.T. walked on ahead (Indian style) with two heavy suitcases. Ruth picked up as many things as she could carry and looked around to see if all the girls had their own things. Linda, two years old, scrambled up and hefted her own private pillow case containing her little potty-chair.

It was an Indian chair woven of bamboo, and they took it wherever they went because Linda was afraid to sit on large toilets. "Lindie," Ruth had said when they were packing at home, "the easiest way to carry your pottie-chair, is to put it in a pillow case." To J.T. she giggled and said, "I know people don't travel with pots in America, but America, here we come." She shrugged. "This doesn't bother me a bit—does it bother you to board a fancy ocean liner with her pot in a pillow case?"

"Not if it keeps Lindie happy."

That day on the dock when Ruth told each daughter to take whatever she could carry, Linda immediately grabbed the pillow case containing her potty-chair. She threw it over her shoulder and striding after J.T., her short legs mimicked his long steps for about a quarter of a mile down the dock to the gangplank. She looked like an animated doll with her red curly hair, freckled face and frilly yellow dress. The pillow case was longer than she was, and with her every step, the chair thumped on the dock behind her. Others lined up waiting to get on board, watched Linda with smiles. Sylvia and Sheila laughed and offered to carry her chair, but she didn't want help from anyone. She'd rather thump it down the dock.

Ruth and J.T. seemed destined never to have a calm voyage anywhere. Loaded with luggage they panted up the gangway, and a fellow traveler asked J.T., "Did you hear anything about the possibility of the whole Italian fleet going on strike?"

"What? No!"

"Well, that's what we heard. I hope we're not in for trouble." Ruth, the optimist, broke in, "Oh, I don't think we need to worry. These people would never let us all get aboard if they were going to strike!"

"I hope you're right," their next-door cabin neighbor answered.

That night the Seamands family greeted the ship's captain and relished a fancy turkey dinner in the ship's beautiful dining room. They hugged the rail and watched moonlight dance over the Arabian sea as their prow split the water with only a swish. They sailed north, expecting to pick up more passengers in Karachi the next day. Reluctantly they sauntered off deck to their cabin below.

Their beds were far better than they'd been used to on troop transport ships and they were gently rocked to sleep. Aaah—so wonderful, no responsibilities, they could relax on their first night of furlough.

Early the next morning they were startled awake by silence. One gets used to hums and vibrations of the ship's engines, so immediately when they are stopped, passengers want to see why. They must have reached Karachi.

Ruth's family got up, dressed leisurely and ambled down the hall and up the stairs to the dining room. Nobody there; no lights on; no activity. No breakfast. A sign posted on the dining room bulletin board announced, "We wish to inform the passengers on this ship that the entire crew is on strike."

Speechless, Ruth read it again. Strike! Having grown up in

Southern Illinois, Ruth was well acquainted with strikes—coal mine strikes. She also knew that sometimes strikes lead to death.

"How are we going to get breakfast, Mommy?"

"I'm hungry."

"That turkey I ate last night is long gone, Mom."

Ruth thought she heard her own stomach growl.

Many other breakfast seekers soon joined the bewildered Seamands family, and they read and re-read the notice. "On strike. ON STRIKE! They *can't* be on strike. What does it mean? How're we going to get anywhere on a strike-bound ship?"

"We paid good money to get to America. They can't get away with this!"

"I'd like to shoot the whole lot of them."

Everyone was bewildered. They were on a silent ship sitting in Karachi Harbor, not able to get off and not knowing what to do. People milled around the dining room door for a while, then turned around dejectedly and went back to their cabins hoping that somebody would soon get busy cooking.

Sylvia said, "Come on, kids, let's go back to the cabin and play some games for a while. They won't starve us forever." She held Linda's hand. "Come on, honey."

Little Linda said, "I'm hungry. I want some breakfast!"

Ruth wasn't optimistic about anybody cooking soon, so she barged pass the information sign on into the dining room. Maybe something had been left in the cupboards. A few other mothers followed her. They began to search the buffet there, looking for any kind of food at all. Ah, ketchup! Ruth helped herself to three half-bottles of ketchup and half a box of crackers she found. The other mothers snatched the rest. Within two minutes, that dining room was as bare as a forest after a grasshopper invasion.

Her family ate a state-room picnic breakfast of crackers and ketchup. "We can pretend," said Ruth, "that we are feasting on chicken and noodles. That's one of your favorite things."

About 10:00 o'clock Linda started to complain, "Mommie, I'm hungry again. I want some warm tea or milk or something."

Ruth was beginning to get huffy about the whole starvation situation, so she marched herself back to the dining room. Still nobody there. Still no food—but she smelled food! *Thank You, Lord, for my good smeller.*

She followed her nose out toward the ship's kitchen, pushed open a sparkling white swinging door, and her temperature rose at the sight. The whole kitchen and dining room crew sat around long, white tables laughing, drinking coffee and eating hot, fragrant Italian bread.

She recognized the head dining room steward from last night, walked straight up to him, controlled her voice and asked, "Won't you please ask your men to get some breakfast, at least for the children? They are so hungry."

He shook his head, his face cold. "Sorry, Madam, no."

Her temper flared. "You and your crew can sit here guzzling coffee and starve your adult passengers to death if you want to, but please do something for the children. I heard lots of hungry children crying up and down the halls."

The steward shrugged and said, "Sorry, Madam, we *feel* for the children, but we cannot break strike."

That did it. Ruth looked at those ten or fifteen big hefty fellows smiling because they were on vacation, drinking and eating. Looking at them she said with scorn, "Yes, I *bet* you all feel for the poor little children. You just *look* like you do. I bet you are even crying in that coffee! All right, then, if you aren't going to do any work, please give me the keys to the cupboards and all of you get out of here. I'll go get some women and *we* will cook some food for our children. We aren't helpless and we're not on strike! We have *paid* for that food."

The steward licked his lips, smiled a little, shrugged again and said, "Sorry, Madam, I can't do that. The whole Italian fleet of ships is on strike—we cannot break strike by doing anything about it!"

Ruth forgot that she was only one small woman in a whole roomful of overweight cooks and waiters. She was so angry that her stomach hurt as she yelled at him, "Well, you'd just *better* do something about it!" Then she started to cry and that made her madder than ever.

Ignoring her rolling tears she shouted, "I'm going out of here and round the women up, and I'm coming in here with every mother on this ship. If you don't give our children something to eat, we are going to wreck this kitchen and dining room. If you lock the doors, we'll break them down. We *will not* sit here, unable to get off this ship and see our children hungry and crying.

"Your crew thinks you are all so lucky because all that food which *we* have paid for is locked up with the keys in your pocket. Well, you won't even *have* any pocket!" She took a deep breath and leered into his face, "You'll never even *recognize* yourselves when the women get through with you."

The head steward stepped back and his Adam's apple

bobbed, but he didn't answer. The crew laughed.

She turned, then looked back, " Now you'd better think about that, for I mean it!" And she stamped, she literally stamped out the kitchen door and started down the hall knocking on doors and yelling, "All mothers, please join me. We're going to get food for our children!"

Mothers and fathers came pouring from every door on that first hall.

The steward must have believed Ruth and called to his happy crew, "Quiet! This is an emergency. . .!" for within just a few minutes a room steward scuttled down the hall and clutched Ruth's arm. "Madam, I've been sent to tell you there will be milk and cookies for the children in the dining room in ten minutes. Please have some mothers come in and help us serve it."

Ruth's voice was steel. "It's about time! Get yourself up and down every hall and call all the children. I don't want to hear that some of the children didn't know about milk and cookies. *Milk and cookies!* Here it is nearly noon, the children have had nothing since last night, and you'd better have *enough* milk and cookies!"

Ruth and the mothers of her hall grimly marched their children into the dining room as some fathers stood watch. Soon they were joined with at least 200 more. All the over-worked kitchen crew did was to shove milk and cookies out the pass-through, while mothers supervised seating children and handing out their big feast.

At least the children were satisfied for a time. They straggled back to their rooms while mothers gathered up all the crumbs and put them into napkins. Not a single crumb on the table was going to waste. Unlike the Bible story, they didn't find twelve baskets full, but some did find a few partially filled milk containers. No matter who had drunk out of the milk boxes, the mother closest nearby grabbed it up. The crew closed the pass-through. Nobody came to sweep up the crumbs from the rug.

The captain, calling over loud speakers directed, "At twelve thirty buses will be leaving the docks for downtown Karachi, about ten miles away. Passengers can go off and have lunch there. Buses will wait and bring you back to the ship. We will have to continue this program until the strike is over."

By this time, the temperature outside was about 115 degrees in the shade, and Ruth's children were exhausted from the morning's excitement. They were not hungry then anyway. "Mommy, I'll stay with Sandy and Linda. I don't want to go out in the heat in an old bus," said Sheila.

Ruth nodded. "All right, watch them carefully. We'll bring you something from town. We'll probably be gone at least two hours."

For Ruth, J.T. and Sylvia (now sixteen), the first ketchup and crackers had long since been digested.

"I'll go with you and Daddy," said Sylvia. "I can't face another ketchup bottle right now."

The three of them went down the gangplank and were waiting on the Karachi dock for buses when another announcement from the captain came over the loudspeaker. "Since this ship is on strike, we cannot remain at this dock. We will be in another position when you return." And the ship was already beginning to move!

Ruth saw it and gasped with sudden panic. Remembering her three youngest children in the cabin, she cried to J.T., "If our kids look out the porthole and see this ship moving, they'll be scared to death! They'll think they're being taken away somewhere and we won't know where they are! I've got to get back on board!" She was already running toward the ship as she shouted.

J.T. called, "Don't go!" and tried to catch her but he wasn't close enough. The ship hadn't moved far yet, the gangplank was only about a foot or so away from the dock, and Ruth was always a good jumper. Jump she did. She leaped off the dock, grabbed the gangplank rail and hung on for dear life. She crawled forward as deck hands were drawing up the plank. One of the sailors at the top reached down and hauled her on board by the back of her dress. "Lady, you sure took a chance that time!"

Ruth looked over the side at the ever-widening water, and down at J.T. and Sylvia's horror-struck faces, and she started to shake. From safety she managed to raise her arm and wave to them, then muttered to the flabbergasted sailor, "Thank you very much. Back to the ketchup bottle!"

The deck hand shrugged, shaking his head. "Americano!"

The next day passengers got together in the big lounge to protest and to elect a committee of four men and one woman to consult with the Captain. Their petition stated they wanted either to get off the ship with their money refunded, or for the Captain to give them the services they'd already paid for. When the talking finally died down they had elected four men and Ruth to be the committee. Some women said Ruth must be on that committee because of the heroic way she had, unarmed and single-handed, stood up to the kitchen crew the day before.

"I hadn't even thought about being heroic!" Ruth said. "I just got good and mad for a good reason. The crew is holding us hostage on a strike-bound ship in the hottest place I know of. They think the steamship company will have to give in to their demands because they have us. And I don't like being hostage material!"

The assembly clapped.

The committee of five called on the captain and laid their petition before him. He said, "I feel sorry for you, but I can't do a thing, because my whole crew is on strike. Even *I'm* on strike. But I promise to negotiate with our Rome office by telephone, and try to get them to charter planes for you. I can't call on other Italian ships because the whole fleet is on strike. This will probably take several days."

The angry passengers stayed for a week on that ship, and it got dirtier and stinkier by the day. Not a floor was swept, they had no brooms. Not a bed changed. Not a bathroom floor or toilet was washed. (No cleaning cloths.) The passengers did their best to keep themselves and their children clean. But the worst thing was that not a clean towel or washcloth was given out.

On the Seamands floor, someone (it wasn't Ruth!) broke into a closet holding cleaning supplies and toilet paper. Ruth noticed the opened door, helped herself to what her family needed, and shared the good news with her neighbors. The women thanked the Lord for the windfall and staged a run on the supply closet. It was emptied in five seconds.

Garbage from the crew's meals lay on the deck because they weren't allowed to throw it overboard. Neither did they sweep it up. Those happy seafarers sat in the middle of their filth with their feet up, enjoying a noisy, alcoholic vacation. They made remarks about the female passengers, so women were afraid to walk near any of the drunken crew. It was the worst week many of them had ever seen.

Every day, buses took them three times a day ten miles into Karachi for meals. That must have cost the ship owners a fortune. Then the United States Embassy came to the rescue of the many Americans on board.

Some staff came on and announced, "We are ordered to give Americans permission to buy things from the PX. You can get bread, candy, condensed milk, canned meat and vegetables, Kleenex, toilet paper and writing materials. Since you cannot come there, you must make your orders one day in writing. Then the next day you must line up on the dock for delivery at twelve noon. You will pay the same PX prices as we do."

Every noon after that, a long line of Americans stood on the dock in the sun, (in June in Karachi!) with the thermometer nearly spewing out its top. People fainted in line. But they did get some supplies, and American food which they could eat cold in the cabins, thus lessening their trips into the city. Of course they even had to order can openers. They gladly did it. Those excursions to town through such heat two or three times a day in slow buses (no air conditioning), were utterly exhausting. Half the time the children refused to go. "We'd rather be hungry," they said.

The fact that Americans had to buy all their food and supplies after already paying their passage home, angered them all.

Finally after a stinky, debilitating week, the ship's loudspeakers crackled. "This is the captain speaking. Planes are chartered for all passengers to go to Europe, beginning tomorrow. Plane numbers and dates of departure are reported on the bulletin boards. Each passenger is allowed only one small overnight bag. Women may also carry a purse. Pack your other luggage and leave it in your cabins. Label it clearly and after the strike is finished, your luggage will be forwarded to you. Please find your plane times and be prompt."

Shouts went up all over the ship. What joy to be prompt! Three of Ruth's family were scheduled to go on one plane, and for some unknown reason, the other three were booked on the next day's flight. Ruth, with her two younger children, would go on the first plane, and J.T. would follow the next day with his two older ones. For her one handbag, Linda chose—what else? Of course, her pillow case with her potty-chair.

When Ruth landed in Zurich, Switzerland with Sandy and Linda, she mumbled, "I've entered Heaven's portals." After suffering in that Karachi heat, Switzerland *looked* like Heaven. Switzerland *felt* like Heaven.

Sandy kept exclaiming, "Mommy, look! Green grass! We don't have green grass like that in India. And this air is so cool. Look at the houses—they all have flowers in their windows."

Ruth marveled at the cleanliness. Living in India for so many years, and on a filthy ship for the last week, she had forgotten how clean and beautiful some places are.

Ruth checked them into a hotel and they went first to the dining room. Oh, the food! She didn't realize that because they'd been on half diet for a week, their stomachs had shrunk. Ruth ordered a dinner for herself, and one child's dinner each for Sandy and Linda. Sandy looked at her heaped up plate and her eyes bulged. "Mommy! I can't eat all that!"

Ruth looked at her own high mounded plate and exclaimed, "My goodness, that's enough to feed our whole family!"

After dinner they ran, stuffed and rejuvinated, upstairs to their hotel room and took baths in the biggest tub they ever saw. After pour baths with a few cups of water for the last six years in India, this tub was like a lake. Ruth was totally amazed at the amount of dirt floating from her children's hair and bodies in that big tub. "What's that tub going to look like after I take my bath?!"

Talk about Heaven—I'm not a'goin' there, I'm already here. Ruth sank into a bed so comfortable she felt she was floating in air. And the room was so cool she had to pull up a blanket. She hadn't even seen a blanket for a long time.

Twenty-four hours later, J.T., Sylvia, and Sheila arrived at the hotel. From her vantage point of being clean, Ruth couldn't help but gasp at how begrimed they were. *To think I looked like that last night in the dining room!* She shooed Sylvia toward the bathtub first. "All of you, just get clean. We're on our way to America tomorrow and we are sailing on the Queen Elizabeth!"

CHAPTER FORTY-SEVEN
Adjustments

The taxi couldn't reach 618 South 18th Street fast enough. As the door swung open, Ruth heard her father Henry shout, "They're here, Pearl!"

He stood waiting, still tall, but shoulders a little rounded, waiting to enclose Ruth in a grip so tight she could hardly breathe. "Ruthie! You look just the same! And where is that little red-headed Linda?"

"Here I am, are you my grandpa?" Linda tumbled out of the back seat.

Henry stooped down and hugged her. "You sure got them freckles!"

Sylvia, Sheila, and Sandy followed, and Henry gasped. "Look at them kids. I wouldn't have known 'em! Well, Sylvia, you're nearly as tall as I am. And you, Sheila, and you Sandy. How you've all grown! How are you, J.T.?" Everybody hugged each other on the sidewalk.

"Where's Mom?"

"Well, Ruthie, she can't walk much. She's waitin' for you in her usual place in the kitchen."

Ruth ran to the kitchen, but stopped for a moment in the doorway to look at her mother, Pearl. A wave of sadness washed over her and tears dimmed her eyes. Pearl's hair was snow white and she was bloated from her cortisone medicine. "Oh, Mom!" Tears ran down their cheeks as Ruth fell on her knees to hug her as she sat wheelchair bound. "Oh, I'm so glad to be home."

"And I'm so glad you're home! I can't hug you much because my arms don't work so well any more. But Ruthie, you look fine—just as pretty as you always were."

"Oh, Mom." Ruth shook her head. "I am so sorry to find you in a wheelchair. But I know you, I bet you make up funny poems even about that."

Pearl laughed. "Well, I did. This is my 'Surrey Without the Fringe on Top.' That's the name of my poem. And though my body looks like a balloon because of the cortisone I have to take, and though my hair is cut like a boy's because I can't comb it, I can still talk and I can still laugh. Thank the Lord it doesn't hurt anywhere to do either one!"

"You're amazing. Oh, Mom, I love you so much. I see you've got a television."

"It's lots of company for us, Ruthie, when we can't do all the things we used to do. Everybody's got TV now."

"Our kids will certainly like that. Nobody has TV in India. It'll probably take another twenty five years for that. Mom! I see Old Ben still sitting up there on his private shelf."

Pearl looked up fondly at their old clock. "We couldn't do without Old Ben. With you and all the kids gone, sometimes things were so quiet we could almost hear our hair grow. Only noise in the house sometimes was Old Ben's tick. And I can still hear it! He keeps me company."

The rest of the family all came into the kitchen. Pearl looked up at them in amazement. "Sylvia! Is that my little Sylvia? Going to start to school to be a doctor?"

Sylvia, sixteen and tall for her age, hugged her. "Yes, it's me, Grandma. How are you?"

"Well, Doc, if my knees would hold me up, and my hands could cook again, and I could turn over in bed all by myself, I think I'd feel better. Maybe when you are a doctor you'll discover something to make arthritic people well. And there's Sheila, our first baby redhead! My, what a pretty young lady you are. And our little Sandy. When you left here after your last furlough, you were only four years old. Now look what a pretty girl you are too."

Linda stood close to Ruth looking up at her grandmother. Pearl, with obvious pain raised her hand to touch Linda. "What a sweet two-year-old you are, Linda. I am your mommy's mommy. I'm your grandmother. You look like your mother did when she was two years old."

Linda looked up at her mother. "Mommy looked like *me*?"

Pearl nodded. "Yes, she did. Only when she was a baby she had blond hair instead of red."

"Mommy likes our red hair."

"We all like your red hair."

Ruth looked up at her father. "Daddy, at last you have some salt and pepper gray in your hair, but you're still the handsomest man in town, I know. Remember when I used to put cream on your face every night and comb your hair? I never wanted you to get any wrinkles, and I remember saying I was rubbing them all away."

"I remember. Ruthie, did you have a good trip over on the big boat?"

The whole family laughed. "Yeah, great!" answered Sylvia.

Ruth shook her head. "Now *that's* a story we'll all tell you when we get settled down a bit. You're not going to believe any of it. But we'll wait for another day." She saw Pearl lean back in her chair; her mother looked tired.

Ruth held Linda's hand. "Come on, kids. I gotta show you everything that I remember about this place. This is home!"

Pearl rested her head against her chair and dozed.

Ruth's family stayed for a few days, and they knew Pearl was happy they were there. But Ruth could see that all the noise and confusion the four children brought to a usually quiet kitchen did upset her mother. Ruth did the cooking and cleaning, with her kids' help, and gave Henry a chance to sit and rest. He needed it. He and J.T. took walks around town and he asked J.T. a million questions about their lives in India.

"It's just so good to breathe American air again, Mom—Dad. How wonderful it is to be home. But we'll have to go soon to Wilmore. We have a house rented there for our year's furlough—we were lucky to find a big furnished house near the college. Of course, Sylvia will start in Asbury College in the fall. But we'll be back to see you often," Ruth said. "I'll try to come up from Kentucky at least once a month. That isn't a bad drive. We're buying a new car when we get there."

* * * *

Ruth's family moved into their comfortable farm-style house and it began to feel like home. The children adjusted to America as if it were the easiest thing in the world, but Linda had a language problem. Having been taken care of most of the time in India by an *ayah* who spoke no English, Linda was proficient in the Kanarese language and didn't want to speak English. She under-understood it perfectly, because her family used English at home. But two-year-old Linda said, "Mommy, I don't want to talk like that. I want to talk like Jothi (her ayah)." Even that was said in Kanarese.

Her problem was that other children on the street didn't know her language. Her special little playmate simply played with her but they didn't communicate very well. Linda would shout at him in Kanarese and he'd pay no attention to her words. She would get disgusted. But he did pick up some of her words. Before long he began calling a bug "poochie," a blanket "cumberlie," and saying "ba" for come and "hogu" for go.

One day it dawned on Linda that nobody was paying any attention to her if she spoke Kanarese, so she decided to try English. She swung into it easily, for she had a perfect English vocabulary all stored up in that red head of hers. Though she spoke in English, she was still thinking sentences in the Kanarese sequence. Right words were in the wrong places. She'd say, "With me come, Mommy. Toy store to the going I am. My blanket taking I am."

Of course, after a while her English improved, but she still had her Indian accent. J.T. and Ruth wondered what her accent would sound like when she got it all mixed up with Kentucky, but she never did sound like most Kentucky people.

They'd been home for a year and in May, 1960 visited Arthur, Ruth's brother in California, before packing to go back to India. But they couldn't enjoy the family get-together because Sandy became ill. She was nine, and began to have a fever every afternoon. "I don't feel good, Mommy. I can't play. And I don't want to eat anything, either. I just want to go to bed."

Ruth suddenly realized Sandy looked pale and drawn. She caught her breath at the thought that malaria might be coming back.

"Sandy, honey, we've got to get you well. We're supposed to go back to India soon. We'll take you to a doctor."

The pediatrician did not appear overly cautious. "Keep her in bed for a few days, she'll be all right."

But she wasn't all right, and slept most of the way as they flew back to Kentucky.

Sylvia decided to start summer school in Asbury College in June. Her major would be pre-med. "I will become a doctor. And because it is such a long process, I'll go summers like Mom did and finish college in three years. Then I can get to medical school a year earlier."

That was nothing new to the family, Sylvia had been saying that she would be a doctor ever since she was six years old and had never once changed her mind about her future.

"And I can't wait to get back to India!" Sheila exclaimed. In May, she started packing her suitcase to go back to Kodaikanal boarding school. She would be a sophomore and school would begin in June. "I will miss you all though."

Ruth hugged her second lovely daughter. "It won't be so long. We'll be back in India in September—all except Sylvia, of course." Ruth sniffed and wiped her eyes. "I don't like this breaking-up-the-family business. We'll miss you so much, honey."

J.T. flew with Sheila to New York, where she joined another family headed back to Kodai School. Sheila didn't seem to be overly upset about leaving the rest of the family. It was Ruth who was upset the most.

Toward the end of summer, Sandy's illness, which had relentlessly progressed, was diagnosed as histoplasmosis. This disease had recently been discovered, but J.T. and Ruth had never heard of it. On x-rays histoplasmosis looked like tuberculosis, but did not respond to tuberculosis treatment. Sandy's doctor told them that Kentucky was full of cases of histoplasmosis because thousands of blackbirds lived in the area. Chickens and pigeons also caused it.

One day when Ruth took Sandy to the clinic, she sat in the waiting room with five men. They all looked pale, drawn and tired, though they were not very old. They were talking to each other and Ruth heard one mention the word 'histoplasmosis.'

"Did I hear you say you had histoplasmosis?" She asked.

"Yeah, we've all got it."

Ruth said, "This is my little girl Sandy. She has it too, and we don't know much about it, or where she got it. We think it might be from the next-door neighbors' chickens. Our doctor told me it was possible." Sandy was leaning against her, listless and tired and half asleep.

The men nodded. "Could be. She looks just like how we feel. Tired all the time, and heart workin' overtime because the disease landed close to heart and lungs."

"How did you all get this disease? Do you all work at the same place?"

Another of the five answered, "Yeah, we do. We're carpenters. We were goin' to build a new church belfrey and had been tearing down the old one. Hundreds of pigeons had roosted in that belfrey for many years. Breathing that pigeon-dropping dust is what infected us. We've all been awful sick."

When J.T. and Ruth's mission board heard about Sandy, they refused to give the family a medical okay to go back to India. The board's doctor wrote, "A cure for Sandy's illness is not known at this time. A high protein diet is all that seems to help histo patients, and maybe Sandy wouldn't be able to have that in India. We are sorry, but we must refuse permission for your return."

Ruth and J.T. looked at each other stunned. Not go back to India? Their missionary life was finished! "How can we not go back to India? Our whole household of furniture and things are there!

And Sheila is already in India," Ruth wailed. "What will we do about her?"

After considering the problem, J.T. said, "Well, let's let her stay through this first semester, then we'll bring her home. We shouldn't interrupt her now. But we'll call her and let her know."

"I can't believe they finally have a telephone at Kodaikanal, on top of that mountain. When Sheila broke her nose, they didn't, and we didn't have a phone—she could have been dead and buried before we could have known about it. Thank goodness for progress out there."

It took them three days to finally reach Sheila by phone. After some preliminary conversation her father said, "Sheila, we do have some news. I'm afraid you won't think it is good news. We are not going to be able to come back to India. Sandy is still sick and the board won't allow us to come back. I'm sorry, honey, but at the end of this school semester, you will have to come back to USA."

J.T. heard Sheila's gasp over ten thousand miles of ocean telephone cables. "Daddy! You mean, *never* live in India any more?"

"Yes, that's the way it is."

"Oh, Daddy! Is Sandy going to get better?"

"We believe she will. Lots of people have been praying for her. It will take some time, but yes, we believe she will get well. The doctor told us to give her all the steak we could afford and all the milkshakes she will drink. She must have a high protein diet and rest in bed a lot. We are so sorry you have to leave your Kodai School, but we want you here with us after this semester. Think you can adjust to that?"

"I can do that. I hope she gets better soon." As Sheila hung up the phone, J.T. and Ruth knew she was crying. But by the end of October she accepted her disappointment and flew back to America.

Sylvia said, "Boy, I wouldn't mind getting a trip around the world by myself at the age of fourteen!"

Four years earlier, the president of Asbury Theological Seminary had asked J.T. to join the seminary as a professor. At that time, J.T. had told him, "I couldn't sit in a chair of missions at the seminary because God has called me to India."

In 1960 the president of the seminary heard about Sandy, and again he asked J.T. to come on the staff of the seminary as professor of missions. J.T. said this time, "God must want me here. If He wanted us back in India, He would heal Sandy now." This time J.T. accepted President McPheeters' offer. The agreement was that J.T. would teach three quarters a year, and during the fourth, he could go anywhere he wanted to go, studying and participating in Christian missions around the world.

"With a job like that," J.T. exclaimed, "I can still be a missionary—and I can also prepare others. Who knows, maybe the Lord can see that I would be more useful here."

"I can hardly believe the turn our lives have to take now," Ruth said. "It's a blow we didn't expect. But I know that Mom and Dad will certainly be happy we're staying in USA. And we are only 300 miles from them. Honey, in spite of our worry about Sandy and our disappointment, God is very good to us.

"We've had twenty years of our lives taken up with India, and I'm thankful. God will direct us in the next twenty. Probably the missionaries that you train right here in your classes will do more than you would ever have been able to do."

"I pray that will be so," he said.

EPILOGUE

The sun is setting with long, red fingers sweeping up from the low western horizon. This morning I cleaned the dusty attic window, and now the whole space is aglow.

Again I'm looking at my albums. I gaze at young Julia as she looked 117 years ago, and wonder how she survived all that life meted out to her. But her faith in God and love from her brothers made her strong. Then when she met Grandpa John, she knew that God's grace still included her.

When Julia's son Henry brought Pearl to meet the family, Julia showed Pearl great love, and a new generation bonded with the old. When I, then my brother and sister came along, we were all in the shadow of God's grace.

Today in 1994 I look again and realize that a hundred years have passed since my father, at seventeen months, jigged his diaper off at a square dance. If my mother were alive she would now be a hundred years old.

But they are both gone. Pearl's arthritis became so bad that by the time she was sixty-six, Dad waited on her and did all the housework.

One day when Mom was sixty-eight, Dad called me and said through choking tears, "Ruthie, a little while ago I went to the grocery store—it's only a block away, you know. Pearl was sitting in her rocking chair in the kitchen. I had just brought in the mail and she was reading a letter from Arthur. I wasn't gone very long, but when I came home, Art's letter was in her lap, and her head was resting against the back of her chair." Dad took a deep sobbing breath. "Ruthie, Old Ben, our clock she loved so well, was still ticking on the shelf, but—she couldn't hear it any more. She'd gone home to Heaven."

My little Linda, then four years old, heard me weeping and looked around the back of her chair. "What's the matter, Mommy—did Grandma die?" She still remembers that day.

Dad lived alone for three more years—so lonely he could hardly eat, even though he cooked well for himself. He missed Mom every day of his life. He died at seventy-six years of age.

These are my roots. As Julia and John watched their children go, as Pearl and Henry watched me go, I too have watched my children go off into lives of their own. Our long shadow is already cast upon the next generation.

Waves of grace rolling through the century, washed my grandparents, Julia and John, and down, down the decades through Pearl and Henry, even on down to me and my J.T. and our children. Amazing grace! Kinfolks, because of such grace, cast long shadows. Thank God.

* * * *

Not long ago I visited Boner Cemetery where Grandma and Grandpa, Julia and John sleep, side by side. Just a few feet away, Mom and Dad sleep together under a simple granite stone, as they slept together for forty-three years in the ornate, white iron bed. And I knelt in gratitude and love to all of them.

An hour later as I walked the quiet summer streets of Herrin, my hometown, I was lost in memory. For I was sure I heard my Mother's happy laughter. I saw us as children playing in a South 18th Street yard, and glimpsed my Father—a tall, straight, proud, handsome man—holding the hand of a skipping, curly-haired little girl.

Until we meet again—Ruth Childers Seamands